No One Home

TIM WEAVER

PENGUIN BOOKS

PENGUIN BOOKS

UK | USA | Canada | Ireland | Australia
India | New Zealand | South Africa

Penguin Books is part of the Penguin Random House group of companies
whose addresses can be found at global.penguinrandomhouse.com.

First published by Michael Joseph 2019
First published in Penguin Books 2020

001

Set in 11.39/13.65 pt Garamond MT Std
Typeset by Jouve (UK), Milton Keynes
Printed and bound in Great Britain by Clays Ltd, Elcograf S.p.A.

A CIP catalogue record for this book is available from the British Library

ISBN: 978-1-405-93949-2

www.greenpenguin.co.uk

Penguin Random House is committed to a
sustainable future for our business, our readers
and our planet. This book is made from Forest
Stewardship Council® certified paper.

For The Linscotts

PART ONE

The Village

I

The sign said: *Welcome to Black Gale.*

It was weather-beaten, rinsed pale over the time that it had stood guard at the gated entrance to the village. Purple crocuses were dotted like jewels along the grass bank it was on, and beyond the sign was a mud track littered with stones, leading to three homes in a semicircle and a farm. The farm itself was modest, surrounded by a crumbling drystone wall dotted with moss and half covered by weeds, which also hemmed in the other homes. But on the other side of the wall, the farm's fields unfurled across the moors like a huge patchwork quilt.

I'd met Ross Perry just outside Grassington, a market town twenty miles south of Black Gale, and had followed him up here. The further I drove, the higher I climbed, daffodils dotted along the banks of the narrow, one-lane roads. Even in March, though, winter hadn't quite vanished. As I pulled my Audi in next to Ross's Range Rover, I looked north, towards the heart of the moors, and could see hills still painted with ribbons of snow.

Ross waited for me next to his vehicle, dressed in a smart black suit and a bright red windbreaker. Stitched into the breast pocket of the windbreaker was CONNOR & PERRY PROPERTY | YORKSHIRE. I'd done a little reading up on Ross: he was young, twenty-six, but already the co-owner of an estate agency, and one of West Yorkshire's most eligible bachelors according to a list in a local magazine. He was stocky, dark-haired and olive-skinned, the latter an endowment from his mother, Francesca, who had been born and raised in Florence.

The three houses were all roughly the same size and the same build too – a mix of stone and render, with slate roofs and double garages, and then a U-shaped garden that wrapped around the front and sides of each. They were separated from each other by wooden fences, wild flowers and vines weaving their way through the slats, so that each property maintained a degree of privacy. But the privacy was more of an illusion than anything: the buildings were beautifully constructed – big, four-bedroomed homes – but they were close enough to one another that it would have been almost impossible to live here if you didn't get on with your neighbours.

The farmhouse fanned out behind one of the houses, a bungalow all on one level. It too was built from stone but it had a thatched roof and was a little less pristine, hay bales randomly, untidily scattered, tractor tyres piled up. There was an overturned animal trough close to the front door and two ruptured water butts. But nothing could quite impair the view: in whatever direction you looked, hills rolled into the distance and the dark spring sky seemed to go on for ever.

'Which one was your mum and dad's?' I asked Ross.

'That one,' he said, gesturing to the house closest to us. I'd seen pictures of the house already in the research I'd done, in the police file I'd managed to get hold of as well, but as they all looked the same, I wanted to be sure. 'They moved in three and a half years ago,' he added.

'They were obviously looking for somewhere quiet.'

Ross smiled, but it was sad and seemed hard to form.

'They loved this part of the world,' he said softly, his eyes scanning the hills. The nearest village was a mile to the east. In between it was just fields and stone walls. Other houses were dotted further out, like smudges against the morning and, way off into the distance – little more than a few strokes of a brush – was the ashen hint of a town. Chimneys. Roofs. Telegraph poles.

'Before this,' I said, 'they lived near Manchester – is that right?'

'About twenty miles away, in a village called Denshaw.'

'They seemed happy there?'

'They were in the same house for twenty-one years. The house I grew up in.' He glanced at me. 'They always seemed happy wherever they were.'

4

His mouth flattened – an attempt to appear stoic – and then his eyes instantly betrayed him as he looked at their home again. He started to blink a little faster, obviously not wanting to stand here, in front of me, in tears. I saved him any embarrassment by moving past him, closer to the house. At the side I could see a grey Mercedes, parked outside a garage, and then a glimpse of the back garden.

'How come the car's still here?' I asked Ross.

He shrugged. 'The police did take it away for a while and then – after they'd completed all the tests they needed to do – they gave it back. I know it sounds weird, but I didn't know what to do with it once they returned it. I didn't want to drive it, because it would only . . .' He stopped. *Bring back bad memories.* 'But I didn't want to sell it on in case Mum and Dad just walked through the front door one day.'

None of that sounded odd. I'd heard something similar, on repeat, in every missing persons case I'd ever worked. The idea that loved ones might suddenly resurface, out of the blue, even after decades, was powerful and impossible to let go of.

I turned back to the house and saw a garden room with skylights and a grey slate roof at the rear, and then somewhere, out of sight, I heard a weathervane move, its gentle squawk like a bird that had injured itself.

'What about the neighbours?' I asked. 'Everybody got on?'

'Yeah,' Ross replied, stepping in alongside me again, his composure restored, 'they got on well. That's why Mum and Dad loved it here so much. It wasn't just the house, it was everything. The eight of them – the four couples – they were always getting together as a group. Dinner parties, nights out, pub lunches. I mean, literally the first year they moved in – when I was in Australia for Christmas – they all got together on Boxing Day.'

I looked to my right, down the remainder of the track, past the third house to where the farm was visible. Each of the properties had driveways and two out of the three had cars parked on them. The Perrys had the Mercedes; the people in the second house had a Porsche Cayenne. There was plenty of money up here, and plenty more at the farm: it might have been less pristine than the houses, but as well as a tractor, and all the farm equipment, there was a new Land Rover Defender parked outside.

'I just don't understand what happened to them,' Ross said.

For a moment, as I looked at him, he was perfectly framed, his parents' house behind him, the grass too long out front, weeds running rampant, the dark windows giving just a hint of the empty hallways within. He told me over the phone that he'd been trying to keep the house together, the lawn mowed, the rooms tidy, but it was hard when even the process of unlocking the front door hurt. His parents had been gone two and a half years, with no answers and no trace.

But they weren't the only ones.

As I looked again at the other two houses, and then back in the direction of the farm, I saw windows that were just as dark as the Perrys' and gardens just as overgrown. That was what made the scale of this case so intimidating.

It wasn't just the Perrys that had disappeared.

It was the whole village.

Before I'd met Ross Perry, I'd met someone else.

I'd arrived late at the drab motorway hotel where he was staying. The drive up from London had been bad, the journey pockmarked by constant roadworks, and as I crossed the empty car park, rain hammering against the tarmac, I glimpsed him at one of the windows, partially formed behind a white gauze curtain. He looked like a ghost, a shape drifting in and out of existence, and in some ways that was what he'd become; but this ghost was what had first got me interested in Black Gale.

His obsession had now become mine.

The foyer was unremarkable, the woman behind the counter uninterested in who I was and why I might be there. She never looked up, didn't even move, her face washed white by the glow from her monitor. Bland music was being piped out of a speaker close to me, but mostly all I could hear above the rain and traffic was the intermittent sound of her fingers across the keyboard.

He was sitting halfway down a corridor housing a row of vending machines, holding a plastic cup of coffee, steam spiralling out of it. He had his legs crossed and, either because of the angle he was at, or because of the light, he appeared smaller than the last time I'd seen him. I tried to remember when that was and realized, despite talking to him on the phone four times a week, every week, for three and a half years, I hadn't actually seen him in the flesh for thirteen months. Before today, we hadn't had much choice: he'd been living off the grid in a fisherman's cottage in south Devon that had once belonged to my parents and now belonged to me, and he'd been doing it in secret, and under the alias Bryan Kennedy. His real name was carved into a headstone in a cemetery in north London, and buried under the earth beneath was a body that was supposed to be his. It was all a lie.

He'd faked his own death, I'd helped him do it, and if anyone ever found out the truth, we were both going to prison. So, in the time since, he'd steered clear of the Internet and mobile phones – anything that put him on the map – all of his bills paid by me because he didn't have a bank account, and we'd agreed never to meet up unless it was absolutely necessary.

I'd spent the three days before coming up from London – and the entire drive out to see Ross Perry – wondering if what we were doing here qualified as necessary.

In the end, I'd come anyway.

He got up and walked towards me. In the time since he'd moved to Devon, he'd been working on a fishing trawler, being paid cash in hand to go out into the English Channel casting for hake, cod and herring. It had made him slender, sinewy, a stark contrast to how he'd looked before he'd fooled the world into thinking he was dead. Back then, he'd been a cop; even further back, he'd been a good one. He'd worked murders at the Met for nearly two decades, overweight and restless, and had existed on bad food and adrenalin. For a while, towards the end, booze had crept in too. He was in his early fifties now, his red hair shaved off, his face covered by a thick beard, but it was hard to say if he looked older or younger: physically, he was in better condition, but his face was marked by more lines than ever, cut into him like nicks from a blade. It gave him the weary look of someone permanently scarred by their history.

'Sounds like you had a relaxing trip up,' he said as we shook hands. He'd called me twice on the hotel's payphone to find out where I was; the second time I'd been sitting in a four-mile tail-back. He picked up his machine coffee and rocked it towards me in a *cheers* motion: 'Still, after all this time, at least we get to meet somewhere really glamorous.'

I smiled and then looked through the curtain to the empty car park. Rain continued to hammer against the ground – a fierce, relentless drumbeat.

'Did you get a taxi here yesterday?' I asked him.

8

'Yeah, from the station at Knaresborough.' He took a sip from his coffee, his eyes scanning the foyer over the rim of the cup, and then – very quietly, his voice deliberately dialled down – he said, 'I checked in at three yesterday and then sat at the window in my room for the entire evening, watching. There were only two other people staying here last night, and they've both already left. No one's checked in this afternoon. There are four cars around the back, all belonging to staff, including her.' He gestured to the woman at the front desk. 'She's the most unresponsive person I've ever met. Literally doesn't give a shit who comes and goes because she's too busy playing solitaire on her computer. It's dead here. I'll be fine.'

I nodded, but checked the car park again anyway.

'Have they closed all the supermarkets in London, Raker?'

I frowned. 'What do you mean?'

'I mean, you're looking lean.'

'I've been running a lot,' I said.

'Yeah?'

'I'm doing the New York marathon in November.'

He broke out into a smile. 'You serious?'

'I've done London, I did Paris with Derryn in 2006. I did the Two Oceans when we were in Cape Town. I'm enjoying all the training. It's keeping me focused.'

He nodded but didn't say anything.

We both knew why.

In November 2009, my wife, Derryn, had died – aged only thirty-four – after a long battle with cancer, and then, three months ago, I'd landed a case over Christmas that had been related to her death. The case had taken everything from me – in fact, it had almost destroyed me – and I'd spent the months since trying to recover from it and return to some sort of equilibrium. So, while I'd always been a runner, mostly I'd do short distances and had only ever used it to supplement gym work – but now I was doing fifteen-mile runs as standard, from my home in Ealing, south into Kew, and then out across the northern fringes of Richmond Park. I liked the singular, solitary nature of running, the time it gave me alone, the way it cleared my head and calmed my thinking; and because I liked it, I'd kept doing more of it.

'We'd better go through the case again,' I said.

'Everything's in the room.'

We headed for the lift. As soon as the doors slid shut, I said to him, 'Your new ID will be ready in a couple of days.'

He only nodded this time.

By now, it was just routine: another new name for another pretend life.

His room was right at the end of a corridor on the second floor. He removed a DO NOT DISTURB sign from the handle, took out a keycard and swiped it through the reader. We both instinctively checked the corridor, and then I followed him inside.

'So are you going to start calling me by whatever name I get next?' he asked, popping the card into the power socket. The lights in the bathroom and bedroom flickered into life. Before this, we'd tried to get into a routine of only calling him by the name we'd arranged last, Bryan Kennedy – but it had never felt natural.

'No,' I said. 'To me, you'll just be Colm Healy.'

Colm Healy.

His real name weighed heavy on the air. There were so many miles attached to it, such anger and tragedy and sadness, and yet – as a smile formed at the edges of his mouth – it was clear that this was what he'd always wanted; he wanted to go back, even if it was only when the two of us were alone, to return to the part of his life that had made the most sense, when he'd had the structure of a family and a career.

'Thanks, Raker,' he said quietly.

I looked at the walls.

He'd moved aside a desk, the TV, a corner table and chair. He'd taken down a painting. In its place, he'd filled the entire wall, every inch of it: tacked-up photocopies, pictures, printouts, a cascade of paper, of headlines and handwritten notes that meant nothing to anyone except us. This was no one else's obsession but ours.

At the top, on hotel stationery, was a title for it all.

Black Gale.

When he'd first floated the idea of looking into what happened at the village, I'd said no. I'd said no a month later when he tried again, even though I knew he was going stir-crazy stuck in a hotel room in the north-east; he'd moved there from Devon as a safety measure when a journalist had started sniffing around my life. Eventually it dawned on me that giving Healy something to get his teeth into made sense, as it was then less likely that he would get careless, and at the time I'd taken ownership of all the information that was now pinned to the wall of this room. So as a peace offering, perhaps as an apology too, I'd couriered everything back to him in Newcastle in an effort to keep him focused, but also to send him a message: I still wasn't ready to get involved. Missing people had always been my life, as essential to me as the blood in my veins, but my last case had almost killed me. I hadn't felt ready for something on this scale, and the idea of working a case with Healy seemed a bad way of acclimatizing.

But that was just the problem: when something was in your blood you could never really get rid of it. I could deny it for a while – or try to – but the compulsion would always remain. So when we'd talked on the phone three nights ago and he'd mentioned Black Gale again, this time I let him tell me about it. I put the phone down afterwards and went looking myself. And then the next day I woke up and I realized something: this job had nearly destroyed me before, but it had saved me as well. It had brought me out of the darkness after my wife had died. It had given me focus, and maintained me, and taught me how to live. It was like breath.

It was how I felt normal.

'We came here once with the kids,' Healy said, the distance in his voice instantly bringing me back, its timbre laced with the anguish of events long past. He was looking at a picture of Black Gale. 'I mean, not here, but the Yorkshire Dales. We stayed at some place near Malham Cove.' Another smile, there and gone again. 'Leanne was always easy; she'd just go along with whatever Gemma and I decided. But the boys . . .' He made a noise through his teeth: amused, then more emotional. 'All they did all week was whine. Every walk, every place we took them.'

I watched him for a moment, the dull light of the room reflected in his eyes. There was no animosity in his voice. Just sadness because of what came after, the things he'd lost.

The family.

'I wish I could come with you,' Healy said.

It was hard to remain silent, harder still to insist that he didn't, but that the best place for him was right here, inside a room booked in a false name, where no one would remember him or ask questions about who he was. When a man wasn't supposed to exist, you risked absolutely everything even by driving into the middle of nowhere.

Even so, it hurt me to deny him the chance; if it wasn't for Healy, we wouldn't have ever got this far. Before he was forced to relocate, in his evenings, at weekends, alone inside my parents' old cottage, with no access to the Internet, he'd spent the money that he'd earned on the trawler paying for photocopies and books, and on bus tickets to the local library. There, he'd kept his sanity by reading newspapers, using their computers to get online, even sitting at ancient microfiche readers, in order to study old, unsolved cases. That was where he'd found this one. If the world hadn't believed him dead, this would have been the sort of case he would have worked. Instead, he'd called me, telling me to look into it, knowing the whole time that – whatever contribution he made – he'd always exist in the shadows.

I'd brought a backpack with me from the car and, as I looked at the walls again, reminding myself of the timeline that Healy had constructed of what had happened out at Black Gale two and a half years ago, I handed him the bag.

'What's this?' he asked, taking it from me.

'A printout of the police investigation. One of my old sources at the Met mailed it over to me, but it just came through this morning so I haven't had a chance to look at it properly.'

He unzipped the bag, pulling out a stack of paper.

'I thought you could go over it while I'm out,' I said.

'This file could be the jackpot, Raker,' Healy said, his face coloured with excitement, his fingers fanning the pages of the file.

I stepped closer to the wall. 'Maybe.'

A cut-out of a front page was pinned in the centre.

Or maybe not.

The photograph was of the farmhouse at Black Gale, shot from the bottom of the mud track with the other homes on the fringes of the frame.

Under that was a simple, two-word headline.

GHOST HOUSE.

3

I was still thinking of the hotel room with the Black Gale case pinned to its walls when Ross Perry asked me, 'Do you want to go inside the house?'

I looked at the other homes in the village and then back to his parents' place. I did want to search it, but first I wanted to spend a little longer outside, looking at the view and getting a sense of Black Gale itself. All the power was off in the homes anyway, which meant they were unlikely to be any warmer. We moved closer, beneath the shelter of the Perrys' porch.

'When did you realize something was up?' I asked him.

'I called Mum on the 1st of November,' Ross said. 'As I'm sure you know, this would have been the end of 2015.'

'But she didn't respond?'

'No. She didn't pick up the landline or her mobile phone, so I tried Dad's mobile instead. But he didn't answer either. Mum was useless on her phone, but for Dad not to answer . . . that was unusual.' He shrugged, eyes watering. It was hard to tell if it was tears or the cold. 'Anyway, I guess I didn't think too much about it at the time. Mum had been to the doctor's a couple of days before because she needed to talk to them about her blood pressure pills – they were making her light-headed – so I was only checking in on how things went. I just figured the two of them were out to lunch or something.' He shrugged a second time, but it was less certain now. 'There was a country club in Skipton they loved.'

The wind picked up again, rattling the fence posts that separated the houses. Rain dotted my skin, and then sleet. I started making notes, sheltering my notebook from the weather.

'I tried them again in the evening and then again the following morning. Nothing. I'm not sure that I was worried by that point . . .'

His voice trailed off, his gaze fixed on a space beyond me. 'I don't know. Maybe I was. It wasn't like we talked every day. It's just, after you send someone two or three texts and you leave them a few messages, you do start to wonder.' His eyes strayed back towards me. 'I live south of Leeds, so it's a seventy-mile drive up here. It wasn't like I could just pop round to see if they were all right. It was a Monday, the branch was open, so I had clients and viewings. I would have been busy.'

He said it like it was a decision anyone could understand him making, but his voice betrayed him. He'd spent every day of the last two and a half years wishing he'd reacted faster, because driving seventy miles was nothing when you were doing it for the people you loved. Would it have made a difference if he'd dropped everything and come here on Monday 2 November? Or, as the police suspected, were the Perrys and the rest of the families in Black Gale long gone by that time? The not knowing was the problem. It was the prickle in his skin, the irritant.

'So when did you finally come up here?'

'When Rina Blake called me on Tuesday the 3rd.'

I flipped back to some details I'd logged the night before, at home in London as I'd gone over Internet accounts of the Black Gale disappearances. Chris and Laura Gibbs, and their teenaged son Mark, were the family who'd lived at the farm. Patrick and Francesca Perry I already knew about. In the house next to theirs had been seventy-year-old Randolph Solomon and his sixty-four-year-old girlfriend Emiline Wilson. And then, finally, in the last house, was a retired couple called John and Freda Davey. He was sixty-eight, she was sixty-five, and Rina Blake was their daughter.

'How did you know Rina?' I asked.

'We'd met a few times when we'd both been up here visiting our parents. She knew I ran my own estate agency in Leeds, so she knew where to find me. She called me and said she'd been trying to get hold of her mum and dad and neither of them had responded. She and Freda were in touch every day – literally, every day. She said her mum would often just call to ask how

Rina's day was going. I think she could be a bit of a mother-hen type sometimes, but Rina said she never minded. She said Freda had been a great mum.'

'Rina lives in Cambridge, right?'

'Right. So she was even further away than me.' Ross looked out at the moors; a storm was coming towards us, the clouds pregnant with it. 'She said she'd tried calling my parents on their home number, then the Gibbses, then Randolph and Emiline, but couldn't get through to any of them, so she asked if I could speak to Mum and Dad – maybe try their mobiles – and see if they could check in on *her* folks. That was when I said to her, "I can't get hold of my parents either." I started to panic. We both did.'

'So then you headed up here?'

He nodded. 'The moment I got here, I knew something wasn't right. It was so quiet. Normally, Chris and Laura were out on the farm: Chris would be repairing machinery, or be working on the tractor, or in the sheds. Mark would be there too, a lot of the time. He was nineteen, at agricultural college, but whenever he wasn't down in Bradford he was helping his parents out.' He stopped, pointing to the house next to his mum and dad's. 'Emiline, she was always outside as well. Loved her garden; would be out there rain or shine. But that day there was no one around. The houses were all locked up. It was dead.'

I stayed silent, looking out at the moors.

The police had done three separate searches of the surrounding area in the weeks following the disappearances – the second and third time with cadaver dogs – and had found nothing. No bodies, no clothing, nothing belonging to any of the nine missing Black Gale residents. Two months in, they took a helicopter out, with cameras capable of revealing recently disturbed earth – and, in turn, potential grave sites – but that came up short too. Before that, they'd found no unidentified tyre tracks in the surface mud on the road in and out of the village, and therefore no evidence that any vehicles – other than Ross's, and the ones belonging to the villagers – had driven up here on the date of the disappearance, or the days that followed. CCTV coverage was virtually non-existent this far out and there were no witnesses to anything suspicious in the villages that circled Black Gale. The police concluded that the last physical contact anyone had had with the village was when a postman delivered mail to the Daveys and the Gibbs on Saturday 31 October.

Or, at least, that was the last contact they knew about.

'They reckon it happened on or just after Halloween night,' Ross said, his voice muted. He looked from one house to the next as if willing someone – *anyone* – to come to the front door. His eyes eventually landed on the farm. 'I couldn't see it from the outside, but when the police broke down the doors on the farm it was obvious that the Gibbses had thrown a dinner party. Although everything had been packed away – all the plates, all the food, the booze – it was still done out in a Halloween theme: you know, cobwebs, pumpkins, that sort of thing.'

'But the rest of the house was tidy?'

'Yes. Immaculate.'

'All the houses were tidy, right?'

'Yes,' he said again. 'They'd all been left spotless.'

But not suspiciously clean – not deliberately wiped down in order to hide evidence – just hoovered and dusted, items packed away, electrical items switched off, as if the occupants were all going away on holiday. Which they weren't, at least not abroad: in the file, investigators said all nine of the missing villagers had taken their wallets or purses with them, their mobile phones too, which never pinged a single tower after Halloween night, and were never switched on. But they hadn't taken their passports.

'And they didn't take any clothes with them, correct?'

'That's right.'

'No suitcases?'

'Nothing,' Ross said. 'Nothing's missing from any of the cupboards – or not that you can tell, anyway. I mean, when you go on holiday, normally you make *some* sort of dent in your wardrobe, but in Mum and Dad's room, in the bedrooms of all the

17

others, it doesn't look like anything's been removed at all. And, like I just said, no suitcases got taken either. No other baggage. It's all so . . .' He shook his head. 'Weird.'

It was certainly weird if it really had been a holiday. But the fact that none of them had used any ATM machines, or credit cards, and that their phones were off – and never came back on – from around 10 p.m. on Halloween night, *and* were all last geo-located to Black Gale, didn't really fit with the idea of a trip, whether it was planned or a last-minute getaway. So why take the wallets? Why take their mobiles?

'The police got hold of a load of photos from the Cloud,' Ross said. 'It's how they knew the dinner took place on Halloween. Metadata, or whatever.' He gave a forced smile. 'On Chris Gibbs's phone there were all these pictures. You know, selfies, that sort of thing. The police showed me a few of them. They looked like they were having a laugh. Relaxed. Like I said, everyone always got on well.'

I'd seen some of the photos that Chris Gibbs had taken too.

On the police database, there would have been the option to view the photos in a higher resolution, but I'd had to make do with the low-res printouts I'd been given. They'd be good enough for now, though. Even pixellated, they backed up exactly what Ross was saying about the Halloween dinner: the four couples – and Mark Gibbs too, who appeared in a number of the shots – had all been having a good time.

'They all had Halloween masks,' Ross said. 'In one of the pictures, I think Chris must have set his phone on a timer because there's all nine of them, with masks on.' He went to say something else and his breath caught. 'Mum and Dad . . .'

I waited for him.

'They wore these stupid zombie masks.'

It seemed a trivial, almost comical detail at first, but this was exactly the kind of thing that swelled and intensified the longer a person was missing. It became the element that the families fixated on when they were left behind, the madness in which they tried to find rational answers. Was there something in that choice of mask? Had it been a sign? Did it mean something? Ross's parents were out there somewhere, maybe dead, maybe alive. The more he thought about that, the more it became significant.

To Ross Perry, the choice of mask was some kind of portent.

In the sky around us, the storm had started to break: there was a charge in the air, and though I could almost feel it on my skin, I wasn't thinking about it.

I was thinking about the Halloween party.

For the media, it had been a gift: three couples, and the farmer and his family, all vanishing into thin air, never to be seen again, on the same night the world celebrated monsters, and ghosts, and the unexplained. It had allowed journalists to push the idea that Halloween might, in some way, be responsible for what had happened at Black Gale, that something this strange, this uncharted, could only ever have occurred on the last night of October. And the longer the police went without something tangible to counter it with – some compelling piece of evidence, some theory that altered the narrative – the more the idea began to take hold.

Two and half years on, the disappearances had long faded from the headlines, and from most people's memories as well, but in the online accounts of that night the concept of Halloween was still deeply embedded, not least because you almost always found the same image republished. It had become synonymous with the case: a front page from one of the country's biggest tabloids, published on 5 November, two days after Ross called the police. The headline was GHOST HOUSE. Under that was a subhead: *Like something out of the Twilight Zone* . . . Beneath both of those was the now familiar image of the farm, abandoned and dark.

It didn't look like a home any more.

It looked like a mausoleum.

4

Inside, the Perry house was clean, the downstairs rooms orderly and attractive. Ross hadn't just kept an eye on the property, he'd kept it looking the same as the day his mum and dad were last there. A refillable air freshener had been left running in the hallway, presumably in an effort to offset the musty aroma of a house without fresh air, but otherwise it appeared exactly like the photos attached to North Yorkshire Police's original investigation.

I wiped my feet on the mat, and then took in the layout: stairs ahead of me, a kitchen beyond that which, in turn, led to the garden room; a large living room on the left with leather sofas in it. The hallway floors were oak, and on the wall beneath the incline of the staircase was a nest of family photographs, shaped like a tree. I could see Patrick and Francesca Perry at the centre, and then what I assumed were extended family at the edges, but mostly I could see Ross. As their only child, he was the dominant fixture in the tree, the pictures charting his life, from the day he was born, to a shot, only a couple of years old, of him in a suit, holding a trophy up at some sort of industry awards ceremony, his parents flanking him, proud, smiling.

I walked to the wall and looked more closely at the Perrys. In a shot similar to the one that had run most often in the media, they were outside a villa in Spain, Patrick in a polo shirt and shorts, Francesca in a dress, but in others the two of them were in the Alps, in Thailand, New York, Dubai. They were attractive, still young-looking even as they got to their late forties, Patrick handsome, tall and athletic, with silver-flecked hair, Francesca dark-eyed, dark-haired and slender.

'They loved to travel,' Ross said from behind me. 'Even after so many years of being married, they never lost that spark. They just loved spending time together.'

That was pretty clear, but while the majority of the photographs of the two of them had been taken on holidays, there were a few that weren't. In one, Patrick was in a pair of shorts, a vest and a hard hat, in the space that would eventually become their porch. Off to the side of the shot, I could see a vague image of the other two houses, less developed than the Perrys' – in fact, little more than concrete beds at that stage.

'Is it right that Chris Gibbs built these homes?' I asked.

'Sort of,' Ross replied. 'I mean, he didn't build them all himself – he brought a firm in to do it – but it's his land and, once they were finished, he sold them through us. That was how Mum and Dad ended up here: as soon as Chris came to me with the properties, I phoned Dad because I knew they would love the house and the area it was in. They were big walkers, always outdoors. It wasn't that they weren't happy in Denshaw, but Dad was working from home by that stage, so there was no need to be so close to the city.'

'I read that your dad was a journalist.'

'Yeah, for the *Manchester Evening News*.'

'Why did he leave?'

'They made him redundant in 2010. He was forty-five, at a bit of a crossroads in terms of his career, so he took the redundancy money, put it in the bank and then caned it for a year as a freelancer. At the end of that, he took out a loan and put in everything he'd earned to set up his PR business.' Ross glanced at one of the photographs of his father; a flicker of a smile. 'He nailed it, David. I knew he would. He didn't stretch himself thin, didn't take on too many clients – he wanted everyone to feel like they were getting the personal touch. By the end of 2014, he was turning *down* work.'

'They didn't struggle to afford this place, then?'

'No, definitely not.'

'I'm guessing Chris Gibbs didn't do too badly out of it either.'

Ross nodded. 'He didn't have to pay for the plot, so that

instantly saves a lot. The houses cost £250,000 to build – and he sold them for four hundred grand each.'

A profit of almost a million.

I'd already wondered if money might be at the heart of this case, and now I thought about it again. Patrick Perry's PR business was flying; Chris Gibbs had made almost seven figures on the houses. Jealousy often shadowed financial success.

'So Chris had a lot of cash burning a hole in his pocket?' I asked.

'He said there was no money in farming any more, so I think he saw it as clever business. A nest egg for Mark. But you know what? Chris was never money-oriented. I know that's easy to say when you've got nine hundred grand sitting in your account, but he wasn't. He bought himself that Land Rover out there, farm machinery or whatever, but Dad said he never lorded it over anyone. You'd never have known that he had all that cash. Mum and Dad really liked him, and Laura too. They were just normal people.'

I looked at the pictures of Ross again. He was an only child. John and Freda Davey's daughter, Rina Blake, had a brother, Ian, but he was in Singapore. Randolph Solomon and Emiline Wilson had never married and never had kids. Chris Gibbs had a sister who lived in London called Tori, but his parents were both gone. Laura Gibbs didn't have any siblings and her mother was in a nursing home in Leeds and had late-stage dementia. What that meant was that there were surprisingly few family connections left behind: Ross Perry, Tori Gibbs, Rina Blake, and then her brother who lived and worked seven thousand miles away and who, with the best will in the world, was going to be of little help in the search for answers. It was why everything had begun to drift. It was *always* the reason cases began to drift. The fewer people directly connected to a disappearance, the more difficult it was for it to stay afloat.

'Have you got keys to the other houses?' I asked.

'Yes,' Ross replied, and reached into his coat pocket. 'Because

Tori's in London and Rina's in Cambridge, they like me to check on the properties when I come up here. I tend to come every couple of weeks or so, just to make sure everything's all right.' He handed me a set of keys. 'The one for Randolph and Emiline's place is on there too. It's still complicated, obviously, because we don't know if any of them are . . .' He trailed off. *Dead.* He couldn't say the word and I didn't blame him. That was the best and worst bit about a disappearance: there was always the chance they were still alive, so you always had hope, but it was the hope that so often inflicted the most damage. 'What I mean is,' he continued, his voice low, affected by what lay unspoken, 'in Randolph and Emiline's will, they state that they want any money from the sale of the house to go to charity, but nothing can be done until we know for sure what happened to them. So, in the meantime, the key is with their solicitors, and because I've worked with the firm before, and recommended them to clients of mine – and because I'm checking on the properties every fortnight or so – Randolph and Emiline's solicitor gave me a copy of the key.'

He looked around the house, his expression dropping slightly, as if he hadn't noticed before how dark it was, how quiet and uninhabited. As I walked through to the kitchen, modern and smelling of surface cleaner, I heard the vent flicker into life. I heard a fence post creak softly in the garden, the weathervane again, and a rumble of thunder. But then all of those noises died away and in their place came an almost suffocating quiet. For a moment, the moors were absolutely soundless, and so were the houses.

I had to find a way to make these walls talk.

5

I headed upstairs.

At the top there were skylights, so it immediately felt lighter and less closed in than downstairs, even if the air was still dry. The main bedroom had an en suite and a walk-in wardrobe, and there were two spare bedrooms either side of it.

The fourth room was an office.

I stopped in the doorway and looked around. On the walls were some framed art, an autographed Manchester United shirt, and a three-tiered bookcase. There was another free-standing bookcase below that. The shelves were filled with classic literature, but there were a few sports biographies in the one on the wall and some books on journalism in both. On top of the mounted bookcase were two picture frames – glossy reprints of *Manchester Evening News* front pages. One was about a violent gangland shooting, the other was about how the leader of Manchester City Council had illegally redirected taxpayers' money to the account of his mistress. The stories had been written in the 1990s and Patrick's byline was on both.

There was a computer on the desk, but the hard drive had been removed from the tower and was sitting next to it, still wrapped in an evidence bag. The fact that it had been returned suggested nothing had been found on it by the forensics team.

I returned to each of the bedrooms, looking for personal possessions that had been left, keepsakes, photographs of any worth, but nothing caught my eye. Heading back to the office, I grabbed the tower and the hard drive and, downstairs, placed them next to the front door. After that, I started searching the living room. I was getting a good sense of the Perrys – what films they liked, the authors they read, the type of art they liked hanging on the walls – but it didn't answer any questions about how and why they had vanished. The only item of interest was a shoebox of photographs in the sideboard. They were different from the pictures on the wall: less staged, more authentic maybe, which in turn meant that they might carry some tiny hints or clues.

After going through the kitchen again, I did another circuit of the house, this time going back to front in order to check access points. None of the windows or the doors had been tampered with. I was looking for clear indications that someone had come back in the aftermath of the disappearances and tried to get into the property, for whatever reason, but there was nothing as conspicuous as a jimmied window and no suggestion the locks had been picked. I grabbed everything and headed outside.

It was raining hard now, chattering off the stone of the cottages and slapping against the mud. As quickly as I could, I loaded the PC, the hard drive and the photos into the Audi and then waited under the porch for Ross to finish a call. I could hear snatches because he had it on speaker, but I wasn't really listening. Instead, I was trying to build a picture of what might have happened here two and a half years ago.

One of the theories the police had initially floated was the idea that the villagers had all headed out on to the moors as part of a dare, or a game, fuelled by booze. From what had been found in the recycling bins at the back of the farmhouse, at least three bottles of wine, eighteen bottles of lager and a bottle of rum had been consumed that night, so even if not all of them were drinking at the same rate, most of the neighbours were likely to have been pretty well oiled by the evening's end. Perhaps they were trying to frighten each other with their Halloween masks. Perhaps it was a drunken game of hide-and-seek. The moors at night, unlit by street lamps or nearby towns, would have been the perfect setting for that kind of thing, especially when there was enough alcohol in the blood. Police surmised that a game could be the sort of thing you might suddenly decide to do when you're intoxicated, the kind of unplanned change of direction that felt like the funniest, most important thing in the world after four or five drinks. But it wasn't a theory that held up to any real scrutiny.

And it was why the cops had ditched it soon after.

A game of hide-and-seek in Halloween masks might have fitted the profile of a group of people in their teens, maybe even in their twenties or thirties, but it was harder to picture a group in their fifties, sixties and seventies heading out on to the moors after dinner, in the dark. Randolph Solomon's medical records showed that he'd had a hip replacement the previous June, and old medication found in John and Freda Davey's bathroom confirmed that she'd had oral chemotherapy the year before and was – at the time of her disappearance – taking painkillers for an ongoing muscle complaint.

And even if they had – even if, for whatever reason, all nine of them went out on to the moors that night, and got lost in a drunken haze, or were injured – why hadn't the police found them in the three searches they'd conducted? Conversely, if someone had come to the house, maybe a group of people, and taken all nine of them against their will – an idea that had to be considered given the length of time they'd been missing, even if it was hard to know what the catalyst for that might be – where was the evidence of it? Where were the tyre tracks from another car? Where were the footprints belonging to other people? Where were the trails on the moors? Where were the signs of a struggle?

And, in the end, all of that ignored something else.

If this had happened straight after – or around the same time as – they'd eaten, why were the houses so tidy? Why were all the bottles of booze already in the Gibbses' recycling bins, all the food packed up and all the plates washed and put away? It was just about possible to accept that the Perrys, the Daveys and Randolph Solomon and Emiline Wilson might leave their homes totally spotless before heading down to the farmhouse for dinner, but there was no way I could get on board with the idea that they'd then helped clear up at the Gibbses' after eating – while probably quite drunk – including wiping down kitchen surfaces, and *then* decided that the perfect epilogue was to head out to the moors with their wallets and phones.

Which was probably why the investigation had ultimately stalled, and why the news stories eventually petered out: the Halloween tie-in made for good copy, but it was largely irrelevant if they had actually left the next morning, not on 31 October, which would also explain how the residents had found the time to clean their houses. There was no explanation for why they left en masse, or where they went, but there were also no signs of a struggle, no upturned furniture, no blood, no damage of any kind. Nothing at the scene implied an actual crime – and to the police, to the media, that was the problem. The crime itself was like oxygen.

When it was there, a case and a story continued to breathe.

When it wasn't, everything withered and died.

6

Thunder rumbled above the village, a low sound like an old engine trying to fire, and, finally, Ross hurried over to me, shielding his hair from the rain with his coat.

I told him what I'd removed from his parents' house.

'Did the police say anything about your dad's PC?'

'Just that they didn't find anything on it.'

I nodded. 'And you've left the house as is?'

Yes,' he said. 'I've kept it tidy but I haven't changed anything.'

I looked at an alarm box, high up on the front of the house, and to similar ones on the other two. When we'd entered earlier, Ross had put in a code. He'd told me that he knew the codes for the other properties too.

'When you arrived here on the 3rd of November,' I said, 'was the alarm set?'

'No. None of the houses had their alarms on.'

It was hard to know whether that meant anything or not. The couples were going to a dinner party less than a minute's walk away and the houses were in a remote location where the threat of crime was minuscule. They'd locked up their homes that night but there were almost certainly times before that when they'd popped in to visit each other and hadn't even bothered doing that much. There were probably times when they'd gone further afield and never bothered setting the alarm either, because of how low risk the area was. I'd noted that the Perrys' alarm – and most likely the others too, because they were all fitted by the same firm – had a police response function on it, which meant that if the alarm went off in suspicious circumstances, the security company informed the cops. But that was irrelevant if they'd never been set in the first place.

I walked over to John and Freda Davey's home. Their house

was much less contemporary, the furniture more functional, perhaps a reflection of the fifteen-year age gap between them and the Perrys. It was lovingly put together, though, photos of their kids – Rina Blake and her brother, Ian – absolutely everywhere, along with pictures of their grandchildren: Rina had a girl and a boy, although the boy wasn't in any of the pictures here because he was only about a month old; Ian had one boy, and in most shots was in Singapore, where he'd lived and worked since 1999.

I lingered next to a photograph of John and Freda on what looked like a cruise ship. He was a big guy, bald, a little overweight, maybe six three. He might have been a rugby league player once, because he had a Leeds Rhinos shirt on and was built like a prop. Freda couldn't have been more different: she was youthful and attractive, mid-height, the top of her head about level with her husband's chin, and had lovely eyes, like the ocean in a brochure. But she was pale and absolutely stick-thin. It could have been her natural build, but it was more likely that at the time the photograph was taken, she'd been sick and was in recovery. In 2013 she'd had treatment for cancer, and according to her medical records had – for a second time – been referred to the oncology department at Harrogate District Hospital in the months before she vanished. Police had managed to confirm with staff there that the cancer had returned and that they were, at the time of Freda's disappearance, exploring the options available to her. There had been an interesting side note too, which had caught my attention in the police file: one of the nurses, who'd known the Daveys through mutual friends, remembered Freda saying that she and John might go on a holiday before she began the ordeal of more chemo.

I wandered through the house, going through drawers, repeating exactly the same steps as with the Perrys' – and in the bedroom found an iPad inside another evidence bag – but there was little else that caught my attention. Both of them had been retired for a while, so their disappearance was unlikely to be linked to anything that had happened in their jobs, and their time as pensioners seemed pretty low-key: they liked to travel, they were both in a bowls team, they went down to Cambridge a lot to see Rina.

I went to the house next door.

Of all the couples at Black Gale, Randolph Solomon and Emiline Wilson were probably the least known. They had no kids and little in the way of close family, so, unlike the others, they had no one fighting to keep their story above water. Randolph had had a brother who'd died when still young, and Emiline was an only child whose parents were both long gone. They were active socially – he was a huge Middlesbrough fan and, until his hip replacement, had always attended home games with mates; she met a group of friends from school in Kendal once a week – and Emiline also had a part-time job at the library in Grassington. But none of that was much help in finding out what had happened to them: they'd said nothing out of the ordinary to people they'd known or worked with in the weeks leading up to Halloween – nothing about taking a holiday; no emergency trips – and Emiline hadn't put in for any time off at the library.

Again, I moved through the house, picking up a Dell laptop from upstairs, and then stopped to look at pictures of the two of them in the living room. Their holidays didn't appear to have been as exotic as the Perrys', a mix of package deals to Spain and Portugal, and some city breaks to places like Berlin and Venice, but there were some shots from a trip they'd made to the States, maybe five or six years back. I got the sense though that, the trip to the US apart, foreign holidays weren't as important to them, something backed up by another picture I found loose in one of the drawers: Randolph and Emiline standing either side of a 2012 Volkswagen camper van, a Caravan Club sticker in the window. It was parked on their driveway. I took the photo out, removed some of the others from their frames as well, and then pocketed them all.

Finally, I headed to the farmhouse.

Inside it was lovely: big rooms with beamed ceilings, white walls, bright, modern furniture; a mix of flagstone floors and carpets, with log burners in both the living room and the kitchen. Despite the power and heating being off, it was easy to imagine it as a home people loved coming to. Quiet as it was now, its former life echoed throughout.

The kitchen was divided by an island, the cabinets on one side, a long oak table on the other. The table was where the four couples – and, presumably, at some point – Mark Gibbs had congregated for the Halloween dinner. It was hard to know whether he'd spent all night with his parents; the only thing that was certain was that, when everyone upped and left, he left with them. I found it hard to imagine that a nineteen-year-old kid would voluntarily want to hang out for an entire evening with his mum and dad and a bunch of people three – and in Randolph Solomon's case, almost four – times as old as him, but he'd appeared in some of the photographs that his father had taken on the night of the disappearances. Maybe he came down for dinner, or just to say hello. Maybe he spent the rest of the time upstairs in his bedroom studying, or playing video games, or texting his friends.

None of the Halloween decorations were up any more, Tori Gibbs attending to her brother and sister-in-law's house the same way Ross had done to his parents', but the rest of the place looked untouched. Clean surfaces, clean carpets, beds made.

I went to the kitchen sink and looked out over the land at the back of the house. Two and a half years ago, there would have been hundreds of sheep, a few chickens in a pen too, but now the fields were empty and the runs were unfilled. The Gibbses had owned three dogs too, but those had been found new owners. In the media, on the twelve-month anniversary of the disappearances, Ross, Rina Blake and Tori Gibbs had tried to re-engage people by giving interviews to the local media, including the *Yorkshire Evening Post*, and it had been in that story that I'd read about Tori Gibbs having to sell off her brother's livestock. She'd admitted to having no idea how much she should ask for them, and hadn't even really been sure it was the right thing to do. *What if he and Laura return home tomorrow?* she'd said. *Chris would have an absolute fit. This is his livelihood.* But Chris Gibbs didn't return home, and neither did the rest of them – so the sheep were sold and the moors became still.

I looked around the rest of the house – the living room, the bedrooms – grabbed an iPad from what appeared to be Laura's bedside cabinet and a laptop belonging to Mark, and then ended up in a utility room at the back of the property. It had a sloped tiled roof and was glassed in on three sides, the views presumably spectacular on a clear day. Today wasn't that day: a fog had begun dragging across the fields, following the swirling curtain of rain.

There was a washing machine and tumble dryer, shelves full of powders and soaps, and a shoe rack, the Gibbses' footwear – their mud-caked wellies, their walking boots, their old trainers – stacked in a mess of upturned soles and snaking laces. For some reason, the image gave me pause, the way they were all discarded there, one on top of the other. It was so mundane: whenever it was they dumped their shoes here, the three of them could hardly have imagined that they might never do it again.

I locked up and went to the barns beyond the house, to a work-shop in which Chris Gibbs had kept tools, and took pictures on my phone. After that, I returned to my car, loading everything in, ensuring it was all secure for the drive back. Ross wandered over, this time holding an umbrella. I held up the property keys.

'Mind if I keep these for a day or two?'

'No,' he said, 'of course not.'

I didn't really want to have to return here with Healy, because any journey with him, anywhere, represented a risk – but I couldn't help thinking it might be useful to get a second pair of eyes on these places. Nine people, four houses, eight rooms in each of the new-builds, ten in the farmhouse, plus barns, a workshop, and that was without even stepping on to the surrounding moorland: I'd been thorough, and was pretty confident nothing major had been overlooked – but that was a lot of ground to cover.

I dug the photograph of Randolph and Emiline's Volkswagen

camper van out of my pocket and said, 'You mentioned your mum and dad's car to me earlier.'

He nodded.

'And the Daveys' and the Gibbses' vehicles are obviously still here too.'

'I think Rina and Tori feel the same way as I do.'

'You all want to keep the cars here in case your families return?'

'Right.'

I handed him the picture of the Volkswagen.

'Any idea where Randolph and Emiline's camper van went?'

'No,' he said. 'It was gone when I got here.'

I'd read the same thing in the official investigation. The other vehicles had all been taken away for testing – and returned afterwards – but the police had never had the opportunity with the camper van. It hadn't been parked here on the day Ross came to the village and realized everyone was missing – and it had never been found in the time since. I studied the photo again. Could they all have left in one vehicle?

'Thank you.'

I looked up at Ross. 'Sorry?'

'I just wanted to say thank you,' he repeated quietly. 'When you called me up out of the blue the other day, when I phoned Rina and Tori and told them that you had offered to look into what happened up here, it was just . . . it just felt so . . . it just felt . . .'

He cut himself short, embarrassed about becoming emotional again, and then looked away from me. I'd worked a lot of cases, and seen a lot of people cry; from the outside looking in, the idea of a brawny twenty-six-year-old man being reduced to tears so easily might have seemed unusual. But I saw it all the time. You grieved for a disappearance just like you grieved for someone you loved when they died, but they weren't exactly the same thing – not quite. When someone died, you walked an upward trajectory, a path out of the darkness, however slow: the grief got easier eventually, or you buried it effectively enough for it not to destroy you every day. When someone vanished, the trajectory

33

went in the other direction: the longer you went without answers, the worse it got. There was no certainty in a disappearance. All of the demons, all of the pain, were in the unanswered questions.

What happened to the person I loved most in this world?

What if someone had hurt them?

'You don't need to thank me, Ross.'

'I want to,' he said, holding up a hand. 'It's just, we thought it was the end of the road, I guess. The police haven't called for a year. They seem to have forgotten us. I mean, I know they have to move on, I get that, but Rina, Tori and me, we just stay where we are. We're stuck.'

He swallowed and expelled a long breath.

'I know you're not doing this for free,' he said, his voice barely audible above the rain, 'I know we're all paying you, so I suppose this is just a job for you as well –'

'This isn't just a job for me,' I said.

He looked at me, blinked.

'It's not just a job,' I repeated, more softly.

He wiped at his eyes, the rain disguising his tear trails, unsure if I meant it, or if I was just repeating myself for his benefit. But I wasn't. I meant every single word.

This wasn't just a job to me.

Missing people were my life.

Joline

Los Angeles | Tuesday 23 July

Her pager started buzzing just before 5 a.m.

Jo didn't register it to start with. Ethan had been up most of the night with a summer cold, his nose blocked, his eyes streaming, and she and Ira had taken it in turns to go through to their son. She'd done the last run, just before 3 a.m., and when she'd returned to bed, she'd struggled to fall asleep again. It was just so hot in the house, so hot everywhere in the city right now, and neither the ceiling fan in their room nor the pedestal fan they'd brought in from the garage seemed to make any difference at all. If anything, as she'd lain there staring into the darkness, they'd made everything worse, recirculating hot air and masking all the sounds beyond the house: the traffic, their neighbours, doors closing, approaching footsteps. Ordinarily, that wouldn't have mattered, but these weren't ordinary times.

People wanted to be able to hear everything now.

Every creak; every whisper.

She hauled herself up, trying to work out how much sleep she'd had. Ten until ten fifty, one to two thirty, and four until almost five.

Just over three hours.

'Urgh,' she said softly, and started rolling the stiffness out of her neck. Next to her, Ira moved, the sheet twisted around him, and when he moved again she felt his hand brush against the small of her back. Taking his fingers in hers, she scooped up the pager and checked the number. It was the night-shift supervisor.

'What time is it?' Ira whispered, his voice dulled by the pillow.

'Way too early.'

She leaned over, kissed Ira on the cheek and went through to the phone in the living room. As she did, she caught a glimpse of herself in the mirror: she was only thirty-four but this morning she looked about ten years older, her eyes puffy and tired, her skin pale, her black hair escaping its braid and plastered to her face where she'd sweated during the night. *Well, you look like shit*, she thought, and – thanks to three hours' sleep – she felt like it too. Ignoring her dishevelled image, she dialled the night supervisor. He picked up after two rings.

'Rise and shine, Kader.'

'Urgh,' she said again.

'I got something for you.'

'Is it a pay rise?'

'Funny. You got a pen?'

'Yeah.' She grabbed one off the table. 'Shoot.'

'Ten-oh-five La Cienega. A motel called the Star Inn.'

She wrote it on the back of her hand.

'And what am I going to find there?' Jo asked.

'A body in a bathtub.'

They lived in a bungalow in North Hollywood, a block from Laurel Canyon Boulevard. Whenever she went out to the car, especially this early in the morning, she could usually smell eucalyptus on the air, cypress too, and hear the fronds of the palm tree in her yard snapping in the breeze. One or two of her neighbours would normally be up as well: Ricardo, opposite them, always rose early – she'd often come out and find him on his front porch, with a coffee and a newspaper; there was a young guy in his twenties too, five houses down from them, a jogger whose name she didn't know, but who always headed east towards the freeway and North Hollywood Park. Not this morning, though.

It was already in the low seventies and there wasn't a breath of wind, not even a murmur. But there were no people outside either, no sounds drifting from open windows or from doorways that had been left ajar. Every single window in the road was shut; every last door locked. For months now, when people slept, their houses were sealed like a tomb and they kept a gun under their pillow.

It was why, before leaving the house, Jo had watched Ethan for a while, standing inside his bedroom as she'd quietly eaten her breakfast, worried about his cold, but worrying more about what sort of world they would be sending their son out into. Would it always be this bad? Deep down, as she'd stood there watching him, she'd known the answer. She saw it every day when she went to work. Nothing got better. Perhaps the best she could hope for was that it stayed the same.

By the time she was done with her breakfast, the emotion had formed like a lump at the bottom of her throat, and when she leaned over the crib and kissed her son lightly on the cheek, a tear blurred in one of her eyes. *I love you so much, baby boy.* She straightened, cleared her head, made sure Ethan's windows were definitely locked, and then did the same with all the windows and doors in their home, the sound of the fans disguising her movement as she went from room to room. She finished in the kitchen, where, bleary-eyed, Ira was busy making eggs.

'I've got to go to a scene in Hollywood first, but I'll be in the office after that.' She put her bowl in the sink. 'Any emergencies, just page me.'

'Emergencies? Like, emergency food orders? Because I was talking to a client yesterday and he said there's a new Italian place on Ventura that does killer takeout.'

'Is that a fact?'

'Yes, ma'am.'

They smiled at each other.

'He'll be fine,' Ira said. 'It's only a cold.'

'I know. I just don't like seeing him like this.'

Ira nodded at her cereal bowl. 'Is that what passes for washing-up these days?'

Jo winked at him. 'It is when you've got a manservant.'

Kissing her husband goodbye, she headed outside, locking the screen door, checking and double-checking it. Popping the locks on their Oldsmobile, she looked out at their street. Four of the houses had been repainted in the last week alone; Ricardo was halfway through doing the same, the original beige exterior giving way to a tepid coral. Because most of the attacks had taken place in beige or yellow homes, people had started to think it was a colour thing: they now had a blue home in their road, a green one, white, grey. Jo had been in a meeting yesterday where Lieutenant Hayesfield had told her there was such a run on guard dogs that animals had to be brought in from neighbouring states. Locksmiths were working twenty-four hours a day. Gun-shop owners were turning up in the mornings to find people already waiting in line. The city was in a perpetual state of fear and panic and it was all down to one man.

The media had dubbed him the 'Night Stalker'.

So far he'd killed eleven people, raped four women, attempted to rape another, beaten a sixteen-year-old girl so badly with a tyre iron she'd needed 478 stitches in her scalp, and gouged out the eyes of one of the victims when she tried to shoot him. He didn't just break into homes, he ravaged them, physically and psychologically. He'd brought terror to the whole city, not just because of the sheer brutality of his crimes, or because he was a satanist, scrawling pentagrams on the walls and making his victims swear allegiance to the devil, but because his hunting ground seemed to be everywhere: he'd started off in Glassell Park, four miles from Downtown, but had since spread out to Monrovia, seventeen miles east of there, Whittier, fifteen miles south, and then twelve miles to the north in Sun Valley. Because of that, the whole thing was a jurisdictional nightmare, with the LA County Sheriff, the LAPD and eight other separate police departments involved. Yet Jo wasn't a part of any of it. Hayesfield had expanded the twenty-five-strong team of detectives at the Sheriff's Department without ever asking Jo to join, and for reasons she knew had nothing to do with her abilities as a cop and everything to do with her being female and having given birth eighteen months ago.

Before she'd had Ethan, most of the men she'd worked with more or less treated her the same, at least to her face. That didn't mean she hadn't overheard discussions about the size of her breasts, the shape of her ass, how she would perform in bed and what her favourite position might be; about how she wouldn't be strong enough to pick up a Remington, the department's shotgun of choice, or how the kickback would probably burst her right tit; and then there were all the barbed comments – dressed up as light-hearted fun – about how she'd never be as effective as a man in chasing down a suspect because, again, her tits would get in the way; and in a high-speed pursuit she wouldn't be able to keep up, or just crash the car completely, because everyone knew how bad women drivers were. It was generally done out of earshot, or when they thought she wasn't around, but even when it wasn't, even when her male colleagues said things directly to her face, all she could do was swear at them or ignore them, because there was no recourse. There was no system of complaint, not even the basic framework for it. There were no other female Homicide detectives to go into battle with, and every senior position was held by a man. So, unless she wanted her career to be over, there had never been any point in protesting about the discrimination before, and – with so much focus on the Stalker, so much tension inside the department, and resources so stretched – it would have been even more suicidal to say something now. All of which meant that, for the past year, she'd not only had to endure all the usual comments, repeated jokes, sniggers and put-downs, she'd had to work some investigations entirely by herself – without a partner – because so many other detectives had been seconded to the Stalker. Worse, it meant she was catching all the shitty cases no one else wanted or got given, and she was having to watch one of the biggest manhunts in the entire history of Los Angeles play out from the opposite side of a squad room. And it was making her angry. It was making her bitter. It hurt.

Starting up the car, she pulled off the driveway and headed south, into the Hills, trying to calm herself by listening to the radio. Tears for Fears played for a while, but when the music stopped, the DJ began talking about the Night Stalker. She switched stations, but the same thing happened again, and then again, over and over, the lulls between songs, the gaps between ads, dedicated to the actions of a depraved animal.

Finally, she turned the radio off completely.

For twenty minutes she revelled in the quiet, the drive into West Hollywood filled with nothing more than the low throb of the engine and the repetitive sounds of the freeway. She thought about the day ahead, about the men she worked with, about the things in her life that she *could* control, and then a picture of her son filled her head, an image of Ethan asleep in his bed, and everything settled. He was her ballast.

Her son was everything.

And, in that moment, Joline Kader found some peace.

She would never find it again.

7

We talked about what I'd found out at Black Gale over dinner in Healy's hotel room, although dinner was something of a misnomer: we were five miles from the nearest town of any size and wedged between the motorway and the main building of a service station, so we'd had to make do with Burger King.

'What did you find in the file?' I asked him.

'It's a pretty thin case,' Healy replied through a mouthful of burger, 'but not because of sloppy police work. They worked all the angles you'd expect them to, they tried to tie available evidence to the biggest questions, but the lack of an obvious crime means some of it feels desperate. I mean, it's not hard to see why they dropped the idea of it being a pissed-up game of hide-and-seek.' He reached over and picked up a thick sheaf of papers; on top was a gallery of low-res shots extracted from Chris Gibbs's phone. Healy waved it in his hand. 'They were pretty well oiled even before they ate, judging by these pictures. Maybe not hardly-able-to-stand bad, but we're clearly in warm-glow-and-stupid-grin territory. The empty bottles in the recycling bins seem to back that up too. And when you're half-stewed, some spontaneous Halloween game *is* the sort of nutty shite some people might find fun. But I don't know . . .'

'Not this group?'

'No.'

'I agree. I think we can dismiss the idea of a game.'

I looked at the printouts that Healy had in his hands, in particular the photo that Chris Gibbs had taken on his mobile phone using the timer: nine faces, partly obscured behind party wear, but all of them recognizable. I tried to force myself to see something in the shot, some minor giveaway, something to help me make sense of what happened afterwards, but there was nothing.

And that was something else that had begun to occur to me as I drove back from Black Gale: everyone had gone. The four couples liked each other, that much seemed to be indisputable, but was it really normal for nine individuals – including a kid of nineteen – to operate with such a hive-mind mentality? Wasn't it more realistic to suppose that one or two of them might have decided they didn't want to leave the village that night?

'What if someone forced them to leave?' Healy asked, as if he knew where my thoughts were at.

'There were no foreign tyre tracks in the village.'

'Maybe whoever it was came in on foot.'

'One person versus nine?'

'The person could have been armed.'

'Still,' I said, 'it's not great odds. You only have to make one mistake, turn your back at the wrong moment. Even with a gun, it's tricky to herd nine people around.'

'Maybe there was *more* than one attacker.'

'If there was, there should have been evidence of it.'

He'd started nodding before I'd even finished my sentence because he already knew it was unlikely to have happened in that way: there wasn't only a lack of tyre tracks, but forensic techs had meticulously matched footprints in and around the properties to footwear left behind in the four homes. That still left the shoes that the nine villagers were wearing at the time they exited the village – which, of course, the investigators couldn't match in the same way – but there were no prints leading up to Black Gale's main gate, suggesting they hadn't left on foot, and the unmatched moulds taken from the scene belonged to nine people and nine pairs of shoes. So, in essence, the police had nine shoe prints they couldn't definitively link to the missing villagers, but it was almost one hundred per cent likely that it *was* them, especially as those footprints all moved in the same patterns around the homes, in repeated loops.

'What's your thinking on the timing?' Healy asked me. 'Did

they disappear on Halloween night? The next morning? November the 2nd?'

I looked at the selfies that Chris Gibbs had taken and then picked up one of the shots: 'It says in the file that none of the clothes they're wearing in these pictures are listed as clothing the police found in any of the four homes, right?'

He nodded, again seeing where I was going: the clothes in the selfies weren't discovered in any of the properties, which heavily suggested that the villagers were still wearing them at the time they left the village.

'I think it happened on Halloween night,' I said.

'Or they woke early and pulled on exactly the same clothes as the night before because they'd been left nearby in the bedrooms and were convenient.'

That was possible too, but Halloween night still felt more likely: their phones were off from ten that night, and none of the alarms had been set, so it seemed like they'd gone to the dinner party expecting to return to their homes at the evening's end. If they'd known what was coming – if they'd known that they'd be away from the village for days, weeks, months – they'd have surely set the alarms. The fact that they didn't seemed to suggest that something had interrupted them that night. The question was what – or who?

'Does this smell like an inside job to you?'

Healy glanced at me, but not in surprise at the question. It had been on my mind from the second I'd first started looking into the case and I could see he'd been considering it too.

'It would explain why there are no other footprints,' I went on, studying the same photos, 'and it explains the lack of suspicious tyre tracks. Chris Gibbs had a Land Rover, the Daveys had that Porsche SUV, and Randolph and Emiline a camper van. They're all big cars, capable of ferrying around lots of people at once.'

He shrugged. 'There could be something in it.'

'But?'

'But which of the villagers had the motivation?'

43

'I don't know. Maybe the same one – or ones – who had the motivation to take the camper van and make it disappear.'

'Randolph and Emiline, you mean?'

'Not necessarily. I mean, it's their vehicle but it wouldn't have been hard for someone else in the village to gain access to it.'

I looked at my notes, at the names of the villagers, at the possible suspects – and the possible reasons – why one or more of them would have taken the Volkswagen. There was little of substance about the missing vehicle in the police file, only that the cops had looked for it and gone through the same thought processes we just had. Ultimately, it was another line of enquiry that had hit a dead end.

I looked at the villagers' jobs again, trying to seek my answers there. Patrick was running a PR firm and Francesca Perry was a nurse in Cumbria. John and Freda Davey were both retired. The Gibbses ran a farm and their son was at college. And Randolph and Emiline were retired and worked part-time at a library respectively. Nothing rang alarm bells in terms of their employment, so – if I was going to run with the idea any further, or make any sort of connection from them back to the unaccounted-for camper van – I'd have to dig down into who they were as people.

'Here's something else,' Healy said, bringing a page of phone records towards him. 'Why bother taking wallets and mobiles if they had no intention of using them?'

'Maybe they *did* intend to use them.'

'But the phones didn't come on after Halloween night and there's been nothing since,' he went on, 'not even a minor blip on the radar. I looked at the phone records here. They only cover the two weeks before everyone went missing, but I can't see much to get excited about. We'd be looking for calls to strange numbers, repeated calls to the same number, that sort of thing, but there's nothing like that here. No issues on Internet activity either: the Gibbs kid is the only one who seemed to use his phone for actually going on websites, and that seems to be a mix of video games and porn. I mean, he was a teenage boy – that's pretty standard, right?' He checked the printouts again. 'The others used a few apps here and there, but it's mostly uninteresting and expected: Mail, WhatsApp, some news feeds – and Patrick Perry used Twitter and Instagram.'

'Anything on them?'

'Nothing.'

'So maybe we need to go back further than a fortnight. Two weeks doesn't give us much of an overview. I've got a guy I can ask.'

He nodded, knowing not to press further. I had sources from my newspaper days that I still used, but I never discussed their identity with anyone, not even Healy.

I gestured to some of the paperwork he still held in his hands. 'Ross said that Chris Gibbs made almost seven figures from the building and sale of those houses.'

Healy nodded. 'So you think this could be about money?'

Our eyes both shifted to a photocopy of a tabloid story – run a couple of days after the villagers went missing – that we'd pinned to the wall. The newspaper had managed to locate a friend of Laura Gibbs who claimed that, five or six years before he vanished, Chris had started to 'get a taste for gambling'. In the same article, Tori Gibbs – Chris's sister – completely disregarded this statement, calling it a lie, but the friend – who wanted to remain anonymous – said Laura had told her in confidence that no one else, not even Tori, knew about Chris's 'demons', and said she had only come forward because she wondered whether the gambling had something to do with what happened at Black Gale. Could Chris have owed someone money?

And did the other villagers get caught in the crossfire?

'There's no evidence to support what's on the wall there,' Healy said, taking another bite of his cheeseburger. 'If Chris was a gambler, I can't see it in these financials.'

'So what did he do with all the money he made from the houses?'

Healy leafed through the police file.

'He invested in some more property in Harrogate and York and rented both of those out, he paid a whopping tax bill, and then the rest of it is all audited and spoken for in black and white. There are no dodgy payments to cryptic bank accounts, no notable transfers in the days before they went missing. He had no accounts with online betting companies. I mean, it's possible that his gambling habit – if there even was one – may have been physical: he could have withdrawn cash, which is more difficult to track and trace, and then gone into an actual bricks-and-mortar bookies – but the nearest ones are in Kendal or Skipton and they're thirty-odd miles away in opposite directions. If he was a gambler, why not just do it online?'

I looked at the article on the wall again. 'So your gut reaction is –'

'We probably shouldn't dismiss it until we know for sure, but I reckon it's pretty unlikely. And, anyway, for the past two and a half years there's been no activity at all in Chris and Laura's accounts and nothing in any of the others either. The cops have got alerts set up with all their banks, so if money had suddenly come out at any point, or if someone had gone into any of the accounts to recoup a debt, it would have been noted. But it hasn't. These accounts have been dead for the entire time the nine of them have been gone.'

He handed me the bank statements and, for a while, we worked in silence, both of us inching our way through the nine missing persons reports.

Eventually, I said, 'What was the weather like at the time?'

Healy held up a finger and worked his way back through the paperwork until he found what he was looking for. 'Dry,' he said. 'On Halloween it had been clear skies in the day, minus temperatures at night, with frost. The day following that was the same; the 2nd of November was cloudy but no rain, and so was the 3rd.' That was when Ross had arrived at the village. 'It rained on the 4th of November.'

'So there was no chance other footprints had been washed away before the police got there on the 3rd?'

'Unlikely.'

I glanced at the wall we'd set up, the cascade of paper shivering as the air from the heating vent whispered across it. I'd pinned up some of the pictures I'd taken from the houses, photographs of the four households, on holidays, at home, living out their lives with no idea of what was coming down the line. In among them was another shot of them all – this time without their masks – gathered around the Gibbses' table. Freda Davey in a floral dress. Emiline Wilson in a red one with blue trim. Chris and Patrick in jeans, Patrick with a green V-neck sweater, Chris in a checked shirt. Randolph in cords and a pair of polished brogues, his right foot inching out from behind a table leg. Everything looked so normal.

But it wasn't normal.

Nothing was normal.

The more of them that were missing, the easier they should have been to find, because nine people meant nine potential trails. Instead, the case was constricting, closing itself off, the trails vanishing. Black Gale had started out as one of the strangest disappearances I'd ever come across.

Now I could sense it turning into something else.

Something much more unsettling.

8

Just after 9 p.m., I video-called Rina Blake and Tori Gibbs.

I'd already talked to both of them before leaving London, but we'd only covered the basics. Rina – John and Freda Davey's daughter – lived in Cambridge and was currently six weeks into maternity leave after the birth of her second child; Tori, Chris Gibbs's sister, was down in Deptford, and wrote about politics for the news website *FeedMe*. When we talked, the two women admitted they'd grown close since the disappearances, and because they were only a fifty-minute train ride apart would often meet up, primarily for Tori to give Rina updates about the case: Tori admitted she'd always had an interest in true crime and was now using that to try and spearhead her own search in her spare time into what happened at Black Gale.

It would have been easy to be cynical about that last part – especially because, if she'd found anything in the last two and a half years that was in any way useful, the search wouldn't still be in deep freeze – but I chose to see it as an opportunity: if it turned out Tori had anything I could use, that was a bonus; if she didn't, I hadn't lost anything. And, anyway, her efforts were driven entirely by the same things that drove me.

Unanswered questions.

The pain of grief.

The people she'd loved.

I'd decided to split the calls, talking to Rina first, then Tori, then both of them together, and when Rina came on, she was in a low-lit living room, with a floor lamp beside her. It was quiet apart from the occasional crackle from a baby monitor.

I started by asking her about the movements of her parents in the weeks and months before they disappeared, and she replied in a soft South Yorkshire accent, her blonde hair scraped into a bun, her face carrying the lines and shadows of a mother whose six-week-old baby was waking up on the hour, every hour, all night. Despite her obvious exhaustion, her responses were lucid, often very detailed and precise, perhaps reflecting the nature of her work as a forensic accountant at KPMG, her face a clear echo of her mum's: I recalled the photo I'd seen of John and Freda Davey on the cruise ship, him in a rugby league shirt, her underweight and pale, and it had been the colour of Freda's eyes that had caught my attention. Rina's were the same vivid blue.

'So your parents seemed all right in those last few weeks?' I asked her.

She picked up a glass of water, sipping from it, thinking. 'They seemed fine. I honestly can't think of anything we talked about that raised any alarm bells with me.'

'How often did you speak to them?'

'Mum, I would normally speak to three or four times a week on the phone, and then we'd text most days. Dad, I would text less often – maybe once or twice a week.'

'I read that your mum had cancer.'

A flash of distress.

'Yes,' she said.

'I'm sorry to hear that.'

She shrugged. 'It is what it is, I guess.'

'This was the end of 2013?'

'That's right, yeah.'

'And it came back a couple of years later, before she disappeared?'

'She went to see her GP in August, I think, and she was back at the hospital in September. She said to me that the doctors reckoned it was early and it was treatable, and so she was due to start chemo in October, but decided to delay for a few months.'

'Any idea why?'

'She told one of the nurses she wanted to go on holiday first.'

That had been in the file too.

'But she didn't tell you that?' I asked.

'I remember her talking about it. She'd always wanted to go to Australia, and it was something she and Dad discussed often, especially after they'd retired, because he was more interested in New Zealand and they always said that they'd just combine the two into one massive trip. But it wasn't something they ever booked – certainly not in the weeks after she got the news about the cancer. I'd bet my house on the fact that what she told the nurse that day was just the same things she'd talked to me about, over and over again – her dream trip, the places in Australia she wanted to go, all that sort of thing . . .' Rina glanced to the side of the camera, as the baby monitor sprang into life. When her eyes came back, they were pained. 'When she said she was going to delay the chemo, I remember thinking, "Just get it done, Mum. A stupid bloody holiday can wait for a few months, this is your *life*." But then I realized she was scared. She was just really scared. The treatment was brutal the first time – and so a holiday sounds a hell of a lot better than the reality of having more poison pumped into your body.'

I gave her a moment and then said, 'What did they do before they retired?'

'Dad was a teacher and Mum worked for the council. She and I were born up in Leeds, but Dad was a southern softie.' She smiled; paused for a second. 'He was born in Dover and grew up somewhere near Margate, but he did his degree in York. He always joked that he couldn't wait to get as far away from home as possible; I didn't know my paternal grandparents because they died before I was born, but from what Dad used to say, my grandfather was a bit of a shit – you know, a drinker, a womanizer, not scared of using a fist or a boot. Anyway, after his degree, Dad worked as a teacher, *then* he wrote this super-hardcore academic paper on the Second World War which, in university circles, got a lot of people in fawn blazers hot under the collar. "Ideology, Exploitation and Extermination: Realism versus Idealism at the Nuremberg Trials". Give it a go. It's an excellent sleeping pill.'

I smiled. 'And your mum?'

'She was much less career-orientated. She used to tell Ian and me that all she really wanted to be was a mum, and that any job she had would always be secondary to bringing us up. Mum didn't work a lot, really, until the early nineties when Ian and I were both at secondary school. She was at the gas board for a while, and then for the last five or six years before she retired she was at Leeds council. Then they both called it a day, bought the house up at Black Gale, and the rest . . . it's just . . .' *History*. She blinked, trying to remain stoic. 'Anyway, like I said, Mum wasn't hugely driven in that way. I think, to be honest, she missed her true calling.'

'Which was what?'

'She was a brilliant runner in her twenties,' Rina said, smiling. 'She used to run marathons all over the place and clocked serious times. Even after she stopped competing, she still ran. She was still running in her fifties. She loved it, and she was bloody good at it too.'

Out of the corner of my eye, I could see Healy writing something down, sitting out of view of the laptop's camera.

'What about Black Gale?' I asked. 'Did they like it there?'

'They loved it.'

'So no arguments or disagreements with the neighbours – even minor ones?'

'No.' Rina shrugged. The baby monitor blinked into life again, the soft sound of her son turning over in his crib. 'They loved all the guys up there. Dad always used to say it was the best decision they ever made.'

I thanked her, told her I would call her back in half an hour, and then dialled Tori Gibbs's number. She answered straight away, sitting in an armchair by a set of bookshelves, the lights of the Thames visible behind her. She was in her early fifties, with dark eyes and dark hair; she was also single, with no kids and no distractions other than her work, which must have been how she'd found the time to dig into the disappearances at Black Gale. Her interest in true crime was obvious too, her shelves packed with books about some of history's most notorious killers. BTK. The Green River Killer. Jack the Ripper. Fred and Rosemary West. The Night Stalker.

We talked for a while about Chris and Laura Gibbs, about Mark too, and then I asked her about the story that had run in the newspapers concerning her brother.

'That was total bullshit,' she said.

'He never had any problems with gambling?'

'No way. In the tabloids in those first few days, it was a feeding frenzy, so they were all searching for an angle. Whoever they spoke to – if it was even a real person – just lied through their teeth. There was another story in one of the other papers about Mark being "fixated" on this girl he went to school with, again using quotes from an "anonymous source". That was a bunch of lies too. He posted some comment on this girl's Instagram feed – like a "You look hot" sort of thing – and that was him apparently obsessed with her. I mean, it was ridiculous. That's how teenagers communicate, right? Mark was a lovely kid.'

'I didn't see that story. Which paper was that in?'

'I can't remember. One of the red tops, I think.'

I glanced at Healy and he knew what I was asking him: *see if you can find the story she's talking about online.* He picked up my phone and started looking.

Turning back to Tori, I said, 'The money that Chris made from selling the houses at Black Gale – do you know what he did with it all?'

The answer was already in the police file, but I wanted to see if the information we had tallied up. The Gibbses had a lot of cash swirling around at the end, and while it all appeared to be accounted for, money could often be the cause of bad decisions, as Healy and I had already speculated.

'He bought a couple of properties as investments,' Tori replied, 'and then rented them both out. I think he might have stuck some of it into fixed-rate savings accounts; the rest they just used for holidays, stuff for the house, that sort of thing. They weren't extravagant people, my brother and Laura.'

That echoed what Ross had told me earlier.

I shifted to the subject of the other residents.

'Your brother never had any problems with the neighbours?' I asked.

'The other people at Black Gale? No, never. In fact, I remember him saying once how lucky he and Laura felt – they'd built those houses, and they'd ended up with three sets of neighbours they loved. I mean, it could have been a disaster. They could have ended up next door to the Manson Family.' She leaned back in her chair and put her hands behind her head. 'I stayed up there for a week when they first put those properties on the market,' she went on, coming back in towards the camera, so her face filled the frame again, 'and Chris was absolutely bricking it. "What if we end up with neighbours from hell? What if this ruins everything?" He could be a bit of a worrier sometimes, my brother, but actually I could see where he was coming from. He'd built those houses so that they could give themselves and Mark a really nice future, but Chris was right: it could have been an absolute bloody mess. In reality, the whole thing was a big leap into the unknown. And that area, it's pretty remote. I mean, they'd only just got decent broadband, let alone fibre, and being that secluded – it doesn't always appeal to everyone, does it?'

She was right. In fact, being so far removed from other people could create problems, and what seemed idyllic to start with could soon become oppressive. I'd wondered, as I'd looked around Black Gale earlier, whether the seclusion might have played a part – could it have led one of the villagers into making an irrational decision? Could it driven them to depression? – but there was no evidence of that and it felt like a stretch. The village was isolated, but it wasn't at the ends of the earth.

I changed direction. 'You mentioned last night that you'd done some digging around yourself on Black Gale?'

'Right.' She instantly looked apologetic, and said, 'What you've got to remember is that – until you picked up the phone to us all the other day – this whole thing was dead.'

'It's okay,' I replied, holding up a conciliatory hand. 'The question wasn't loaded. I was just wondering what you'd found. To me, the police seem to have done a pretty decent job. What do you think?'

'Don't ask how I got hold of the file,' she said, 'but I've seen the investigation and I'd have to say that – broadly – I agree with you.'

'Only broadly?'

She looked down into her lap and I heard the sound of pages being turned: she must have had a notepad of some kind. When she looked up again, she said, 'What do you make of the fact that there are no suspicious tyre tracks or footprints?'

'It could mean a couple of things,' I replied. 'Either they all piled into the back of the missing camper van and left voluntarily – *or* it wasn't so voluntary.'

'You're talking about it being an inside job?'

I glanced at Healy. We'd discussed the same thing earlier.

'I think we have to consider it,' I said.

'What about Randolph and Emiline?'

'What about them?'

'No one knows anything about them.'

'That's not entirely true.'

'But it's almost true,' she said, and then stopped herself, frowning. 'Sorry, I wasn't . . . Look, I didn't mean to accuse them of . . .' She sighed. 'You know, the crazy thing is, I've spent five years standing up to politicians, holding them to account, picking apart their lies and skewering them on our website, and I've become pretty bloody good at what I do. But what happened to Chris and Laura, to Mark, to all the others, it's the first time I've ever felt uncertain of myself.' She paused again. 'I guess what I mean is that, when it comes to Randolph and Emiline, everything's just less . . . clear.'

'In what sense?'

'Asking around, even among friends of theirs, it's like you get a surface sheen of detail but, when you dig a little deeper, no one really, properly, knows them.'

'Okay,' I said. I was being deliberately non-committal, because I didn't want to accuse Randolph and Emiline of anything ahead of the facts. They had no family and no kids – they'd left their house to charity in their wills – and the majority of the time, families were how the most lucid memories of someone were built. They were also the connections that, quite often, maintained the entire momentum of a missing persons search. So I was less concerned that their friends didn't know every detail of their lives – or that, unlike the other residents of Black Gale, they appeared, on the surface, more opaque – and more bothered by the fact that theirs was the only vehicle that was missing. That was evident, inarguable, and the longer it took for that camper van to resurface, and the villagers alongside it, the more it seeded doubts about who Randolph and Emiline were.

Out of interest, I asked Tori what she made of the missing vehicle.

'It's pretty bloody weird, that's what I make of it. I mean, it was the only vehicle that wasn't there the day Ross turned up at the village.' She opened out her hands, a gesture that said everything about Randolph and Emiline that I'd just been thinking myself. 'Have you got any leads on it?'

'Not yet.' I glanced at Healy again. 'I've got someone trying to trace it.'

'You won't find anything. It's like it vanished, the same as Chris and Laura, the same as all of them. It wasn't sold on to anyone, there was no SORN declaration made, so if it's off-road somewhere, it's being kept that way illegally. It's a total dead end. The police couldn't find it – and neither could I.'

'All right,' I said, 'leave it with me.'

We talked about the chronology of the house moves – the Perrys were first in, then Randolph and Emiline a month later, then the Daveys a month after that – and then I dialled Rina's number again and began a conversation between the three of us. It was obvious the two women were comfortable with each other.

'When was the last time you talked to your brother?' I asked Tori.

'That would have been by text three or four days before Halloween, but I spoke to Laura on the phone on the 30th of October, because I was going to this house party in Peckham and I wanted to get a cheesecake recipe from her. Laura was great at all that sort of thing. She was really artsy and creative, a talented cook.' Tori paused, taking a long breath. 'Laura was never just a sister-in-law to me. She was a sister. I used to talk on the phone to her more often than to Chris.'

'And you didn't get the sense that anything was wrong?'

'No, nothing.'

'What about with Mark?'

'No,' she said again, even more decisive this time. 'Like I said, he was a good kid; a little awkward sometimes – your typical teenage boy – but he was polite and sensible, and he loved his mum and dad. Especially his dad. There were only two things Mark wanted to do after he finished school – be a farmer like Chris, and play video games.'

Things petered out after that, so I thanked them and waited for their video windows to snap to black. Rina leaned forward, grabbed her mouse and disappeared.

But Tori didn't.

'Is everything all right?' I asked her.

She'd moved back a little and I could make out more of the background: right angles and blocks of light on the Isle of Dogs, and then the distant towers of Canary Wharf.

'Tori?'

'I didn't want to mention it in front of Rina,' she said quietly, not looking into the camera, as if she felt guilty about what she wanted to say. 'I'm not sure if I should mention it at all, in fact, which is why I never said anything when we talked before. I mean, it's probably nothing and I've never been able to prove it one way or another, anyway.' She looked up now. 'I deal in facts. Gossip and rumours, I hate all that shit.'

She stopped.

Out of the corner of my eye, I saw Healy, a pen still clamped between thumb and forefinger, turn around at the desk and shift forward, eyes glued to my laptop.

'It's fine,' I assured her. 'What is it you want to say?'

'It's about Patrick Perry,' she said.

9

I glanced back at the wall, at the photos of Patrick and Francesca Perry.

'What about Patrick?' I asked.

'It might be nothing,' Tori said, and began moving in her chair, shifting from side to side: she was hesitant, obviously still conflicted about whether she should say anything. 'It's why I haven't mentioned this to Rina, and especially to Ross, because I don't want to make a big deal if it's nothing. I don't want to be making accusations I can't back up. I mean, he could have just been doing exactly what he claimed to be doing . . .'

I shifted closer to the laptop.

'You'd better spell it out for me, Tori.'

'Okay,' she replied, the word pushed out with a sigh. 'Okay, so like I said to you, it could be nothing at all, but I remember being on the phone to Laura a couple of months before they disappeared, and we were right in the middle of this conversation when she just stopped dead, like someone had interrupted her. I asked her if she was all right, and she was fine – she just said something odd was going on with one of her neighbours.'

Healy and I glanced at each other.

'What did she mean by "odd"?' I asked.

'Patrick. He kept going for these walks out on the moors.'

I frowned. 'As in hikes?'

'That's the thing: Laura didn't know.'

'So he *could* just have been going for a hike?'

'He could have.'

'But Laura didn't think so?'

'She said he never went out with a backpack, or in hiking shoes. He never bothered with a coat – and he was never gone longer than an hour.'

'So he was going somewhere close by?'

She held out her hands. 'I guess.'

'And in which direction did he head?'

'Out beyond the back of the farm, into the valley.'

'Cross-country? Not out of the front, where the main gate into the village is?'

'No,' Tori said. 'Out into the fields.'

'Did Laura say how often this happened?'

'I think she said it had happened about three or four times by then.'

'So not very often at all?'

She could see what I was driving at: because she was so wedded to the idea of it being relevant now, it was hard for her to see how prosaic this revelation was. Three or four times, Patrick had gone out on the moors for an hour – so what?

'But why wouldn't he go out with any of the right gear?' Tori asked. 'No walking shoes, not even a coat. You don't think that's odd?'

'Did Francesca ever go with Patrick?'

'Well, that's the other thing. I think that's what caught Laura's attention. He'd head out on to the moors without his wife, and he'd often do it first thing in the morning, or early evening, when the sun wasn't properly up yet or it was just about to set – like he didn't want anyone to see him.'

'But Francesca must have noticed his absence?'

'She worked over at Westmorland Hospital in Kendal – she was a senior nurse there – so she always did irregular hours, shift work, all that.' Tori paused. 'This is just what Laura said to me. I don't know a lot about the Perrys, really. But Laura said Patrick was a good-looking guy, charming – not that that means anything, but you know . . .' Even unspoken, it was clear to her that Patrick being attractive *did* mean something. 'Anyway, point is, he would only go out like that when his wife was working. Whenever she was home they'd go out together, and when it was the two of them they'd have all the right equipment: the shoes, the coats, the backpacks. When it was just him, that was when it was different.'

As Patrick and Francesca Perry stared back at me from the wall, I thought of something Ross had said to me earlier: *Even after so many years of being married, they never lost that spark. They just loved spending time together.*

So where could Patrick have been going when he was on his own?

Sneaking around like that, if that was even what he was doing, and especially going out so unprepared for a hike, would normally lead to an obvious conclusion: he was going to meet someone; he'd established a relationship in secret, an affair. It happened, even within a successful marriage. But why head out the back, where there were no roads and the moorland went on for miles? Other than the main track in and out of the village, Black Gale's surroundings were a knotty sprawl of fields, woodland and valleys, not particularly easy to navigate, and the nearest village was a good fifty-minute walk away. Laura Gibbs had told Tori he'd gone and come back inside an hour. There was a sporadic network of narrow back roads, all of which had passing areas, which meant waiting points for a car and whoever he might have been meeting, but it seemed like a lot of unnecessary hassle: if Francesca was at work and he really *was* having an affair, why wouldn't Patrick just jump in his own car and drive to where he needed to go?

Could he have been meeting someone else from Black Gale?

I looked at the wall, at the faces of the other residents, mulling over the idea of an affair conducted within the confines of Black Gale. It would have been risky, hard to hide and potentially easy to expose in an environment where all the villagers lived so closely, physically and socially. How could you ever do anything in secret when even something as simple as a walk got spotted? But that didn't make the idea impossible. And if Laura was the one who'd actually spotted Patrick, and Patrick really was cheating on his wife, that meant he could have been seeing either Freda Davey or Emiline Wilson.

'Did Laura ever say anything to Patrick?' I asked.

Tori nodded. 'He told her he was trying to get into photography, and that he thought sunrise and sunset would be the best times to get the most dramatic photos.'

'Which is perfectly plausible.'

'It is, yes.'

She seemed a little defeated now, as if – for the first time – she understood the arguable nature of this line of enquiry. The decision not to mention anything to Rina or Ross looked like a good one.

Tori moved, her chair squeaking gently. 'For what it's worth, he told her he was practising taking photographs on his phone with a view to getting a proper camera later on down the line – which is what he *did* do. Laura said he showed her the pictures he'd taken, and they were beautiful, and then he showed her a camera he'd bought a few weeks later that he started carrying on him. So, whatever else was going on, he wasn't lying about that. He *did* go out there and he *was* taking pictures.'

'And did you tell the police what you just told me?'

'Yes. All of it.'

Except it wasn't in the file, which meant they clearly didn't see anything worth pursuing. It was easy to see why. As I thought about that, out of the corner of my eye I saw Healy holding something up. It was a six- by four-inch picture he'd lifted out of the shoebox full of photographs that I'd found in the Perrys' living room: taken from the moors, it was a shot of the village, the four properties just silhouettes against the red stain of a sunrise.

'What about Francesca?' I asked. 'Did Laura ever speak to her about it?'

'Yes. She said, after the seventh or eighth time it happened, she casually dropped it into conversation with Francesca, but Francesca seemed to be pretty accepting of the explanation Patrick had given her.'

'That he was out there taking pictures?'

'Right.'

'Okay, Tori,' I said. 'I appreciate you mentioning it.'

We said goodbye and rung off.

I turned and looked at Healy. He was going through the shoe-box, picking out and setting aside other photos that Patrick had taken: there were at least six of them.

'What do you think?' I said.

He stopped and looked up, one of the pictures – a shot of a valley, a woodland in its cleft, the sky a deep, vivid mauve – pinched between his thumb and forefinger.

'We forget it and move on,' he said.

'You don't think there's anything in it?'

'In a guy going out with a camera and taking pictures of the countryside?' He placed the photo on to the pile. 'It's like Chris Gibbs being a gambler, or no one knowing anything about Randolph and Emiline, or Mark Gibbs being "obsessed" with some girl he went to school with. None of it means anything until we can prove that it does.' Healy held up my phone so I could see what he was looking at: onscreen was the website for one of the red-top tabloids and the story that Tori had been referring to: GHOST HOUSE KID 'STALKED' INSTAGRAM GIRL.

'"Stalked". Is that in any way accurate?'

'Not based on what's in the story. He was "obsessed" with her because he wrote three separate comments under one photograph she posted.' Healy checked the story again. 'First comment: "You look hot." Second comment: "Do you still live in Skipton?" Third comment: "How are your family doing?"' Healy shrugged. 'She didn't reply to any of the comments.'

He threw me the phone and I started going through the story. On the surface there was nothing in it. There was nothing in Patrick going out to take photos either, or in Chris's history as an alleged gambler. But when you were looking for missing people, the answers were rarely, if ever, bobbing around on the surface.

The truth was never in the shallows.

It was always somewhere much deeper.

10

We called it a night.

I went downstairs to reception and booked a second room, next door to Healy, and then began the process of taking the computers and tablets upstairs. That meant the hard drive and tower from the Perrys', laptops belonging to both Mark Gibbs and Randolph Solomon, and the iPads that had been on Laura Gibbs's bedside table and in John and Freda Davey's home. Healy didn't argue – computers had never really been his strong point as an investigator, technology had moved on since he was at the Met, and he'd always been more effective in the field, anyway – so we'd make more headway if I did a first sweep of them in the morning. In reality, though, I didn't expect to find much: if all the tech had already been released from evidence, that was normally a fair indication of its worth.

While I was outside at the car, I also put in a call to the old newspaper source I'd mentioned to Healy. His name was Spike. He was a hacker, hidden away at an address he'd never given me, using a name that wasn't his. We'd never met in all the time we'd known each other, and when I paid him, I left the cash in a locker at a sports centre close to where I lived. But when it came to getting beyond firewalls and never leaving a trace, Spike was the best there was. I asked him to get me the mobile phone records for the nine Black Gale residents, starting two months before they vanished. The police had only gone back a fortnight.

'Wow,' he said, 'that's a big job.'

'Yeah, I know. Reckon you can handle it?'

'Ha ha. This is me you're talking to. You want landlines as well?'

'Yeah, across the same period of time.'

'What about after they disappeared?'

'None of the handsets have been used since 31 October 2015, so I don't think there'll be calls into or out of them after that – but if you see anything, let me know.'

I hung up and headed back to the room.

As I was letting myself in, my phone sprang into life again. I expected it to be Spike with a question he'd forgotten to ask, but instead it was my daughter, Annabel.

I pushed the door shut and hit Answer.

'Hey, sweetheart.'

'Hey, how are you?'

'I'm good. How was your day?'

'Not bad,' she said, although she sounded tired. I'd only known her for around five years, her entire existence kept secret from me – and mine from her – until she turned twenty-four. But while I sometimes worried that we'd never capture the bond that flourished and matured between a father and daughter, I knew enough about her now to pick up on the things that were concerning her. Often, she would try to hide those things from me because she believed they were unimportant when compared to what I dealt with in my work. But they were never unimportant to me. Those things were everything I'd missed for twenty-four years.

'Is Liv okay?' I asked.

'Yeah, we're both fine.'

She lived with her thirteen-year-old sister, Olivia, in the house in south Devon that they'd grown up in; a house that had been left to them by the people Annabel had – for nearly a quarter of a century – believed were her parents. Biologically, Liv wasn't mine, but it had never felt that way: I treated her exactly the same way as I treated Annabel.

'So what's up?' I said.

'I think I might have done something I shouldn't have.'

I pulled a chair out and sat down.

'What do you mean?'

'I messed up before school this morning.'

64

Annabel was a teacher.

'Messed up how?'

'Liv's being a pain in the arse at the moment,' she said, her words soft. '"School's boring, I hate school, I hate learning" – all of that. I try to laugh it off, try to tell myself it's just a phase she's in, but it grinds me down. I had her in one ear, and then all this lesson prep, and I just . . .' A pause. 'Someone called this morning.'

'What did they want?'

'He said he was a friend of yours.'

A low-level alarm started to grip me.

'Okay. What did he say his name was?'

'That's the thing, he didn't, and I didn't ask. I know that's stupid.'

'It's all right,' I said, attempting to sound calm, even though I didn't feel it. I tried to imagine who'd call Annabel claiming to be a friend of mine, without offering a name.

I could only really think of one person.

'Did this guy have an accent?' I asked her.

'Yes,' she said. 'He sounded cockney.'

Shit.

'What did he ask you?'

'He just wanted to know if I knew where you were. He said you and him had been working on an investigation together but he hadn't been able to get hold of you on your mobile. He said, in those circumstances, you'd encouraged him to call me because, if you weren't in London working, you'd generally be staying here with us.'

That was a complete fabrication.

The alarm started to turn to anger now.

'Did you tell him where I was?' I asked her. There wasn't a hint of accusation in my voice, but it still felt like some kind of an attack on her, especially as I'd phoned her yesterday evening to tell her I was working a case in the Dales. Apart from Healy – and the calls I'd made to Ross Perry, Rina Blake and Tori Gibbs to offer to help – Annabel was the only person who knew where I was heading.

'No,' she said. 'I didn't tell him you were up north.'

I felt the relief wash through me.

'Okay,' I said. 'Okay, that's good.'

'After he asked me that, I thought to myself, "Something's not right." I realized he hadn't offered his name, and when I began asking him who he was, he tried to talk his way around it again – and when that didn't work, he hung up on me. Have you got any idea who it was?'

'No,' I said, trying to make light of it. 'Probably some chancer.'

Except it wasn't.

It was a journalist from the *Daily Tribune* called Connor McCaskell. He'd been the one who'd started sniffing around my life in the weeks after I'd completed the case at Christmas, but unlike other journalists who'd pursued me in the aftermath, McCaskell hadn't been interested in the case itself. His interest was in me, my life, my background, my history, and it had eventually led him to the cottage in Devon and to questions about the man called Bryan Kennedy who was living there. McCaskell was the whole reason the cottage was empty now, why we'd shifted Healy out of there so quickly and then begun the process of changing his name for a second time.

He hadn't called me since early January, he hadn't left any messages, or sent any emails. I'd hoped he'd forgotten about me, or decided my life wasn't actually that interesting. I'd even started to believe that might really be the case, to the point where – when Healy had asked me about him in our weekly calls – I'd assured him everything was fine. I'd floated the idea we might be in the clear.

But now I knew we weren't.

McCaskell was still after me, and still after Bryan Kennedy.

He still had the scent of a story.

The Motel

The entrance to the Star Inn was off Santa Monica Boulevard, although nothing of the building was visible from the street. The parking lot was accessed via a ramp, itself small and easy to miss, and only then – once you'd passed under part of the second-floor corridor – did you even realize you were in a motel. The courtyard was narrow, with five parking spaces on either side, and kicked out in an upside-down L-shape, with rooms all along the right and directly ahead. Now, though, there was no access for potential guests, if anyone would ever, truly, choose to stay here: instead, everything was cordoned off with yellow crime-scene tape and the lot was filled with vehicles from the Sheriff's Department, a van with a blue stripe along its flank that belonged to the county coroner, and a Dodge Charger driven by Dan Chen, a pathologist from the medical examiner's office. Jo levered down her window, showed a waiting, uniformed deputy her badge, and then pulled in alongside Chen.

The moment the a/c died and she opened the door of the Oldsmobile, hot air rushed her. She left her jacket in the car and, as she moved across the lot, looked up to her right, where – on the second floor – she could see activity in a room at the end.

She rolled up her sleeves and took the stairs.

The closer she got to the room, the more she could see and hear of what was going on – the blink of a coroner investigator's camera flash, voices, the occasional, subdued hum of laughter – and, on the air, there was a smell too: fetid, decayed. She checked the courtyard for any dumpsters, wondering if the smell might have been exacerbated by torn trash bags, by spoiled food rotting in one-hundred-degree heat, but it was more out of hope than expectation. She knew exactly what the stench was, and she knew why it was so bad. She'd joined Sheriff's Homicide in 1978, had spent every day of the seven years since turning up to murders, and when she finally arrived at the open door of Room 17, the smell hit her as hard as it always did.

The room was small and tired, everything bleached by age, the drywall punctured. Bed sheets were lying in a pile on the floor and on the nightstand was a bottle of bourbon and an open bag of potato chips. Some of the chips were on the floor, crushed into the carpet, next to a soda can and a pile of clothes. The clothes looked male: Jo could see some boxer briefs and a big pair of white sneakers.

Just inside the door, in a wide semicircle around the bed, were Greg Landa, a detective from the LASD, a forensic tech – already suited up – who identified himself as Austin Davis, and someone from the ME's office who was here to assist Chen. Jo didn't know Davis or the guy who'd come with Chen, but she knew Landa: he was a twenty-year veteran who'd spent his career working murders in West Hollywood, East LA and Compton. Because of that, Jo always tried to afford him the proper respect, but it was hard because she detested him. It wasn't because he was fifty pounds overweight and permanently flushed, or even that his face was always beaded with an unsightly sheen of sweat, even when it was in the low forties outside; it was because he would always try to use his size to intimidate her, subtly stepping into her personal space, presumably in some primal effort to show her where the power lay. No woman in the LASD needed reminding of that: Jo was the only female detective in Homicide and everything she did was analysed and judged, joked about and criticized through the prism of her sex. Male detectives were allowed ten mistakes before anything got written up, but she'd get ripped for one. So Greg Landa wasn't different from any of the other men she shared a building with, he was just one of the worst: she'd never seen him drink, and because he sucked on extra-strong Altoids the whole time, she'd never smelled it on him either, but his cheeks were criss-crossed with a mesh of prominent blood vessels and a few people in the office called him 'Grog' behind his back. If that was true, if he really did drink heavily out of work, Jo knew that Landa would be the worst kind of drunk – slimy, hostile, violent.

As soon as Landa saw Jo, he started to sing the Dolly Parton song 'Jolene', the words softened by the smacking of his lips as a mint moved around his mouth. The song was a long-running joke he liked to reanimate every time the two of them met.

'How you doing, Greg?'

'I'm doin' fine,' he said, his Texan roots still evident even thirty years after he'd moved to California. He quickly but unmistakably looked her up and down, a smirk on his face, and then nodded towards the bathroom. 'Hope you didn't eat breakfast.'

Jo ignored him. 'I thought you were on the Night Stalker task force.'

'I am. I was close by, so Lieutenant Hayesfield wanted me to make sure the vic ain't one of ours, because some of the injuries' – he tapped a pudgy finger to his forehead, signifying that the victim in the tub took a bullet there – 'are consistent with what we've seen.'

That was total bullshit: LA was a city of guns, and wherever there were guns there were murders. People were taking a bullet to the head in this city all the time.

'Anyway,' he said, 'turns out he ain't one of ours. I mean, the Stalker don't off 'em in hotel rooms for one thing, and while he's pretty messed up in there, it ain't the kind of messed up the Stalker likes.' He shrugged indifferently, as if he were talking about someone stealing a few bucks out of a cash register, not the murder of a man.

And that was probably the real reason Jo disliked Landa so much: not his stupid, predictable rendition of the song; not even the way he'd tried to suggest that she'd puke as soon as she saw the body, or that he got here first because Hayesfield thought it might be related to the Stalker, rather than the truth, which was that Hayesfield frequently sent male cops out to assess Jo's crime scenes before she arrived. Instead, what she disliked about him was that he'd become detached. He'd lost his sense of obligation to the victims. He wasn't receptive to the loss of life in the way a cop should have been, even if a cop's only burden extended as far as a promise to find the killer. She'd heard Landa talk about a son, but she couldn't imagine he'd spent a single day at the door of his boy's bedroom while the kid was growing up, wishing the world were a little safer. To Landa, after twenty years behind a desk in a squad room, after hundreds of killings, the man lying in the bathtub was just another face to forget.

'Anyway,' Landa said, pushing the mint to one side of his mouth, 'thought I better hang around until you got here in case these assholes screwed up your crime scene.' He winked at the two men: Davis, the forensic tech, clearly didn't know how to react to that, so smiled at Landa and then looked uncertainly at Jo, while the guy who came with Chen erupted into laughter, as if Landa had delivered a joke for the ages. 'I was tellin' Bobby here about a case I worked out in Wellington Heights where a –'

'Thanks for coming down, Greg,' Jo said, cutting him off and letting him know that he could get the hell out of her crime scene now. She didn't wait for a response, just stepped past him and headed to the bathroom. Behind her, she heard Landa say something quiet to Bobby, the guy who'd come with Chen, and they began laughing.

She ignored it and paused outside the bathroom.

This close in, the smell was horrible.

Two more men were inside: one was knelt beside the tub with a camera, taking pictures; Dan Chen was watching from the opposite corner. The bathroom was gloomy, the faucets speckled brown with a mix of mould and rust, the walls slick with trails of water. Chen stepped away from the wall and moved towards Jo.

'What's up, Kader?'

'How's it going, Danny?' She looked at the tub. 'Can I come in?'

'Just let us finish up and it's all yours.'

She nodded, her eyes still on the tub.

'Landa said he took one to the head?'

'Yeah, looks like it,' Chen said. 'But he was put in here afterwards.'

The tub had been filled up. The man was face down, his buttocks, his shoulders and the rear of his skull the only parts of him that weren't submerged. Something weird had happened to the water, though: it was slightly misted, as if the victim had been washing with soap, and there was a thin, almost creamy substance floating on the surface. Jo wondered if that was the reason why the scene smelled so bad. Dead bodies never smelled good, and decomposition was a stench you never got used to, but there was something different about this one.

The camera flashed again, and then again.

'What's that on the surface, Danny?'

'Fat,' Chen replied.

'Fat? You mean, from the body?'

'Exactly.'

Jo frowned. 'How come it's leached away like that?'

'Because it's not water he's in,' Chen said. 'It's acid.'

11

At 2 a.m., I woke with a jolt.

I'd been dreaming, my head full of images of moorland, an endless ocean of crests and plunges, the fields absolutely empty except for the silhouettes of nine people. They moved slowly in a line, almost shuffling, one following the other, and yet they always stayed just out of reach, even when I was running; and then, when the sun came up and the night flickered out like a candle, everyone simply vanished.

I sat up, rubbing the sleep from my eyes. It had been a long time since I'd dreamed, a longer time since I'd had one as forceful and vivid, so I felt almost disorientated, my heart thumping in my ears, sweat at the arc of my hairline and all the way down my back, as if I'd woken with a fever. Eventually, though, I felt my body begin to relax, the tension easing out of my bones, and once it did, I hauled myself on to my feet, poured a glass of water and stood at the window watching the rain fall across the emptiness of the car park.

I turned on a light, sat down at the desk and began going through some of the photos I'd removed from the houses. Patrick and Francesca Perry, mid-hike, rolling hills beyond them. Chris, Laura and Mark Gibbs gathered around a table in a restaurant somewhere, smiling for the camera. John and Freda Davey in the same photo I'd seen earlier, on a cruise, Freda, in remission, small against her husband, John looking small too against the backdrop of the vast ship. And then Randolph Solomon and Emiline Wilson on their holiday in the States, the two of them pointing from either side of the photograph at the Hollywood sign way off in the distance. I thought again about all the things that could have led to nine people disappearing – an affair, a gambling debt, the awkward comments of a teenager on social media, the fact that two of the nine were much less known than the others – and then switched my attention to the computers and tablets. I'd planned to wait until the morning to tackle them all – but then I hadn't banked on being awake at 2 a.m.

Once I started going through them, I quickly discovered that most had nothing useful to offer, but I got to know each person a little better: Randolph Solomon, the Middlesbrough fan, was into football in a big way generally, his web history showing repeated visits to an online fantasy league; his girlfriend, Emiline, as her job at the library suggested, was a big reader, as well as a keen gardener and landscaper, and she'd uploaded photographs of her work to a horticultural forum where she'd been an active member; Laura Gibbs was interested in interior design and had created a Pinterest page full of things she'd decorated and bought for the farm, and Chris's hobbies lay in areas related to his job – machines, agriculture, countryside; John Davey wasn't only a big rugby league fan, he was into cricket too, and played golf a couple of times a week; and Freda would often use the web to go to running forums – which echoed what Rina Blake had told me about her mother being a gifted athlete – where she'd read about marathons and trail running, about routes people had found and places she'd maybe still dreamed of trying for herself one day, however unlikely it may have seemed. She also spent a lot of time on travel websites, including plotting the locations in Australia where she wanted to go on her dream holiday.

The most used piece of tech was Mark Gibbs's, but only because his laptop was powerful enough to run computer games, which he seemed to have sunk hours into. He used the Internet a lot, as a nineteen-year-old would be expected to, but nothing in his browsing habits rang any particular alarm bells. Chrome had remembered his passwords for both Facebook and Instagram, though he obviously hadn't been on either for two and a half years, and all his notifications were from friends of his. I went back through some of his posts to see if anything stood out, or if any comments rankled, but he uploaded rarely and posted even less. One of his friends had created a 'Find Mark Gibbs' account on Instagram and Twitter, posting pictures of him; a few had DM'd him directly on Facebook in the immediate aftermath of his vanishing, begging him to come home. I took down their names. There were a few similar messages in the email accounts of the Daveys and the Gibbses too, from friends and family. A week after her parents had vanished, Rina had sent John and Freda Davey an email begging them to get in touch.

I love you both so much, she'd written. *Please, please call.*

My eyes lingered on that second part, feeling the emotion in it. Eventually, I started examining the Perrys' PC.

Tearing the evidence bag off the hard drive, I set up the tower next to the TV, clicked the hard drive into one of the bays on the reverse and used an HDMI cable to connect the PC to the hotel room's TV. It took a couple of seconds for the TV to work out what was going on, but before long I had an image of the PC's desktop onscreen.

It was tidy, a series of applications in three vertical lines on the left. Most were of little or no relevance, except for Firefox. I clicked on the icon and then went to History. The last Internet activity was at the end of November 2015, a month after the disappearances at Black Gale. But there was nothing suspicious about that: it was a forensic tech. They'd been back over the same websites that Patrick Perry had been looking at before he vanished. I checked his email, which automatically opened at start-up, and then moved the cursor to the bottom left and selected File Explorer. Soon, it became a cycle of repetition: Powerpoint presentations, Excel spreadsheets, invoices, pitches he'd made, letters on headed notepaper, the same stuff duplicated over and over. I also found folders full of photographs – landscapes, hills, valleys, the village at sunset and sunrise. Was this the evidence that finally proved his trips to the moors – witnessed by Laura Gibbs – were genuinely to take pictures and not for some other purpose? One thing was for certain: not a single document even remotely suggested something illicit had been going on between Patrick and anyone else.

Drained, I got up and went back to bed, crawling beneath the duvet again. The mattress was lumpy, cold, two singles pushed together with a ridge along the centre where they met. I tried to still my thoughts, and slowly I began to drift, images of Black Gale – of nine untold stories – giving way to fatigue.

Silence. Darkness.

And then a sound from the corridor.

I got up again and went to the door, opening it. There was no sign of anybody outside. Halfway between my room and the lift was a skylight, reduced to a square of blackness now: the rain was making a machine-gun sound against it, harsh, forceful, like pebbles scattering.

Had that been the noise I'd heard?

I paused there for a moment, holding the door open with one hand, and then grabbed my keycard, let the door click shut behind me and went to Healy's room. I stood there, listening for a while, and then heard it again: the same noise as before.

It took me a couple of seconds to place it.

And, once I did, my heart dropped.

Inside his room, Healy was crying.

12

He opened the door halfway.

He was dressed in a T-shirt and boxer shorts, but it was clear that the delay in answering had been because he'd tried to clean himself up. There were still beads of water on his cheeks where he'd washed his face, droplets in his beard too, and he was standing straighter, more upright than normal, as if he were trying to offset some of the sadness. It was an act that he barely seemed to have the energy for.

'Are you okay?' I asked, despite seeing the answer.

He went to speak and then swallowed, his reply failing to form properly. After a couple of seconds, he nodded and said, 'Yeah.' Sniffing, he wiped some of the water from his face, and then his body relaxed. He couldn't be bothered with the act either.

I looked past him.

The wall of paper was still intact. The Black Gale file was on a table at the window, empty coffee cups and fast-food wrapping dotted around it. He'd kept going after I'd left, evidently returning to the start, the file open at a point about a fifth of the way in. Beside the file was a series of photos that didn't belong in the investigation, or on the wall, and had nothing to do with Black Gale.

They were pictures of his family.

He watched my gaze, saw that I'd zeroed in on the portraits, and then stepped back from the door, letting it swing open fully. Wandering across to the table, he slumped into the chair next to it and drew the pictures closer to him.

'Do you want to talk about it?' I asked him gently.

He shrugged. 'What difference does it make now?'

I perched myself on the edge of the bed.

'I don't know,' I said. 'Maybe it might make some.'

He didn't say anything for a moment.

'Healy?'

Finally, he muttered, 'When I was down in Devon, I read this book.' His forefinger was tapping out a gentle rhythm against a photo of his daughter, Leanne. Even from where I was, at the edge of the bed, I could see her face, her smile, a teenage girl frozen for ever in time. His finger eventually stopped next to her face, as if he were trying to scratch his way into the shot and touch her. 'Anyway, this book, it was written by this scientist – he was trying to explain physics and quantum particles and how the universe works, all that shit. He wrote it for morons like me, who'll never have a hope in hell of ever understanding these things properly, but it was still a bit of a headfuck. I managed to follow some of it, managed to get confused by most of it, but there was this one thing that really stuck with me.' He paused, fanning out the photos slightly. I could see he had five in total. The one of Leanne, one each of his sons, Ciaran and Liam, one of the three of them together, and then one of the Healy family as it had once existed: the three kids, Healy and his ex-wife, Gemma. He glanced at me and then back down at the pictures. 'This one chapter, it was all about how quantum mechanics describes the world in terms of probabilities, not definite outcomes. I mean, I left school with half an education, maybe not even that much, so I only really get the basics, but the mathematics of a theory like that means that all possible outcomes of one particular situation – one choice – can occur. In other words, in this outcome right here, we went across the road and got Burger King tonight; but in another, we didn't get Burger King, we got a sandwich; in yet another, we only bought ourselves coffee.'

'You're talking about parallel universes.'

He nodded. It was obvious where this was going now.

'It sounds like some bullshit out of *Star Trek*,' he said, 'but this physicist, he works at one of the big universities in America, and it's an actual thing. It's real. A lot of the most incredible human beings on the planet say it's real. It's to do with string theory, particles, the substance of the universe, the infinity of space – something, I don't know. But like you say, parallel worlds. Basically, what this guy is saying is that in each possible outcome, in each universe, there's a copy of you that thinks their reality is the correct reality. Which means, somewhere out there, you and me are sitting in a room just like this one, but with sandwich wrappers all over the floor.' His eyes moved to the remnants of our burgers, to the wall full of paper, to me, and then to the photos of the family he'd once called his own. He lifted the shot of Leanne away from the table. 'And somewhere out there, there's a version of me that still has this.'

It was difficult to know what to say to that. I'd been down this road myself, when I'd mourned Derryn, when I'd landed the case at Christmas that had brought all those memories back to the surface, and it was so hard to push past grief when it was this intense; it may have been harder for Healy than anyone I'd ever met because he'd left so much unsaid. I, at least, got to say goodbye to the person I loved. He hadn't. His daughter had been murdered, his sons had disowned him, and – ground down by years of Healy maniacally working cases, of putting his job ahead of everything else, of hurting her emotionally and once, to his shame, physically – his wife finally left in the aftermath of an investigation that snapped him into pieces: an obsessive search for the murderer of a mother and her twin girls.

'I remember a dinner I had with Gemma once,' he said. His voice was still small, distressed. 'It was for one of our anniversaries. I turned up late as usual. I was right in the middle of a case. I guess I was a mess, but I never saw it then. Anyway, I remember she left me at the restaurant because we got into an argument, but before she did, she said, "You're a good man, Colm. There are lots of days when I loathe you, but you do the right things for the right reasons, and that's more than a lot of people do." She was talking about how the work would consume me. I didn't think about it at the time – didn't even consider it, really – but that was the moment.' He sniffed, looked up at me. 'That was the moment

I should have walked away from the Met. All the shit I put her through, all the times I wasn't there for her or the kids, and she still managed to tell me that. That was my exit, I can see that now. That was the universe I should be in. But I'm not. I stayed because I think, as weird as it sounds, my life at the Met made more sense than my life at home. I didn't know how to handle teenagers, but I knew how to run a murder investigation.'

And that was why, when he was fired, when the central pillar of his life collapsed, when he ended up entirely alone, with no family and no work colleagues left to hear his cry for help, he had to start again as someone else. He'd had an idealistic notion of disappearing and becoming someone better, but the reality had long proved to be different. It was playing out in front of us tonight. I aided him in getting to this point, perjuring myself in front of the police in order to help him stay hidden, because I suppose, for a time, that same idealism had captivated me. I'd seen at first hand what he'd become and I wanted a better life for him, and I didn't see how it could be any worse than it was. But this – this room, this wall full of paperwork, this concealed existence that meant even his walking outside to the car in the morning was a risk to us both – this was the reality of the life he'd chosen.

'You did what you thought was best,' I said.

'Did I?'

His gaze was still on Leanne. She'd been gone over seven years now. Neither of us moved for a long time and then he looked up and I could see he'd finally given in, the control gone, the attempt to seem impassive: tears filled his eyes.

'I liked that book,' he said, the tears carving into his words, breaking them as they formed in his mouth. 'I liked the idea of her being alive somewhere, of us being together.' He stopped, wiping his eyes. 'She'd be twenty-seven. Can you believe that? My baby, twenty-seven.' Again, he paused, brushing his cheeks with his sleeve, pinching the photograph of Leanne so hard between his thumb and forefinger it was starting to crease. 'Maybe – somewhere – she's married. Maybe she has kids.'

He forced a smile.

'Maybe I'm a grandfather.'

I nodded, smiled, watching as he held on to the picture for a moment longer, before placing it down on the table again, next to the other memories of his family.

'I hope I'm a better father in that place,' he said.

He looked up at me.

'I hope I always tell my family that I love them.'

PART TWO
The Deer

13

By 8 a.m., we were on the mud track leading in through the gate at Black Gale. The rain of the day before was gone, and under a perfect blue sky the colour of the fields seemed so bright, so different from my first visit, it was like seeing it through some kind of filter. Snow still clung to the hills, but it was a perfect spring morning.

Ross had left me the alarm codes for the houses, as well as the keys, so Healy and I went around unlocking the properties, and then I gave him an overview of what I'd found – or hadn't – inside each the previous afternoon. I'd also brought a copy of the police evidence inventory, and a checklist I'd written of items most likely to have been taken by the villagers, alongside their wallets and phones – jackets, hats, beanies, torches, practical belongings that might help with a planned disappearance and tell us a little more about where they were headed. It was, in truth, going to be impossible to account for any missing effects definitively, but piece by piece we might build a bigger picture.

'I'll help you when I get back,' I said to him afterwards.

'Back from where?'

'I'm going to see where Patrick went for his walks.'

I left Healy and headed down the track, around the farm and out past the barns. The Gibbses' garden ran at an angle, its gentle slope finally ending at the moss-dotted drystone wall that marked the northernmost edge of Black Gale.

I climbed over a stile. The moorland on the other side was boggy, the grass saturated from the storm the day before, but two worn trails were immediately visible, marked out by years of passing hikers: one headed east to west, the other directly north from the village. I followed the northern path out from the wall, across land belonging to the Gibbses and then beyond the boundaries of what was theirs, into the dip of the valley. Occasionally, I would stop and take a picture in an effort to document the area – so that I could remind myself later on of the surroundings and the route that Patrick may have taken if he'd pursued this exact trail every time he came out here – but mostly I just walked. As the valley dropped, more trees started to emerge, gathering in the folds of the hills, and after a while, when I stopped and looked back, I realized the moors had sloped so dramatically that I was actually below the level of the village now; all I could see of it was a chimney stack on the side of the farmhouse, rising above the spine of the hill.

I checked the time, saw that I'd only been going for about fifteen minutes and decided to carry on for a while, switching my thoughts back to Patrick and his trips out here at sunrise and sunset in the weeks and months before he, and the others, had vanished. A clump of trees was up ahead, their branches dense and tangled, the leaves yet to form. As I got closer, I could see glimpses of exposed roots, with muddy pockets of water between the trunks.

I stood for a moment, looking around, trying to see if I recognized this part of the moors from Patrick's photographs, but it didn't seem familiar. It was cooler here, though, the sound more muted, the light greyer because the sun had slipped behind the eastern flank of the valley. In among the trees there was a narrow sliver of a trail, snaking between the knotty roots. I decided to follow it in, curious about where it ended up, and as I did, what light there was fell through the canopy and created patterns on the ground. The effect was mildly discomfiting: everything seemed to be moving, dancing, but if you were looking for a place to lie low, to not be seen – and somewhere only a twenty-minute walk away from Black Gale – this was perfect.

I headed back up the slope, the way I'd come in.

At the drystone wall, I took the east–west trail, the route much flatter as it followed a tiny stream towards a braid of peaks. After half a mile of going west, I double-backed on myself, came up and around the edge of the village and entered through the main gate. As I did, I saw Healy moving from the Perrys' house to the one next door – the Daveys' – writing something down as he walked.

'Find anything?' I asked once I'd reached him.

He shook his head. 'Nothing so far. You?'

'No. There's a good meeting spot down there, though.'

'Yeah?'

'Only twenty minutes away, but properly isolated.'

He looked towards the valley.

'You really think he was having an affair with Freda or Emiline?'

'I don't know,' I said, because we didn't.

I worked in the opposite direction to him, starting with the farm, then Randolph Solomon and Emiline Wilson's, then John and Freda Davey's house, and finally Patrick and Francesca Perry's. In each of them, I emptied out drawers and went through wardrobes and cupboards, ensuring I hadn't missed anything, but by the time I returned to the Perrys' hallway, the smell of the plug-in strong in the air, I'd found nothing.

'No luck?' Healy said, meeting me outside.

'No. You?'

He shook his head.

I glanced at Randolph and Emiline's place.

'You didn't get anywhere tracing that missing camper van?'

'No,' Healy said. 'Total dead end, just like Tori Gibbs said.'

So where was it?

I looked at the other cars and then at the single empty driveway.

'We should probably go,' I said.

He didn't respond, because it was obvious he was reluctant to. He liked being out here, even if he hadn't found anything, because it wasn't the confines of the hotel we were in, or the hotel he'd been forced to flee to in Newcastle before that, or the house he'd rarely left down in Devon. This was freedom of a sort: a wide open space where he didn't have to look over his shoulder the whole time; perhaps more than that, a place where he could think like a cop again.

I gave him a moment and headed back to the car.

A few minutes later, we left, cloud beginning to build, the sun drifting in and out of view as we headed south to the B road. Healy talked to me as we drove, and I listened to enough of it to respond to his ideas, his theories, ways in which we could push forward on the case – but in the puddles on the road, in the dew-soaked grass on either bank, I also found a repetition that helped me forge a separate path in my own thoughts, back to the moorland I'd walked, to all the unanswered questions.

It meant I was seeing the road, but I wasn't concentrating on it.

A second later, I hit something.

14

The deer seemed to come out of nowhere.

It was suddenly there, in front of us, frozen in the centre of the road. I had time to see its antlers, the black glint of its eyes, to watch its body begin to shift away from us – and then I slammed into it. The left-hand side of the Audi crunched against the rear flank of its body, the impact seeming to tremor through to the dashboard. The sound was horrific: the dull tear of metal, the hiss of a radiator, the terrible, prolonged squeal of the deer itself; and then the car hit a bank.

The airbags exploded out at us.

I wasn't sure if I blacked out entirely – it felt like I could hear the car creaking and rasping around me the whole time – but when everything came back into focus, thirty seconds had passed and I could feel blood running from my nose and mouth. I looked across at Healy. He was conscious but dazed, staring out of the windscreen as it began to mist up. I touched a hand to his arm. 'You all right?'

'What the hell just happened?' he muttered.

'We hit a deer.'

I opened my door, undid my belt and got out, passing the broken body of the deer on the road, and then went around to Healy's side. After sitting him down on a bump in the bank, I looked him over. He was worse off than me: there were two big cuts on the left-hand side of his face and he was holding his arm at the elbow, where it must have crunched against the door. He might even have been in shock: he was staring ahead, past the body of the deer, to the other side of the track.

I checked my phone, looking for a signal, but we had to be in a black spot. I wasn't sure what I would have done even if I'd had any bars. Was I really going to call an ambulance? Doing that would endanger both of us. Healy had a fake passport identifying himself as Bryan Kennedy, but hospitals meant questions, and not just about who he was and how he'd got injured, but about why he didn't have an NI number and didn't exist on the system. Worse, it might mean hospital staff deciding to phone the police.

He looked up, his expression replicating everything I'd just been thinking. But one of the gashes on his face was bad. It would need to be treated – and ideally not out here on exposed moorland with the light drifting in and out. When the sun was shining, it was fine. When it went in, the temperature dropped like a stone.

I went to the body of the deer, held a hand flat to its belly and checked that it was definitely dead. It had suffered already and I didn't want it to suffer any more. Once I was sure, I grabbed it by the legs and started dragging it in the direction of the grass bank. Normal procedure was to call the police, so that someone could come and retrieve the body, but that would create the same problems as taking Healy to hospital, so I made sure the deer was as far from the road as possible and then returned to the car and fired it up again. It spat, the chassis kicking, rocking from the front, but then it gently began to idle. It didn't sound right – something was ticking loudly in the engine – and when I put it into reverse and tried to pull back from the bank, the front wheels spun on the gravel.

I asked Healy if he could get into the driver's seat and try to reverse the Audi while I gave it a push from the front. It took a long time, both of us becoming frustrated, but finally it worked: gravel ricocheted off the car, mud flecked my trousers, then the wheels gripped.

We swapped seats, I turned the car around and we headed towards the village again. I'd noticed a first-aid kit in the farm-house, and there were blankets, flannels and hand towels in the airing cupboards at all four homes.

Five minutes later, we were back at Black Gale.

We drove all the way down the track, pulling up outside the

farm. Helping Healy out, I opened the property and we headed inside, and then I left him on one of the chairs in the kitchen as I went searching for the first-aid kit. I found it in the utility room. The box of plasters was a little under half full and, as I looked at them, I wondered when they were last used. Months before the Gibbses disappeared? Weeks? The night they went missing? I grabbed the plasters and then a dressing, tearing it out of its packet and returning to Healy, telling him to press it to the cuts while I went to fetch water.

'Where are you going to get water from?'

He was right: the taps hadn't run here for two and a half years.

'Don't worry, I've got some in the car.'

Once I'd grabbed a bottle I kept in the boot, I returned to the house, told Healy to lean over the sink and started to empty the water over his cuts. They'd begun to clot already and most probably only required the plasters, but the gash at his eye was pretty deep.

'You need to learn to drive straight, Raker.'

It broke the charged atmosphere.

'But that grass bank came out of nowhere,' I said.

He returned my smile.

It took me a couple of minutes to clean and dress the wounds, then I grabbed a blanket from the airing cupboard upstairs and handed it to him. I pulled out a chair and sat down opposite him at the table. I'd barely had time to stop and think about myself, but now, as I finally began to relax, I could feel pain all along my neck – the effects of whiplash – and real discomfort, perhaps bruising, across my front, right shoulder to left hip, where the seatbelt had locked hard.

'How are you feeling?' he asked.

'I'll survive.'

He nodded. 'I guess that's what we do.'

I looked out of the kitchen window at my car. The left-hand edge was badly damaged, the headlight smashed, the grille bent, some of the bumper pushed back in towards the engine. I needed to find the number of someone local who could repair it for me; there was no way I could drive back to London with it looking like that. If I'd been on my own, I might have taken the gamble. But if I got stopped by the cops on the motorway, there was a chance they would work a trail back to here, to the hotel, and ultimately to Healy. Everything had to be looked at through the same lens, every decision taken on the basis of whether it might expose him.

'So what now?' he asked.

I took a moment before replying, steeling myself.

'I think it would be a good idea if you stayed here.'

He frowned. 'What are you talking about?'

'The car's a mess. It's a fifty-mile drive back to the hotel, and thirty-five miles of that is motorway. If there are cops out, there's every chance they'll pull us over and that means having to explain everything. It's safer if you're not a part of that.'

'I'm not staying here.'

'It'll be for a day,' I said. 'Two at the most.'

'Two days in *this* place? Forget it.'

'I need to get the car repaired.'

'Then I'll come with you.'

'I just told you, that's not a good idea.'

'I'm not staying here, Raker. There's no way I'm sitting on my hands for the next forty-eight hours staring at the walls. Even if the sum total of my contribution to this case is locking myself in that hotel room and going through paperwork for you, it's better than staying in a house that no one lives in, in the middle of nowhere. I can't do that any more.' He paused, squeezing his eyes shut, his fingers going to the wound I'd dressed. 'Look,' he said, his voice quieter, more contained, 'I spent a long time living on my own in Devon. You know that. I've barely had contact with anyone but you. I've had no life, just this secret. I know you're looking out for me, I know what you told me on the way up here in the car this morning about Annabel, about how we've still got that arsehole McCaskell on our tail, I know the risks. I do. I understand them. But what *you've* got to understand is that these past two days have been better than *any* of the days I've had over the past three and a half years. So don't make me do this, okay? Please don't leave me here.'

I looked at him and then back out of the window again, annoyed, sympathetic, conflicted. The sun had disappeared completely now, cloud knitted together in the sky, the light greyer and more sombre. My gaze drifted from the car, up to the main gate of the village, the legs on the Black Gale sign rocking in their bed as the wind picked up.

And then I realized it wasn't the legs that were moving.

It was a person, coming out from behind it.

There was somebody else here.

Caraca

Los Angeles | Tuesday 23 July

'My name's Detective Kader. I'm with the Sheriff's Department.'

Jo held up her badge.

The manager of the Star Inn was a Latino man in his late forties with a week's beard growth and a pot belly. He looked from her photograph to her face, then back to the photograph. 'We don't get so many lady police detectives coming in here.'

He said *lady* like he was trying to come on to her.

'Well, this is what we look like,' Jo replied. A scarred walnut counter lay between her and the manager, and in a room out the back she could see a couch malformed by age and a TV playing old reruns of *I Love Lucy*. The guy had dragged in a fan from somewhere and set it up where he'd been sitting, and it was on so hard it was gradually blowing a half-eaten jelly doughnut across a plate.

'The a/c's broke,' he said, seeing where her eyes were at.

'Ever thought about getting it fixed?'

He shrugged. 'Yeah, when I win the state lottery.'

It was hot as hell inside, hotter than the second-floor room she'd just left, but she'd take the heat in here to the scene upstairs any day of the week. Once Dan Chen and his assistant had got the young man out of the tub and on to a sheet on the bathroom floor, they'd been able to see the full extent of what the acid had done to him, and it had been difficult to look at. The kid had been shot through the cheekbone from close range, the bullet entering just under his right eye, and livor mortis – the way blood had pooled inside his body – seemed to confirm that he'd been dropped into the tub, face down, pretty soon after. Chen believed the acid was added once the man was in the bath, and that the body had been there for between thirty-six and forty-eight hours, based on the amount of damage the acid had already done to the corpse: it had eaten away at his front, turning his face, chest, groin and shins into a creamy mulch; a paste that had begun to slide away from the bone. A few more days and they would have been picking him out of the tub in bits; after seven, they would have needed a shovel.

Jo got out her notebook.

'You called in the scene upstairs, is that right?'

'That's right,' the manager said.

'What time did you find him like that?'

'About 4 a.m. The couple in the room next door came down and said they could smell something bad.' He shrugged again, as if he heard that complaint all the time. 'Place like this, that usually means a blocked drain, a blocked toilet – or a dead body.'

'So you knocked on his door?'

'Sure. Went up and knocked about twenty times.'

'And there was no response?'

'Nothing.'

'Which is when you let yourself in?'

'Correct.'

It was the same story he'd given the first responders.

'What's your name, sir?'

'Rivaldo Torus.'

'You got a guestbook here, Rivaldo?'

Torus reached under the counter. The guestbook had leather covers, but the pages had yellowed and there were coffee stains all over the front. He opened it up about three quarters of the way in, today's date printed at the top, and then flipped back a couple of pages.

Spinning it around, Torus pointed to the second-from-last guest name.

'There he is.'

Gabriel Wilzon.

'Did he show you any ID?' Jo asked.

'No,' Torus responded, as if the idea were absurd. 'Most of the guests here, they pay cash. I mean, we ain't exactly the Chateau Marmont, you know what I'm saying?'

'So he checked in last Friday?'

'That's what it says.'

Today was Tuesday. He'd been here four nights, and if Chen was right, the kid had been lying in a tub full of acid for two of them. There was no way he was actually called Gabriel Wilzon – after Torus had told the first responders what name the guy had used to check in, Jo had done the legwork and tried to find someone with that name, matching the guy's general description or approximate age. But there were no missing persons reports, and no one in their early twenties with either a social security number, driver's licence or criminal record using the name. There might be something to be gained in finding out why he chose *Wilzon* for a fake name, especially with the unusual *z* – in Jo's experience, these things were rarely selected at random – but that relied on knowing more about him, and at the moment they couldn't lift his prints because his fingertips had dissolved, and they didn't have a face because his features were like melted wax.

'He paid for seven nights up front,' Torus said, bringing Jo back into the moment. 'Fifteen bucks a night, hundred and five bucks for the week – but I called it a round hundred.' He nodded at Jo as if he expected something in return – perhaps congratulations, or a positive reinforcement of his generosity.

'Did you see him much after he checked in?' she asked.

'Not once.'

'He didn't come out of his room at all?'

'I'm not saying that. I'm saying, I don't watch my guests.'

She looked around. 'Is that why you don't have any cameras here?'

'We had one out front for a while,' Torus said, waving a finger in the vague direction of the courtyard, 'but the VCR got screwed up and the wires burned out.'

'Better get that done after the a/c, then,' she said.

Torus made a *hmph* sound.

'Do you remember what this "Gabriel" looked like?'

A frown. 'Ain't you just seen him upstairs?'

'He's been in there a while,' Jo said, keeping it vague. Torus made an *oh* with his mouth, obviously taking that to mean natural decomposition. That reassured Jo: he couldn't have snooped around the room before calling the cops, or had any direct contact with the body – or, worse, actually been involved somehow – because he clearly didn't realize the tub was full of acid and that the issue wasn't decomposition, it was corrosion. 'Anything you remember about his face? Scars? Marks? Teeth? Maybe he had a harelip or a distinctive pattern of freckles?'

Torus leaned forward and put his elbows on the counter, drumming both sets of fingers against the walnut. 'Not really,' he said. 'I mean, I saw him for a couple of minutes on Friday night. He handed me the money, I gave him the key, *y completo.*'

Jo walked to the door in the hope there might be a breeze. There wasn't. The morning was absolutely still.

She looked back across the courtyard, in the direction of the second floor. A uniformed deputy was standing guard at the doorway, and below, at ground level, Chen and his assistant were reloading equipment into the back of the coroner's van.

'Reckon you could describe him to an artist?'

Torus shrugged. 'I guess.'

'He hasn't got a car parked out there, so did you see anyone drop him off?'

'No.'

'No vehicles? A cab maybe?'

'No.'

'See any vehicles coming and going that didn't belong to guests?'

This time, Torus didn't respond.

'Rivaldo?'

He looked conflicted. 'I don't know. Maybe. There was this red station wagon on Saturday or Sunday night. I ain't sure which. Didn't see who was driving it either.'

Jo took a step closer.

'It didn't belong to any of the guests?'

'If it did, they didn't put it in here,' he said, pointing to the column in the guestbook where occupants were asked to write down their licence plates. 'It must have only been here a few hours, though, cos I was checking some couple in, then I went to watch a movie out back, and next time I came through to here the car was gone.'

'You remember the make or model?'

'No,' he said.

'Nothing at all?'

'No. But there was a sticker in the windshield.'

'Yeah? You remember what the sticker said?'

'Caraca something or other.'

'How you spelling that?'

Torus spelled it out for Jo.

'And you don't remember the rest of what it said?'

'No. The Caraca bit was big and bold, the rest was small as shit.'

Jo's eyes went to the second floor again as another deputy began knocking at a door halfway along, hoping for an answer that wasn't going to come. Jo had already found out that the same seven people had been staying here since the night Gabriel Wilzon checked in: two couples, a guy on his own, a lone female and Wilzon himself. The deputy had already talked to all six remaining guests – and none of them had seen anything. Now he was reduced to knocking on empty rooms.

But maybe this wasn't going to be a total dead end.

Jo just had to find out what Caraca was.

15

Someone else was at Black Gale with us.

It was a man, barely more than a silhouette at the top of the track. He didn't look towards the farmhouse – and even if he did, it would have been hard to see the Audi: it was parked behind one of the tractors, in the shadows of the barn.

'Healy,' I said quietly. 'Look.'

We both got up and went to the window.

'Who the hell is that?' he muttered.

The man had started to move: he walked down the mud track, pausing at the beginning of the Perrys' driveway. For a second he just stared at their house, his head turning to take in the others as well, and then I realized he was holding something in his hands.

A phone.

He started taking photographs of the houses with it.

Healy glanced at me, frowning, but I kept my eyes on the man. He'd stopped at a rut in the track, a dip adjacent to the third house belonging to Randolph Solomon and Emiline Wilson, and, as he did, sun briefly punctured the cloud and he became a little clearer. From where we were, it was hard to tell his age – forties maybe, or early fifties – but he was tall, well built, had dark grey hair, and was dressed in jeans and a suit jacket. He took more pictures, and then walked up the driveway to Randolph and Emiline's front door to check if it was locked.

When he was done there, he returned to the track and started going further up, pausing outside the Daveys' to take even more shots. Instinctively, Healy and I both backed away from the glass, conscious of being seen now, at least until we figured out what was going on – but, as we did, the movement registered with him. For the first time, he glanced at the farmhouse, his eyes quickly shifting from window to window, to the tractor and then the

Land Rover. From where he was, he still wouldn't have been able to see my Audi, but the fact that he'd clocked our movement, as slight as it was, instantly told me enough. Whoever this guy was, he was alert.

Then something else got his attention.

This time, he looked the other way, up towards the Black Gale sign – a fast, abrupt movement. Had he heard something? Or thought he had? He moved quickly, pocketing the phone and hurrying up the track, only slowing a few feet ahead of the entrance. From where we were, it was impossible to see the road in because the village was built on a downward slope, but there was no sound other than the faint whine of the wind; certainly no rumble of approaching cars. A few moments later, the man swivelled around, looking down the track, his gaze lingering on the farmhouse yet again. After that, he made a beeline for the side of the Perrys'.

He disappeared from view.

Leaving Healy at the window, I quickly moved through to the living room, which had a partial view of the three gardens. The man wasn't in any of them. I watched for a moment, waiting for him to appear, but then Healy called me back, his voice deliberately low. By the time I returned to the kitchen, the man was out front again, trying the door on the Perrys' house.

He returned to the Daveys' again, heading along the side of their property. Once he was done there, he repeated the same routine at Randolph and Emiline's, trying the front door before disappearing out of view at the side of their house, and then reappearing a minute or so later.

What was he doing?

Finally, he emerged again and took a few steps up the slope in the direction of the main gate. He looked like he was getting ready to go.

But he didn't.

Instead, he began coming down the track towards us.

'You need to go upstairs,' I said to Healy.

'What?'

He stared at me like I'd offended him.

'We don't know who this guy is and you're supposed to be dead, so I think it's better if he doesn't find you in here, because I don't fancy going to prison – do you?'

I gave him a look that said everything, but he still lingered for a moment, his stubbornness an echo of the man he'd been before this, when every decision he didn't like became a battle. Eventually, though, he went, his path upstairs a series of creaks.

I switched my attention back to the window.

The man was continuing his approach, his pace slowing as he got closer to the farmhouse. I'd retreated further, using the darkness of the interior to disguise myself, but even though I knew it would be difficult for him to see me, I felt no particular comfort in knowing that: there was a severity to his expression that set me on edge.

Twenty feet from the front door, he finally saw the Audi.

His whole expression changed, his body tensing, his eyes narrowing, and then his gaze switched between the kitchen window, the living room and the upstairs bedrooms. By then, I'd already started moving, heading out into the hallway.

He knew someone was here.

I didn't have any choice but to confront him.

16

The man's eyes were already on me as I stepped out of the house. He tilted his head, watching me from under his brow.

'Can I help you?' I asked.

'I don't know,' he replied with a smile – but it looked awkward on his face, discordant. 'I didn't realize there was anyone else here.'

'Neither did I until a minute ago.'

'Is that your car?' He gestured to the Audi.

'It is, yes.'

'Let me guess: you hit a deer?'

He must have spotted the animal in the undergrowth at the edge of the road on his way in. The question was odd, though: even as he asked it, something else moved in his face. I couldn't work out what it was, but it stuck with me as he once more glanced at the windows of the farmhouse and said, 'You here by yourself?'

'Yes,' I replied.

'I see.'

I wasn't sure now if his question had been genuine or some kind of test to see how honest I was prepared to be.

Did he know Healy was here?

How?

'I'm Isaac Mills,' he said, the change of direction wrongfooting me. Somehow I'd expected to work harder for his name. 'I'm from a company called Seiger and Sten. You might have heard of us. We're the legal firm looking after the estate of Randolph Solomon and Emiline Wilson. We gave Ross Perry a set of keys and, very kindly, he comes to check on everything, but once a quarter we like to do the same.'

That, in part, tallied with what Ross himself had told me the day before: that Randolph and Emiline's solicitors had given him a key. I couldn't say for certain if the second part was true. Was this guy simply here doing a quarterly check? Or was he here for something else?

'What's with the photographs?' I asked him.

A flicker in his face.

Now he knew I'd been watching him.

'We feel it's important to document any changes. Lovely as these places are, they're remote and they're vacant, and that makes them very attractive to criminals.'

He was from somewhere in the north-west, well spoken, but that was about as much of a mark as I could place on him.

'You don't check the insides of the properties?'

He shrugged. 'Sometimes, if we feel it's necessary.'

'But not today?'

'Apart from the farmhouse, they all appear to be locked up tight.'

It was almost accusatory, as if I were the one out of place here, not him. I said, 'So how come you were looking at the other houses?'

This time, he didn't respond straight away, seeing exactly where this was going: if he was looking after the affairs of Randolph Solomon and Emiline Wilson, why had he been taking photos of the other homes? And what had he been doing for so long at the sides of the houses? Taking a step closer, he said, 'I'd have to be a pretty callous individual to drive all the way up here and not show any interest in the upkeep of these other houses, don't you think? We might not be representing their interests in the same way as we do Mr Solomon and Ms Wilson's, but if there was something wrong – if one of the homes had been broken into, or a roof tile had come loose, or a fence panel had fallen over – it goes without saying that I would let Mr Perry know. That's the decent thing to do. I mean, I'm sure any of us would do the same, given the circumstances.'

'I'm sure we would,' I said.

'And what is it you're doing here?'

I tried to weigh up whether telling him mattered or not.

'I'm helping the families.'

'Helping them.' He nodded once and looked at the Audi again. 'Helping them how?'

'By trying to find them.'

'I see,' he said for a second time, but there was a flicker in his eyes that didn't quite conform with his expression, and I started to realize something.

He'd never asked for my name.

He took a step closer to me. 'And how's that going?'

'It's early days.'

'Of course.'

His words suggested a measure of sympathy for the complexities of a missing persons investigation, especially one on this scale, but again his eyes shifted briefly to the upstairs windows and I wondered if he knew for sure that I wasn't here alone. The thought made me nervous.

'Well, I'd better be going,' he said finally.

But he didn't go.

He stayed where he was and carried on looking at me.

'I didn't catch your name. Mr . . . ?'

'Raker.'

'Ah,' he said.

If I'd been willing to believe he had no idea who I was, I might have considered it an odd response. But I didn't. Because this was exactly what I'd seen in his face all along – the dissonance in his expression, the movement in his eyes. This was why he'd never asked for my name until now.

Because he already knew who I was.

He'd known all about me before he ever turned up here.

17

Isaac Mills headed away from me, back along the track.

Halfway up, he glanced over his shoulder and I wondered if he was trying to work out how long I'd been watching him before he discovered I was here. He looked a second time as he got to the apex of the road, where the Black Gale sign stood.

Then he was gone.

I immediately broke into a run. My neck hurt, my shoulders, the bruising across my chest, but I ignored all of it and headed after him. As I got to the wall beside the sign, I slowed, dropping to a crouch and moving in against it, using a break in the stones to peer through to the other side. His car was parked forty feet down the slope, in a natural lay-by. It was a dark blue Lexus. He'd started up the engine – a low rumble against the relative stillness of the moors – and was on his phone.

I took a photo of the car, zooming in on his registration plate, and by the time I was done he'd finished his phone call and was pulling the car out. The brake lights winked as he snapped the handbrake off, and I heard the dull sound of the radio being turned up. After that, he hit the accelerator.

As soon as he was gone from view, I hurried back down the track, towards the Perrys' house, and took out my phone, accessing the address book and zeroing in on the name Ewan Tasker. Just like Spike, Tasker was a source from my days as a journalist; unlike Spike, Task had gone on to become one of my best friends. He'd worked for the NCIS for a long time, a precursor to the National Crime Agency, and – even now, in his late sixties – he was still doing consultation work with the Met. If Spike was my key to things like bank statements, to information that existed on servers that I couldn't access, Task was how I got into the police database.

'Raker,' he said as soon as he picked up.

'Hey, Task. I'm not disturbing you, am I?'

'No. I wish I could tell you I'm on the way to the gym, but the truth is, I've just picked up a latte and a chocolate muffin.'

'Living the dream.'

'And what a dream it is.'

I could hear traffic, people, the hum of the city – and all of it felt a million miles away from here.

'Thanks for sending over that file.'

'No problem,' he said. 'Is it helping?'

'Hard to say yet. I'm still going through it.'

'I remember reading about that case in the papers when it happened. Didn't they vanish on Halloween night? "Like something out of the *Twilight Zone*", right?'

I looked around the village, at its stillness, its solitude.

'Right.'

'So I'm guessing you need something else?'

'I'm sorry to have to ask,' I said, and that wasn't a lie: I really did feel bad about pressing him for another favour. However careful we were – and we always were – every time he went into the database he was risking his work, his reputation, even his pension, so while I tried to even things up in whatever way I could, turning up to his charity golf days in order to be humiliated over eighteen holes, ultimately I could never repay him completely.

'What is it you need?' he asked.

'I was hoping you could chase down a car for me.'

'All right, give me a sec.' The noise of the street dulled just a little: he'd clearly found a spot that was quieter and was digging around for a pen. 'Okay,' he said.

I read out the registration plate for the Lexus.

'I think it belongs to a guy called Isaac Mills.'

'Mills?'

'Yeah. Or it could be a company car.'

'Who's the company?'

'Seiger and Sten. It's some sort of legal firm.'

After a short pause, I heard him start walking again.

'Is there anything that's going to burn me here?'

'There shouldn't be,' I said.

'That's not the most reassuring response you've ever given me.'

'It may or may not be tied into the investigation you sent me. To be honest, it's probably more "may" than "may not". There's something going on here.'

'"Something going on"?'

'This guy just turned up at Black Gale.'

'All right,' Task said. 'I'll call you back in a bit.'

Looking along the side of the Perrys' house, I tried to get a sense of what had caught Mills's attention. I walked it out: it took five seconds to go from the front to the back and yet Mills had spent much longer here – at least a minute at each of the homes. The electric meter – enclosed within a grey plastic box – was at the back of the house, the gas meter below that, but when I opened them up, there was nothing else inside. There were some empty recycling bins here too, and a group of flower pots, but whatever had been growing in them was long dead.

I moved down the slope to the Daveys'. They had some broken trellising propped against the side of their house, the rusting hulk of an old barbecue a bit further along, and the same electric and gas boxes and recycling bins. I checked the bins and boxes but, as at the Perrys', couldn't find anything amiss. It was the same story at Randolph and Emiline's: their recycling bins were stationed at the side, instead of around the back like the others, but they too were empty and the gas and electricity boxes seemed fine.

I returned to the Perrys', confused, frustrated.

There had to be something.

I dropped to my haunches next to the flower pots, trying to see if there might be something hidden under one of them. The only things I found were woodlice and weeds.

'You got anything?'

I looked up: Healy was standing at the corner of the house. He glanced over his shoulder, past the entrance to Black Gale then out to the moors, presumably making sure we were definitely alone, and took in the granite path that connected the front of the house to the back garden, the pots, and then me.

'No,' I said. 'Nothing.'

'Something here got his interest.'

'I know. I just don't know . . .'

But then I stopped.

We both saw it at the same time: a half-brick in the wall, right at the bottom of the house, with no cement around it. It had been completely disguised by a couple of the flower pots, and was partly covered by the drainpipe, which sat flush against the edge of the brick. I shifted my weight and leaned in; Healy dropped down beside me.

'So what have we got here?' he said under his breath.

Gripping the brick, I started trying to lever it out. It wasn't easy: even without the cement around it, there was very little space to get my fingers along the top, but I kept at it, gently rocking it from side to side and pulling towards me every time it did.

Eventually, it dropped out, clinking against the granite.

I grabbed my phone, switched on the light and shone it into the dark of the cavity wall. At first I couldn't see anything, but then I spotted it: a small black unit, almost entirely hidden from view on the extreme left of the hole.

'What can you see?' Healy asked.

'Something's been put inside here.'

Reaching in, I grabbed hold of the unit and brought it out. It was roughly the size of a mobile phone and, because it was clearly switched on, it was warm to the touch. As I held it in my hand, showing it to Healy, it buzzed gently, alive; from one end of it, wires snaked off into the cavity wall, still connected to somewhere else.

'What the hell is that?' Healy asked.

'It's a hard drive.'

He frowned. 'A hard drive? For doing what?'

I looked at the wires coming out of it.

They were audio leads.

'I think someone's been listening to us.'

Late-Night Call

Los Angeles | Tuesday 23 July

As soon as Jo got back to the station, she started ticking boxes. All detectives had to fill out a form that outlined the basic components and elements of the murder they were investigating, which acted as a memo to the Sheriff and, in theory at least, would be read by every officer in the department so that patterns could be spotted and acted upon more quickly.

It took her an hour, and then she spent another hour going over teletypes, the overviews of crimes that had taken place within Los Angeles County, looking to see if she could find any links between the man in the tub and other murders that had occurred inside the nearly 5,000 square miles that the department covered. There was nothing.

Pretty soon after, the phone on her desk burst into life.

'Jo, it's Dan Chen.'

'Danny. What you got for me?'

'Looks like the tub was filled with muriatic acid. I thought it might be as it's easy to get hold of. You can pick it up in any hardware store with no checks at all.'

'That's a cleaning compound, right?'

'Yeah. Folks use it for brightening concrete, masonry, that sort of thing. It's in pool solutions and drain cleaners as well. I'll know for sure once we've done a proper autopsy but I'd say he was in there two days max. Muriatic acid is a lower-grade hydrochloric acid, less pure, but it still does the job. If he'd been a week in that stuff, we'd have been scooping him out with a spoon.'

'Our killer must have used a shitload?'

'Well, it was a twenty-five-gallon bathtub, and we estimate that there was about ten gallons of muriatic acid in there. That's just a best guess for now, but I don't reckon we'll be far off. Generally, you can only pick up one-gallon containers in your local hardware store – so that might make it easier to find out who left him in there.'

Jo understood what Chen was driving at: someone buying ten one-gallon containers of muriatic acid was going to draw attention to themselves. She tried to think of the quickest way to run down that lead. Probably grabbing a Yellow Pages, getting the numbers for as many hardware stores as possible, and just phoning around until she got a hit. There was a caveat, though: it relied on the acid being bought all in one go and recently enough for someone to recall it. If the killer was smart, he'd have picked up the acid from different hardware stores over an extended period of time.

'Did you manage to lift any prints?' Jo asked.

'No. The hands are too damaged.'

'Dental?'

'You might be able to get something from that. Forensics are coming over to take casts this afternoon. Bone takes longer to break down, so if we're lucky our vic's teeth will still be pretty good. I'll let you know as soon as I've got anything else.'

'I appreciate it. When are you cutting him open?'

'Maybe tomorrow.'

'"Maybe"?'

'We've got three Night Stalker victims on the slab here, and half the suits in the city turning up later because everyone's shitting their pants about how this is playing out in public. It's a circus, but I just do what I'm told.'

'All right, Danny.'

'Sorry, Kader.'

He meant the apology, too, she knew that.

'You know I'd rather be working with you, right?'

Jo smiled. 'Who wouldn't?'

She made light of it, but it was frustrating. Everything was subordinate to the Stalker. She understood it, but it hurt cases like hers and made them more likely to fail, because time frame was everything, always. The irony was, standing in a mortuary for eighty minutes was the last thing she wanted to do, but detectives were legally mandated to attend autopsies. And if she was going to have to watch the guy being carved open, she'd rather have just got on with it.

'One last thing, Danny,' she said. 'What about the bullet wound?'

'Ah, yeah. Stippling suggests the gun was close to the cheekbone when fired – an inch at most – and the bullet is a .22. But it's damaged. You want a best guess?'

'Always.'

'Ballistics won't be able to do much with it.'

And even if they could, Jo thought, something told her it wouldn't get her very far. If a man took the trouble to try and dissolve a body in a tub of acid, he'd take the time to buy an untraceable gun for thirty bucks from some fence at the bus terminal.

'All right,' she said, 'keep me up to date, okay?'

'I will.'

'And enjoy the visit from City Hall.'

'I won't.'

She put the phone down and returned to the teletypes she'd already been over. This time, though, she changed direction, pausing in her efforts to try and ID Gabriel Wilzon, or match details of his murder to others in the county. Instead, she focused on possible sightings of a red station wagon with a Caraca car sticker on it.

Again, she came up with nothing.

Undeterred, she headed downstairs to Records and started going through the archives, only coming up for air an hour later when she hit another wall. Back up at her desk she grabbed a White Pages, even though – in her gut – she knew Caraca was unlikely to be a surname: windshield stickers tended to celebrate sports teams, cite political campaigns or slogans, or foist humorous messages and jokes on to the world. What they didn't do was announce your family name in big, bold type.

But then she had a thought.

What if it was the name of a family *business*?

Jo quickly amassed the details of the twelve Caracas living in the greater Los Angeles area and then switched to the Yellow Pages, feeling a charge of electricity as she did. Business names were just the sort of thing you'd put on a windshield sticker.

Inside a minute, she'd found something.

Caraca BuildIt.

They were a supplies yard, out in the City of Industry. And there was something else: when she ran a DMV check, she discovered they owned a fleet of seven vehicles. One of them was a Volkswagen Quantum.

It wasn't red, it was maroon.

But it was a station wagon.

She grabbed her phone, dialled their number and asked to be put through to the manager. When he finally picked up, she introduced herself and asked his name.

'Paolo Caraca,' came the gruff-sounding response.

'Were any of your vehicles out and about on Saturday or Sunday night, sir?'

A confused pause. 'What do you mean?'

'I mean, any chance you or one of your employees took one of your vehicles for a spin on the weekend?'

'What?' He made the question sound like an affront. 'No, of course not.'

'Because a vehicle matching the description of the Volkswagen Quantum you have registered to Caraca BuildIt was seen at a motel over in West Hollywood, is all.'

'Is this a joke?'

'No, sir, it's definitely not a joke.'

'Well, whoever told you that is a liar,' Caraca said.

'You don't own a maroon Volkswagen Quantum?'

'Yes, I do, but all of our vehicles – including the one you speak of – are locked up by me every afternoon from five until we open the next morning at seven. And Sunday we close, so it's impossible that my staff would be out on a Saturday night or Sunday.'

Jo paused, looking down at her notes.

His anger sounded real, virtuous.

'Anyone else have keys to the garage?'

'No, just me.'

'And you weren't in West Hollywood on the weekend?'

'West Hollywood? I live in *Fontana*.'

He meant it was a sixty-mile, ninety-minute drive away from his house, so what the hell would he be doing at the Star Inn? Jo looked down at her notes, thinking, any charge of electricity gone. 'How many employees do you have over there, Paolo?'

'Twenty-three.'

'Okay. I'm going to need you to send me over a list of them.'

Jo got home just after eight.

Ethan was already asleep, his bedroom warm and dark, the fan on its fastest setting. He was only wearing a diaper and he'd long since discarded his blanket, kicked off to the side of the crib. She watched him for a while, thinking about the motel, about the body in the tub, and then – feeling as if she were, in some way, contaminating the purity of her son's room – she left again, ghosting along the hallway to the living room. Ira was on one of the couches watching the Angels, a bottle of beer held in place on his stomach. It was so hot in the living room – so shut in, the door to the yard closed, the windows locked – she was only wearing a vest and panties. Ira was in even less – just his boxers.

'Your dinner's in the oven,' he said.

'Thanks. I'm starving.'

'How was your day?'

She shrugged.

Ira shifted on the couch as Jo removed a plate of quesadillas from the oven, the tortillas stuffed with refried beans, avocado and tomatoes. She got a beer for herself.

'Jo? You all right?'

She collapsed on to the sofa next to him, and he put an arm around her. 'These taste great,' she said finally, wolfing down the quesadillas, and when Ira saw that she didn't want to talk about her day he gave her another squeeze and they sat watching the ball game in silence.

'I've had such a headache today,' Ira said eventually.

'Aw, sorry, honey. There's some Excedrin in the bathroom.'

'Yeah, I grabbed some earlier.'

'Is it any better?'

'Well, luckily I'm a big, strong boy,' he said, 'so I've just about pulled through,' and then he squeezed her again. 'Although they say massages are good.'

'Do they?'

'Good for the head, apparently.'

'And which head are we talking about here?'

That made Ira laugh. She put the side of her face against his shoulder, brought her knees up on to the couch and closed her eyes for a while. She felt absolutely beat.

Five minutes later, her pager started buzzing.

'Shit,' she said quietly, sitting up.

'Just leave it,' Ira replied.

She thought about it for a moment, about all the reasons not to haul herself up off the couch and see what Lieutenant Hayesfield wanted now, but then she set down her plate, kissed Ira on the cheek by way of an apology and retrieved her pager.

But it wasn't Hayesfield.

It was Bennett, one of the detectives who worked the graveyard shift. She liked him about as much as she liked Greg Landa; they were both misogynists, it was just Bennett – in his fifties and newly divorced – never bothered trying to hide it. He wasn't snide and devious like Landa; he was uncomplicated, wearing his lasciviousness like a badge. She went through to the phone in the bedroom and then paused, taking a long, preparatory breath before punching in the number.

Bennett answered after three rings.

'Ben, it's Jo Kader.'

'Kader. What you up to tonight?'

'Not much.'

'I bet you were snuggling up to your man, right?'

'It's way too hot for that, Benny.'

'Too hot? What, for a young woman like you?'

'I got your page,' she said by way of a response.

Bennett audibly sighed, as if she'd disappointed him.

'A guy just phoned for you,' he said, abruptly.

'Who was he?'

'Some cop from the LAPD.'

She frowned. 'The LAPD? What did he want?'

'He wants you to call him.'

'Yeah,' she said. 'I got that part. But did he say what about?'

'It's about your bathtub case.'

That stopped her. 'What about it?'

'He reckons he knows who your killer is.'

18

The Perrys' house seemed quieter than ever.

We stayed where we were at the front door for a moment, looking along the hallway towards the kitchen, and then took off our shoes – using the softness of the carpet to our advantage – and split up: Healy headed upstairs; I went through to the living room.

I didn't move furniture, didn't touch anything for now, I simply looked, only climbing on to the sofas at the end of my search, to peer along the upper edges of picture frames and the tops of dusty bookcases. I couldn't see anything suspicious, but the wall cavity in which we'd found the hard drive was on this side of the house, and if it was wired up to some other device – perhaps more than one – the wires either had to come through here, or through the bedroom above me.

I looked again.

This time, I moved books on shelves, cushions, ornaments, picture frames. I did it all quietly, as slowly and as carefully as I could, but then I opened the lid on a cigar box, now being used to store pencils, pens and paper, and the lid came away entirely in my hand, its mechanism totally broken. The whole thing clattered to the floor, the contents spilling out.

Shit.

Upstairs, I heard Healy shift.

I moved into the hallway and looked up the steps to the landing. He was at the top, a frown on his face, arms out in a *What was that?* gesture. I held up the empty cigar box and rolled my eyes, then returned to the living room, getting down on my hands and knees and scooping up the spilled pens, the pencils, paper, an eraser.

That was when I heard something.

It was a very gentle hum, a noise that faded into the background, but one I was certain I hadn't heard when I'd first entered. It was coming from the floor. I pushed the cigar box aside and, still on all fours, hands pressed into the carpet, leaned down and looked under the sofa closest to me.

A light was blinking on its underside.

Getting to my feet again, I grabbed the bottom of the sofa and – as carefully as possible – tilted it back enough to see underneath. Screwed to the base was a small device, a digital readout on its front showing a series of red vertical bars. It was an audio equalizer, like the kind you'd find on an old stereo. A barely visible lead ran from the back of the device down and through a pinhole in the carpet.

That was why I hadn't been able to find any wires.

They ran under the flooring.

Gently, I placed the sofa back and checked the rest of the room, then moved through to the kitchen. Another device, exactly the same as the one I'd found in the living room, was hidden inside the plastic casing of a strip light, its connection to the hard drive snaking off through another minuscule hole, this time in the ceiling. I had to take the entire light fixture apart in order to find both the device and the connecting wire, but they were there, the readout on the device bobbing up and down in response to my actions, even when they were minor. Afterwards, I stayed exactly where I was on a chair in the middle of the kitchen, silent, motionless, just observing it, and quickly realized that every sound registered, no matter how faint. We'd come into the house with no shoes in an attempt to conceal our search, but it had been a completely worthless act: even the softness of my breathing was getting a response, the equalizer pulsing into life.

Back in the hallway, I stopped, my gaze falling on the photographs under the stairs, the pictures hanging like fruit. There was no device here, no place to disguise it, but it was clear that the technology in the living room and kitchen would have been powerful enough to register conversations at a distance. It would have recorded the exchange I'd had with Ross the day before as we'd stood in front of the picture tree. I didn't remember us saying anything revelatory – but that hardly seemed the point.

Someone had been listening.

Someone wanted to know what I was saying.

A creak on the landing. I came around the stairs and looked up. Healy was standing at the top, waving me towards him. He'd found something. I was pretty sure I knew what it would be, and when I got to Patrick Perry's office I saw that I was right: another device, attached with duct tape to one of the legs on Patrick's desk, hidden from view.

I pointed to the device, then to the floor, and held up a couple of fingers, indicating I'd found two more downstairs.

Healy mouthed, *What the hell?*

I put a finger to my lips and cupped my ear.

They can hear everything.

Inside ten minutes, we'd found two more.

One was in Patrick and Francesca's bedroom, hidden in a false panel at the top of one of their fitted wardrobes; a second was in an air vent in the bathroom, placed there – I was guessing – because the bathroom represented the midway point of the first floor and would therefore be able to pick up sounds from all directions.

I led us downstairs, put on my shoes and headed out of the house, out of the gate that marked the start of Black Gale and beyond that for forty feet.

'What the hell's going on?' Healy said, once we'd stopped walking.

'You really need me to answer that?'

'You think that Mills guy put those things in there?'

'I don't know,' I said, 'but he seems like a pretty good place to start.'

I looked at the Perrys' house and then at the others. Were there bugs inside all four properties? We'd need to make sure, but – given the way Isaac Mills had checked the sides of the other homes in the same way as the Perrys' – I was willing to bet there were. It explained something else too that I'd been trying to figure out: how Mills had seemed to know who I was, even before asking. It was because those same bugs had recorded my visit to Black Gale the day before and he'd heard Ross using my name.

'How did the police miss these?' Healy asked.

'Because there was no crime here.'

He looked at me, instantly understanding.

It was the thing that every retrospective failure in the case – every oversight – would always come back to: if there had been upturned furniture, or damage to the walls, or blood, if it had looked in any way like someone had been hurt here, then the houses would have been pulled apart, top to bottom. But it didn't. It looked like four households had cleaned their properties, locked up and then left. And maybe they had, or maybe they hadn't, but it was why the bugs – leaving aside the fact that they were so well hidden – were never found when investigators arrived here. It was eventually why the case lost momentum in the media as well: because as compelling a mystery as Black Gale was, as much as the papers would have loved to have continued running stories on it, there had never been any evidence of wrongdoing. People had the legal right to disappear – the legal right never to be found too – and that was a hard reality to swallow when you were looking for a headline to sell.

'Maybe the bugs weren't even here two and a half years ago,' Healy said, his thoughts echoing ones I'd had myself. 'Maybe they were installed afterwards.' But then he stopped and we looked at each other, the same question in both our faces. *Why install a bug in an empty house?* It was of value now, when someone was actually looking into what had happened, but – apart from a few true-crime bloggers, and amateur sleuths like Tori Gibbs – no one had been actively looking into Black Gale since the media lost interest and the police investigation hit a wall. It was much more likely that the bugs were in here before any of the villagers left – and that, in turn, changed the entire perspective of the case.

It made it something else.

Something worse.

I thought about the hard drive in the cavity wall, about the devices dotted around the house, and about the way the technology monitored and reacted to our sounds. The soft hum I'd heard, the sound creeping out from under the sofa that had helped me zero in on the first bug, didn't seem to start until I'd strayed within range.

Before that, the device had been silent.

'I think the bugs have got motion sensors in them.'

Healy frowned. 'How do you figure that?'

'It would explain why Mills arrived here when he did. These devices go into hibernation when there's no movement in the house, so when we returned here this morning and began looking around, we set them off again. And as soon as we did, they sent out confirmation that there was fresh activity in the village. Some kind of pulse.'

'A pulse?'

'I don't know exactly. Maybe that hard drive isn't just a hard drive; maybe it's a communication device too. Maybe this whole village is still on the grid, switched on even if the phone company don't know anything about it. The thing is, we can't remove the hard drive and check, or Mills will know for sure that we've found it. But it makes sense. Think about it: once we were done here this morning, once we'd left the village, once – if I'm right – the bugs went into sleep mode again, they, or the hard drive, sent out a second pulse, confirmation that we were gone. Because of that, Mills – who must have been listening in – thought we'd left, so he heads up here to see what else we've been up to, to make sure everything's still in place. But then, a half-mile down the road, we hit a deer.'

'And we decided to come back.'

'If there are bugs in the farmhouse, they'd have come to life once we returned here to dress your wound – but, by then, it was too late for Mills to notice as he'd stopped listening to us.'

'Because he was already driving up here.'

I nodded, looking at him, seeing the sense in it. Right now, Mills was probably still in his car, so he wouldn't realize we'd found the bugs yet. But if there was more than one person listening in, someone else might.

And then I realized something else.

'Shit.'

'What?' Healy said, seeing my face drop.

'*Shit.*'

Dread pooled in the pit of my stomach.

'What is it, Raker?'

Except, a second later, he got it too, and when he did, it was like he'd been hit by a wrecking ball, his feet slipping on the mud as he stumbled back against the wall, his skin blanched, whatever he was trying to say lost on his tongue. He looked at me.

'What the fuck are we going to do now?' he shouted.

At the farmhouse, Healy talked about living in Devon. He'd talked about hiding out down there, in secret. But worse than both of those was what I'd said: that he was supposed to be dead – and if he didn't hide from Mills, we were both going to prison.

And we couldn't deny any of it.

We couldn't hide from what we'd said.

Because everything was on tape.

19

'I never used your name,' I said, trying to sound in control.

'He's got us on *tape*, Raker.'

'I know, but I never used your name,' I repeated, more firmly this time. And that was true, I didn't: I'd talked about his death being faked, but I'd never used his name.

'So – what? – everything's all right now?'

'No, I'm not saying that. Just . . .'

'Just what? Calm down?'

'Just give me a moment to think.'

I turned away from him, trying to clear my head, and as I did, I started to realize how cold it had got, the wind whipping in off the moors, the sun lost behind streaks of bruised cloud. Somehow, the drop in temperature – the chill in the air – all felt right. I needed to come up with something. I needed a plan.

I needed to head this off.

Suddenly, my phone shattered the silence. I looked down at the display: it was Ewan Tasker calling me back about Mills, about the registration plate I'd given him.

'Hey, Task.'

'Raker,' he said, by way of a response.

There was something in his voice.

'What's the matter?'

'I don't know. I've just had déjà vu, that's all.'

'Déjà vu?' I frowned. 'What do you mean?'

'Your guy, Isaac Mills, he's an ex-cop.'

I quickly processed the information and started making it fit. If he was an ex-cop, that probably meant he was on the payroll at Seiger and Sten as an investigator.

'Fifteen years in Lancashire Constabulary,' Task went on. 'I've been into the PNC and he's got no record, no cautions, no formal warnings or reprimands; there's nothing pending. No court orders, no driving convictions. His only registered vehicle is the Lexus you gave me the plate for. Like I say, fifteen years in the Lancashire Constab and a pretty good reputation from what I've been able to find out. A guy I used to know on a Major Investigation Team down in Lambeth works up in Preston now, and he's done some asking around for me. He says people remember Mills as a good cop. Professional, hard-working, smart. Could be a bit of a loner sometimes, didn't socialize much, but then that doesn't mean anything. I've known plenty of cops who socialize. They're normally the biggest arseholes.'

He paused briefly, obviously reading from some of the notes he'd made.

'Anyway,' Task went on, 'he's divorced with no kids, and it says down here that he was at Lancashire Constabulary from 1996 to 2011, and spent most of that time working major crime. His current address is in Keighley. You want it?'

'Yeah, definitely.'

He read it out to me.

'Oh, and his DOB is the 4th of November 1966,' Task said.

'Did your guy say what Mills went on to do after he left the police?'

'Private sector, apparently.'

'Any idea what?'

'My guy didn't know, but he thought it might have been some sort of security job. You know, advising on surveillance and protection, that sort of thing. A lot of ex-cops go that route: the pay's better, and you leave most of the stress at the door. But he wasn't a hundred per cent sure. The day Mills left was the last day any of them ever saw him.'

Surveillance and protection.

That just about fitted with a law firm like Seiger and Sten.

'What did you mean earlier about déjà vu, Task?'

'I mean, you told me when you called that you thought something was going on, and that something turns out to be you looking into an ex-cop. We've done this dance before, Raker, and I know you're going to tell me everything's fine, but whenever you do, a few days later I discover that you've walked into some shitstorm. I'm not going to be giving you this information, then turning up at your funeral next week, am I?'

Tasker's concerns weren't overblown: I'd come close to losing my life before, been dragged so far into the shadows I'd wondered if I'd ever get back, but I quickly tried to allay his fears, as convincingly as I was able, and shifted our conversation on.

My daughter, Annabel, would often raise similar worries about my job, about the risks it posed to me, to our lives together, but she was a dance and drama teacher, far removed from the world that I existed in, and which Tasker was a part of as well, so my reassurance carried more weight with her than it did with him. Task had been a cop, in one form or another, for the best part of fifty years. He'd seen everything the world was capable of, all its lies and its devastation, all its violence and its blackness, and he'd seen it repeated over and over, time after time. That made him perceptive, it made him cynical and wary – but, most of all, it made him realistic.

So I knew he was right: sooner or later, a case would come for me and pull me back into the shadows.

And maybe there would be no way back.

I just had to hope it wasn't this one.

20

There were five recording devices in each of the homes, concealed so well that it took us over ninety minutes to find them
all. The only difference was the design: the Perrys and the Daveys
had one type – theirs smaller, and more difficult to find – while
Randolph and Emiline and the Gibbses had another: a little
larger, possibly newer, but without the audio equalizer bars on
the side of them.

Neither of us talked about it until we were clear of the village,
the car rattling and whining as we made our way back down the
track. It was too risky to leave Healy at Black Gale now, so we'd
made sure the four properties were exactly as we'd found them,
light fixtures screwed in, picture frames returned, the feet of
the sofas placed into the same indentations in the carpets. We'd
been quiet and we'd been careful, but ultimately none of that
really mattered much: we'd talked enough before we realized we
were being recorded, and our complete silence in the aftermath
of Mills's appearance would almost certainly arouse suspicion
once the recordings were played back, as would the minor snaps
and clicks close to the microphones. Those noises would appear
like someone trying to suppress the sound of their movements,
which was exactly what it was: it wouldn't take a genius to realize
we'd found the hard drive and then gone looking for the bugs.

'So what now?' Healy said.

It was obvious from his voice that he was battling to stay
focused on anything other than the fact that his voice was on
tape somewhere, three and a half years after his name had been
etched into a headstone. His gaze was fixed on the road and
his fingers were forming a fist and then opening again, like a
pulse, something that happened when he was nervous. It was

a hangover from his days as a smoker, when he'd have already sparked up at this point.

'I have to get the car fixed,' I said.

'And where does that leave me?'

'You need to disappear for a few days. I don't know who the hell this guy Mills is. I don't even know if he's the one that put bugs in those houses. So while I'm trying to figure it out, I can't be worrying about you.'

Healy looked at me. 'You don't think Mills installed the bugs?'

'I'm saying I don't know for sure.'

But he could see what else lay unspoken in my face.

'Wait a second, you think *Ross* might be involved?'

I didn't reply immediately, because I was still trying to get my head around the idea, to figure out why Ross would do something like that. But one thing was certain: Ross had keys and alarm codes for all four houses.

'I need to look into Mills and I need to speak to Ross,' I said, 'so until I know either way, I think it's better for both of us if you lie low.'

He nodded, seeming to accept his fate.

'The nearest town between where we're staying and here is Skipton,' I went on, 'so I'm going to try and find a garage there. I'll drop you at the station before I do. I suggest jumping on a train to somewhere like Leeds: a big city; busy, lots of people. We need you to fade into the background. I'll give you my other bank card for a hotel room: don't go for some shithole, but avoid a top-of-the-range one as well. The blander and more anonymous the better. Once you're settled, call me from a payphone and give me the details. In the meantime, while the car's being repaired, I'll go back to the hotel and box up all the Black Gale paperwork. As soon as the car's ready, I'll meet you.'

After that, we were both quiet, the car filled with the defective tick of whatever was broken in the engine and the sound of rain on the roof. Eventually, Healy shifted in his seat, and I saw him glance at me, poised as if to say something.

'What's up?' I asked him.

He made a grunt of disbelief. 'What do you think? We've been listened to, maybe watched as well, and some arsehole's got me on tape when I'm meant to be six feet under the ground.'

But it didn't feel like that was it.

'What else is on your mind?'

We were a couple of miles outside Grassington now, where I'd met Ross Perry for the first time the day before, and where Emiline Wilson had worked at the library. I turned to Healy and said, 'He doesn't have your name, okay?'

'Maybe he doesn't need my name.'

'If he doesn't have a name, it's much harder.'

'Much harder to what? To find out I'm actually alive?' He shrugged to himself. 'All this bullshit should have been secondary, you know that? We should have been coming up here to find out why nine people vanished into thin air and why this prick has planted bugs in their homes, not worrying about how much he knows about me.'

His face was turned away from me now, the reflection of him in the window as pale as a phantom. 'All the cold cases I looked into,' he said softly, 'all the months down in Devon I spent researching them at the library . . .' He glanced at me. 'I mean, I had to do *something* to maintain my sanity. I was working on a trawler with a moron and his son, I had zero access to the Internet at home, I couldn't talk to other people, and I either started trying to do something useful, something I was actually good at, or I went home and stared into the void and felt like topping myself. So you know something? When I told you about this case, when I said we should look into it, when you actually *arrived* here yesterday, for a brief moment I allowed myself to think that things might be different.' His gaze returned to the window, to the scenery passing in a blur at the side of us, his reflection blinking in and out on the glass. 'For a second there, I actually thought my life might be worth something more than this; that for a few days, it might not be the same monumental fuck-up.'

I didn't know what to say to that, so we didn't speak again until we were almost in Skipton – the emptiness of the moors gradually giving way to the outskirts of the town – and, when we did, it was simply a repeat of the arrangements for the next few days. We went over them again as I idled outside the station – and then Healy headed inside the building.

He didn't look back.

He simply vanished behind the windows.

A ghost, once again.

Pioneer

Los Angeles | Wednesday 24 July

The next day, Jo woke early, before the sun was up, and – as had become her routine – ate breakfast standing in the doorway of Ethan's bedroom. After she was done, she wandered back through to the kitchen. Ira was catching a flight out to New York for a lunchtime meeting and wouldn't be back until the next day, which was why he'd reluctantly crawled out of bed so early. He still had to eat, shower, pack, drop Ethan at the day care in Van Nuys and then get down to LAX.

'You know where it is, right?' Jo asked him.

'LAX? Yeah, I think I can find it.'

She rolled her eyes.

He smiled. 'This ain't my first rodeo, cowgirl.'

He meant he'd dropped Ethan off at the same day care the last time he'd had to go out of town on business. Ira was a graphic designer, so usually worked from home, and the two of them generally stuck to the same routine: if she was on a day shift, he would work evenings – and vice versa – and whoever was off would look after Ethan.

'So what has Detective Kader got on today?' he said, pulling a chair out from the kitchen table. He sat down, toast in one hand, coffee in the other. He'd left a second cup on the side for Jo. She clipped her holster to her belt and started drinking.

'There was a body in a motel off Santa Monica Boulevard yesterday,' she said. 'I'm meeting a guy this morning in the Hills. He reckons he knows who my killer is.'

'That's good, right?'

'It could be.'

'So why don't you sound convinced?'

'I don't know. I guess I prefer to err on the side of pessimistic.'

He laughed. 'That's the spirit.'

She took another mouthful of coffee.

'How's your headache today?'

Ira shrugged. 'Better, but still there.'

'You taken something for it?'

'It's fine. I'm just stressed about this meeting.'

'You'll nail it, like you always do.'

'That's what I'm worried about. This pitch, if it's successful, it'll pay for a nice vacation next year – but it'll also mean a ton of hours between now and the deadline.'

'Don't worry,' she said, 'we'll make it work.'

She finished her coffee and placed the mug in the sink next to the bowl, then paused for a second, looking along the hallway at Ethan's bedroom door. Ira noticed.

'Something on your mind, Kader?' he asked.

'He'll be all right in Van Nuys, won't he?'

'Ethan? He'll be fine.'

'It's just, he hasn't been to day care for a while.'

'He'll be *fine*, Jo. Honestly.'

'Okay,' she said, although it didn't sound convincing and now Ira was studying her, his jaw working as he ate. She tried to alter the direction of the conversation and switched on the radio, hoping to hear some song the two of them liked, but everyone was still talking about the Night Stalker. More details were emerging about his latest attacks on 20 July: in Glendale, he'd shot and killed a couple in their late sixties, mutilated their bodies with a machete and then raided their home for valuables; in the hours after that, at around 4.15 a.m., he broke into another home in Sun Valley, where a family of four were sleeping. His first act was to shoot and kill the husband, and then he repeatedly raped the wife while their eight-year-old son lay bound and gagged in the next room and the two-year-old daughter slept. As she listened to the part about the woman and the kids, Jo pictured Ethan in the day-care centre and she felt a short, irrational flutter of panic at the idea of leaving his safety in the hands of people they barely knew; when a city was being laid siege to like this, when a man was so depraved he would sodomize a mother while her children were in an adjacent room, nothing was sacred.

'Jo?' Ira said. 'You all right?'

She looked at her husband but didn't really take him in. Ethan had been to day care before and he'd been fine every time he'd gone. He'd loved it, in fact – all the toys they had out for the kids; the kindness of the staff – and it was, in theory, extremely safe, with locked gates at the front and the back of the building. They took the children's security seriously, and if there were any problems, Jo knew they had her pager number, her work number too.

'Jo?'

'Sorry,' she said, forcing a smile. 'I was miles away.'

But Ira wasn't buying that.

'Don't let them grind you down,' he said, and abandoned his breakfast, coming across to her, pulling her in. 'Don't doubt yourself. You can do this.'

'It's not that –'

'It *is* that,' he said softly. 'It's exactly that.'

She sighed gently against him.

'You've been a cop for ten years already.'

'And there are still as many assholes as there were at the start.'

'What can I say? It's a gift men have.'

She squeezed him.

'You're a pioneer, honey,' Ira said. 'Remember that. You're out there in your wagon, crossing those plains by yourself, having to deal with all the dangers of unexplored territory. You're Davy Crockett and Daniel Boone – just with better hair.'

Jo squeezed him again and broke away.

'You're the strongest person I've ever met, Detective Kader.'

'I don't know if I'm strong or not.'

'Of course you are.'

'I worry about Ethan all the time,' she said, looking back along the hallway to his room. 'I'm worried about him going to the day-care centre. I'm worried about this damn cold of his. I'm worried that all of this . . .' She stopped.

Ira frowned. 'All of this what?'

'I'm worried all of this makes me weaker, not stronger.'

'What, you mean being a mom makes you weaker?'

She looked down at her holster, at the gun clipped into it. 'No one else walks into that squad room worrying about their kids. The men in there, they don't spend one single second worrying about whether the people at day care are going to take proper care of their children. They don't worry about the sleeping rou-tines, or the allergies, or rashes, or vaccinations, or *any* of it. Their wives do it all.' She glanced at Ira, winced. 'That came out wrong. I don't mean you're not an amazing father. I don't mean you don't help me and aren't with me every step of the way. I'm so lucky you do the job that you do, that you run your business from here, sup-port me and fit around my hours. I just . . . I just . . .' She stopped again. 'I just love Ethan so much. That's all.'

'And that's exactly why you're a great cop.'

'Because I love my son?'

Ira sat again, picking up his toast.

'No,' he said. 'Because you care so much about someone that isn't you.'

She went over and kissed her husband, hugging him, staying like that for a long time. Afterwards, she washed her bowl, went in and saw Ethan again – pausing beside his bed, taking him in, his size, his vulnerability; the fan not directly on him but moving his hair nonetheless – and then, finally, she left.

The Hollywood Freeway was already busy as she wound her way south, a blur of grey concrete and bright headlights. A cassette played music, the a/c was cranked all the way up to polar, and for a while it kept her focused. But then the monotony of the journey began to kick in and her mind began to loop back again, to Ira, to Ethan.

Was it normal to worry this much about your kids?

Or was her experience exacerbated by being a cop? Was it worse because she turned up at crime scenes and read reports every day of every week that made her skin crawl?

She didn't know for sure, but she knew something: Ethan was only eighteen months old, and he'd barely even scratched the surface in terms of what was to come. Jo wasn't even close yet to the kind of worry that buries itself in your bones, the throb of pain when your kid was really sick, the frustration of loving them and watching them make bad decisions, the impotence of knowing they were grown up, maybe many miles from you, and there was nothing you could do to protect them. Maybe it got easier over time or maybe it got harder, but she knew, eventually, it was up to the kids to keep themselves safe. It was up to them to lock their doors at night when a monster was terrorizing their city.

Because, in the end, it didn't matter how much you loved a person.

Eventually, you had to let them go.

PART THREE

The Student

I used to think I knew what silence was.

But now I realize I never had a clue.

In this place, it feels like I'm outside of time. I don't know where I am because all I can see is blackness. I can't make out an exit. Sometimes I think I can hear what might be the hum of a generator, and sometimes, on the edges of my sleep, the sound of it seems to hang in the air: this low, long buzz, like an insect. But mostly it's just this.

This place.

This darkness.

This silence.

I don't know where I am or how long I've been here. I tried to count it out at the beginning, tried to chart the passage of time, but I eventually lost track. The only thing I know is that it can't possibly be days any more. It must be weeks. A fortnight. In my most unguarded moments, I even start to worry it might be worse than that.

What if it's been a month?

What if it's been two?

When I woke up here the first time, I no longer had a phone on me. My watch and bank cards had been taken as well. It didn't register with me at first that the clothes and the shoes that I was wearing weren't mine — that they were different; that I'd been changed into someone else's property while I'd been unconscious. But after my voice started to become hoarse from constantly shouting for help, it hit home how uncomfortably tight my shoes were, and how badly the clothes fitted. When I touched them, I realized I was wearing a pair of trainers, not the boots that actually belonged to me. I had on tracksuit trousers, not jeans; a hooded top, not a sweater and a T-shirt. Everything I was wearing smelled of mildew and felt old.

I've lost count of the number of times I've got to my feet and, in order to keep warm, tried to build some sort of picture of this room in my head, using my hands to touch and my steps to pace it out. At the start, I would do it often, sometimes consecutively, one exploration after the next, trying to recreate the same route in order to map everything out. But there's no furniture in here, nothing to even bump into. There are no landmarks. I know there must be a way in and a way out because food is left for me in the same place every day, on a paper plate, alongside a bottle of water, but I can't feel any doors. I can't feel the ridges of a frame anywhere. I hear no breeze escaping in, and see no chink of light – not even a single, solitary pinprick.

There's just blackness.

When I first found the food and water, I didn't eat and drink any of it, wary of what I might be taking down. Now, though, I'm less fussy and I try not to think too hard about it. I accept the clothes and the blanket that have been left for me because, if I didn't, it would be even worse than this. I'd be weak. I'd be sick.

Or I'd already be dead.

The longer it goes on like this, the more frightened I become – not just about dying here, not about what might happen to me in this place, although both of those things do scare me. They scare me so deep into my bones, I can feel the fear vibrating inside my skin. No, hard as those things are to face down, they aren't the reason I feel like I can't breathe sometimes. They aren't why tears fill my eyes, and my heart thumps in my ears, and my blood runs cold. What scares me is simpler.

I'm frightened I won't ever get to speak again to the people I love.

I'm frightened I'll never hear their voices, or see their smiles, or even be in the same place as them. I'll never hug them, or laugh with them, or listen as they ask my opinion. I don't want to become so disorientated that I lose sight of who I was, or forget simple things like the way my family made me feel, the images of them that are burned behind my eyes, the emotion of knowing them, even of losing them. Maybe once I would have chosen to forget that last part completely – erased it in its entirety. Maybe once I would have traded everything in my life to delete the memories I have of standing next to their graves. But not now. I want to remember. Remembering doesn't frighten me in here.

Forgetting does.

The more time that passes, the more I exist within the permanence of these shadows, the more I worry that I will relinquish my history. It will begin to vanish from my head. Everything I did, the places I went to; any joy I've managed to bring and any comfort I could give; any sadness I've caused and regretted; any mistakes I made and vowed never to make again; all the things that became a part of who I am, the love, the grief, the agony and the beauty — deep down, it's that which frightens me.

I don't want to lose my moorings and begin to drift.

I don't want to surrender my identity.

Please don't let me forget who I am.

21

There was a garage on the south side of Skipton, about a mile from the train station, its workshop concealed inside a tatty brick building with corrugated-iron gates at the front. Inside, a couple of cars were being worked on, but it didn't look like they were rushed off their feet, and when one of the mechanics came out, he told me to bring the Audi straight in. I parked it up next to a Mondeo on blocks, and explained to the guy what had happened. For now, all I needed was for it to look less conspicuous and be safe to drive.

I headed into the centre of town, following a path that fringed the old shipping canals. In an arcade off the high street, I found a coffee shop, grabbed a table, removed my laptop and put in a search for Isaac Mills. I quickly found him online – but what there was amounted to very little.

He had no social media presence at all – no Facebook, Instagram, Twitter or LinkedIn; not even the shell of a profile that he'd set up but never filled out. There were no photographs of him, certainly nothing as crude as a selfie, and all of that fed into the description of Mills that Ewan Tasker had given me over the phone: when you weren't much of a socializer, someone who preferred not to go to the sort of get-togethers that led to pictures and postings, social media was never going to be a priority. I was surprised, though, not to find a mention of his name in relation to Seiger and Sten, the law firm he told me he worked for.

Instead, the only results of any significance were three newspaper stories, all different accounts of the same event. I clicked on the first. It was uploaded to the *Mail Online* in October 2009, and had the headline: OFF-DUTY COP HAILED A HERO FOR STOPPING ARMED ROBBERY ON HIS DAY OFF. Underneath that was a series of pictures, all taken in what appeared to be the same street in Keighley, the town in which Mills lived. He was smiling broadly for the camera as he shook the hand of the store owner whose shop had been targeted.

> An off-duty police officer was hailed a hero on Tuesday after disarming a gunman who held up a convenience store in West Yorkshire.
>
> Detective Sergeant Isaac Mills, 42, was out walking his dog when he decided to stop for milk at a corner shop run by Mirat Pridesh, 66, in his hometown of Keighley. What Mills didn't know was that, inside the shop, 22-year-old Anthony Snead had a pistol pointed at Mr Pridesh's head.
>
> 'I didn't realize what was going on to start with,' Mills admitted. 'The first thing I remember seeing was Mirat emptying out the till, which I thought was odd, and then I came further in and looked around the end of one of the shelves, and I could see a young lad in a hoodie pointing a gun at him.'
>
> Because Snead was wearing a hooded top, he failed to see Mills enter the store – a stroke of luck that Mills used to his advantage: 'I looped around one of the rows of shelves and came up behind him. I don't mind admitting my heart was beating fast, but I managed to grab the gun, get it out of his hand and get the kid on to the floor.'

The story went on for another couple of paragraphs and included quotes from the store owner about how thankful he was for Mills's help, as well as from two senior officers – one from West Yorkshire Police, where the crime had taken place, and the other from the Lancashire Constabulary, where Mills worked in an MIT – who said they were putting Mills forward for an award. I read the story again, and then a third time, and by the end I was still unsure exactly what to make of it. This wasn't what I'd expected to find on Isaac Mills, and neither the picture of him in the paper or the quotes he'd given quite tallied with the man I'd met at Black Gale, or the man Tasker had described to me over the phone. Outside the farmhouse he'd been cold, withdrawn and guarded; Tasker had suggested he might have been introverted. In the article, in the photograph of him smiling broadly for the camera, he wasn't that man at all. He was a courageous off-duty cop, a gallant community hero, warm and apparently sociable.

So was he both?

Or was one of them an act?

I saved all the pictures of him to the desktop and then went back to Google. There were no more answers when I used both 'Isaac Mills' and 'Seiger and Sten' as keywords, but on the law firm's own website I discovered that their one and only office was in the heart of York, at an address off the Shambles. I'd only been to York once, but I remembered the Shambles: narrow and cobbled, it was one of the city's most famous streets, a tourist trap packed with beautifully preserved, uneven timber-framed buildings that dated back to Elizabethan times. When I switched to Street View, trying to seek out an actual image of the company's unit, I quickly hit a dead end: the firm was based in a doorway-sized lane, between a sweet shop and a café, and the lane wasn't mapped. All I could see of it on my screen was a slender, gloomy artery, an overhanging upper floor, and a pale green sign with gold lettering.

I stayed on their website for a moment, flicking between three tabs at the top: *Home*, *Who Are We?* and *Contact*. The home page was in the same green as the sign hanging above their door in York, and the company name was in the same gold seriffed font. Below that, it said: LEGAL AFFAIRS | EST. 1896. On the *Who Are We?* page there was a short description of their recent history, with no specifics about what 'legal affairs' meant, just an invitation to call them. I knew, though, at least based on what Ross had told me, that they dealt with the complexities of house moves, and if they were looking after the interests of Randolph Solomon and Emiline Wilson – if their will was on file somewhere inside the walls of the firm – then the company obviously handled areas like probate, inheritance tax and distribution of estate.

I thought about Randolph and Emiline. There were bugs in

their house, the same as the others', but they were the only ones in Black Gale with an actual connection to Seiger and Sten, their vehicle was the only one unaccounted for, and something that Tori Gibbs had said to me the previous night had lodged in my mind and was tricky to shake off.

No one knows anything about them.

The bugs made me think of someone else too: Ross. He had keys to all the houses, knew all the alarm codes, and was directly associated with Seiger and Sten through his business. The question was how and why that association had come about. York was an hour's drive from Leeds, so it wasn't even close to his estate agency, and there were twenty law firms in Leeds – and twenty more in the areas surrounding it – that would have been a much more convenient recommendation to his customers.

I grabbed my phone and dialled his number.

'David,' he said once he'd answered. 'How are you?'

He sounded optimistic, as if he were expecting good news, a break in the case, something fresh and positive. If he'd told me the truth the day before, I didn't want to crush him inside the first ten seconds, because I needed him candid and clear-headed. But if he was lying to me, I needed to be able to hear that plainly too, so I said I was calling to check on a couple of things and then gave him a very broad overview of what I'd found out so far. It didn't amount to much – certainly, nothing about the bugs – just enough to assure him things were moving.

'I wanted to ask you about Seiger and Sten,' I said.

'The law firm?'

'I've just got a few things I need to get straightened out.' My eyes went to the laptop, where their pale green home page was still showing. 'You said to me yesterday that you'd often recommend Seiger and Sten to homebuyers looking for a solicitor?'

'Well, we don't officially recommend anyone . . .'

'Unofficially, then?'

'Some people come in, especially first-time buyers, and they have absolutely no idea about how the process works. In those circumstances we might give them a list of solicitors that we've worked with before. Whether they actually choose to pick from the list or go through someone they've found themselves is entirely up to them.' He paused, as if he couldn't understand the relevance of the question. 'Why do you ask?'

'Seiger and Sten are in York, right?'

'That's right.'

'So how did they make it on to your list?'

'Well, we have a satellite office in Harrogate. It's only small – a poky first-floor unit in the middle of town – and we only have one person manning it, but it allows us to sell property in North Yorkshire: Harrogate itself, the whole of the borough, the western edge of York – basically, a lot of high-priced homes. Most of those enquiries won't be drop-ins, they'll be people who find us through the web, so as a small operation it's actually been quite profitable.' He stopped, realizing he'd strayed from my original question, but if what he was saying was true it explained his connection. 'Anyway, whenever we sell a property inside the A1237, it qualifies as York, and that's when we might suggest a solicitor that's based in the city. Seiger and Sten are just one name.'

'So there are others you recommend?'

'Yes, we've got five or six York firms on our list.'

I relaxed a little.

'Okay,' I said, 'so have you ever been to see them?'

'Seiger and Sten? Not at their offices, no.'

'What about the member of staff who works for you in Harrogate?'

'I seriously doubt it. I can give you the details of Karen, our manager there, and you're welcome to call her, but I'd be surprised if she's driven all the way into York just to ask them a question about a house move. She'd generally talk to them on the phone.'

'Who is it you talk to when *do* speak to them?'

'The guy who runs the place, Jacob Pierce. He's been there years. You remember I told you that they were looking after

Randolph and Emiline's estate? Well, Randolph told me one time, when I was up seeing Mum and Dad, that he remembered using Seiger and Sten when his father died – this was in the eighties – and Jacob Pierce was already working there then.'

'So Randolph used Seiger and Sten for his dad's estate?'

'Correct.'

'Any idea what made him choose them?'

'I think he lived in York until he moved to Black Gale.'

It was hard to know what to make of any of that because it was all so utterly perfunctory. I considered again what Tori Gibbs had told me.

'What did you make of Randolph and Emiline?'

He didn't respond immediately, as if he didn't understand the question, and then: 'Randolph and Emiline? They seemed like nice people.'

'Did you talk to them a lot?'

'About as much as all the others at Black Gale, I guess.'

I flicked back through my notes again.

'And you said Randolph used to live in York?'

'I think so,' Ross said, 'although I'm not one hundred per cent sure.'

Tori was right: people didn't seem to know as much about Randolph and Emiline as the other villagers, but being represented by Seiger and Sten didn't mean a thing unless I could prove that it did. At the moment, their ties to the law firm were there, but – if Ross was right – they were pretty overt. However, I made a note to confirm where Randolph had lived before moving to Black Gale.

And there was still the missing camper van.

'What about the name Isaac Mills?' I asked him.

'Who?'

'Have you ever heard of him before?'

'No,' he said, 'never.'

And yet Mills had claimed he talked to Ross frequently about Randolph and Emiline's property. That meant one of them was lying to me – and, for now, I was more inclined to believe it was Mills.

'He never called you on behalf of Seiger and Sten?'

'Not that I ever remember, no.'

'Maybe Jacob Pierce mentioned him to you?'

'I don't think so. Jacob and I just talk about houses.'

I'd idly written Mills's name down on the top sheet of my notebook, circling it so many times the paper had begun to wear thin. I didn't want to cold-call Seiger and Sten or turn up at their doorstep asking questions until I figured out what Mills's interest in Black Gale was, and if he even worked for the law firm. I was having a hard time reconciling the genial hero cop in the papers with the man I'd talked to at the farmhouse – the same man who might have bugged the homes of nine missing people – so if part, or all, of his persona was an act, it was just as possible that he'd lied about his employer. Perhaps the only way to be certain of who he was, and what he might be hiding, was to see him in his own environment, when his guard was down: his home in Keighley was eleven miles south; from here, that was an easy twenty-minute drive.

I changed tack.

'Your dad was a keen photographer, right?'

'Yes,' Ross said, 'he enjoyed taking pictures.'

'When did that start?'

'Late on, I guess; definitely after he left journalism.'

I thought about Patrick Perry heading out on to the moors, and always when Francesca was on shift at the hospital. I thought about Laura Gibbs seeing him, and telling Tori all about it – and I thought about the idea that it was some kind of affair.

'Did he say why he started taking photos?'

'Not really, no. I guess it was just something that interested him.'

'Ever hear him talk to your mum about it?'

'Not that I remember,' he said, 'but Mum was the one who

mentioned it to me. I had no idea he'd got into photography until she brought it up.'

'So she was one who told you, not your dad?'

'Yes. She said he'd become obsessed with taking pictures.'

Ross laughed. He'd interpreted it innocently, as a light-hearted comment that Francesca had made to him. And maybe it was.

Or maybe it wasn't.

'Your mum used the word "obsessed"?'

'She was joking,' Ross assured me. 'He wasn't obsessed. It was just a hobby for him. He started off using his phone, and then he picked up this cheap camera from a charity shop in order to practise with the real thing.' He laughed again. 'Dad wasn't serious about photography, he just enjoyed trying. I mean, how can you be serious about photography when your only camera is broken?'

I frowned. 'What do you mean, "broken"?'

'I mean, the camera he bought was a dud.'

I thought of what Tori had said, about how Patrick had shown Laura Gibbs the camera – how he'd carried it on him – before he'd headed out on to the moors.

'It was only some cheap thing from a charity shop,' Ross continued. 'Actually, thinking about it, I don't know if Mum ever realized that it was busted.'

'But, presumably, your dad then got the camera fixed?'

'No,' Ross responded, still amused by the story. 'Not as far as I know. That's probably why he kept it quiet from Mum. That's just the sort of thing that she would have found hilarious and then absolutely roasted him about for weeks.'

'So the camera *never* worked?'

'No. In the end, it just sat on a shelf in his office. I'm not sure he ever took a single picture with it.'

22

The camera had just been a prop.

Patrick Perry had pretended to Laura Gibbs that it worked, even showed her the camera before he headed out into the valley. So did that prove he was having some kind of affair? There were certainly easier meeting places than the moors, much simpler routes for him to take to the main roads – if a car was waiting somewhere for him – but the fact that he hadn't dressed for a hike did seem to play into it. Laura had told Tori that Patrick would go out without a coat. No backpack. No food or map. Not even hiking shoes. So if he *had* been going out there to meet someone, who? And if it was someone else from the village – if it was Freda or Emiline – why hadn't Laura seen them heading out the same way?

I finished with Ross and went to some of the pictures I had logged of Emiline Wilson and Freda Davey. The one of Emiline was from the trip she and Randolph had made to California five or six years ago, and was a shot of her under a street sign on Rodeo Drive. She was in her late fifties, attractive, in good shape, a half-smile on her face that seemed almost playful. I looked at her, trying to imagine how an affair might have started between her and Patrick and how long it might have been going on. The fact that she and Randolph were the least known of the villagers – and that their vehicle was missing – fed into the idea of something illicit, even if there was no proof, and between her and Freda, Emiline seemed a more likely fit for something like this. In a picture of Freda Davey close to me, she was in a running vest, a number pinned to her top, at the start of a half-marathon. It had been taken seven or eight years before she was diagnosed with cancer for the first time, her face fuller, unburdened by the fear and dread that would come for her later. Even in remission, though, Freda had been struggling with ongoing complaints, niggling illnesses, and when she was diagnosed with it a second time, such a profound and life-changing event made it hard to imagine that she'd gone looking for, let alone been open to, something as consuming and emotionally complex as an affair.

I tabbed between photos of Patrick and Emiline, trying to seek out the tethers between them, and then a moment later my phone started humming.

I thought about not answering, still trying to unravel the lie that Patrick had told, and who else was a part of the fiction, but when I looked at the display, I saw Spike's number. I remembered that I'd asked him to get me two months of phone records for all nine residents of Black Gale.

If I was trying to untangle a lie, phones were a good place to start.

We spoke for a few minutes as he filled me in on what he'd done and how he'd structured the file, and then I switched to my inbox and saw a PDF already waiting.

I dragged it on to the desktop.

The document ran to 102 pages and was divided into nine sections. I kept my pad next to me, and a pen, and methodically worked through it all, looking for anomalies – numbers that didn't fit, activity that didn't make sense, red flags, unexplained calls, irregular numbers, anything. Spike had done me a big favour by listing the name of the person who had received or made the call from or to the individual Black Gale resident, or at least who the phone number was registered to. Sometimes the name listed was only a business. Sometimes the number was for a helpline at a huge company that bore no relevance to the case. Even so, they helped me to dismiss a lot of the calls that had been made out of and into the nine mobile phones, as well as the landlines at all four of the homes. It was slow work. There were so many calls listed in the document that I had to work hard to stay focused – one line blurring into the next – as I went through all nine itemized bills.

In the end, it took me almost ninety minutes, but once I finished I had a list on my notepad of thirteen numbers that either didn't tally up or felt anomalous.

Again, I worked through them in the same way, cross-checking them against the other numbers in the document that Spike had sent me, as well as against a long list of names I'd already compiled of friends and relatives that the residents had had.

By the time I was done, I'd whittled it down to one.

I'd found the number buried among almost nine hundred calls that one of the villagers had made. It was repeated eleven times: nine calls from the villager to the number, and two calls from the number to the villager.

The number had a central London area code.

The villager was Patrick Perry.

As I looked at the PDF, I thought about Patrick going out on to the moors, the broken camera he pretended was working, the idea he was having an affair.

And now there was this.

I spent a moment double-checking, just to make sure, but the London number didn't tally with the numbers of any existing contacts of his that I knew about, and anyway, as far as I could tell, Patrick had done almost no work in the capital during either of his careers. His PR clients were mostly based in Manchester and Liverpool, with a couple in Birmingham, and while he did do some PR work on a DVD release for a small independent film company in Soho, the number for them wasn't a match. There was something else too, the reason that the police hadn't picked up on this: the conversations between Patrick and the number – one of them lasting over sixteen minutes – had stopped three weeks before the Black Gale disappearances.

The police had only searched as far back as a fortnight.

I googled the number, but it failed to provide me with anything coherent, just a clump of sites where people could log cold-callers and scam artists in an effort to help others avoid them. The London landline that was listed in Patrick's phone records didn't match any number recorded as a nuisance call, and it didn't tally with any bona fide company listed in the search results further down. That meant it was probably for a home or a work extension. I punched in the number and pressed Dial.

I wasn't sure what I was expecting.

But it hadn't been this.

'This is Detective Inspector Kevin Quinn. I'm afraid that I can't get to the phone at the moment – but if you leave your details, I'll get back to you as soon as possible.'

Confused, I hung up without leaving a message.

Patrick had been calling the police.

And the police had been calling him.

Going back to Google, I went looking for Detective Inspector Kevin Quinn and found brief mentions of him in a number of media stories dealing with investigations in London. A murder. An assault. A robbery at a jewellery store in Hatton Garden. I read through each of them, but while they were dealing with serious crimes, they seemed relatively unambiguous and I couldn't see a link to Black Gale.

I began tapping out a rhythm on the edge of the laptop, trying to imagine how or why Patrick would have contacted a cop in London and if it was actually relevant to my search. Even if it wasn't, it was odd, an irregularity I didn't like: he'd never lived there in his life, and had spent his entire career in Manchester and the north-west.

Returning to the document, I wrote down the duration of each of the eleven calls between Patrick and Kevin Quinn, trying to spot a pattern. The first call had been the sixteen-minute one, and that was the longest. The others varied in length, some lasting as little as fifty-two seconds and as long as eleven minutes. When I switched to the dates the calls were made, they were haphazard too: they started on Wednesday 2 September, nearly two months before Halloween, and continued at apparently random intervals over the course of the next five weeks. The last contact between Patrick and Quinn was on Friday 9 October at 9 p.m.

Where had this relationship come from?

Had I missed something in my background check on Patrick?

I went back through my original notes on Patrick, on Francesca, on their house, their life together, his PR business, even her work as a nurse at Westmorland Hospital in Kendal. I tried to link the calls from Quinn to anything the Perrys had done in the time leading up to them going missing, but every route soon hit a dead end. Neither of them had connections to London. So why was Patrick making these calls?

I checked my watch, saw that I'd been going almost three hours, and knew the car would likely be ready now – but as I started to pack up, something stopped me.

What if I've got this the wrong way around?

I couldn't see the connection between Patrick and Kevin Quinn, didn't get why Patrick would pick up the phone that first time and call a detective in a city he had no association with, let alone how that conversation would go on to last sixteen minutes.

But what if Quinn hadn't always been based in London?

I redialled the same number for him, heard it ring the same amount of times, and then, as soon as his voicemail kicked in again, I got my answer in Quinn's voice.

I hadn't noticed it the first time, because his accent was so soft.

He was from Manchester.

It could have meant that, before he made the switch to London, Quinn knew Patrick; he could have been a friend, a schoolmate. It meant they could even have grown up together. But given how little they talked to one another over the two months I had records for, how long Patrick had been a journalist, and the type of crime stories he'd written during his time at the paper, something else seemed much more likely: before Quinn went to the Met, he'd been working for the Greater Manchester Police.

He was one of Patrick's sources.

As that hit home, something else pulled into focus: if Patrick had re-established contact after Quinn's move south, it wasn't to catch up, or to relive old times. The sort of relationship they had didn't work like that, however much they might have got on.

Rather, it meant Patrick needed something from Quinn.

Something only a cop could get him.

The Suicide: Part 1

Los Angeles | Wednesday 24 July

Jo approached Runyon Canyon Park from Mulholland.

When she pulled in through the north entrance, there was only one other car waiting. It was a white Toyota Camry, parked next to the trail that led out to the East Ridge. She slipped the Oldsmobile in beside it, her wheels kicking up red dust as she braked, and inside the Camry she saw a man in his sixties, trim, with a moustache and grey hair. It was hard to see much more than that: the sun was starting to come up now, cutting across the eastern flanks of the Santa Monica Mountains, and it filled his front windows with colour. Jo killed the engine and got out at the same time as he did.

'Detective Kader?' the man said across the roof of the Camry.

She nodded. 'Yeah, that's me.'

'I'm Ray Callson.'

They met beside the trunk of the Camry and shook hands. He was over six feet, in good shape, handsome in a weathered, fatherly sort of way, but when he moved it was slowly. Somehow, to Jo, it didn't feel like it was down to a physical impairment – his stride was smooth, his grip strong, his green eyes sharp and focused; instead, it felt like something else was affecting him, something more abstract and hidden. He had the kind of look that cops got sometimes, especially after a lot of years: a fatigue that wouldn't wash out, a slow, corrosive burn. Maybe it was a case. Maybe it was this case. Maybe this was what you became when you worked in a city like this your whole life.

Callson popped the trunk of the Camry and took out a blue

three-ring binder. It was an LAPD murder book. On the other side of their cars, the trail split, one of them heading south, pretty much through the centre of the park, the other immediately climbing west. He used the binder to gesture to the western branch.

'You up for a walk, Detective?'

She nodded. 'Absolutely.'

He locked up his car and led the way. July had been so hot that the trail had baked hard, a spider's web of cracks levering open the ground beneath them. It was still early – not yet 7 a.m. – but it was light, the sky streaked amber and pink, and, as they walked, Callson remarked on the unexpected clarity of the morning. She listened to him talk about the weather, about the colour of the mountains in the sun, about how beautiful the city looked on days when it wasn't sitting under a blanket of smog, and she thought how different he seemed from the men she worked with, how unlike a cop he sounded. She'd never met Callson before, and had only spoken to him briefly on the phone the previous night, but there was something benign about him, in his manner, that made her feel instantly at ease in his company. It was the total opposite of how she felt most of the time in the squad room.

'How long you been a detective?' he asked her, his fingers still clamped on the binder. She noticed he didn't wear his wedding ring on his hand, but on a band around his neck. He had a shirt on but no tie, and the ring swung gently in the V at his collar.

'Since '78,' she replied.

'You enjoy it?'

'Yeah,' she said, but then thought of the body she'd found in the tub the day before, of the panic that had gripped her on the way out this morning. 'Most of the time.'

'That's about as much as we can hope for, right?'

'Right,' she said, and watched him for a moment, just ahead of her, his breath coming more quickly now but the smoothness of his gait hardly changing. Whatever was up with him, whatever it was that she'd glimpsed back at the cars, it definitely wasn't physical. 'What about you? How long have you been working for the LAPD?'

'I joined in 1950.'

'Thirty-five years. Wow.'

'Wow is right. A long time. It's not technically thirty-five: there was three years in Vietnam somewhere in all of that and, believe it or not, I actually retired at the end of '83 and spent last year playing golf. But then they got so overloaded with all the shit that's going on in this city at the moment that they came back to me in February with a better deal – more money, not so many hours. So here I am again.' He smiled at her. 'I actually know a couple of the guys over there with you in the Detective Bureau. We worked the Hillside Strangler back in the day.'

'You were on the Strangler team?'

He nodded. 'Reminds me a bit of this Night Stalker stuff: total jurisdictional nightmare, everyone wanting a piece of the pie.' His lips flattened; a flash of defeat. 'Anyway, like I say, I know a few of your people. You met Gary Perez?' She nodded. She knew Perez but had never really talked to him. 'He's a good kid, Gary. Decent. Principled. What about Greg Landa?'

Landa.

She pictured him, obese and smirking, chewing on another Altoid as he'd stood there in the motel room the day before.

'Yeah,' she said, 'I know Greg.'

'I've worked with Greg on a couple of things.'

Jo forced a reply: 'That's cool.'

Callson watched her for a fraction of a second.

'I think we can both agree that Landa's a Grade-A asshole,' he said.

A smile twitched at the corner of Jo's mouth.

Callson returned it and then continued climbing the trail. 'You need to play the game,' he said, 'and pick your battles. Just know that we're not all like Greg.'

She didn't know if the *we* he was referring to was men or cops – or both – but whichever one it was, she could tell Callson meant every word of what he was saying. She'd never heard a cop talk like this in her ten years at the LASD.

Ahead of them, the trail levelled out, the path bending away to the south before starting another, gentle climb, and as it did, the hillside dropped away on their right to reveal the summits and hollows of the Hollywood Hills. Jo couldn't remember the last time she'd been up here but, whenever it was, the weather had been nothing like this. She could feel sweat running off her face, on her arms, down her back. Callson, too, was perspiring: a long, thin patch had darkened his shirt, the stain tracing the ridge of his spine, and every so often he would wipe sweat from his hairline with a finger.

A few minutes later, he pointed ahead of them, to where the path got steeper, the scrub closing in on either side, thick knots of black sage and buckwheat forming waist-high walls, and said, 'It's just up here.' The path dog-legged back on itself again, into another climb, but Callson didn't go any further; he stopped, pointing to a tiny, trampled offshoot from the main trail.

'That was where they found him,' Callson said.

They walked over to it, Jo trying to prevent the sweat getting into her eyes, and then took a couple of steps along the new path. It didn't lead anywhere, just into a thick tangle of scrub, but she soon spotted crime-scene tape, tied to the branches of a tree twenty feet from her and hanging like a noose.

'Donald Klein,' Callson said from behind her.

'That was his name?'

'Yeah. Monday morning, a woman was out walking her dog here and found his body lying about where you are now. Klein had eaten his gun. The bullet was a .22.'

Suicide.

And not only that. The same type of bullet that Donald Klein had used to blow his brains out had also been used to kill the man that Jo had found in the acid bath.

So had she found her murderer?

Could it really be this easy?

As she looked at the spot in which Klein had been discovered, she thought of Lieutenant Hayesfield. Cases involving murder-suicides, domestic homicides, killings witnessed by police, or when suspects were caught fleeing from the scene, he called 'self-solvers', as they were straightforward, self-explanatory and progressed through the system easily, from the squad room to the courtroom. There was an added bonus, too: they also quickly improved Hayesfield's clearance rate.

'It was definitely suicide?' Jo asked Callson.

'The ME says yes.'

She looked back at him. 'And what do you say?'

'I'd say it's the most likely scenario. The trajectory of the bullet – the way it travelled so close to the nasal cavity – that would be hard, though not impossible, to replicate if you were trying to make a murder look like a suicide. If someone killed Klein, they'd have had to press so hard into the chin with the gun – in order to get the bullet to go where it did – that there probably would have been evidence of the weapon on his face: scratch marks from the rear sight, maybe an imprint from the barrel or ejection port.' Callson paused, then shrugged. 'Like I say, suicide is most likely . . .' He faded out, turning in order to take in the view. They could see even more of the city from up here: the skyscrapers of Downtown; Griffith Park; the mountains and the valley beyond. 'Suicide also makes sense given what was in the trunk of Klein's car.'

He stepped towards her, handing her the binder, before returning to the path again, mindful of crowding her while she worked. Jo nodded, appreciating the gesture, and opened the murder book. Her eyes zeroed in on what was found in the trunk of Klein's car, and then the photograph of him, the sun glinting off its glossy surface.

She studied Klein's face. He was twenty-three, red-haired and awash in freckles, his eyes flecked green and brown and his nose crinkled at the bridge where it must have been broken and badly reset. The picture of him in the file was an arrest photograph, taken in 1983, when he was caught with six ounces of marijuana in a parking lot at the back of a Trader Joe's in Toluca Lake. He was given a ninety-day sentence. As Jo flicked through the pages of the file, she could see that that had been his only arrest. Since his release in May 1984, he'd been working in the kitchen of a steak and seafood restaurant in Sherman Oaks.

'Anything more on the vic?' Callson asked.

Jo looked up, shaking her head. 'No. He called himself Gabriel Wilzon in the guestbook at the motel, but – like I said on the phone last night – that wasn't his real name. That alias, it's a dead end. There are no prints for "Wilzon" because the acid managed to leach the skin from his fingers, and Chen at the ME's office said dental analysis was going nowhere fast. But, you know . . .' She shrugged and watched Callson nod. He understood where her thoughts had landed: if Klein was the guy who'd tried to dissolve a body in a tub of acid, maybe their chances of ID'ing Wilzon just improved.

She looked from the book to the patch of scrub where Klein had shot himself, then back to the book again. Callson was the lead detective, arriving at the scene an hour after the discovery of the body on 22 July, and his work was easy to follow and exhaustive. As she turned a couple more pages, she saw that a pale blue 1983 Ford Fairmont was registered to Klein and that had been the car he'd left in the lot, in pretty much the exact spot in which Jo had left her Oldsmobile. Photos showed the Fairmont in situ, doors open, the cream-coloured interior visible. It was a mess: soda cans, wrappers, the red-and-black uniform he wore at the restaurant. Callson had already confirmed the chronology: Klein finished his shift at 11.30 p.m., and two separate witnesses saw the Fairmont pulling into the north entrance of Runyon Canyon at around midnight.

Her eyes shifted to the photos of the Fairmont's trunk.

Inside were ten one-gallon containers of muriatic acid. It was the same acid that had been used in the tub at the motel. All ten containers were empty.

'His prints are all over them,' Callson said. 'Whatever else is going on, Klein definitely handled that acid.'

Jo looked up. 'Whatever else is going on?'

'Bad choice of words,' Callson said, smiling.

Except now she remembered what Callson had said to her earlier, his turn of phrase when she'd asked him if it was definitely a suicide: *The ME says yes*. She took a couple of steps closer to him, coming back on to the trail, as her Casio watch beeped to announce the half-hour. Seven-thirty, and it was hotter than any day she could ever remember. She pinched the material at the front of her shirt and began to fan it back and forth, trying to circulate some cool air. Callson glided a finger across his brow, a thick band of sweat beaded across his skin. She waited for him to say something else, to expand on his last comment, but he didn't, so she pushed him: 'Detective Callson?'

He looked at her.

'You don't think this is cut and dried?'

He didn't reply for a moment, and she could see a minor conflict playing out behind his eyes. He grimaced a little and glanced out at the view.

'Detective Callson?' Jo asked again.

'Ray's fine,' he said to her, not changing position, except for a slight narrowing of his eyes. Finally, his gaze strayed to the spot where Donald Klein had been found.

'Ray, you don't think this is cut and dried?'

'Well, I definitely think Klein was involved.'

She eyed him. 'But?'

'But I don't believe he was working alone.'

24

The town of Keighley was only a short drive from Skipton so, as soon as I picked up my car, I headed south to the address that Ewan Tasker had given me for Isaac Mills.

The vehicle was fixed to the extent that it no longer whined or hissed as I drove it, and the front looked better, but it was still misshapen and easy to spot, so I parked it a couple of streets away from Mills's house and walked the rest. Rain dotted my face as I approached his road, a cul-de-sac on a slope with a park at the top. Halfway up I spotted his home: a large cottage, set behind an imposing set of gates. His Lexus was on the driveway and there were shutters at the windows.

On my left was a sheltered bus stop, one side of it Perspex glass, so I pulled up the hood on my jacket and moved under the roof. The rain was getting harder now, but I could see enough, and as I watched Mills's home – satisfied I was at a safe enough distance – I got out my mobile phone and switched focus.

Scrolling back through the call log, I found the landline for Kevin Quinn, the detective that Patrick Perry had been in contact with in the months before he vanished.

His former source.

I saved the number and then called Ross again, asking if he'd ever heard of Quinn before. He hadn't, and he said Quinn wasn't a friend of his dad's.

There seemed little point in pressing him because I was already fairly certain that Quinn wasn't someone Patrick had been to school or university with, so I hung up and gave myself a moment to think. If I called Quinn, I could ask him outright what his connection to Patrick had been and see where it took me – but there was a decent chance I'd spook him and then he'd bring down the barricades. I paused, my thumb hovering over Dial. It was a risk, whichever way I went, but then it was a risk standing here in the rain, three hundred feet from the front door of a man who might have bugged the homes of nine missing people – so I called Quinn's landline.

His voicemail kicked in again.

This time, I left a message: 'DI Quinn, my name's David Raker. I find missing people. I wanted to talk to you about Patrick Perry. I'd appreciate a callback.' I kept it at that, left him my mobile number and hung up. I didn't have to wait long for a response: three minutes later, my phone started chiming, the display flashing PRIVATE, and when I answered and said my name, I got nothing in response except silence. In the background, I heard phones, conversation, the low drone of an office.

Finally, a voice said, 'This is Kevin Quinn.'

'DI Quinn, I appreciate –'

'What do you want?'

He was already on the defensive.

'I've been asked by Ross Perry and the families of the people who lived at Black Gale to look into what happened to them.' I stopped for a moment. I was banking on him knowing all about Black Gale already, but I doubted he would be prepared for a voicemail message out of the blue about it, two and a half years on, especially as it had never been a case at the Met, let alone a case he'd worked himself. Not that he wouldn't already have followed this entire exchange to its natural end point: I'd worked out that he was Patrick Perry's source, and now I wanted help.

I quickly tried to allay any sense of enmity or panic he might have been feeling: 'Just so we're absolutely clear, I've got no interest in anything other than finding out where Patrick went. I'd like to ask you some questions, I'm hoping you can give me some answers – and, once you have, I'll hang up this phone and we'll never speak again.'

More silence on the line.

'DI Quinn?'

Nothing.

'DI Qui—'

'I'll call you back.'

The line went dead.

The rain was crunching off the bus shelter now, off the road too, creating a fine gossamer mist between Mills's house and where I was standing. I checked the windows of his home and nothing had changed. The shutters were closed, no lights were on. I didn't even know if he was actually home.

My phone started ringing again.

This time, the number wasn't private, it was blocked.

'What do you want?' Quinn said, straight out the gate.

Wherever he was now, it was quieter.

'I just want to talk to you about Patrick Perry.'

He didn't answer immediately, maybe wondering whether he could deny ever knowing Patrick. But then he must have realized it was pointless: 'What about him?'

'He called you in the months before he vanished.'

No response.

'Eleven times,' I pressed him, trying to keep my voice passive. 'Patrick made nine calls to you, including an initial sixteen-minute one, and you made two to him.'

I wanted him to know that I had everything I needed to con-nect the dots, but I also wanted him to talk to me – so I chose to wait for him, our silence long. In reality, I had zero interest in turning this into a conversation where he either talked or I prom-ised him the world would know what he'd done for Patrick Perry. But if he thought it was a possibility, I might get him onside.

'So what do you want from me?' he said eventually. His tone was suspicious.

'You were his source when he was a journalist, correct?'

'Sounds like you know the answer to that already.'

'That was when you were both in Manchester?'

'Yes.'

'But then you moved south and you stopped talking?'

'I moved south,' he said, 'and then Perry went into PR.'

'So what made him pick up the phone to you again?'

He let out a long breath. 'He wanted some information about someone.'

'Who?'

'Some woman.'

'A woman? What was her name?'

'It was two and a half years ago – how the hell am I supposed to remember?' But then he sighed, and I heard him moving, doors opening and closing. 'Hold on.'

Another prolonged period of quiet followed – and then, suddenly, there was an explosion of voices, the sound of a drawer squealing on its runners, before the voices faded all over again. He'd been back to his office for something. A notebook, perhaps.

'Beatrix Steards,' he said.

'That was the name of the woman Patrick asked about?'

'Correct.'

'How are you spelling that?'

He gave me her surname and I wrote it down.

'Who was she?' I asked.

'I don't know.' There was an aggressive slant to his voice now. He was starting to get impatient, angry at himself for being compromised. 'Some university student.'

Again, I felt thrown.

Why would Patrick call Kevin Quinn about a university student?

'So – what? – Patrick wanted an address for her?'

'No, he wanted to take a look at her file.'

I frowned. 'Her file?'

'Thirty years ago, Beatrix Steards vanished into thin air.'

25

The rain eased off for a moment, the wind dying. I glanced up the road to Isaac Mills's house, checking no one was watching me, and then dug out my notebook and a pen.

'Beatrix Steards is a missing person?'

'Like I just told you,' Quinn replied sharply.

'When did she disappear?'

'1987.'

Thirty-one years ago.

'Do you know how?'

'She was at some house party in Lambeth.'

'Lambeth in London?'

'Do you know any other Lambeths?'

He made it sound like a stupid question, but it wasn't: why would Patrick be looking into the disappearance of a woman in a city that he'd never worked or lived in?

Why would he be looking into a disappearance at all?

'So she was at university in London as well, then?'

'Yeah,' he responded gruffly. 'King's College, it says here. She was at a house party in March 1987, left about 11.45 p.m., and that was the last time anyone saw her.'

I tried to clear my head. At the time he went missing, Patrick hadn't worked as a journalist or freelancer for over three years, had shown no signs of ever wanting to go back, and in fact was riding high on the success of his PR firm. Not only was the growth of his company taking up his entire working life, financially its rewards far outweighed any writing work he might have been – for whatever reason – hoping to pitch. So, whatever it was he saw in the story of Beatrix Steards, it couldn't have been commercial, and it was even harder to imagine that he was doing it in order to get back into journalism. Off the back of that, I remembered an interview Ross had given to the police where he recollected a conversation he'd had with his father only weeks before Halloween. I didn't recall it verbatim, but I remembered enough: Patrick had told Ross that setting up the PR business was the best decision he'd ever made.

So why the sudden interest in Beatrix Steards?

'Did he say *why* he wanted her file?' I asked Quinn.

'No,' he replied. 'He just said he wanted to look into it. I wondered why at the time, but not enough to get involved. We caught up, he asked for the file, and then I sent it to him. The arrangement we had back in Manchester was a two-way street, and he no longer had any column inches to give me, so I agreed to help him out for old times' sake, and because it sounded like it was important to him, but I told him that was it. I couldn't do it again. The other calls he made after that were all questions about the file – terminology, acronyms, that sort of thing. The file was put together in 1987, when the Steards girl first vanished, so some of the lingo we don't use any more. It was mostly calls to clarify that – except for one, when he asked about a guy called . . .'

I heard the crisp snap of pages being turned.

'Adrian Vale.'

I wrote the name next to *Beatrix Steards*.

'Who was he?' I asked.

'He was the last man to see Steards alive. Perry asked if I could dig around and find out more about this Vale guy – aside from what was in Steards's file – but I remember the search went nowhere because Vale died a long time ago – in 1989.'

'Did Vale have a record?'

'No, he was just a student, like her. Same university, same course.'

'Do you know if Beatrix Steards has ever been found?'

'Not as far as I know.'

'And Patrick definitely never said why he was looking into her?'

'I just told you, didn't I?' His voice was rising again, but I got the sense this time that his impatience wasn't a reaction to me asking him questions, or even to the way he'd allowed himself to be manipulated, it was a reaction to his own, lingering feelings of guilt. He'd given Patrick exactly what he'd asked for, and had done it not thinking for a minute it would lead to this moment; to the possibility that, somewhere in the months between that first phone call and Halloween was the reason Patrick and eight others had disappeared. And it might have been the Steards case that acted as the trigger. It might have been the reason Patrick was heading out to the moors.

It might be why he'd lied about the camera.

Even so, I struggled to make any links. There had been no evidence of Beatrix Steards in Patrick's Internet history, no evidence of her anywhere in his life. This had come completely out of left field. So why did she matter to him? Twenty-eight years after she went missing, and over three years after he left journalism, why would Patrick suddenly become interested in this case?

'You got a DOB for Steards?' I asked.

'Fourth of March 1965.'

'And where was she born?'

'Hammersmith.'

So she was born in London, presumably grew up in London, and then went to university in London too. What could have led Patrick to her? Had they met at some stage? Could she have been based in the north for a period of time? In 1987, at the time of her disappearance, Patrick would have been twenty-two, so was it possible they were involved romantically?

'Are we done?' Quinn asked, disrupting my train of thought.

'Yes,' I said. 'I just need one more thing from you.'

Quinn made a sound: he knew what was coming.

'I'd like the file on Beatrix Steards.'

He took a moment, drawing in a breath that crackled down the line, and then he said, 'Look, if I do this for you, I don't ever want to hear from you again, you got it? I just about managed to survive this whole shitstorm by the skin of my teeth the first time round because investigators up north never looked back far enough into Perry's phone calls. I got sloppy back then, letting him call me at work like that, but it's never happening again. It felt like I didn't sleep for months when that was going on. So if I send this to you, that's it. You get the file, you delete my number, and it's goodnight.'

'I told you at the start that was what I'd do.'

'Yeah, well, I've heard of you before, Raker – you're like a swear word in this place – so forgive me if I find it hard to believe the word of a man the Met despises.'

I didn't bother trying to defend myself or argue the point, because I'd already got what I wanted and attempting to convince a cop polluted by the opinions of other cops was an unwinnable battle. I'd worked cases that had ruffled feathers at the Met. I'd picked up and solved missing persons searches that had long been consigned to a drawer there. That had made me enemies in London I hadn't intended, didn't want, but had to accept. So I asked Quinn to get me a digital version of Beatrix Steards's missing persons file and gave him the URL and password to a website where he could drop the file securely. He grunted in response and hung up.

The rain started lashing down again.

Going to Google, I tried to find any mention of Beatrix Steards's disappearance online. There was very little: just one account on a website dedicated to long-term missing people, and it didn't add anything to what I'd already found out from Quinn. The paucity of articles didn't concern me, because cases that predated the Internet and the digitization of media outlets often didn't have corresponding stories online, but it meant – if I got nothing from the file Quinn sent me – I'd probably have to start tapping into national newspaper archives.

There was only one photograph of Beatrix Steards online.

It was small and low res but, despite the quality, I could see enough. She was petite and slim – maybe five three, maybe eight stone – and, at the time the picture was taken, presumably at some point in the mid eighties, she had a short, dark bob and was dressed in a spandex miniskirt and black leather jacket. Her eyes were difficult to define because of how the sunlight was falling across her, but I could see a distinguishing mark just below her right eye – a mole, perhaps, or a minor scar.

Who are you?

I continued to stare at her, trying to make sense of what I'd just learned, trying to figure out the connections to Patrick, to the others at Black Gale, and then, out of the corner of my eye, I noticed something through the rain: movement at the front of the house.

Isaac Mills was leaving.

26

As soon as I saw him unlock his car, I moved, heading back down the road, leaving the refuge of the bus shelter behind. The rain was fierce now, carving in at a horizontal, the wind screaming in my ears. I'd left my Audi two streets along, parked out of sight, but – although he would get a head start on me – I wasn't going to be far behind him.

I got to the car, slid in at the wheel and started up the engine, and then saw his Lexus pass the bottom of the road I was in. Pulling out, I fell into line four vehicles back.

He headed south-east, in the direction of Bradford. I let a couple of cars out at a junction on the edge of the town, playing it safe by putting more distance between us, even though the rain was a useful veil: it had eased off, but the wind had got up, and it created a swirling grey curtain as we hit a dual carriageway.

He went as far as Bingley, midway between Keighley and Bradford, and then took the turn-off. It was another mile before I realized that he was following the signs for something called Keygrave Mill. I had no idea what was there, but the signs for it were brown, which meant it was a tourist attraction.

Now I was even less certain what he was doing.

I managed to keep at least three cars behind him the whole time, and knowing the rough direction he was headed meant I could drop right back: after a while, I was two or three bends off the pace, and only catching the occasional glimpse of his blue Lexus up front – which meant, unless he stopped dead, he'd never see me tailing him.

Finally, I got to the turning.

The mill was immediately visible the moment I came off the road, a restored stone building with two vast chimneys and a waterwheel on the side. It was flanked by fields on the left and a maze of old, terraced cottages on the right, and the car park was rammed. As I came down the drive towards it, I could see Mills's Lexus already pulling into a space next to a pair of huge windows: on the other side of the glass was a restaurant, mothers at tables with young babies, and a play area for toddlers at the far end.

What the hell is he doing here?

I slowed down, not wanting to enter the car park as he was heading for the mill, but once he'd gone into the main doors I found the first space I could and swung the Audi in, front end first, so the damage was hidden from view. I grabbed a baseball cap from the boot and swapped my sweater – the same one I'd been wearing when Mills and I met at Black Gale – for a windbreaker. It wasn't much of a disguise, but it was something.

I made my way inside.

Keeping to a wall, so I only had to be aware of what was around me on one side, I moved through the mill from front to back. The restaurant was heaving, every table occupied, but I couldn't see him seated anywhere, or in the queue for food; he wasn't in the next part of the building either, where a gift shop occupied one side and a museum the other. I couldn't get into the museum without paying, but I could see enough of it through a series of windows.

I got to a set of stairs, with signs directing visitors to conference and reception rooms, and then realized I'd missed a door: it went through to a temporary exhibit full of black-and-white photos documenting Keygrave's years as a textile mill.

He was in there.

I backed up, watching him through a small glass panel in the door. There was no one else in the room except him. At first I assumed that was the whole point, that he was here because he was meeting someone and knew the exhibit would be quiet, but he didn't seem remotely interested in anything but the photos.

So was this really what he'd come all this way for?

A photography exhibition?

About ten minutes later, his mobile chimed.

He got it out, checked his texts and then pocketed his phone again, and after a final look at one of the last few photographs started coming towards me. I nipped up the stairs and out of sight, waiting for him to pass, and then came back down again to merge with the crowds behind him. He headed straight past the museum and the gift shop to the restaurant. This time, it was obvious that he was looking for someone – maybe the person who'd sent the text – his eyes switching from one table to the next.

I tried to see ahead of him, tried to imagine who was waiting for him.

He stopped at a table midway into the room.

There were four seats, three of them occupied, one by an attractive woman in her mid forties, the others by a girl of about fifteen and a boy of maybe ten or eleven.

The woman got up as soon as she saw Mills approaching and, when he reached the table, they exchanged a kiss on the cheek. He then said hello to the kids and they responded politely. They weren't his, not only because I knew already he didn't have any children, but because none of them – not Mills or the kids – hugged. The woman wasn't his wife either, because he was divorced, but they were much more at ease.

They looked like a couple who'd just started dating.

He said something to the woman and then started speaking to the kids, rolling his eyes and pulling a face, and they responded in kind, smiling, the boy laughing a little. Mills was so different from the man I'd seen at Black Gale this morning – so warm, his face so expressive and mobile – I barely recognized him. When we'd spoken earlier, he'd hardly moved a muscle, his eyes fixed on me; here, he was the hero cop the media had reported on.

I stood there watching, unsure what to make of it all, as he appeared to ask the three of them what they wanted before heading across the room to the canteen. After he was gone, I watched the mother and her kids, watched how they reacted, waiting for them to look in Mills's direction and say something about him. But if they did, it could only have been good: they all smiled and the mother made the boy laugh again.

I left the restaurant and headed outside to my car.

They parted company at the mill an hour later. I watched in my rear-view mirror as Mills kissed the woman on the cheek again and said goodbye to the kids, then, as they both left the car park in their vehicles, I let Mills go and fell into line behind the woman. She was heading in the opposite direction to Mills, towards Bradford.

On the outskirts of the city, she pulled into a petrol station.

Apart from us, it was deserted.

I pulled into the pump beside hers, then unscrewed the cap on my Audi. The kids were in the back, the girl on her phone, the boy playing a game on a tablet. I started filling up my car, waiting for her to make eye contact with me, and – as soon as she did – I smiled and did a subtle double take.

'Sorry for staring,' I said. 'It's just, I'm sure we've met.'

She frowned. 'I don't . . . I don't think so.'

'You're Isaac's friend, aren't you?'

She looked surprised.

'Um . . . Yes. How did you . . . ?'

This time, she was embarrassed that she hadn't remembered me.

'How *is* Isaac?'

'He's good,' she said, still confused. 'We just met him, actually.'

'That's great, uh . . . Sorry. This is terrible. I can't remember your name.'

'Melia.'

'Melia. *Right*. I'm Mike.'

'Hey,' she said, and grimaced. 'I'm so sorry, Mike. When was it we met?'

'Oh, a few weeks ago. In town.'

She nodded politely, as if she remembered.

'So how long is it that you two have been going out now?' I asked, not giving her the chance to ask me specifics about our last meeting.

'It'll be three months yesterday.'

'Wow, that's great. Isaac's such a lovely guy.'

She nodded. 'He is. The kids love him too.'

I glanced at her children. 'Yeah, he always was good with kids.'

A lovely guy, who was good with kids.

Who might have bugged nine missing people.

Who might know where they are.

I filled the rest of our conversation with bland talk about the weather, and once her tank was full, Melia went in and paid. While she was inside I got out my notebook and wrote down her registration plate. I wasn't sure what I planned to do with it.

I wasn't sure what to do about any of this.

Because now more than ever, I had no idea who the real Isaac Mills was.

The Suicide: Part 2

1985

Los Angeles | Wednesday 24 July

The two of them found some shade beneath the crooked branches of an elderberry tree fifteen feet from where the body of Donald Klein had been discovered. Jo still held the blue murder book in her hands, the photo from Klein's first and only arrest staring out at her. She glanced at Ray Callson and said, 'You really think Klein was working with someone?'

He shrugged. 'He had the acid containers in his car and I'll bet, over the next few days, the techs who worked that scene at the motel will also find a bunch of prints belonging to Donald Klein on surfaces in that room. It'll be a slam dunk.'

'But?'

Callson eyed her, saying nothing.

'Is it Klein's rap sheet that's eating at you?' she asked. 'The kid got busted with six ounces of grass. The way things are right now, the way drug sentencing works, that means ninety days down in Terminal Island. But it was only weed – it wasn't like he was slinging dope – and being a pothead is a pretty long way from being a killer.' She looked at the crime scene. 'Is that what you don't like?'

He smiled at her, clearly impressed by her instincts.

'The sort of shit you saw up in that motel room yesterday,' Callson said, 'I've seen stuff like that before. For my sins, I've seen it over and over.' He stopped himself, obviously wondering if he should continue. He swallowed, using a finger on his right hand to smooth out the edges of his moustache. 'Trying to dissolve a body in acid . . .'

'It takes a certain type of killer.'

'Right. And a certain way of thinking.'

'And that's not Klein?'

'I don't know. I didn't know the kid. All I know is that he lived with his disabled mom in Van Nuys and he looked after her real good. Like, this kid cared for her, he was kind and thoughtful. Sure, he smoked some grass, maybe dealt a little, but when I told her Klein was dead, his mom hit the floor. Literally, dropped like a stone. He was everything to her.' Callson held out his hands. 'I also picked up the phone and spoke to one of the guards down at Terminal Island. It's a low-security prison, so the very worst person Klein could have shared a cell with was some white-collar criminal who stole a bunch of money from a pension fund. But this guard, he said Klein was shit-scared for the entire time he was inside. I mean, he reckons this kid was crying himself to sleep every night.' Callson looked at the spot in which Klein had been discovered. 'Does any of that sound like a killer to you?'

'Not really, no.'

'It doesn't sound like much of one to me either.'

'It sounds like someone who could be manipulated easily.'

'Or blackmailed.'

Jo nodded, looking at the file again. 'The manager at the motel reckons he saw a station wagon there around the time Gabriel Wilzon died. I think I've managed to locate the vehicle: it's registered to a supplies yard over in Industry. Except, the guy who runs it is the only one who has access to the cars, and he just doesn't feel like . . .' She faded out.

Callson eyed her. 'Like our killer?'

'Right.' She tapped the file with a finger. 'I asked for an employee list and he's mailing that over to me, so it should be in the office by the time I get back. But I don't know.' She shrugged. 'Klein had a blue Fairmont. He's never been employed by this place, Caraca BuildIt. The witness that puts a station wagon at the motel in the first place is . . .' She paused, thinking of the Star Inn manager. 'I don't think he's lying to me, but I don't think he's completely credible. I guess what I'm saying is, I get what you're telling me about Klein, and I agree, but I can't prove it.' She smiled. 'Yet.'

A smile retraced the corner of Callson's lips too, and then he blinked some of the sweat away from his eyes. 'That binder you got there, I haven't put all of what's written in it into the system yet, which is probably why you didn't get a hit on the teletypes for the acid when you were looking for it yesterday, or on the NCIC. I'm sorry about that. I'm old, set in my ways. I'm sure computers are gonna make our lives a whole hell of a lot easier in the future, but I'm a paper guy. I started with paper back in the fifties and I'm going to finish with it. I prefer to get it down in black and white because it helps me to see straight, and once I can see straight, I can see what's off. So when I started to get the scent something wasn't right here, I picked up the phone and called your office because I figured, if there was no link to any open-unsolved *we* had, the Sheriff's Department was a good next bet. My only hope – when I picked up that phone – was that, if someone in your place had something for me, it would be someone like you.'

'Someone like me?'

The light gradually started to vanish from Callson's eyes, and something else moved into its place: a cloud, pregnant with pain.

'It's not in there either,' he said quietly, pointing to the murder book, his hands opening and closing as he talked, like he was restless, or frustrated. 'What we just talked about, I mean. I haven't put in my suspicions about Klein not working alone. To be frank, no one gives much of a shit about anyone except the Night Stalker at the moment, plus it's the same old story at our place as I'm sure it is at yours: we're way down on our clearance rate because we're so understaffed and crimes aren't getting solved. *So*, if I go to my LT and float this idea in front of him – that Klein was just a support act; that whatever he did in that motel room, he either did *with* someone else, or did because someone else *made* him, and that I need more time to push it all the way to the finish line – I'm going to get ignored, or reprimanded, or most likely laughed out of the room. And you know, I'm just . . .' His words ground to a halt. 'I'm exhausted.'

This was what she'd seen when she'd first met Callson: the slowness he'd had in his stride, the weight he carried, it wasn't a physical impairment, but damage that was deeper, more difficult to shift. He was tired because something was hurting him.

He smiled again. 'Sorry. I'm maybe being *too* honest here.'

'It's okay,' Jo said.

'It's just, after all these years, I've learned a few things, and one of them is the ability to call a person right, to get an accurate read on them.' He used his fingers to flatten his moustache again. 'And this case, it'll need someone like you to take it on.'

She frowned at him.

'Someone tough,' he said, 'but someone who cares.'

'What do you mean, "take it on"?'

'The men I work with, a lot of them are corrupt, most of them are racist, and all of them are out for their own. It's about whatever they can get for themselves first, and solving crimes second. I knew it before I retired and came back, and I definitely know it now.' He glanced at the view again, as if drawn to it, but all Jo could do was stare at him, transfixed, shocked by his words. 'You know, sometimes you can come to a place like this and the air is so unexpectedly still, so clear, that for a while you can forget all about the imperfections, all the shit that makes your life less bright than it should be. On a morning like this, it's easy to see that beauty in so many things, and see it with absolute clarity: the colour of the sky, the warmth of the sun on your skin before it gets too hot, the immensity of a view like this, the purity of the sound. You can see it all, and you're suddenly as far away from the pain in your life as it's possible to get.' He stopped. 'But it never lasts long.'

Jo didn't know how to respond to that.

To any of it.

'I'm sorry,' he said, holding up a hand to Jo, and for the first time she could see something else: he had tears in his eyes. 'I know I'm making you uncomfortable. I'm sorry. This is so unprofessional.' He took a long, deep breath. 'It's just . . . it's my wife.'

Jo took a step forward. 'What about her?'

He swallowed, tried to blink the tears away.

'Ray?'

'She's dying,' he said. 'She has Alzheimer's.'

'Shit, I'm so sorry.'

'They reckon she maybe has a week left.'

'*Shit*,' Jo said, the word like an exhalation, 'that's terrible, Ray,' and as she took another step towards Callson, drawn to the sadness flowing out of him, she spun back to this morning, to the drive in, and of her final thought before she'd got to the office.

It didn't matter how much you loved a person.

Eventually, you had to let them go.

Callson forced a smile. 'I've made a fool of myself.'

'No,' Jo said, stopping short of him, uncertain if she should reach out and offer him a hand. In the end she did, squeezing him above the elbow, and he smiled at her again. 'Shouldn't you be where your wife is?' she said. 'Don't you want to be with her?'

'My girls are there,' he replied softly. 'I'll go after this.'

They stood there for a moment, the sun baking the mud, the grass, the hills. From their left, a couple were approaching, a black Labrador running ahead of them.

'I got a couple of daughters,' he said, smiling again, trying to put her at ease. 'One of them is about your age. You remind me of her, actually. They're tough girls. They're beautiful and loving and kind, and I'm so proud of them both, but they're tough. I brought them up to be like that, because women get treated like shit, every day, all the time, which I always find ironic. Because whenever we bring couples in – the parents of kids who've been killed, or husband-and-wife teams who've robbed a bank, or abused children – it's always the man that breaks first. *Always.* Men, they're weak, that's what I've come to learn doing this job. We cry first and we confess first.'

He wiped his eyes.

'I guess I'm here proving my point, right?' He dabbed his eyes again, forcing a smile. 'In a week's time, my wife's not going to be around any more and, man, that's just hurting me so much . . . It's hurting me so much, I can barely even think straight . . .'

'Is there anything I can do to help?' Jo said.

Callson nodded, pointing to the file.

'Find out who really killed that kid in the tub.'

'Donald Klein is an LAPD case, Ray.'

'You find out who killed that kid, you won't need Klein, or the LAPD. That motel is in West Hollywood and that's your patch. That's all that matters here.'

She looked down at the file.

'And you?' she asked.

'I'm just glad you landed this,' he said, by way of a response.

'Look, Ray, that's kind of you, but you don't even know me.'

'I know enough,' he replied, and glanced again at where Donald Klein had been found. 'I should never have come back after I retired. I've been coasting in this job for too long. I can barely concentrate any more, barely even function. When I get home in the evenings, and I think of Georgette in that nursing home, I just get drunk and cry. I'm fucked, that's the truth of it. I'm an old man, standing here, confessing everything to a woman I only met an hour ago. So I'm sorry you had to hear this. I'm sorry you had to be the one that was standing here when all this bullshit finally poured out of me. But you know what? I stopped believing in providence a long time ago. Maybe I stopped believing the first time I ever turned up to a crime scene and saw the damage one person could inflict upon another, and then I definitely stopped believing when Georgette got sick. It's hard to believe in divine government when the person you love doesn't even recognize you. But you landing this case, of all the cases you could have landed . . .'

Jo stared at him.

'There's something about it,' he said, looking at her in the eyes now, suddenly focused and serious, despite the tears. 'This case,

I mean. There's something about it. After thirty years, you get a sense for these things, and this' – he gestured to the file – 'it's giving off all the wrong vibes. So it'll need someone strong and relentless to work it, someone who can give it the time it needs. It'll need someone like you. Because if there's one thing I know for sure, it's this: the person who forced Klein to help him, the person who *really* came up with the plan to dump that body in a tub full of acid, is still out there somewhere – and whoever they are, they're really fucking dangerous.'

27

Pulling the Audi into the near-empty car park of the motorway hotel, I switched off the engine and peered through the doors into reception. I thought about Isaac Mills, about the possibility that he'd already been here, using the audio recordings of Healy and me as a springboard for finding out where we were staying. In my head, on the drive over from Keighley, I built a picture of him tearing the paperwork off the wall of the room.

But then it began to blur.

And, as it did, I pictured the photograph of him, in the days after he'd stopped an armed robbery, and I saw him at the mill with the family, and replayed the words of the woman he was dating, and the image I had of him reduced to a shadow.

All I was left with then was what I knew for sure: Patrick Perry had called an old source at the Met in London and asked him for information on a missing student.

Beatrix Steards.

Getting out of the car, I headed up to the room. An intense flood of relief hit me when I found everything we'd collated – all the paperwork, the cuttings, the notes – exactly as we'd left them.

As quickly as possible, I began packing it all up, until I was left with just the photograph of the villagers at the Gibbses' dinner table. I held it in my hands for a second, pinched between my fingers, my eyes moving between the nine villagers, their clothes as ingrained in my head as the expression on their faces. Freda's floral dress. Emiline's red-and-blue one. Chris's checked shirt. Patrick's green V-neck sweater. Randolph's dark brown cords.

Where are you all?

I dropped the photo into the box, on top of everything else, and headed back out to the car, loading it all into the boot. Once

I was done, I paid the bill for both rooms and then nosed out of the services and on to the motorway.

This time, I drove east.

I'd already called ahead and paid for two nights in a holiday cottage on a farm south of York, and once I found it, I unloaded everything again, chatted politely to the owner of the cottage, and then began the process of sticking everything on to the wall of the living room.

Half an hour later, Black Gale filled every inch of it.

I took a moment to make myself a coffee and then returned to the wall again, to the reminders of the course Healy and I had been trying to plot, and to Beatrix Steards's name, which I'd now added. Seconds later, my phone started ringing, shattering the quiet of the cottage. I grabbed it, looking at the display.

It was a Leeds area code.

'It's me,' Healy said as soon as I answered, almost shouting the words, his voice swamped by the sound of passing traffic. He must have been at a phone box on a main road.

'Is everything okay?'

'Yeah, fine. Managed to find a place just outside the city centre with a bed like concrete. Anyway, I've been thinking about what we found at the house,' he said, changing the subject instantly, trying to retain his connection to our search, 'and about Randolph Solomon. He's the only one with a proven connection to this Seiger and Sten, right? Randolph was using them to handle his legal affairs. Then this Isaac Mills, he *works* for Seiger and Sten – so what if Randolph and Mills knew each other? Or what about if it's worse? What about if they were working together?'

'What, you think Randolph is behind all of this?'

'I know you've been thinking the same thing.'

It was true, I'd considered it – not least because of the missing camper van – but, according to Ross, Randolph's connection to Seiger and Sten was simple enough to follow: he'd lived in York before Black Gale – although I still needed to confirm that – and he'd then used the company to wind up his father's estate in the

181

seventies, and for other legal issues in the time since, including his and Emiline's move out to the Dales. But the longer I went without being able to disprove Randolph's involvement, the longer suspicion would linger, so, for now, I decided to focus on what I knew for sure, and what I could control: Patrick Perry, the lies he'd told Laura Gibbs about his camera, his moorland walks, and his search for a student who'd been missing for thirty-one years.

I gave Healy a quick overview of everything he'd missed.

'Shit,' he said quietly. 'You got any idea who this Beatrix Steards girl is?'

'Only what I've read online. I'm waiting on her file.'

'And Isaac Mills? Do we know anything else about him?'

'Only that he's an ex-cop and he *says* he works for Seiger and Sten.'

'He told you his name at Black Gale and that turned out to be true. Why give you his name – knowing you'd go looking for him – and lie about where he worked?'

It was a good point, one I didn't have an answer to. But something wasn't right about this. I didn't like how easily Mills had given up his name and what he did. What if him giving up his name, as well as the company he worked for, was bait?

What if he *wanted* me to come to him?

What if he knew I'd followed him today?

'I need to look into him some more,' I said. 'And Seiger and Sten.'

'I can look into them for you.'

'It's fine.'

'I said I can do it, Raker.'

'I *know* you can do it,' I shot back, and this time I heard the sharpness in my voice, 'but at the moment you're hiding out in a hotel room trying to make sure neither of us goes to prison. So I think it's best if you sit tight, don't you?'

He didn't respond this time.

'Look, Healy, I don't want it to be like this but –'

'I just feel helpless,' he said quietly.

I stayed silent, any anger vanishing instantly.

'I don't want to be here, hiding out in this dump; I want to be there, with you, working this case. This was *my* case. I spent two months collecting all that stuff you've got there, and now everything's gone to shite.' Even over the traffic noise, I could hear him clearing his chest, the emotion forming a ball in his throat. 'Whatever I had before this in Devon, it wasn't much, but it *was* a life. It was better than this.'

I couldn't think what else to say to him, didn't know how else to frame the same response I'd given him, over and over again, during the last three and a half years. There was a revisionism to his memories of living in Devon because, mostly, he'd absolutely hated it, the loneliness and isolation, the back-breaking manual work, the lack of interaction, and the fact that there was no returning to the police force, to the investigations that he'd loved. But he was right: Devon had been something; imperfect and solitary, but still a routine in which he'd found a measure of comfort.

A chime on my laptop brought me back to the present, and when I used the trackpad, I saw that the icon for my file drop was flashing in the top bar of the screen.

Kevin Quinn had delivered.

He'd sent me the file for the Beatrix Steards disappearance.

28

The missing persons file for Beatrix Steards looked every day of its thirty-one years, the scanned pages in the digital version duplicating the flaws of the paper original exactly: its tears, its marks, the way the typewriter produced imperfect letters – some black and crisp; others soft, undefined or barely there at all. The overriding poverty of the search was much easier to see, though: there were few clues, even fewer leads, and the whole case had begun stalling about two weeks after Beatrix vanished. It was hard to say if that was down to a lack of focus, a lack of care or a lack of ability – it may even have been a combination of all three – but it was there on the page, stark and undeniable, the last update of any significance added in October 1989.

The lead investigator was a DS called Stuart Smoulter, who – after a couple of phone calls – I discovered had died of a stroke in 2009, aged sixty-nine, which meant there was no way of mining his memories of the case. His work was solid, mechanical, a series of ticked boxes that had ultimately resulted in minimal forward movement. I was, though, able to confirm some of the details that Kevin Quinn had already provided me with: Beatrix Steards had been twenty-one at the time of her disappearance, she'd got a first in History at King's College and had then stayed on to do a Politics postgrad in September 1986, and the night she went missing – 3 March 1987, the day before her birthday – she'd been at a house party in Lambeth. The last person to see her alive was a 22-year-old man called Adrian Vale, who Quinn had told me about over the phone, and who Patrick Perry had asked him about as well: in the middle of the file was an interview that Smoulter had conducted with Vale. I gave it a quick look but decided to leave a detailed read until the end, concentrating instead on trying to fill in as much of the background on Beatrix Steards as possible.

Smoulter didn't offer much on her childhood, but I managed to fill the gaps I had using a combination of what he'd found out and what was written in the one article about Beatrix I'd discovered online. She was born in Hammersmith on 4 March 1965, had lived in Fulham and then further out in Woking, and although her parents, Dave and Mira Steards, weren't around any more – they were killed in a car accident in 1990 – she had had, by all accounts, a happy, settled upbringing. In terms of geography, the details also seemed to tally: Beatrix had never been based anywhere except the south; certainly never in the northwest, where Patrick Perry lived. The two of them were around the same age at the time of Beatrix's disappearance, but they'd lived out their lives in separate cities, two hundred miles apart.

The idea that they might have been romantically involved was one I couldn't dismiss, but I put it on the back burner for now. Instead, I rang some old newspaper colleagues of Patrick's, using numbers I found online, trying to get some sort of idea of when his interest in Beatrix Steards might have started. Could it have begun while he was still working at the *Manchester Evening News*? It was a theory that almost immediately got dismissed.

'Why would he be interested in a girl who disappeared in London?' his former editor asked me when I finally managed to track him down. 'Pat ran plenty of stories past me in the time he was with us, but she wasn't one of them. And even if she was, why would I ever publish it? Tragic as it sounds, we deal with news in Manchester.'

I spoke to a couple of other journalists who said the same thing, and then started trying to work another angle, cross-referencing King's College courses at the time Beatrix vanished with ones offered at Manchester University, where Patrick had studied English, at the same point in history. It was slow, difficult work – both on the net and on the phone – because of the amount of time that had passed, and impossible to answer anything conclusively, but there was no hint of a collaboration or exchange programme between the two universities, no hint at all that Patrick and Beatrix may have moved in the same circles in their early twenties.

I tabbed back to the start of the file and looked at the photo of Beatrix Steards at the front. It was exactly the same as the one I'd seen already online, just a better-quality version. I zoomed in a little, trying to get a clearer sense of her face, of the colour of her eyes: they were light green, almost grey, and her mouth was turned up into a hint of a smile, framed perfectly between the two vertical lines of her bob. And then, on the right-hand side of her face, just below her eye, was what I'd thought might have been a mole, or perhaps some minor scarring. But, in fact, it was neither.

It was a birthmark, pale brown and oddly shaped.

Almost like a butterfly.

I picked up the phone to Ross again. It had only been a matter of hours since I'd last called him, asking if he'd ever heard the name Kevin Quinn, but he told me I could call when I needed, and he was stuck in traffic on the way home, anyway.

'Can you remember when your mum and dad met?' I asked him.

'Mum said she was nineteen, so that would have made it . . .' He stopped, trying to do the sums. 'About 1986. They dated for four years and got married in July 1990.'

'Your mum was from Italy originally, is that correct?'

'Florence, yes.'

'When did she move here?'

'When she was fifteen.'

'And her family moved from Italy to where?'

'Liverpool.'

He was smart, so even if he didn't know where the questions were going, he knew they were loaded. I was looking for reasons why Patrick might have headed south, even if it was only briefly, around 1986 or 1987. But if Francesca had been based in Liverpool, he would have been travelling back and forth to see her.

'Did your dad ever mention a woman called Beatrix Steards to you?'

'Who?'

'Beatrix Steards. She was from London.' I spelled out her name for him. 'Maybe it was a friend of his, or a girlfriend. This would have been when Patrick was about twenty-two.'

'When he was twenty-two, he was dating Mum.'

I looked at the wall of photographs; didn't say anything.

'Wait a second, are you wondering if Dad was carrying on with this woman behind Mum's back?' The thought seemed to rattle him, the confusion evident in his silence, but then he came back hard: 'That never happened. Honestly, I'm telling you, Dad never spent time down south. His education was up here, he was working for a Manchester newspaper – he had no reason to be in London, ever. Plus, he'd only started dating Mum the year before. Why would he go off with someone else and come back and marry Mum? How would he have met this woman in the first place?'

They were both valid points, but people did all sorts of things for all sorts of reasons, and made all sorts of connections. And, anyway, an affair wasn't the extent of my thinking. I'd decided against voicing it in front of Ross – because if he struggled with the idea of his dad cheating, he would never contemplate something even worse – but could Patrick have had something to do with Beatrix Steards going missing?

Based on most of what I'd read and heard about Patrick Perry so far, the idea didn't necessarily land, but then he'd lied to Laura Gibbs, and more importantly to his wife, about why he'd repeatedly headed out to the moors in those last few months, so was it really so hard to believe he might lie about this?

I thanked Ross, hung up and called Tori Gibbs.

'You told me the other night what Laura said to you about Patrick,' I started. 'Did Laura ever say anything else to you about him? By that I mean what sort of person he was.'

'You mean was he the cheating type?'

'I don't know,' I said. '*Was* he?'

Tori's breath crackled in the phone. 'She said she didn't think so — she said his wife was a real beauty too, and they seemed devoted to one another — but then it's weird, right? Heading out to the moors like that, but only when your wife isn't home.'

'Maybe he did it because that made most sense: when Francesca was home, he could spend time with her; when she wasn't, he could spend time taking his photos.'

Except his camera didn't work.

And Francesca had called his hobby an obsession.

So was her comment, as Ross believed, a bit of light-hearted fun? Or had she actually started to suspect her husband was up to something?

I heard Tori moving. 'I mean, anything's possible.' A door opening and closing and then the sound of paper — a file maybe, or a pad. 'I'm just flicking through my notes here . . .' Another pause. 'After they all disappeared, I tried writing down everything I could remember Laura saying about the neighbours.'

I brought my own pad towards me.

'To be honest, though, most of it's pretty good.' She sounded disappointed, but it wasn't surprising: the fact that everyone in Black Gale had got on, and that the neighbours had all liked each other, had been clear from the start. 'She said Patrick was handsome, charming, funny — basically, she said he was the type you could imagine women dropping their knickers for, and after Laura kept seeing him going out on to the moors, we talked about whether he could be having his end away. I said to her it sounded like it had all the hallmarks of an affair, but I've written that Laura said — and I quote — "If Patrick was having an affair, I bet it's weighing heavy on his conscience." It's definitely possible that I've massively paraphrased that, because I wrote this down at least a month after Halloween, but even if the words aren't right, the sentiment is. Patrick might have been having an affair, but whatever pleasure he got from it would have been offset against the guilt he felt at cheating on Francesca.'

I looked at the photograph of Patrick I had on the wall.

'Do *you* think he was having an affair?' Tori asked me.

It was still hard to say for sure, but I had to consider it, just as I had to consider something else: that whatever happened to Beatrix Steards in 1987 had eventually had a knock-on effect in Black Gale two and a half years ago; that whatever he'd been looking for in her case, he'd found.

And it was the reason he disappeared that night.

And the reason eight others did too.

29

The interview with Adrian Vale, the main suspect in Beatrix Steards's disappearance, took place with DS Smoulter in Walworth on 6 March 1987, two days after Beatrix was reported missing by two friends she shared a fifth-floor flat with in Bermondsey.

He'd been six months older than Beatrix and was doing the same postgrad in Politics as her. In total, there had been six people taking the course, and while Vale stated in his interview with Smoulter that only Beatrix and another student, Robert Zaid, had actually known each other before the start of the year – Beatrix and Zaid had done the same History degree – he said that all the students had got to know each other relatively quickly after the postgrad course began in September 1986. They weren't best friends necessarily, Vale said, but they knew each other quite well. That meant that, when Beatrix had left the house party in Lambeth at around 11.45 p.m. on 3 March, and she'd come across Adrian Vale on the steps outside, smoking, they'd had a short conversation.

> SMOULTER: What was the conversation about?
> VALE: We talked about the course, about some mutual friends, and then I think we just talked about movies. She asked me if I'd seen *Ferris Bueller's Day Off* and I said I hadn't seen it yet, but I had seen *The Fly*. She joked that she didn't have the stomach for that one, and I told her she should definitely go to see it because the special effects –
> SMOULTER: Okay. What else?
> VALE: That was it, really.
> SMOULTER: That was literally all you talked about?
> VALE: Yes.

SMOULTER: Which friends did you discuss?

VALE: Uh. I think we mentioned Robert.

SMOULTER: That's Robert Zaid?

VALE: Yes.

SMOULTER: He was the one who did the same History course as Beatrix – is that right?

VALE: That's right, yes.

SMOULTER: Anything else?

VALE: No. Like I say, it was a fairly short conversation. Maybe five minutes. Perhaps ten.

SMOULTER: Five or ten?

VALE: Uh . . . closer to ten, I guess.

It was clear from the transcript that Smoulter's alarm was going off: he didn't like Vale, maybe saw something in his manner that put him on edge, so a lot of his questioning was hostile. Yet even though Smoulter had come straight out the gate and piled into Vale, Vale had remained polite, his answers consistent and rational, and he rarely appeared evasive.

SMOULTER: How did she seem?

VALE: Seem?

SMOULTER: When she left the party. Was she drunk? Was she upset? Did it look like she'd been crying?

VALE: No, not really. She seemed fine.

SMOULTER: So you're saying she wasn't drunk?

VALE: If she was, it didn't seem like it.

SMOULTER: Had you seen her drinking that night?

VALE: Yes. Everyone was drinking. It was a party full of students. That's what most students do.

SMOULTER: Are you saying you don't?

VALE: No. I don't drink.

SMOULTER: You don't drink alcohol? Why not?

VALE: My father was an alcoholic. He died when I was fifteen. Alcohol doesn't hold much appeal to me.

Even reading the words on the page, shorn of their delivery, the nuances of expression and inflection, it was obvious that the response put a hitch in Smoulter's stride. At that point, he asked if Vale wanted something else to drink – a coffee or a tea – and the interview was temporarily halted.

When it started again, Smoulter picked up where he left off.

SMOULTER: Did you chat to Beatrix at any point while you were both inside the property at the party?

VALE: No, I didn't.

SMOULTER: So the first and last time you spoke to Beatrix Steards was when she left the party?

VALE: Yes.

SMOULTER: Why did you go outside to smoke?

VALE: It seemed like the polite thing to do.

SMOULTER: What's polite about it?

VALE: Well, not everyone likes the smell of cigarette smoke. I try to be cognizant of that.

SMOULTER: But it's not a crime to smoke inside.

VALE: I didn't say it was. I said not everyone likes it, so I thought it would be polite to –

SMOULTER: Did you go outside to smoke because you'd seen Beatrix getting ready to leave the party?

VALE: No, I did not.

SMOULTER: Was her 'bumping into you' on the front steps of that house actually part of your plan?

VALE: I didn't have a plan.

SMOULTER: So you just got lucky?

VALE: That's not what I meant.

SMOULTER: We spoke to Robert Zaid and he told us that you had previously admitted to liking Beatrix.

VALE: Liking her?

SMOULTER: You fancied her.

VALE: I don't remember saying that.

SMOULTER: So Mr Zaid is lying?

VALE: No. You're twisting my words.

SMOULTER: You didn't find Beatrix attractive?

VALE: I don't believe that thinking she was attractive is the same thing as 'fancying' her. You can admit to finding someone attractive without it meaning that you want to date them or ask them out.

SMOULTER: So you *did* find her attractive?

VALE: Do I remember telling Robert that? No, I don't. Does it mean I didn't say it to him? No, it doesn't mean that either. I probably did say that to him in passing. But, as I said, admitting a person is attractive isn't the same as having something to do with them going missing. It's not the same at all. Beatrix and I, we talked for ten minutes, and then she headed towards the Tube station at Kennington. That was the last time I saw her.

Smoulter tried to push the same agenda for a while, tried to catch Vale out by mining for inconsistencies in his account of the night, but the interview began to wane shortly after and, towards the end, it became a painful exercise in repetition as Smoulter desperately attempted to unearth leads that clearly weren't there. After two hours, Vale's solicitor began to get more involved, and by the end he was cutting into Smoulter's questions every time they were posed, querying relevance, objecting to veiled accusations and highlighting a lack of evidence tying Vale to any crime.

Finally, at 9.37 p.m. on 6 March 1987, the tape was turned off.

It was the one and only interview conducted with Vale.

Police appealed for other eyewitnesses: people who might have been on a night out in the area at the time, or perhaps been waiting on the platforms at Kennington station, where Beatrix had told Vale – and friends at the house party – that she'd been headed. There was no footage of her on CCTV, because her disappearance had taken place at a time when security cameras were nowhere near as prevalent, especially not within the concourses and corridors of the Underground, so the appeal eventually led nowhere. The more his investigation stalled, the more Smoulter went back to Vale, securing financial statements from his bank account at the Midland, as well as an itemized bill from the phone line he'd had at his flat near Clapham High Street.

Again, they were dead ends.

After that, Smoulter started digging into Vale's upbringing, his background, his family, including the father Vale said had died when he was still only fifteen. That felt especially irrelevant, but I imagined it was done not because Smoulter distrusted the story that Vale had painted about his dad and his alcoholism – though he may have done – but because, by that stage, Smoulter and the Met were desperate. They had nothing. But, this time, the search failed for another reason, and it wasn't down to the information not being there, it was down to it being hard to access.

Vale, it turned out, was in the UK on a scholarship.

He was American.

Clear: Part 1

The squad room was quiet, the graveyard shift gone, all of the desks empty except for one at the back where a member of the Night Stalker team was already in place and screaming into his phone about a detective he'd had to deal with at Glendale PD.

Jo had overheard enough shouting the day before to know that Homicide at Glendale were on an LASD shitlist: two of the Stalker murders on 20 July had happened inside the city's thirty-square-mile boundaries, at a house close to the Ventura Freeway, and – a week and a half on – the task force believed detectives over there were still withholding important information they'd gathered at the scene because they wanted to make headlines for themselves. Jo didn't know if those suspicions were correct or not. She only knew that the LASD was supposed to be acting as the lead agency because of the chronology and location of the initial murders, that cops were territorial, in the same way as they could be intractable, driven, disingenuous and entirely self-serving, and that the frenzied hunt for the Stalker had brought out the worst in a number of them.

She wheeled herself in under her table and opened the top drawer of her desk. Inside was a Walkman. She put the head-phones on and pressed Play, not caring what tape she'd left in last time, just wanting to tune out the sound of the detective, who was now threatening to drive to Glendale and get someone fired. The irony wasn't lost on Jo. She'd had to watch more resources being poured into the Night Stalker, and more attention directed his way, than any case she'd ever orbited in seven years as a detective.

But all that extra money and manpower hadn't acted as a glue. If anything, it had turned the city on itself.

She took her investigation into the motel killing and the xeroxed copy of Ray Callson's murder book out of her tray and placed them on her desk. In her ears, Marvin Gaye was singing like an angel.

She started going through the suicide first, leafing through photos she'd already seen of Donald Klein's body, his skin marbled, his eyes glazed, the top of his skull missing. The day after she'd met him, Ray Callson had mailed over the full forensic report, and she'd since got one hundred per cent confirmation that the bullet Klein used to kill himself with came from the same gun used to murder 'Gabriel Wilzon' before he was dumped in the tub. On a scrap of paper in the same envelope, Callson had written down numbers for both his pager and his house, and had told Jo to call him any time she needed. She'd tried to do so once, to clarify something minor, but Callson had never picked up, so she'd left a message on his machine.

She was still waiting for a callback five days later.

She pictured the man she'd met the Wednesday before up on the slopes of the park. He'd been tired, grieving, in pain. He'd told Jo his wife only had a few days left.

Maybe those days were over already.

It didn't matter how much you loved a person.

Eventually, you had to let them go.

Between the vertical edges of the binders, under the glass top of her desk, a photo of Ethan looked out. He was smiling and had an ice cream in his hand, while Ira was holding the camera up, at the end of an outstretched arm, in order to fit them both into the frame. Light shone in the perfect blue of Ethan's eyes, his skin unblemished. She switched cases, flipping open the front of the motel binder, and shifted the paperwork across the desk so that it completely covered the portrait of her son's face. Ethan had looked different this morning when she'd left at six, less angelic, his diaper sagging, his nose still blocked from the cold he couldn't shift. He'd been crying too, trying to escape from his high chair as Ira attempted to feed him. But healthy or unwell, laughing or crying, even-tempered or difficult, she didn't ever want him – even his photograph – to come close to the world contained inside the binders. Not now. Not ever.

She refocused.

The full autopsy report from Dan Chen was due this morning, but Jo had seen and heard enough the day before to know she shouldn't expect much. She'd spent ninety minutes in a white room in the basement of the county coroner's building as Chen carved apart Gabriel Wilzon, and she'd still come away with nothing.

Leafing through the shots of Wilzon, she looked at the artist's sketch that had been made from what the manager at the Star Inn could remember, but so far it had got her very little. Wilzon was Hispanic – Chen had confirmed as much – but the sketch made him look Caucasian. It felt like she'd studied the sketch and the photographs a thousand times over, one half of Wilzon liquefied, the other half showing more traditional signs of decomp: at the Star Inn, his back had a sheen to it where the breakdown had begun and blisters had formed and ruptured on his skin; in pictures that Chen had taken at the autopsy, he was cleaned up, his face like wax, his body bloated from the gases.

Odontology had proved just as worthless as everything else: there was no match for the teeth, and so far no indication that Wilzon had received treatment at any clinic in Los Angeles. Jo had started to send out teletypes to agencies further afield, in an effort to see if Wilzon had come from somewhere else in California, but it was a long shot, she didn't expect to get any hits, and she wasn't convinced that that was where the answers lay, anyway. Forensics believed it was much more likely that Wilzon just hadn't attended a dentist regularly, or perhaps at all. Chen had said that, judging by the condition the skin, bones and internal organs, Wilzon was in his early to mid twenties, and during the transition from high school to college it often happened that as kids became adults, and moved away from home, they forgot to get their teeth checked regularly. Or perhaps, as Jo believed, there was another reason his teeth came up blank.

He never went to a dentist in America.

Because he wasn't American.

From her in-tray, she took a sheet of dot-matrix printer paper that had been mailed over to her by Paolo Caraca, the owner of Caraca BuildIt. It was the details of all thirty-six members of staff he'd employed since 1982, when he'd bought out and changed the name of the supplies yard. Including former members of staff as well as current ones was more than Jo had asked him for so she'd spent the previous day running background checks on all of them. As much as she'd appreciated the gesture, though, it was still a dead end: none of his staff, former or current, had a record. A few had some minor traffic violations, but nothing to raise the pulse. What had been more interesting than the names, though, was what else she'd found out about Paolo Caraca's business: it dealt in the supply of corrosive chemicals for industrial use – and one of them was muriatic acid. He told Jo that, at any one time, he could have as much as six hundred gallons in the yard, so she'd asked him to do a stocktake to ensure all containers were accounted for. He hadn't liked it, because he felt he'd already done her a big favour with the employee list, but he'd agreed to do it anyway. Now she was waiting for the results.

She felt someone moving her chair.

Taking off her headphones, she swivelled around and could see that it was Lieutenant Hayesfield: he was walking past, clicking his fingers at her and pointing towards his office. Jo put the headphones down and looked at the clock. She'd lost all track of time. It was after 9 a.m. and the squad room was now full.

Closing the binder, she grabbed her notes and followed Hayesfield. His office was small and unimpressive. There were blinds at the window, which he never closed, a green, black and yellow flag in a frame on the wall – the official flag of the Los Angeles County Sheriff's Department – and a detailed map of LA County itself, with sticky notes all over it indicating the active crimes that detectives were currently investigating. Jo noticed that there was no sticky note anywhere close to the Star Inn.

'Take a seat,' Hayesfield said, easing himself into his own chair. He was in his late forties, mixed race, burly and strong, an amateur boxer who'd won heavyweight belts all across the state in his twenties. He reached for a plastic cup of black coffee on the desk, steam smoking out of it, and said, 'So where we at, Kader?'

She looked at his map. There were three sticky notes with her name on them: one in Altadena where a woman had been raped and shot outside a country club, another at the fringes of the Angeles National Forest where a man had been found by a trail head on State Route 39 with a bullet in his chest, and a third next to a burger joint on the corner of Sunset and Palm where two men had got into a fight and one of them killed the other.

'Ortiz, the kid who popped his pal on Sunset, has his arraignment later on this morning,' Jo said. 'The case is a slam dunk. We've got eyewitnesses all over the place, we've got ballistic matches, his prints are all over the gun – it's going all the way.' She took out her notebook and leafed through to what she had on the killing at Route 39. 'The guy we found up in Azusa has been ID'd as Gerald Krysinski. After I'm done at the arraignment, I'm going to head out and talk to his family. His sister told me over the phone they hadn't seen him for months.' She flipped through more pages. 'The rape: we all know it was Kyle Hansen – we've just got to prove it, so I'm speaking to the DA later.'

'Okay,' Hayesfield said. 'So that's one down, two to go.'

Jo glanced at the map.

'I need those other two closed, Kader.'

'I hear you, LT.'

'I hope so, because I've got Santos crawling up my ass about our clearance rate while I'm dealing with the biggest manhunt in the history of the department.'

This time, Jo just nodded.

'Something on your mind, Kader?'

She switched her attention back to Hayesfield and saw that he'd come forward at his desk, pushing his cup aside, his eyes fixed on her.

'Actually, I think it might be one down, three to go, LT.'

Hayesfield searched the map for a case of hers he'd missed.

'What are you talking about?'

'The murder I caught last week at the motel.'

He frowned. 'The body in the tub?'

'Yeah.'

'We already cleared that.'

'Well, we found out who handled the acid.'

'Like I said, we filed on it already.'

'Klein was in that motel room when it happened; he almost certainly emptied the acid into the tub, because his prints are all over the containers. But he was there under duress. I've got together a working theory that, whoever was with him, was threatening to hurt Donald Klein's mother as a way to force Klein to –'

'Are you kidding me, Kader?'

She paused. 'His mother's got type 1 diabetes.'

'And?'

'And they're close. He really cared for her.'

'So? So what?'

'So that, combined with his personality, makes him easy to manipulate –'

Hayesfield held up a hand, stopping her.

'I want you to think carefully about what you say next.'

Jo looked at him, confused.

'LT, I'm not sure I underst–'

'I want you to think *really* carefully about what you're going to say, okay?' He returned his hand to the desk. 'Because I promise you, Kader: if I don't like the sound of what comes out of your mouth next, you'll be clearing your fucking desk.'

30

It was late, the clocks in the cottage reading 11 p.m., the windows showing nothing but absolute darkness. Upstairs, I collapsed on to the bed, my laptop still in my hands. I was tired, fried from hours of sitting in front of a screen and staring at the collage of photographs, cuttings and theories I'd tacked to the walls of the living room. But I wanted to finish going through Beatrix Steards's casework before I tried to sleep, because I knew, if I didn't, I'd never drop off.

The background information on Adrian Vale in Beatrix's file was thin on the ground, the result of a phone call that DS Smoulter had made to the Home Office – and then to King's College – five days after the disappearance, but it managed to fill in some gaps. He discovered that Vale had been born on 2 November 1964 and that his parents were both from Honduras: it meant his first name was pronounced *Adri-ahn* and his surname *Vah-lay*, but from what I could tell, no one, including him, appeared to have bothered correcting people in the UK who assumed Adrian was the anglicized version and *Vale* rhymed with *male*. He'd grown up as an only child in a house on St Louis Street in Boyle Heights, which, I found out via the web, was a 1. 2-mile road, running north to south, from the I-10 to the bottom of Hollenbeck Park in central Los Angeles.

Los Angeles.

I looked at the wall, at a photograph I'd pinned up of Randolph Solomon and Emiline Wilson pointing at the Hollywood sign. Was it simply coincidence that, for one of the only long-haul holidays they'd chosen to take, they'd opted for the same city that Adrian Vale had been born and brought up in?

Or was there something worth looking for here?

On the wall next to the shot of Randolph and Emiline was a

picture that Patrick Perry had taken of the moors, presumably on one of the unaccounted-for 'hikes' he'd made. I thought again about the idea of him having an affair with Emiline, even floated the possibility that I might have called it wrong and that it wasn't Emiline but Freda Davey he was seeing, despite her health issues, and then I looped back around to the LA link and felt no closer to an answer for any of it.

Returning to the Beatrix Steards file, I refocused on Adrian Vale and began reading about how his father had been a manual labourer and his mother had cleaned rooms at an old hotel on Main Street, close to Union Station in downtown LA. I read about how he went to local elementary, middle and high schools, and had been such an outstanding student, and achieved such impressive results, that he was able to apply for and secure a full scholarship to Stanford University, where he studied at their prestigious Law School. After completing his degree there, he then applied for another scholarship, the Marshall, which at that time awarded thirty US-based students a bursary in order to continue their studies at a British university for up to two years. When Vale was selected, he chose to do Politics at King's.

According to Home Office records, he flew into Heathrow on 28 June 1986 and had listed a house in Clapham as the place where he was staying. That was backed up by a contract that Smoulter had pulled from the local authority in Lambeth, which included Vale as one of three tenants paying rent on a house in Cask Lane, a road at the south end of Clapham High Street.

Much of the rest of the information that Smoulter had gathered on Vale felt at best extraneous and at worst irrelevant: other places that he'd travelled to on the same passport; a history of part-time employment he'd listed on an application he made for a weekend job at a pub near the Elephant and Castle; the contact details of his mother, who was – by 1987 – a widow; and purchases he'd put on a debit card, which rarely got more exciting than weekly grocery shopping and ATM withdrawals.

There was one photograph of him.

It was taken from his passport, the whole first page photo-copied. Dark-haired and handsome, he appeared athletic, his chocolate-brown eyes pinpricked with tiny blobs of light, his jaw strong and square, the muscles at his neck developed enough to confirm a love of working out. In fact, he looked more like a poster boy for weight training than an academic superstar, but a superstar he obviously was: one of his lecturers told Smoulter that Vale was 'one of the brightest and most purely talented students I've ever had the pleasure to teach'. When the lecturer was asked by Smoulter how he would describe Vale as a person, the response was just as unequivocal: 'He's a lovely young man: humble enough to sit and listen when he doesn't know something – and admit that he doesn't, which takes just as much modesty – but confident enough to argue a point when he strongly disagrees.'

I wrote down the quote and switched tack.

Smoulter had tried to pursue the idea that, because Vale had admitted to finding Beatrix attractive, it in some way implicated him in her disappearance. In the days after his interview with Vale, he'd returned to Robert Zaid, another of the students on the Politics postgrad, and the person who first suggested that Vale might have liked Beatrix; or 'fancied her', in Zaid's words. It was a comment that Zaid, from what I could see, had made only in passing, and without being one hundred per cent certain it was true, but it was a comment that Smoulter had zeroed in on and which, over the course of those first few weeks, became a central pillar of his search.

Unlike Adrian Vale, Zaid hadn't come from a working-class family: his father was from Iran, a multimillionaire who'd made his money in oil and construction, and who – after the 1979 revolution – had settled permanently in Camden Town. Zaid's mother, whom his father had originally met at Princeton while they were both studying there, was a former model from Budapest. Robert Zaid was born in Tehran but had been educated in England from the age of eleven, attending a boarding school in Gloucestershire. After A levels, he chose to read History at King's.

That was the course on which he'd met Beatrix.

Smoulter hadn't conducted an official interview with Zaid, but there were a few notes, including one quote that Smoulter had directly attributed to Zaid, and that he'd written in the margins of the file, verbatim: *I didn't mind Adrian. I never had a problem with him at all. But he could be a bit weird sometimes. Like, there was this night when Beatrix, me and a couple of others were walking back from the pub and one of the guys turned around and said, 'Isn't that Adrian?' And we all looked around, and it was definitely Adrian, but when he saw us, he darted off into this side street and didn't appear again. I remember saying to Beatrix, 'That was a bit odd,' and she said, 'Not if you know Adrian Vale, it isn't.'*

So was this the reason that DS Smoulter had dug his nails into Vale and refused to let go? Zaid's comments seemed to suggest that Vale might have been following – possibly even stalking – Beatrix, and it wasn't only Zaid who believed Vale liked her: a couple of other friends were spoken to by Smoulter and they all said similar things. Ultimately, it didn't amount to much more than hearsay, and it would never form the basis of any genuine prosecution, but it built a broader picture, and especially showed how Vale seemed to exist on the periphery of the group. Still, even if Vale had liked Beatrix, even if he had followed her, did that make him responsible for her disappearance? The quote Smoulter had written down from Zaid made Vale's behaviour sound weird, but being weird didn't make Vale guilty.

I could see that the investigation started to stall pretty soon after. A week passed, and then a month, and then three, and the search for Beatrix Steards continued to go nowhere. The last entry of any significant kind – rather than bland statements about there being nothing new to report – was on 12 October 1989.

That was when Adrian Vale died.

31

Vale had still been living at the same address in Clapham, was unmarried with no children, and, apart from a short stint in April and May 1989 working part-time as an archivist at the British Library, appeared to have struggled to find work after finishing the postgrad in June 1988.

Despite his academic brilliance, he'd also had few, if any, close relationships. When interviewed by police, the two men he rented a room from in Cask Lane said they barely talked to him, or saw him, in the entire time he was sharing with them. Perhaps that, and the lack of employment, was a contributing factor in what happened next, perhaps the fact that he was so far away from home, or perhaps none of it, but somewhere in the time after he ceased to be a student, his life must have taken a turn, because Vale hadn't passed away due to a physical disease. He hadn't become a victim of a crime or been in a car accident. He'd lost no battle with his bones, or his blood, or his internal organs; just his head.

He'd committed suicide.

His body was found on the East Sussex coast, where majestic chalk cliffs rose out of the sea to heights of five hundred feet. The actual date of his death was hard to pin down because there were no witnesses, but after a father and son – sailing past an isolated cove in their boat – spotted a body on the shore, a pathologist suggested it could have been there for up to two months. It was hard not to feel sorry for Vale, despite the lingering suspicions that Smoulter had had about him: not a single person had reported him missing, even the people he shared a house with, and about thirty feet from his body, police found his wallet. There was a suicide note inside that he'd failed to finish. It talked about how lonely he was and how much he missed his mother, who'd died the January before.

I leaned back on the bed.

There was nothing in the casework that directly connected Beatrix Steards *or* Adrian Vale to Patrick Perry or the other residents of Black Gale. There wasn't even a hint of a geographical tie-up either: the disappearance of Beatrix Steards, the suspicions about Vale, as well as his subsequent suicide, had all taken place hundreds of miles from the Yorkshire Dales. The timings were all way off too: when Beatrix went missing in 1987, when Vale jumped to his death in 1989, Black Gale didn't even exist. It would be three decades before its residents vanished.

So why the hell was Patrick so interested in Beatrix?

I began robotically tabbing back through the pages of the file, but I was only half concentrating. My mind was turning, full of static and noise, heavy with questions that still lacked answers and didn't look any closer to getting them. Where were the links? Where was Patrick's motivation for digging around in a thirty-year-old case? Where were the reasons for what happened at Black Gale, for the hidden audio devices inside the houses? Who was Isaac Mills?

And then everything shifted into focus.

I was on the first page of the interview transcript, looking at the questions from Smoulter and the answers from Adrian Vale. I'd already been over them once – but now I realized I'd missed something.

In the transcript, the three people in the room during Vale's interview were listed as SMOULTER, VALE and SOLICITOR. But, at the top, in a line along the edge – the point size not just small, almost imperceptible – was a list of their full names: *DS Stuart Smoulter. Adrian Garcia Vale*.

And then the third.

The name of Vale's solicitor.

Jacob Pierce.

It took me only a second to place the name, and when I did,

I felt a prickle in my scalp. Pierce was the person that Ross had mentioned on the phone to me earlier.

He was the man Isaac Mills worked for.

The man who ran Seiger and Sten.

Clear: Part 2

Los Angeles | Tuesday 30 July

In a flat voice, Hayesfield said, 'You don't think Donald Klein's our killer.'

It was a statement, not a question.

'No,' Jo replied. 'I don't believe Klein was the one who shot Gabriel Wilzon.'

'So he helps some asshole fill a tub with acid, watches as this mastermind puts a bullet in the Wilzon kid's face, and then Klein drives up to Runyon Canyon, goes for a midnight walk and pops one in his own skull because – what? – he feels so guilty?'

'Or he couldn't see an end to it.'

'An end to what?'

'To the killer threatening his mother.'

'Klein cares so much for his mom that he blows his brains out?'

'If he's dead, he can't be blackmailed.'

She kept her voice calm, quiet, as if she absolutely believed that she was right, but here, in this moment, as Hayesfield glared at her from across the desk, as she articulated her thoughts for the first time, her certainty began to grey: she was frightened that she'd called it wrong, frightened that the sympathy she'd felt for Ray Callson had helped cloud her judgement; she was frightened that she'd just set herself back months, maybe years, and that all the reservations that had been expressed about her, about her abilities as a cop, about the limitations of her sex – all the things that had been discussed in front of her and behind her back – would now be used as a way to articulate her inadequacy.

'Look,' she said, 'LT, I know it's not what you want to hear.'

'You're damn right it's not.'

'There's just something off –'

'I'm going to pretend I didn't hear that,' Hayesfield said. 'I'm going to pretend you haven't marched in here and tried to screw up a perfectly good case with some half-baked, feel-it-in-your-waters horseshit about an evil genius. Your wit at the motel is a creep who says he *might* have seen a station wagon, but will have no credibility on the stand. Ballistics match. Klein's got a record and his prints are all over that acid. It's done, Kader. You closed this thing last week.'

'I'm not sure Wilzon's American.'

'So? Do you need to know where he came from to know who killed him?'

'That's what I'm saying: I don't think Klein killed him.'

Hayesfield's gaze didn't shift an inch, even as his mouth stiffened and his lips blanched. In a tight voice, he said, 'Wilzon's an illegal – is that what you're saying?'

'We lifted a partial from one of his fingers,' Jo replied, 'and it matches another we found at the motel – so we've managed to build a clear, usable print. But that's been a total dead end. Nothing from dental either, nothing from the autopsy, and I spoke to the INS and no one matching his description has entered the country through any airport or –'

'So he was here illegally?'

She paused, nodded. 'I think he might have been, yeah.'

'And he was Hispanic – that's correct, isn't it?'

She knew exactly where this was going now.

'*Is* he Hispanic?' Hayesfield said again.

'Yes,' she replied.

'So you're telling me that we're going to unravel an entire case – one in which we can put the killer *at the scene* – because you want to go on some crusade to find out the name of an illegal who probably swam across the Rio Grande last month, and who you'll never be able to ID anyway because most of his face

209

is melted off? We don't even know if he came from *Mexico*, Kader. He could have come from anywhere. And even if he did, the Mexicans literally won't give one single shit about helping you.'

'It's not necessarily about ID'ing Wilzon.'

'Then what's it about, Kader? Enlighten me.'

'It's about finding the person who really pulled that trigger.'

He smirked. 'This "mastermind".'

Hayesfield's gaze didn't leave hers.

'And what are the LAPD saying about the suicide?'

'The detective there believes the same thing I do,' Jo replied.

'*Great*. And what's his name?'

'Ray Callson. He's a detective over in Hollywood.'

Hayesfield frowned. 'Callson?'

She nodded again.

This time, Hayesfield didn't say anything. Instead, he peered out through the blinds, as if searching the squad room for something, and then tapped on the glass. A few of the detectives on the floor looked up from their desks, including a well-groomed, grey-haired Latino man in his late forties, who Jo knew was called Gary Perez. He was the one Hayesfield was trying to alert. And then, as Perez got up and started coming towards the office, she remembered something else: Perez had been one of the detectives Callson had told her he'd worked with before at the Sheriff's Department. *He's a good kid, Gary*, Callson had said. *Decent. Principled*.

'Bring that copy of the *Times*,' Hayesfield shouted at Perez.

Perez double-backed, looking confused, and scooped a copy of the *LA Times* off his desk. When he got to the doorway of Hayesfield's office, he nodded at Jo and then reached across her and gave the paper to the lieutenant.

It was yesterday's edition.

'Perez, you said last night that you worked with Ray Callson, right?'

Perez looked between them again, thrown.

'Right?' Hayesfield pushed.

'Ray?' Perez said. 'Yeah, we worked on a body dump last year. The vic was left on Lake Hollywood Drive, but she lived up in Santa Clarita, so Callson called me and –'

'You rate him?'

'Callson?' Perez nodded. 'Yeah, he was good police.'

Hayesfield had begun to leaf through the *Times* and, as he found the page that he was looking for, something registered with Jo, something that Perez had just said.

Callson was a good cop. *Was.*

Hayesfield laid the paper down in front of her and pointed to a column on the right-hand side, halfway in. COP 'COULDN'T LIVE WITHOUT LOVE OF HIS LIFE'. Jo saw the words, the opening paragraph, but barely took any of it in. She looked up at Hayesfield, at Perez – still standing in the doorway – and back to the article. *No.* Ray's wife, Georgette, had died in a nursing home in Hancock Park over the weekend. When staff had found her, they'd found Callson too. Jo looked at Perez again, and he shrugged at her, still not understanding what was going on. *No, this can't be true.*

Callson had been found lying next to his wife, holding her hand.

He'd deliberately overdosed on sleeping pills.

'You can go.' Hayesfield's voice brought her back, and she saw Perez leave, taking the newspaper with him. 'The case is cleared, Kader.'

Callson is dead.

The sadness lingered for a second, and then the anger took over. It filled her head like the impact of an explosion – static, noise, heat – and she shot a look at Hayesfield, one he immediately saw the animosity in. His own expression tightened.

'You got something you want to say, Kader?'

She didn't respond.

'You don't think I've got the balls to fire you – is that it?'

Again, she said nothing.

'Your man Callson is dead, so the LAPD are going to be

about as interested in his theory as I am in yours. You've got Klein, you've got Wilzon – the case is finished.'

She looked at the map, at the scene where a sticky note should have been.

'He was in a tub of acid,' she said. 'He was shot in the face.'

'We got people being shot in the face all over the city.'

'He's a victim, regardless of where he came fr–'

'Don't play that weepy shit with me.'

She pressed her teeth together, rage pulsing in her throat.

'Klein went down for possession,' she said.

'So?'

'He was just a pothead in the wrong place at the wrong time –'

'I don't give a *shit*, Kader. *Okay?*'

He yelled the words at her this time and, out of the corner of her eye, she saw a few of the men – out on the floor – look their way. The argument on the Stalker team died down. Everyone was listening. Aware of it, Hayesfield lowered his voice but lost none of his steel: 'I got thirty-seven unsolved homicides where we can't get witnesses to cooperate with us because they're so shit-scared of gang reprisals. One in three of the murders we actually proceed with is getting kicked back to me by the DA because they don't think we've got enough evidence. We're digging week-old gunshot victims out of rock houses, we've got ODs absolutely *everywhere*, I've got drugs on every block and bodies on every sidewalk. I haven't got enough cops to deal with *that*, let alone this son of a bitch who's running around breaking into people's homes, raping and murdering anything with a heartbeat and then disappearing into the night like David fucking Copperfield. I mean, I assume you've *heard* of the Night Stalker, Kader? I just want to be sure here, because I know you didn't make the cut, so maybe you're struggling to understand the sheer *scale* of the manhunt we've got going on here, but if you think – given everything I just said – that I'm going back to Santos today with one less closed case than I had yesterday, you're out of your fucking mind. So do me a favour: save the Sherlock Holmes shit for playtime, when you get home to your kid. The case is done. Forget it – or clear your desk.'

She got up – so angry she could barely breathe – and headed out, ignoring amused looks from the men closest to Hayesfield's office. Two tables down from her, Greg Landa had wheeled himself away from his desk and was singing 'Jolene' again, smiling as he did, except he'd changed the words of the chorus to *I'm begging you, please don't fuck this case*. Some of the others laughed.

She glared at Landa, at everyone else, a whole floor's worth of eyes burning a hole in her.

And then she grabbed her jacket and walked out.

PART FOUR

The Envelope

32

I was still awake at 2 a.m.

Since the case at Christmas, I'd consistently failed to sleep well. The echoes of that, of how personal it had been, of how close I'd come to completely losing my grip, all still reverberated, feeding and massaging my fears. Some nights, like this night, the fear was so completely overwhelming, all I could see as I stared up into the darkness was defeat – all the questions I had no answers to, all the things I'd failed to figure out.

All the ways in which I'd never solve Black Gale.

I flipped back the covers and sat up.

Through the window, I could see cows in the field opposite, gathered along the fence, creamy streaks against the dark. Somewhere else, an owl hooted, the night so still that the sound carried undisturbed, as clearly and distinctly as if the bird were inside the room with me. I finished the water next to my bed and went to fill it again.

And then paused.

Was there something else out there?

I stayed where I was, the carafe at an angle in front of me. My gaze switched from the roof of my car – just about visible from where I was sitting up – to the fence hemming in the paddock. It was so dark on the farm that I couldn't see much further, or much more, than that: in the far distance was a dim glow from the main road, maybe three quarters of a mile away; beyond that, there were tiny pinpricks of amber from the nearest village; then, finally, there was an outside lamp on the main house, two hundred feet up the track from me. It was sallow, a weak half-circle of orange light extending about four feet from the property, framing the porch and part of the lawn.

Putting down the carafe, I got up.

At the window, using the curtains as cover, I looked down at my car, checked the glass and doors were still intact, and then watched as a few of the cows – who'd strayed out from the barn – continued to graze at the spot across from me. They looked undisturbed, unworried.

So was it just them I'd seen moving?

I grabbed a pair of tracksuit trousers, slipped on a T-shirt and headed down to the living room. There was the faintest of carry from the lamp on the main house, a low-level grey that allowed me to make out the corners of the furniture around me, and then a hint of the papers and photographs I'd mounted on the wall.

I went to the front door and looked out at my car, and then both ways along the track. There was no one out there. I rubbed at an eye, tired suddenly, trying to think of the last time I'd been in a place like this, one that was so soundless and dark. I'd spent pretty much my entire adult life in London, and after so many years there I hardly noticed the noise and light any more; there was no escape from it – even in the dead of night – and it had become so written into me now that, in a place bereft of both those things, I felt unsettled.

I made my way back upstairs, my bones aching from exhaustion, and perched on the edge of the bed. I took off my T-shirt and finished a third glass of water. Fully awake now, my mind started moving, rewinding through the things I'd read before bed: the death of Adrian Vale; the interview DS Smoulter had conducted with him after Beatrix disappeared; and Vale's connection to Jacob Pierce, the man who ran Seiger and Sten.

And then, in the field opposite, I really did see something.

One of the cows to my right, close to the barn and barely visible in its shadow, had turned away from the fence and had suddenly broken into a run. Seconds later, another did the same.

Something was spooking them.

Or someone.

33

Grabbing my shirt and a coat, I hurried downstairs.

At the side of the cottage was a series of footprints.

They were freshly fossilized in the mud and moved past the front of my car, on to the track and across to the fence: a clump of daffodils was now lying flat to the grass, where they'd been trampled upon.

I looked left, up the track to the main house. The security lamp was on but there were no internal lights. The farmer, his wife and their kids were still asleep.

The footprints didn't belong to them.

I clicked the door shut behind me and stepped on to the track. Stones gently crunched under the soles of my boots. I saw they were unlaced and dropped to one knee to do them up – and, as I did, I heard the low of the cattle in the barn.

The cows were responding to something.

I followed the direction of the footprints. They went to the fence and then transferred to the slats themselves: wet mud stained the posts where someone had climbed over into the field.

I'd brought a penlight with me, could feel it shifting around in my coat pocket as I clambered over the fence and into the field, but I didn't switch it on for now. The darkness was so thick ahead of me, it was impossible to see much more than a few feet, and the further from the main house – and its security lamp – that I got, the less I was able to make out. Before long, I could hardly see anything at all, even where my feet were landing. But if I couldn't see anything, neither could whoever was out here.

They would have a torch, the same as me.

I just wanted them to use theirs first.

Pausing for a moment, I listened to my surroundings, the thump of my heart in my ears. I'd come in what felt like a straight line, using the main house as a mooring, but it was hard to be certain, even as I looked back. Somewhere off to my right was the barn, and as I stared at the dark, I thought maybe I could make it out now, its huge corrugated iron walls and the maw of its main doors. I thought I could see a vague hint of white as well – one of the cows.

And then I realized it wasn't an animal at all.

It was a person.

By the time it had registered with me, they were gone, vanishing inside what I was certain now was the barn. Immediately, I heard cows start to react – confirming that someone was in there – their noises softened by the fluted walls of the structure.

I picked up the pace, almost turning my ankle in the bumps and crags of the grass, but soon the barn began to emerge, painted a deep, charcoal grey against the night. At the doorway I saw cows moving around inside, their chalky coats making them easier to spot, even if the shadows still hid the majority of their bulk. The farmer had told me they were truly free-range, able to wander and graze wherever they wanted, except in the depths of winter, and as one came out towards me, forming out of nothing, the others passed behind it like phantoms. The smell was strong here, a mix of hay, manure and water, and for the first time I could hear a breeze: it was faint, barely strong enough to register against my skin, but as it passed through the panels of the barn it made a feeble whine, like a cry for help.

Suddenly, a light flicked on.

Automatically, I stepped back, behind the edge of the main doors, and looked across the barn. It was torchlight, a pipe-shaped beam coming from the opposite side. In between were gates and runs for the cattle, as well as the cows themselves, so it was hard to see much else, let alone who was holding the torch. And then, whoever it was had gone again, a thin shape passing out through a door in the far corner of the building.

I backed up and hurried around the barn, walking parallel to it, my hand out at my side, my fingers brushing the corrugated skin of the structure in order to keep me in a straight line. When I got to the corner, I leaned around: at this end, the barn opened out into more pasture, hemmed in by wooden gates. On the far side, maybe four hundred feet from me, I could see an ivory column of torchlight.

Whoever it was, was heading away from me.

I moved quickly across the field, stumbling slightly, and then again as I got to the fence. Just down from me, six feet away, a cow emerged from the darkness as I scaled the barrier, and once I landed on the other side it made a long, low sound like an air-raid siren.

Ahead of me, I saw the torch swing back in my direction.

Whoever was out here was trying to find me – or, at least, the reason why the cow had made a noise – but it was much harder now because, I realized, we were in a different part of the farm: not a field any more, but a series of smaller, open-sided barns, linked together by concrete paths. Inside the barns were the skeletons of old machinery: tractors without wheels, ploughs, a field sprayer, rust-eaten vehicles and equipment whose shapes I couldn't identify, all of them sitting dormant in a sea of blackness, like the torso of some sleeping giant. As the torch came back in my direction again, trying to seek me out, I moved behind cover and watched the beam continually vanish and reappear as it passed countless openings and doorways.

They couldn't find me.

There were too many hiding places.

I stayed behind one of the barns, moving along its flank, using the torch like a point on a map. The owner of the torch was moving slowly now, back in the direction they'd come, either drawn towards the noise the cows had been making, or aware that they'd hit a dead end. Beyond the barns, from what I could see, circling them like castle walls, were huge laurel hedges, and I realized that, though we were at the edge of the farm, there was no way out from here.

It was a dead end.

Whoever was here would have to come back.

I stayed where I was. The torch swung left to right, the owner little more than a swipe of black paint, the beam of light leaking a fraction of the way up their arms, across their coat and down to their legs. They were all in black, their coat tight-fitting, the silver zips at the pockets glinting. Shadows moved either side of them; doorways lit up and darkened.

It was definitely a man.

He stopped.

As soon as he did, I instantly sensed something was wrong, the movement so sudden and unexpected that it had to have been deliberate. And then – out of the very corner of my eye – I saw another blink of light. I turned, looking along the barn, into the dark. From here, there was no way I should have been able to see the cottage I was staying in, not only because it was too far away, but because I'd left all the lights off.

Except all the lights were on now.

Someone was inside the house.

This whole thing was a trap.

34

I had a second to register that the man was wearing something on his head – was it a beanie? – and then he killed the light.

Darkness.

Absolute darkness.

He'd wanted me to follow him.

Which meant he'd led me out here on purpose.

I stood there, sealed in by the night, my bones throbbing with every heartbeat. I didn't try to walk, to run, to hide, wary of making a noise; instead, I took a fractional shift to my right and looked in the direction of the cottage again. Its windows were minuscule squares of yellow, perforations in an infinite wall of black. I couldn't see anything inside. From here, I couldn't even see a hint of the nearest town any more, or the glow from the main road.

It felt like I was adrift on an ocean.

And then I heard a sound.

It seemed so out of place among these fields and barns, alongside the dying hulks of old machinery, that I didn't identify it for a moment. But then there was a follow-up sound, a smaller, almost identical noise – electronic, like equipment was being turned on – and I remembered seeing a beanie on the man's head.

Except it hadn't been a beanie, I realized that now.

It had been a set of night-vision goggles.

I stayed where I was – the panic like a fire – trying to come up with something: a plan, a move, a way out. He would be able to see me, but I wouldn't be able to see him. I had no idea if this was all purely a distraction – a ploy to keep me out here while someone went through my things at the cottage – or if he was planning something much worse.

I listened, trying to push the sound of my heartbeat into the background, and thought I could hear movement – perhaps the scattering of stones underfoot – on the opposite side of the barn. Moving parallel to the wall, I retreated to the next doorway along. In the darkness, I thought I could make out a tractor, or maybe a plough, a tiny dusting of light falling against one of the wheel arches, and then the clouds thinned, the moon making its escape, and suddenly everything had a deep, lead-grey outline.

I started to move, making use of the fact that I could see, following the concrete path I'd come in on. At the corner of the building, I stopped again and peered around its edge.

No one was there.

There was ten feet of space between me and the next barn, so I bridged it quickly, passing the old corpse of a harrow and then a pile of tools, lying on the ground, discarded. I stopped again, reached down to grab a shovel, and then the light altered.

The clouds thickened; the moon vanished.

Black.

I listened for any approach, any sign he was close to me or using the sudden switch in light to his advantage. When nothing came back but more silence, I slowly inched the shovel out from the pile.

But I never got the chance to use it.

There was the scuff of a sole against the uneven concrete path and then a fist crunched into the side of my head, releasing my grip on the shovel instantly. I stumbled sideways, my cheek on fire, my ears ringing, and then I was struck again, an attack from the darkness I couldn't see and couldn't defend. I staggered off the path, clattering against a rake. It clanged as it fell and hit the concrete, and then I lost my footing and landed hard on the grass. When I looked up, hands in front of me for protection – bracing myself for more – no one was even there: it was just a swathe of black, no shape to it at all.

Fast footsteps.

I dragged myself up on to all fours, turning on my hands and knees, following the sound of him. He was heading back in the direction of the cottage. I heard his feet pounding against concrete, and then the dull thump of the grass.

Clambering to my feet, I switched on the penlight and used it to guide myself out of the maze of barns. I could smell sweat on myself, dirt, manure, could feel blood running from my hairline, but I kept going, ignoring it all, focused entirely on the cottage: all the lights were still on inside and, as I got closer, I could see the front door was open.

Were they still in there?

I hit the final fence, climbed over it and then switched off the penlight.

Approaching slowly, I moved on to the porch and stopped in the doorway, leaning in so that I could see most of the living room. None of the furniture had been moved. To anyone else, it probably looked like nothing had changed at all.

Except it had.

My laptop was gone: I'd left it charging, but all that remained now was the cable, plugged into the wall and snaking across the floorboards. My phone was missing. My notebook was still on the table, open to a page halfway in, but I knew straight away that it wasn't untouched: inside, along the gutter of the book, pages had been torn out, and when I picked it up and started going through it, I could see that the only pages that remained were the ones on which I'd made notes in shorthand, or in a form that only I understood.

I looked across the room.

It got worse.

Everything on the wall had been torn down. Photographs, cuttings, paperwork, theories – it was all either scattered on the floor, ripped into pieces that I could never put back together, or gone entirely.

'Stop looking into Black Gale.'

I turned, almost dropping the notebook, startled by the voice, the pages of the investigation like confetti under my feet.

A man was standing in the doorway of the kitchen.

He was holding a shotgun.

Monster

Los Angeles | Thursday 1 August

They met in a coffee shop on Broadway. Downtown was busy, the sun baking the city's streets again, Jo watching from one of the booths at the back as a fight broke out on the sidewalk opposite, two bums pushing each other as their shopping carts blocked a lane of traffic.

Larry O'Hara turned up shortly after.

Jo had already gone ahead and got herself a coffee and was picking at some eggs. She'd missed breakfast with Ira to get here for 10 a.m. O'Hara slid in at the booth without even saying a hello.

'Morning, Jo,' she said to him.

He rolled his eyes.

'I'll skip the pleasantries if that's all right.'

'Suit yourself,' she responded, and watched as he started going through a bag he'd brought with him. O'Hara was in his late thirties but looked like he'd done a ton more miles, the bags under his eyes like permanent scars, his hair already gone in its entirety. He slid on a pair of reading glasses and brought out a personal stereo.

'What you got for me, Larry?'

'First,' he said, 'let's establish some ground rules.'

'We already did that on the phone two hours ago.'

He shook his head, as if the conversation she'd had with him this morning hadn't ever taken place, and then laid a hand over the tape slot.

'If, and when, you get this guy,' O'Hara said, 'you give me what I want.'

She frowned. 'Is there an echo in here? I already told you that.'

'Don't screw me over, Jo.'

'Have I ever screwed you over before?'

He didn't respond, because the answer was no.

'Did you see the story?' he asked.

She nodded. It had been in yesterday's *Times*, on page four: an update on the suicide of Donald Klein, looping in his connection to the Star Inn, the body in the tub, the acid, the red station wagon and the fact that the victim at the motel still hadn't been ID'd. The moment she'd stormed out of the squad room two days ago, slighted, boiling with rage, she'd got on the phone to O'Hara and set the wheels in motion. The story he'd written was, in truth, a zombie, full of no new information, but it served a purpose for both of them: first, Klein was an LAPD case, so Jo had an insurance policy if Hayesfield ever came knocking as she could claim that – because the story had led with Klein – it had come from the LAPD, not from her; second, it got the details of the motel murder fully out into the open, where it would get seen by the public and, in turn, by potential witnesses to whatever had happened on the night of the killings; and, third, it was a bridge to carry O'Hara to what he ultimately wanted.

Not answers to the motel murder. He didn't care about that.

What he wanted was the Night Stalker.

Jo had told him that she wasn't working on the task force, but he didn't care: he wanted colour, not details. He already had another source who was on one of the teams – Jo suspected at Glendale PD – and so what O'Hara needed from Jo was the soap opera: how the task force looked, the stress levels, the kind of hours they were pulling, dominant personalities, arguments, all the bullshit that would add shade to what his insider gave him about the actual Stalker murders themselves.

Jo hated having to do it, because the Stalker was no game.

But the real killer of Gabriel Wilzon was still out there.

O'Hara pushed the personal stereo towards Jo, handed her a pair of headphones and pressed Play.

In Jo's ears, the tape whirred into life.

'*Sorry about that. I just wanted to move somewhere quiet.*' It was O'Hara, and he was feeding the caller some bullshit; he'd put whoever had phoned on hold because he was setting up a recording device.

'*So you're the dude that wrote that article about the bathtub case?*'

It was a woman, maybe Hispanic.

'*Yeah, that was me.*'

'*What's the name of the cop that's dealing with it?*'

'*Why, do you know something about it?*'

'*You got the name of the cop or not?*'

'*Joline Kader,*' O'Hara said, and read out her number.

'*You said a witness saw a red station wagon?*' the woman asked.

'*That's right. Do you —*'

But the woman hung up.

Jo looked across the table at O'Hara. 'That's it?'

'That's it.'

'You made me come all the way down here and eat these shitty eggs for *this*?' She took off the headphones and tossed them at O'Hara. 'If she actually calls me, we might be in business, otherwise this is worth less than nothing, Larry, you know that.'

'Just see if she calls.'

'If she doesn't, our deal is off.'

'Just see if she calls first,' O'Hara repeated.

'Yeah, well, she's had my name since 2 p.m. yesterday.'

He shrugged. 'Maybe she's waiting for the right moment.'

The right moment came just before 7 p.m., as Jo was leaving the office.

'Kader,' she said, picking up her phone and putting on her jacket.

'Uh, are you the one looking into that motel thing?'

She quickly sat down again. 'Yeah, that's me.'

'I read that a witness at the motel saw a red station wagon. That right?'

'That's correct.'

Jo grabbed a pen and her notebook and looked in the direction of Hayesfield's office. She could make him out behind the slats of the blind.

'Hello?' the woman said. 'You still there?'

'Yeah, I'm here.'

'And this guy who blew his brains out up at Runyon Canyon Park – this Klein guy – you think he was the same dude who did all that shit with the acid and stuff?'

'Can I get your name, ma'am?'

'No. No, you can't get no name.'

'I need your name to –'

'Do you think he did it or not?'

She felt her pulse quicken as she said, 'I don't know.'

'Well, I think you got it wrong.'

'Got it wrong how?'

There was no response this time.

'Ma'am?'

More silence.

'Ma'am, are you there –'

'I think someone else did it.'

Jo tried to still her emotions.

'Why would you say that, ma'am?'

Jo could hear the hesitancy in the woman now, like a series of staccato breaths.

'Ma'am, it's okay,' Jo said.

'Maybe this was a mistake.'

'It's not. You're not making a mistake.'

'All this Night Stalker stuff,' the woman said, and for the first time there was a tremor in her voice, 'I know it's bad. I got eyes. I can read. I can see how messed up it is. And, I don't know, maybe he ain't as *loco* as this Stalker nut, but he's still . . . he's . . .' Her sentence trailed off.

'Who are we talking about here, ma'am?'

Silence.

'Ma'am?'

229

'I used to see him driving around in that red station wagon sometimes.'

Jo's adrenalin spiked. *Shit. I might actually have found him.* She grabbed the printout from her in-tray with the list of all the employees Paolo Caraca had hired since 1982, and pushed the woman again: 'Who did you see driving around, ma'am?'

Nothing.

'Ma'am? What was the name of –'

'Adrian.'

Jo checked the list: there was an Adrian on it.

'Adrian Vale, that's who you need to look into,' the woman said, more quietly this time, as if his full name had spooked her. 'He's a total fucking monster.'

35

Isaac Mills emerged from the shadows.

He held the shotgun across his front, the barrel tilted towards the floor, his fingers fixed to the fore-end. Around his neck hung the night-vision goggles. He watched me for a second before he edged forward, still shadowed by the angle of the stairs.

'Close the door,' he ordered.

He used the barrel of the gun to gesture towards it and, once I'd shut the door, he pulled out a chair for me and backed away, the two of us standing either side of the table.

'Sit down,' he said sharply, the shotgun turning in my direction as he used it to point to the chair. I sat, watching him closely, and as he came further into the light I saw mud and manure caked around his boots and then something else on the hem of his sleeves. It was dotted across both of his hands too.

Blood.

He stopped at the other side of the table, leaning against the wall, adjacent to the breakfast bar that separated the kitchen from the living room, and then his eyes shifted to the space on which I'd mounted the casework, and he said, 'It's a real shame about your wall, there.' He said it flatly, without any expression or emphasis at all, and when he returned his gaze to me, it was equally neutral. I thought of the man who'd come to Black Gale the day before, evasive and opaque, asking questions he already knew the answers to and lying about his reason for being there; and then I pictured the other Isaac Mills, the one who'd been so warm with the woman and her two kids, who'd stopped an armed robbery and had stood there for photographs afterwards, smiling and benign, before going on to collect a bravery award. I couldn't get a read on him then, I couldn't get a read on him

now either – and if I didn't know who he was, I couldn't antici-
pate him. He was unknown and unpredictable.

And both of those things scared me.

For the first time, he dropped his hand away from the fore-
end of the shotgun and went to the pocket of his coat. Initially,
inside his closed fist, it was hard to make out what he'd removed.
But then I saw a headphone jack at one end.

He placed the mobile phone down on the table and, as I looked
at it, confused, he reached forward and pressed something on
the screen. The Speaker icon. Someone was listening to us at
the other end. I tried to get a look at the number he'd dialled
but it simply said PRIVATE. Mills glanced at me and shrugged,
an almost imperceptible movement, but one that left something
behind in his face: it took me a second to work out what it was,
not only because he was difficult to read but because I thought,
to start with, I was mistaken.

Was it regret?

'You need to stop,' he said, and when he took hold of the fore-
end again with his spare hand, he stared at me and anything
conciliatory was gone, like it hadn't ever been there. 'You need
to stop what you're doing.'

'What am I doing?'

He smiled. 'That's cute.'

I glanced at the empty wall again, and then to the laptop lead
on the floor. 'I'd say you've done a pretty bang-up job of stopping me already.' I pointed towards the mobile phone. 'You and
whoever you came here with.'

He smiled again, but it was different this time.

And then the smile faded, he cleared his throat and he said,
'Look at you: still playing detective, even now; even as you sit
there with a shotgun aimed at your face.'

Except he wasn't aiming the shotgun at my face.

He was pointing it at the floor.

I glanced at the phone again, saw the minutes still ticking over
on the display, and then back to Mills. He was staring at me, his

head tilted slightly, eyes narrowed, as if he were trying to work me out – or waiting for me to catch up.

'Stay the fuck away from Black Gale.'

He delivered the words with such ferocity, it almost felt as if they'd come from someone else. I looked him in the eyes, lingering on their stillness.

'Or don't,' he said. 'But that wouldn't be a good idea.'

I felt myself push away from him, my back pressing hard against the chair, the weight of his words – his articulation of the threat – like a physical force. He watched me for a moment longer, and all I felt was disconcerted: it was like he really was two different people, the aggression in his voice not matching the expression on his face. That was just a blank.

Mills came forward, disrupting my train of thought.

I shifted around in my chair, following his movement, still trying to work out what was going on and who he was. Was this all a game to him?

Or was this imbalance in his personality a sickness?

He stopped a couple of feet short of me.

'I imagine you've been in this situation before,' he said, his voice small, quieter now. 'A man like you, the job you do. You kick enough hornets' nests, you expect to get stung, right?' He glanced again at the empty wall, clearly not expecting an answer from me. 'You've developed a tough hide. I mean, you have to. The kind of cases you take on . . .' He trailed off. 'You've clearly already gone digging, so you know I used to be a cop, and let me tell you, Raker: people like you, they're a cop's worst nightmare.'

I didn't say anything.

'Someone with determination,' he said, 'someone who can dig around and not worry about getting dirty – worse, someone who can pick up failed cases and unlock them . . . No police force in the land is going to like that. They're frightened of you, you know that? And probably with good reason. You make people nervous. It's a quality.'

I watched him, but he really seemed to mean it.

233

'I'm glad you think so,' I said. 'Is that why you've brought a shotgun with you?'

It came out of nowhere, a movement so fast I barely even registered it, nerves exploding in my face as he jammed the heel of the weapon into my cheek. He used it like a battering ram, pain exploding in the right side of my face, in my eye socket, sparks of the same fire flaring in my ear and jaw. The force of the strike sent the chair rocking back on its legs, the whole thing tilting and then falling; I went with it, slamming against the wooden floorboards, the whole room seeming to pitch. Dazed, I instinctively put a hand up to protect myself from another attack.

But there wasn't one.

He just stayed where he was.

I shuffled away from him on my hands and feet, like a spider scuttling for the shadows. But again he didn't move, just watched me, the shotgun back in position.

'I could kill you here,' he said, looking from me to the weapon. 'I could put a hole in your chest the size of a dinner plate, but that's problematic when you've got a journalist sniffing around.' He meant Connor McCaskell from the *Tribune*, the man Healy and I had talked about – and been recorded discussing – at the farmhouse. Mills stopped, running a tongue along his teeth, like something sour was in his mouth. 'If I kill you here, or make you disappear, it means questions, and journalists are like bacteria. Questions are what they feed on. You can try to stop the spread, try to cut off a food source, but they just keep coming. This arsehole looking into you is a case in point.' He paused and let out a frustrated breath. 'No, men like you, you need to be brought to heel in other ways.'

This time, he took a couple of steps closer to me, kicking aside the chair I'd been sitting on. I scrambled to my feet, looking around for something I could use as a weapon, something I could fight back with. But how could I beat a shotgun?

'How I get to someone like you is I use your pressure points,' Mills said, and stopped adjacent to the sofa, eight feet from me, his voice unsettlingly even, as calm as a lake without wind. It was as if nothing had interrupted him, as if he'd never attacked me with the shotgun and split my face. 'We've all got pressure points. When you do all these heroic things for families, when you get confident, when you follow people around and they never see you watching' – he flashed me a look and it was obvious why: he knew it was me who'd talked to his girlfriend at the petrol station – 'you start to think you're absolutely invincible. But you're not. You're still vulnerable. You've got a daughter, right?'

A butterfly escaped in my chest.

'Stay away from her,' I said, my voice groggy.

He nodded, but not because he was agreeing to; it looked like he'd been expecting the exact response that I'd given him. His face had changed again and I realized I was even further away from understanding him than when he'd first walked in here. He looked at me like he felt some semblance of compassion – but he'd attacked me with the end of a gun, opened up a cut under my eye, talked about murdering me.

'Your daughter is a pressure point,' he said, 'we both know that. But what would I achieve by kidnapping her, or threatening her, or killing her? It would crush you. It would rip your whole life apart, all over again.' He stared at me, letting me know that he'd read up about my history and knew all about Derryn. I'd got to my feet already, forcing myself to face him down. 'But, if I hurt Annabel,' he went on, using her name now, his voice exactly the same pitch, tone, volume, 'you'd get really fucking angry, and that determination I talked about earlier, that ability and willingness you have to play dirty, that would probably come back to haunt me. Maybe you'd end up in a shallow grave somewhere because you'd be so messed up with grief and rage and revenge that you'd be sloppy and easy to handle. Or maybe your rage would be the fuel that keeps you sharp, the fuel that means you come for me and kill me, you come for everyone I work with; and this thing we don't want you to unravel gets unravelled, and getting rid of your daughter turns out to be the worst decision in human history.'

His eyes flicked to the kitchen door he'd emerged from.

'So you know what your real pressure point is, Raker?'

I stood motionless, trying to figure out where this was going.

'It's freedom,' he said. 'It's the independence your job gives you, the latitude it has, the way finding these missing people fixes you and repairs you, filling the gaps left behind by your wife. I get it, I do. Closing cases, getting people answers, it's liberating. It gives you a sense of immunity; nothing touches it.'

He rocked forward again, as if he was about to come towards me, but instead he turned on his heel and retreated, heading past the sofa, towards the kitchen door.

What the hell is he doing?

He stopped there, in the shadows of the stairs.

'Your real pressure point,' he said quietly, 'it's not your daughter, much as I'm sure you must love her. I'm not even certain it's the idea of losing your life. I look at the things you've done in the past, and I believe you made your peace with death a long time ago. I'm not saying you aren't frightened by it – we all are at the end, especially when we actually have to face it down – but sticking a gun in your mouth, threatening to pull the trigger, that's never going to work, is it? If that was a viable option, you'd have stopped looking for missing people a long time ago, because – from what I've read – you've had plenty of guns pointed at you plenty of times.'

He looked into the blackness of the kitchen.

'No, it's the thought of being contained, that's what you're truly frightened of. It's the thought of all of this coming to an end, of never feeling that immunity again.'

He eyed me, feeding on my confusion.

And then he vanished into the kitchen.

Immediately, I came around the sofa to the table, slowing my footsteps in case it was a trick. The closer I got, the more I could hear: a back door opening and shutting, movement, furniture shifting around.

A soft moan.

He re-emerged, dragging something.

The shotgun was in one hand; his other was clamped on to the back of a shirt collar. It was another man, blindfolded. As Mills hauled him out of the blackness of the kitchen, the man made a wordless noise like a wounded animal. I could see blood on his clothes, understood now how it had ended up on Mills's knuckles – and then Mills released his grip and the man rolled, slumping sideways.

'The thing that scares you,' Mills said, using his foot to turn the man on to his back, 'is the thought of your work being cut short. All that the missing bring to your life, the comfort you find in the search, the way they hauled you free of your grief and helped you survive. It keeps you sane. Being forced to stop would be worse than any bullet. Being contained, walled in, being in a situation where you had no control over your life, where you have no agency any more and, worse, no freedom, it would kill you. So you want to know what your pressure point is, Raker?'

At my feet, the man moaned again, his beard specked with saliva, his lip split, his shaved scalp matted with blood.

'It's your fear of going to prison.'

36

On the floor, Healy tried to move.

His wrists were tied in front of him. The cut above his eyebrow had reopened. His nose looked busted, the straight line of the bridge puffy, the skin purple where he'd been struck. But while he was obviously dazed and half-conscious, his stunted actions and soft, continual moaning was coming from something more than just his injuries.

He'd been drugged too.

He must have fought, which was exactly why Mills had been forced to give him a sedative: he'd been surprised by Healy, by his will to survive, to resist. As I dropped to my haunches, placing a hand against Healy's arm, I felt him flinch. When I told him it was me, there was a fractional delay, and then he frowned and started repeating my name. His voice crackled with the pain of his injuries and the first swells of a fever.

I looked up at Isaac Mills.

'You need to stop,' he said again.

'Where are they?'

'Who?'

I stood up again, facing him down.

'The villagers. The people from Black Gale.'

He sighed, closing his eyes for a second.

'Just tell me what happened to them.'

Mills shook his head, as if he were dealing with a child, and then he turned the shotgun – moving it in an arc – so that the barrel was pointed at Healy's chest.

'Haven't you been listening to me, Raker?'

'Was it to do with what Patrick Perry was looking into?'

Mills didn't respond.

'Was it something to do with Beatrix Steards?'

238

This time, he glanced at the phone, still recording our conversation from the living-room table, and then – when his eyes switched back to me – something was in them, something different: a hint of definition, as if they'd coloured at the mention of Beatrix Steards's name.

'Mills?'

'Shut up.'

'*Was* it something to do with Beatrix?'

'Shut your mouth.'

I watched him for a second, but whatever had been in his eyes was gone now. I tried a different angle: 'Why is Randolph and Emiline's camper van missing?'

He broke into a smile this time.

'What's so funny?'

'You,' he said. 'You're what's funny. "Where's the camper van?" What a total waste of fucking time.'

That stopped me – and he could see it.

'I had it crushed.'

I frowned. 'What?'

'The camper van. It's history. No one will ever find it.'

'Why would you –'

'No,' he said, cutting me off, his voice harsher than ever. 'No more questions. This is how it's going to play out from here on in, okay?' Once more I wondered if he was sick, his nature – his actions, his expression and his voice – so inconsistent. 'You're going to go back to London, and anything you've got squirrelled away down there on Black Gale, any notes you've made about anything, you're going to rip up and flush away. Before that, and after I'm gone, you're going to set up a nice little fire in the chimney over there and burn all the shit that was on the wall as well – every last scrap of paper. I want this place so spotlessly clean, so free of any reminders of the digging around that you and your Irish friend on the floor have been doing, that it'll be like you were never here.' He glanced at Healy, on his side now in a foetal position, still moaning gently, and then used the toe of a boot to prod him in the ribs. 'You'd better make that clear to Seamus here because, judging by the trouble he gave me in Leeds tonight, he obviously has a hard time understanding basic English.'

He returned his gaze to me.

'Are you following me so far, Raker?'

I just stared at him.

'I'm sorry, I can't hear you?'

I nodded.

'Okay,' he said. 'Good. So you're going to do all of that, and you're never going to ask another question about Black Gale again, *ever*, or things start going wrong for you. Because I will start digging around in your past cases and find all the shit I *know* you covered up, all the lies I bet you've told the cops, and then I will call the police, and I will do the same with Connor McCaskell, and I will tell them everything. I'll tell them you illegally obtained the paperwork from this case as well – an open investigation – which will, in turn, compromise your sources and end with them in the dock too. And who knows? Just because I can, I might even throw in the fact that you hit a deer and failed to report it.' He used his boot again, pressing down at the side of Healy's head, crushing his face into the floor. When I moved, automatically trying to stop him, he swivelled the shotgun around and pushed the barrel into my chest. Its weight rocked me back. 'Don't think that I won't do it. Even after everything I've said, don't think I won't cut you down. If it's me or you, you'd better believe it'll be you that goes in the ground first, whether that means some journalist sniffing around me or not.' He prodded my chest with the barrel again. 'Step back.'

I did as he asked.

As he released his foot from Healy's face, he turned to me again, a smile twitching at the corner of his mouth. 'You're a clever bastard, you know that, Raker? I've gained a new appreciation for you since yesterday. All the moves you've been making, they're moves I'd have made, or moves I maybe wouldn't have even thought of. Sending Bryan here down to Leeds, now that was a smart idea.'

'Obviously not smart enough.'

'Well, everyone's a genius in hindsight,' he said, shrugging, and something moved across his face, brief, ephemeral, like the flicker of a candle flame. 'The year before I left Lancashire Constabulary – this would have been October, November 2010 – I landed this case: a killing in Preston. It was a family of four: Dad, Mum, son of nine, daughter of eleven. I walked in there and that place was like a bloodbath. In fifteen years as a cop, I'd never seen anything like it. The *anger* of the killer – it was fucking scary. You think you've seen everything, you think you've pushed it all so far down that nothing will ever bother you again, but it does. That family, they all got to me so much, I was seeing crime-scene pictures of the kids every time I blinked.'

I watched him, confused now.

Why was he telling me this?

'When I think back,' he continued, his voice humming with the after-effects, even now, of what had been left behind of that family, 'turning up there, having to process that, it was probably the moment I realized I was done. Cops who go on for ever, seeing shit like that all the time, I admire their resilience, but that wasn't me. I wasn't being paid enough to lie there awake every night, staring into the dark, seeing images of a nine-year-old's brains up the walls and his guts on the bed sheets.'

'But what you're doing now is better?'

'I guess it's easy to leave your principles at the door when the money's good.' He smiled, but there was no humour in it. 'Anyway, a couple of days in, a case comes up on the computer that bears a resemblance to mine. I'm thinking to myself, "Could they be connected? Could this be the same killer?" This one was down in London, though – in New Cross.' He was eyeing me, seeing if I'd caught up with him – and I had. I knew exactly where this was going now, and as it hit home, the entire room felt like it was spinning. 'I figured it was worth a closer look,' Mills went on, 'so I got one of my team to call up the detective who was handling the case and they asked him about it, to see if we could help each other, but he just shut us down. He was fucking rude. He told my DC that our cases were different, they happened miles apart, that there weren't enough similarities, that he didn't have time to go chasing false leads and false hope. I mean, he was right, because in the end, they *weren't* connected, but I had a family of four and he had a family of three: a mum and her twin daughters. You can see why I got someone to call him.'

We looked at each other, the room silent.

The detective that Mills's team had talked to had been Healy. The mother and her twin daughters had been the case that had destroyed his life. His marriage. His career. It was the case that had set Healy on the road to a breakdown, to homelessness, a heart attack, to perpetual thoughts of suicide – until, eventually, he'd faked his own death and started again in Devon. That case was the reason he'd *become* Bryan Kennedy.

And Mills had figured it out.

Maybe not everything, but enough.

'I highly doubt if he would even remember that call,' Mills said, looking at the prone figure on the floor. 'He was so consumed by that case, and we only ever talked to him on the phone.' That explained why Healy had never mentioned knowing Mills when his name had come up: not only because the call from Mills's team had happened almost a decade ago, but because it came in the midst of a search for a child killer, a search that was going nowhere, that remained unsolved for over three years, and that Healy was being crushed under the weight of, even back then. He didn't know Mills. He barely recalled anything from that period except loss.

Mills's gaze came back to me.

'Anyway,' he said, and stopped again.

And then something weird happened.

'I don't know exactly what my point is.' His eyes fixed on mine, and I knew straight away it was a lie. He knew exactly what his point was. All of this, the whole account of how he'd landed the murder of the family in Preston, had been a prelude, a lead-in to the revelation that he knew it was Colm Healy lying on the floor between us, not Bryan Kennedy, and that if I ever asked another question about Black Gale, if I pinned another piece of paper to a wall, he wouldn't only dig into my cases and expose my sources, he would tell the world that Healy wasn't dead. I would lose my freedom, my cases, my oxygen.

I would go to prison.

'That hack McCaskell is on to something,' he said, his words not matching his eyes again, his voice not aligning with his expression, 'and whoever this is lying here – whatever his actual name, because I haven't been able to find this Bryan Kennedy *anywhere* – he's clearly important enough to land you in trouble, which is why I'm guessing McCaskell is so interested in him.'

I frowned. Why was he pretending he didn't know Healy's real name?

'Don't come back here again, Raker,' he said, stepping around Healy and going to the table. He stopped, looking down at the mobile phone. 'As soon as the sun is up, you leave. I don't want to hear the words "Black Gale" coming out of your mouth – not now, not ever. I don't want you asking questions about the people who lived there, their lives, their histories, what they used to like, what they didn't. Nothing. I don't give a shit what you tell the families, what excuse you make for not carrying on with the search, but you're going to tell them it's over, and make it sound convincing, and then you're going to forget you ever came here. Because if you don't, I promise you this: I'll go looking for Bryan Kennedy, and I'll find out who he really is, and one way or another, I'll take the freedom from both of you.'

I frowned at him, thrown, misled. 'Why are you –'

But he shook his head at me.

I stopped, my sentence half-finished.

'Why am I *what*?' he fired back, his voice sharp, but this time I could see it for exactly what it was. Not a game. Not a sickness either.

An act.

243

An act for whoever was listening to us.

'How much simpler do I have to make it for you?' he said. 'Get rid of what's left in here, make the phone calls to the family, then go home.'

He watched me for a moment, and then his eyes went to Healy, lying on the floor a few feet from me: still, except for the rasp of his breath.

I glanced down at him myself.

Blood had formed in a pool under his cheek.

When I looked up again, Mills had the phone in his hand and was at the door, opening it up. We were still being listened to, the numbers still ticking over on the display. But now he held up the mobile and gave me a single nod of the head.

He was saying, *You're right.*

This whole thing was a performance.

'Don't make me come back for you, Raker.'

He lingered in the doorway, his eyes on mine.

And then he headed into the night.

37

I stood there, eyes on the blackness of the doorway, trying to figure out what had just happened. And then Healy moaned softly, barely more than a whimper – as faint as the wind at the windows of the cottage – and I snapped back into focus.

Reaching down, I slid my hands under his arms, removed his blindfold, and tried to hoist him to his feet. He was a dead weight. He moaned again, one of his eyes twitched open and he started trying to say my name. The more he tried to say it, the less coherent his speech became, until he gave up altogether. Blood had begun to clot inside his nose, thick and gummy, and it had dried to one side of his face, a streak of it, like the roots of a plant creeping out from the corner of his mouth.

I walked him over to the sofa.

He slumped sideways, his head hitting one of the cushions, and every part of him seemed to exhale, his whole body contracting as if every last breath had escaped. A second later, though, he shifted again, eyelids flickering, body tilting as he tried to get a sense of where I was in the room. I dropped to my haunches at his side, and after a second he zeroed in on me, his eyes glazed, and he said, 'I'm sorry, Raker.'

'It's okay.'

He blinked.

'Do you know what sedative Mills gave you?'

'No,' he managed, the noise like an expiration.

Even if he'd known, it wasn't going to make much difference: the best thing he could do now was lie here and let it wear off. I went to the kitchen, filled a glass with water and then started searching through the cupboards for a first-aid kit. Even if I couldn't do anything about the sedative, I could try to repair the damage to his face.

As I searched, I felt a moment of déjà vu, a second where Healy and I were in the farmhouse at Black Gale, after we'd hit the deer out on the road, and I'd been trying to find a first-aid kit for the cuts on his face. The thought of that, of being in the village, of being in the middle of a case that I didn't want to let go of, sent a spike of anger through the centre of my chest. The anger was for Mills, for the people he worked for, the *we* he talked about when he baited me with the idea of going after Annabel – but as I looked at the empty wall, at the paper on the floor, I realized that wasn't all of it.

I felt anger for Healy too.

I'd helped him start again – to construct a new life, however simple it might have been – because I'd believed, at the time, it was the right thing to do. But there hadn't been many days since when – in my most unguarded moments – I hadn't wondered if it might have been easier to let him destroy himself.

Because the lies I told for him had just cost me a case.

And it had cost nine people even more than that.

By the time I returned to the living room, he was asleep, breath rasping in his throat, bubbles of snot and blood forming at his nose. I took a moment to clear my head, to try and douse some of the anger, and popped open the lid of the first-aid kit.

Slowly, I started to clean him up.

He reacted a couple of times, wincing – even in his sleep – as I wiped the blood from the bridge of his nose, from the cut at his eyebrow which needed re-dressing. His nose wasn't broken, but he'd been punched there and a puffy ridge of purple had already formed in the corner of one of his eye sockets. When I was done, I used a mirror inside the lid of the first-aid kit to examine my own face, the cut on my right cheek from where Mills had jammed the shotgun, the bruising that had already begun to colour at its edges. I cleaned it but didn't dress it for now, and then packed everything away again.

When I was done, I looked over at the doorway again.

Who had been listening to Mills and me on the mobile phone?

Was it Jacob Pierce? Someone else at Seiger and Sten? Or did this have nothing to do with the legal firm at all? It was obvious that Mills had come here with at least one other person, because at the same time he was leading me out to the barns, someone had been going through the cottage – so why hadn't that person stayed behind? Why listen on speakerphone?

I could think of only two reasons.

They didn't want me to ID them.

And they didn't fully trust Mills.

I felt a spark of energy at the thought of the second, even as I looked at what was left of my casework, and it only burned stronger when I remembered how Mills had been throughout our conversation: violent in words and actions, but not in the way he'd looked at me. Not in the nod of his head at the end. Not in the act he'd put on for whoever had been listening.

'I'm sorry, Raker.'

I looked down at Healy again.

He blinked up at me, struggling to focus.

'Just rest,' I said to him.

'This is my fault.' His voice was weak, strained.

I got to my feet, thinking again about Mills, about why he'd tried to sound authentic to whoever was listening, but I couldn't work out whether he'd genuinely betrayed his employers – and why he'd ever do such a thing – or whether this was another component in some ornate trick I couldn't see properly. Uncertain, I glanced at the table again, to the place in which the mobile phone had sat, recording us both.

And I realized I'd missed something.

An envelope.

I hurried across to the table and, as I did, remembered a moment, just before Mills had exited the cottage, when he'd picked up the phone. At the same time as he'd done that, I'd looked down at Healy, lying still, blood on his face, and had wondered what was going on, why Mills wouldn't admit that he knew who Healy was.

I'd looked away for a second.

I stopped next to the table, staring at what Mills had left behind. There was no writing on the front of the envelope and, when I turned it over, I could see that it had been properly sealed. I glanced at Healy, asleep again now, unaware of any of this, and then scanned the rest of the living room, shadows still clinging to every surface. Was this legitimate? Or was it all part of the same trick?

As soon as I scooped up the envelope, I could feel something solid shifting inside, sliding from one end to the other, and knew straight away what it was.

A key.

I ripped open the seal.

The key's design was unusual: it had the familiar lines on the blade but was moulded entirely from hard plastic. It was also extremely thin – perhaps only two millimetres in width – and had a tiny magnetic square at the point of the key. Whatever door it opened, the lock on that door was using a mixture of technologies – part tumbler, part electronic reader.

There was something else in the envelope too.

A folded piece of paper.

It was headed, crowned with a now familiar company logo and an address in York. Below that, handwritten in the middle of the page, were six numbers: *459822*. I looked from those to the key – and a dizzying surge of adrenalin hit me.

The key was for Seiger and Sten's office.

The numbers were their alarm code.

Martina: Part 1

Los Angeles | Monday 5 August

The property was a single-family tan stucco with a raised porch, a bay tree in the yard and a rust-eaten fence between the sidewalk and the lawn. A brick driveway ran along one side of the building to a garage.

As soon as Jo pulled up outside, she could hear the low drone of the freeway; a slanted bank opposite the house, and a high concrete wall – its surface peppered with the ghosts of old graffiti – were the only things lying between the houses and the lanes of the 710. The moment she switched off the ignition, it got even louder, a perpetual wall of vehicle noise from which there would never be an escape, even in the dead of night.

She sat there for a moment looking at the house, the white bars at the front window, the terracotta pots in a line on the porch, wondering whether she was doing the right thing in making this detour. She'd spent the afternoon in Monterey Park, talking again to the family of the guy who was murdered on State Route 39, and now had a couple of solid leads that she knew she should be chasing down and reporting back to Hayesfield on. Instead, she was here. Hayesfield had already hauled her into his office and asked her if she'd had anything to do with the Larry O'Hara story in the *Times*, so Jo knew that he'd go nuts if he found out she was still pushing the idea that Donald Klein wasn't the real killer. Yet here she was, off the back of a tip from a woman who refused even to ID herself, a woman who made her call from a phone booth so she'd be impossible to locate, and whose accusations, about a man called Adrian Vale, Jo had failed to find one shred of evidence for in the three days since. He'd worked at Caraca BuildIt, which was why he'd sometimes driven their maroon VW Quantum in the past, but as he hadn't been employed there for two years, she had no idea if Vale was genuinely a monster or just some asshole the caller had a problem with.

She locked the car, opened up the gate and headed along an uneven stone path towards the porch. There was a table on it with a drying rack next to that, damp laundry hanging from it, positioned so that it was in the full glare of the late-afternoon sun. Even now, a couple of hours before sunset, the city was still like a furnace: she could feel sweat, frozen to her body by the a/c in the car, now beginning to thaw, the heat a constant, irritable prickle in her skin. She brushed a finger across her brow and knocked a couple of times on the metal screen door: it was secured, and padlocked for good measure, but the front door beyond it was ajar.

Birds squawked on a nearby utility pole. A siren faded in and out again on the freeway.

'Can I help you?'

Jo turned to find a Hispanic woman in her mid to late fifties standing behind the grey bars of the security door. She was short and plump, her black hair scraped back into a messy ponytail, her face etched by tiny brown sunspots and fine age lines.

'Mrs Vale?'

'*Sí*,' the woman replied.

'We spoke on the telephone earlier.' Jo removed her ID wallet from the pocket of her pants and flipped it open. 'I'm Detective Kader from the Sheriff's Department.'

'Ah, *sí*. Yes. Of course.'

Mrs Vale began unlocking the security door.

'Adrian, he isn't home yet,' she said in lightly accented English.

Jo had found out as much about Adrian Vale as she could, which wasn't a lot, but she knew that his parents had emigrated from Honduras in 1959, and Vale's father had died when he was only fifteen, having drunk himself into oblivion. She knew that

Valeria Vale had brought up her son alone for the last five years, that she cleaned rooms at a downtown hotel, and that Adrian was currently at Stanford on a fully paid scholarship. Right now, however, he was back in LA for the summer break.

'Do you know where he is, Mrs Vale?'

'He called to say he was running late ten minutes late and would be home at six,' she said, unlocking the security door. 'He has a summer placement at a law firm in Pico Rivera.' She smiled, nodded, as if she were telling Jo that, no, she hadn't misheard: he really *did* have a summer placement at a law firm. Jo returned the smile, not wanting to destroy the pride that Valeria Vale clearly had for her son. The security door swung gently out. 'Please,' Valeria said, using an arm to invite Jo inside. 'Please come in and wait.'

The living room was small, the furniture old, the carpets thinning, but it had a cared-for, comfortable feel. On a mantel were photographs of Adrian Vale as a boy, his father, the three of them together, and then other, extended family members. Jo could see ornaments and trinkets elsewhere, books in Spanish and English, and on a wall above the mantel a walnut cross, rosary beads hanging from the horizontal limb.

'Can I get you something to drink?'

'Just some water,' Jo replied. 'Thank you.'

After Valeria went through to the kitchen, Jo moved across to the mantel. She hadn't been able to find any decent photographs of Adrian Vale. He didn't have a record, so had never been arrested, which meant his picture wasn't on file at the LASD or LAPD, and it wasn't in the system upstate either. From home the previous night, she'd made calls to the Sheriff's departments in Santa Clara County – where Stanford University was located – Santa Cruz County, San Mateo County and to the San Francisco Police Department and he'd never got into trouble anywhere in that part of California in the three years he'd been living there. He had no passport, because he'd never travelled abroad, and the photo on his driver's licence was three years old and poor quality, so a DMV search hadn't been much help either.

Until now, Jo had barely even known what he'd looked like.

She picked up one of the pictures closest to her. In it, Adrian Vale was about eighteen or nineteen, and sitting on the front porch of his mother's home, a glass of water perched next to him, a book open and face down on the wall that hemmed the porch in. He was smiling. Expressions in photographs were so often faked, but the lie in this, if it existed, was hard to pick: the smile reached from Vale's mouth to his eyes, out into the rest of his face. He was a handsome kid, dark-haired and well built.

'That was the summer before he went to Stanford.'

Jo turned and found Valeria standing next to her. She smiled again, the swell of joy she had for her son and his academic achievements so obvious, it seemed to inflate her somehow. Jo put the picture back down and looked at some of the others: Vale as a child, being led across a strip of white sand by what must have been his father; him with his mother, the portrait two or three years old, the two of them in a park, the sun going down behind them; and then Vale in his early teens, in a high school photograph, smiling for the camera.

They sat, Jo taking the water.

The house was warm, a fan going in the corner of the room, clicking very softly every time it hit the limit of its arc. Valeria had left the windows open, the back door too, but the windows were all protected by bars and the rear entrance had the same security door as the front. As she'd driven past, Jo had noticed that a lot of the other houses on the block were the same, a necessary measure in an area with a high crime rate. A year ago, having to put metal bars at your windows and steel doors front and back would have been viewed as undesirable and ugly. It would have been the antithesis of a home, a confirmation of where not to own a house if you could afford it. But, then, a year ago, the Night Stalker wasn't killing people in their sleep. The irony of the situation wasn't lost on Jo, as it probably wasn't lost on Valeria and her neighbours: if you gave people the choice now, most of LA would have preferred to be in a house like this.

'I hope Adrian isn't in any kind of trouble,' Valeria said.

Jo returned her attention to Vale's mother and could see the worry already forming in her face, stark as neon. 'I have a case,' Jo said softly, trying not to set off any alarms before Vale had even got here, 'and it might be one that Adrian can help me with. That's all.' She smiled at Valeria reassuringly and, in the silence that followed, Jo thought of the phone call she'd had with the anonymous woman three days ago.

'Why would you call Vale a "monster"?'

'Because that's what he is. The thing is, though, not many people have seen that side of him. In high school, mostly he was just this quiet, book-nerd loner.'

'You were in high school with him?'

'Yeah, but I didn't know him. I didn't know him at all. That's the point. No one did. He was good-looking, crazy smart, but he'd always just go about by himself, listening to music, reading, all that sort of shit. He was polite, would always talk to you if you talked to him, but he never had any friends, far as I could tell. He was never at any of the parties we went to. I never saw him out at all, ever. I bet no one he went to school with could tell you a damn thing about him – except for Martina.'

'Who's Martina?'

'She's the girl whose life he destroyed.'

Valeria Vale moved in her armchair, coming forward to the table where she'd left a glass of water for herself. She looked at Jo. 'Is it something to do with the law?'

'I'm sorry?'

'Is Adrian going to help with your case?'

Jo was touched by the woman's naivety, the absolute faith she had in her son, the love she carried for him, and felt distressed at the thought of having to crush it in her home.

'I think it's easier if I just talk to Adrian, Mrs Vale.'

'*Si*,' she said. 'Of course. I'm sorry.'

'Not a problem.'

'I'm so proud of him, that's all.' She paused, looking at Jo, a flicker of emotion in her face. 'He's never had it easy. He's had to fight for everything. His father and I, we never had any money. We arrived in this country with just the clothes on our backs. We never took Adrian on vacation . . . It was hard.' She blinked, let out a breath. 'Adrian's father, he was . . .' She stopped again. *An alcoholic.*

Jo nodded. 'He died in 1979, is that correct?'

'That's right.'

'And he worked for a building supplies company?'

'*Si.* The same one, for ten years.'

Valeria didn't ask how Jo knew about Lautaro Vale, his death, and the way in which he'd died, or about why Jo might have gone digging around for information on the Vale family. Maybe she just assumed that that was what a detective did before they turned up at someone's house.

But the truth was a lot more complicated.

'Adrian had a part-time job,' the caller had told Jo. *'Martina said that he worked where his old man used to work. It's this building supplies company somewhere over in Industry. But his old man got him in there when he was, like, fourteen or fifteen, working on weekends and over the holidays, and Adrian stayed on there – even after his old man died – until he went to Stanford.'*

In theory, when Vale had returned to LA two months ago for the summer break, he might not have been working for Caraca BuildIt any more – as it became known in 1982 – but he would have known where to find enough acid to dissolve a body: as much as six hundred gallons of it. In theory, that might also explain why the company that first Lautaro and then Adrian Vale had worked for might not have immediately noticed if ten one-gallon containers were missing from their vast stock. *In theory.* Jo was still waiting for Paolo Caraca to get back to her about whether any containers were missing from the yard, the whole thing protracted by the fact that Caraca himself had been admitted to the ER two days ago with pneumonia, so the request had been pushed down the line to his deputy. Jo had called him, and he promised he'd get it over as soon as possible.

'The drinking was hard.'

Jo looked at Valeria, back in the present.

'Not for me. It wasn't hard for me. I got used to seeing Lautaro like that years ago. What I mean is, it was hard for Adrian. Having to watch your father like that – unable to stand; angry, or passed out; missing all these things that Adrian was doing at school – that's hard for a boy growing up. A boy shouldn't have to see his father like that. He shouldn't have to bury his father at fifteen.' Valeria blinked, tears in her eyes. 'It made him quiet. He found it hard to make friends. He wasn't unsociable, I just don't think he could find anyone he related to, or anyone who understood him. I mean, which other father drank himself to death in their child's first year of high school? So he just studied hard and immersed himself in his school work.'

Jo looked at the mantel.

The photo of Adrian Vale looked back at her.

'So how did Vale destroy Martina's life?'

'I don't know the exact details. I mean, I never really knew Martina at school – she always hung out with different people to me – but we both dropped out in '81 and ended up working in the same Kmart up in Temple City the year after. Total coincidence. Anyway, then we started talking sometimes, lunch breaks, on the way out at the end of our shift, and sometime after that she started telling me things . . .'

'About Adrian Vale?'

'Yeah.'

'What about him?'

'She started off by asking me if I remembered him from school, and I said I did, just about. She said they met again, end of '81; bumped into each other at some drugstore down in East LA and then went out for a while after that. Like I say, we weren't buddies – we didn't know each other that well – but even I could tell she wanted to talk about it. She obviously wanted to get it out. Like, what's that word? Articulate. She wanted to articulate it. I guess maybe it was easier doing it in front of someone like me that she didn't know;

255

basically, a stranger. Or maybe she was like Adrian used to be: quiet, lonely, didn't have many friends. Maybe that was why those two ended up together in the first place. Whatever. I don't know. All I know is she wanted it out.'

'Out?'

'She wanted to exorcize that shit.'

'And what shit was that?'

'The shit he pulled on her up at the lake.'

'Are you a mom, Detective?'

Jo glanced at Valeria.

'I'm sorry?'

'Are you a mom?'

She was looking at Jo's wedding band.

'I am, yes.'

'I thought so. I admire what you're doing.'

'What I'm doing?'

'This job. It must be a difficult job when you have a child.'

Jo shrugged. 'Every job is hard when you're a mom.'

'You know, you can always tell.'

'Tell what?'

'You can tell a mom, just from the way she looks.'

'Yeah?' Jo frowned. 'How's that?'

'We can never quite let go of the worry.'

Valeria smiled, her expression changing, making it difficult for Jo to interpret that comment. Was it just a general remark? Or was it some sort of coded message?

Just then, they both heard a car pulling on to the driveway, the rumble of old, loose bricks under its tyres, the tick of its engine. Valeria shuffled to the edge of her armchair and hauled herself out of it. 'That'll be Adrian,' she said, going to the security door. Jo stood, watching from the living room, as a rust-speckled mini-van pulled in.

'What lake was this?'

'Big Bear.'

'Okay. So what happened?'

'Martina, she said he drove them up there one weekend in the spring.

256

They're just chilling out next to the water when, suddenly, late in the after-noon, Adrian tells her they should go hike one of the trails so they can watch the sunset from the top. She thinks he's being romantic, so she agrees, and follows him all the way up this trail to the top. They watch the sun go down, just like he says, and then he tells her he needs to piss, so he leaves her there, in the pitch black at the top of this damn mountain, surrounded by bears and bobcats, coyotes, rattlesnakes – who the hell knows what else? – as he goes off to find a spot. Except he never came back again.'

'At all?'

'Or, at least, that's what she thinks, anyway.'

'So he did come back for her?'

'No. Not exactly.'

'I don't get it, then. What happened?'

'She's shit-scared, making her way back down the side of this mountain, with no torch, no food and no idea where she's going – and then she realizes something.'

'What?'

'Adrian is watching her.'

Jo heard the door of the minivan open and close, and a male voice – softly spoken, gentle – say, 'Hey, Ma. Sorry I'm a little late.' Footsteps followed, first out on the driveway, then on the porch, where he filled the frame of the front door. He was just like his photograph: handsome, broad, muscular.

His eyes searched the living room for Jo.

'Oh, hello,' he said, smiling, his tone warm. 'I'm so sorry I'm late.'

'This is my boy.' Valeria beamed from behind him. 'My Adrian.'

'So Adrian remained out there in the woods with Martina?'

'He was just watching her. Like, following her, out of sight.'

'She couldn't see him?'

'No. No, she couldn't see a thing.'

'Did she say anything to him?'

'Yeah, she kept calling his name.'

'But he didn't respond?'

'No. Not once, even when she tripped and fell, and busted up her ankle

257

real good. I mean, she said it blew up like a balloon and she could barely put one foot in front of the other. She could hardly even walk, she was scared out of her fucking mind, screaming his name into the darkness, begging for him to help her out.'

'But he still didn't help her out?'

'No. It was like . . .'

Jo got to her feet.

'Hello, Adrian,' she said, shaking his hand. 'I'm Detective Kader.'

'It was like what?'

'She said it was like Adrian was hunting her.'

PART FIVE

The Room

38

Twenty-four hours later, York was a ghost town.

It was 2 a.m., the vast Gothic spires of the cathedral climbing so far into the night they appeared to almost dissolve. Rain drummed against doorways and windowsills, water rushed and gurgled in gutters, and the skies were perfectly black, except for the occasional flash of lightning. In those moments, the narrow streets and bowed, crooked buildings would come alive – blinking like a strobe – before retreating into darkness again.

As I approached the Shambles, I double-checked my pockets for the key and the piece of paper with the alarm code on it, and then slowed my pace, looking behind me. Healy and I had spent the day since Mills left us at the cottage talking this through, arguing the risks, batting everything back and forth, and he'd never wavered once: he believed the whole thing to be an ambush, a juicy piece of bait that would either destroy me or kill me, and do the same to him. Why would Mills put on a performance like the one at the cottage? Why help me? Why would he go against the person or people he worked for? It was certainly simpler to dismiss it as an ambush – but Healy hadn't seen Mills with the mother and her kids, and he hadn't seen the expression on his face at the cottage.

I kept moving, the rain unable to breach this part of the city as effectively, the cramped Elizabethan buildings on either side barely feet from one another. The empty streets and silent rooms put me in mind of Black Gale, another ghost town, and then a little way along – as signs whipped and wheezed in the wind – I found a small entrance between a sweet shop and a café: a void filled only with darkness. There was no signage on the main thoroughfare, no indication that this led to a law firm, but as I took a few steps in, under an archway, I found myself in a courtyard, beneath an overhanging second floor, and spotted the sign out front.

Pale green with gold lettering.

Seiger and Sten.

Despite the archaic building, the door was modern: heavy oak, a silver lock and letterbox. Yet, new as the door was, straight away I realized something was off. I paused there for a long moment – the plastic of the key pinched between my thumb and forefinger – and tried to convince myself everything was fine.

But it wasn't.

The key was wrong. It wasn't even vaguely compatible with the lock. I tried to slide it in but got nowhere. It was too thin, the cuts on the blade weren't right, and the lock was a traditional tumbler: there was no electronic reader on it, or inside it, so there was nothing to read the strip on the key.

Instantly, I thought of Healy, of how I'd overruled him and his concerns about coming here. So had he been right all along?

Was this a trap?

But why would Mills place the key inside Seiger and Sten note-paper if it wasn't *for* Seiger and Sten? And if the key didn't open the office, what did it open?

I tried to look through the front window, but all I could see was the vague shape of a long desk, and the curve of a sofa on the left. As I stepped back, I felt my wallet shift against my leg and knew that, inside one of the zip pockets, were my picks. I looked again at the door: it was big, heavy, and would be hard, maybe impossible, to break open with physical force. The lock was different, though. It was just a pin tumbler. I could get past that.

But now I was doubting myself.

The key didn't fit, so what if the alarm code Mills had given me didn't work either?

I looked at the door, at the piece of paper in my hands with *459822* written in the middle. I thought about Black Gale, about the nine people who'd called it home.

There was only one way to find out.

I dropped to my haunches at the door and pulled on a pair of latex gloves. The wind died, the place becoming quiet again, except for the perpetual lap of water in the drains, and babble of the gutters.

Thirty seconds later, something clicked and the door had come away from its frame.

Straight away, the security system started to chirp.

As quickly as possible, I moved inside the building – leaving the door open in case I needed a rapid escape – and searched for the alarm box. About five feet from me, on a wall adjacent to the front desk, its fascia was blinking with blue lights. It was near black inside the office but the lights produced an intermittent wash, enough for me to see that the alarm box had a small, flip-down section housing the number pad. I pulled it open and punched in the code. For a split second, nothing happened: the LEDs were still winking, the sound hadn't stopped.

I turned to the door, ready to run.

But then everything snapped to silence.

39

I clicked the main door shut, and everything retreated into darkness. I could just about make out the reception desk, a curved piece of pale wood – built on to a slight platform – and a sofa and a couple of tub chairs.

As I switched on my penlight, shadows shifted, forming in the corners of the room and around a doorway to the right of the reception desk. It was pulled most of the way shut. On the walls were photographs of a man who I assumed was Jacob Pierce. He was different from how I'd imagined: in his late sixties; a full, thick head of grey hair swept back from his forehead; bright blue eyes, smooth skin, clean-shaven. I'd expected him to look older, maybe less polished, as if his desire not to publicize himself on the company website, or anywhere else, was down to something physical – his age, or an impairment, or some odd tic. But he had none of those things. In most of the pictures he was at social events, the names of charities on banners, Pierce shaking hands with people and presenting them with oversized cheques. In one, he was standing next to Kate Middleton.

I made a beeline for the corridor leading off the reception area and, as I crossed the room, noticed for the first time how low the ceilings were, how the lines of the interior were all slightly off, and how there were three further doors.

The first was on my left and led to a small room with two desks facing each other and a wall stacked entirely with ring binders. I moved inside, sweeping the light across the shelves. The ring binders were arranged alphabetically, the surname of the client on the spine. I searched for Perry, Davey, Gibbs, Solomon or Wilson, but none of the nine villagers were up on the shelves.

The desks each had a PC on them, three-tiered in-trays and a desk diary. There were four photos on one of them, the same woman in all the shots, with the same kids; and on the other desk was a small cactus, with Post-its stuck to the monitor, reminders scrawled all over them. I booted up both computers, taking a closer look at the photographs of the woman: she was in her forties, with two daughters about fourteen and twelve. The other desk belonged to a man: in the top drawer, I found some hair gel as well as a can of Lynx. I couldn't completely dismiss either person as irrelevant, but somehow I doubted they were a part of whatever might be going on here, and I became more convinced as I started going through their PCs. Neither was password-protected, the inboxes were full of bland work emails, and there was nothing in either Internet history that was even vaguely connected to Black Gale.

I returned to the corridor.

Through the second door, opposite the office I'd just been into, was a small, closet-style toilet. In front of me, at the far end of the corridor, I could see a solid, bricked wall. Between that and where I stood was the third door I'd spotted earlier. It had a nameplate on it.

JACOB PIERCE.

As I pushed open his door, I found myself in a bigger, much nicer office, divided almost in two. One half was set on a raised platform, where Pierce had placed an eight-seater table, and a sideboard with a TV screen above it and video-conferencing facilities. In the other half was his desk, shelves full of more binders, and a line of five filing cabinets behind his chair.

I went through the binders in the same way as I had in the other office – and this time I actually found something: a file for Randolph Solomon.

It was a history of the work Seiger and Sten had undertaken on his behalf, all the way back to when they'd dealt with the estate of his late father. I could see Jacob Pierce's name throughout, his signature at the bottom of forms and letters, some so old they'd begun to yellow, and then at the back was the paperwork associated with the move that Randolph and Emiline had made to Black Gale. I began to leaf through the pages more carefully, but couldn't spot a single letter, form or agreement that might in any way be tethered to my case. There were none of the photos that Mills had taken on his phone when we'd seen him at the village – photos that Pierce must have asked him to take in order to ensure that nothing at Black Gale had changed, that no one was on to them – and there was no indication that the property had been bugged.

Frustrated, I switched to the cabinets behind his desk. Inside each of the files, I found an increasingly predictable mix of probate, house moves, divorce paperwork, employment law and business disputes. Nothing even remotely connected to the village.

I looked around the office, confused.

Why would Mills give me the alarm code if there was nothing here?

Maybe for the same reason he gave me a key that doesn't open anything.

I glanced at Pierce's desk, at his computer, and switched it on. As it chimed into life, I went through the drawers of the sideboard at the other end of the room and then fired up the video-conferencing equipment. It made a soft ping as a large, fifty-inch monitor blinked on, and then I reached for the camera underneath and turned it away from me just to be safe.

Picking up the remote control, I began cycling through some menus on the left of the TV. At the bottom was an option for Recent Calls. Most were the names of local businesses I recognized from the binders that I'd already been through, but a couple of them had red dots next to their names. Pretty soon, I realized why: they were recordings.

I pressed Play and got my first look at Jacob Pierce in action.

In a square box at the bottom left of the screen he was talking to two men and a woman from an insurance company in Selby about a redundancy process they were about to embark upon. He was smartly dressed in a shirt, grey waistcoat and mauve tie, and spoke in a soft northern accent. He was urbane, stylish, engaging, even about subjects that were tedious, and had the appearance of a

266

figurehead, of someone who could gain business based on nothing more than his good looks and personality. So why was his presence online so subdued?

'Any other questions you have,' he said to the trio, writing something down, 'just send them over.' I watched him, his ease with them, his humour. 'I've recorded this session because I know you guys like to have a copy of all our correspondence, and because the legalities of employment law are *obviously* a very exciting subject, so you'll definitely want to watch this again.' They laughed, and then again as Pierce looked into the camera and straightened his tie, insinuating that – if they ever *did* watch it back – he'd be looking his best. 'I'll be back in touch very soon.'

They said their goodbyes and the screen went blank.

I stood staring at the television, still asking myself why a man like this was so determined to spend so much of his life below the radar. When I played the second recording, I discovered it was the same three people from the same insurance company, Pierce as smart and gregarious as before. After watching it through, I switched the whole system off, reset the camera and returned to his PC, sliding in at the desk and firing up his email.

Unlike his employees, Pierce had password-protected his inbox. It didn't necessarily mean anything – most people did the same; it was rarer to find an email client open – but while there was little of interest among the documents on his hard drive, when I switched to the Internet, I instantly saw something was off.

He was using two different browsers.

In Explorer, his history was littered with uninteresting stop-offs, all related to work he'd been hired for or was advising on. There were brief detours to other websites, unrelated to his profession, but they weren't exciting either. Online newspapers. Shopping. Sport.

Chrome was different.

Before I'd even got to his history, I could see he'd added an extension. Its icon was in the corner of the browser window and, when I clicked on it, I realized he'd downloaded a proxy and VPN service.

It was software that let him mask his IP address.

A menu was showing his location as somewhere in Sweden.

For a second, a buzz of excitement charged through me, but then I went to his history, expecting a waterfall of websites, confirmation of why I was here, of why Mills had handed me the alarm code, and found nothing.

There was no Internet history at all.

I sat there for a second, staring at the screen, frustrated, panicked. Did Pierce erase his activity every time he used it? Or had he done it because he knew I was coming?

And then I happened to look down.

The carpet was the only part of the room I hadn't paid attention to, but now, as I used the penlight, I saw that there was a small rug, laid at one end of the row of filing cabinets stationed behind Pierce's desk. It looked weirdly out of place.

I got up and kicked at it with the toe of my boot, pushing it away from the cabinets, and – as soon as I did – I realized there was something underneath: two metal plates, snaking out from under the last of the five cabinets. They were thick and ridged. I crouched down, trying to get a better angle with the torch.

Runners.

Standing again, I went to the first of the filing cabinets and pressed two hands flat to its flank, pushing at it. It jolted, almost bucked against me, but then the whole thing – all five of the cabinets – began to slowly move along the tracks embedded in the floor, squealing softly as they did. I'd got the cabinets about three and a half feet when I finally hit a buffer.

Behind the cabinets was an entranceway.

It opened on to a set of ten steps, akin to a cellar staircase, that dropped down to a metal door. I moved inside, having to duck as I did, the ceiling low, the walls so thick around me that it instantly seemed to deaden all sound. When I got to the bottom, I looked at the lock.

The keyhole was minuscule – maybe only a couple of millimetres wide – and around the circumference of the lock plate, equally spaced in an upside-down triangle, were three LEDs. I reached into my pocket, fished out the key that Mills had left for me, and tried inserting it into the lock. It went all the way in.

The second I turned it, something buzzed.

The LEDs all lit up.

And then, with a click, the door opened.

40

I moved past the door, into the room beyond.

It was small, cramped, about ten feet across, even less from left to right, and like everywhere else in the building, its ceiling was low. Brown watermarks crawled above me like vertebrae, and – all along the walls – the plaster was punctured and broken. There was no window, just a tiny square of thick, opaque glass in the roof. I swept the torch from left to right, looking for a light switch, but there was no electricity either. There was no heating system. There was no other way into this place except through the coded door.

In front of me were two shelving units.

On one was a series of long, rectangular metal boxes with flip-up lids. On the other were two very large cardboard ones. All of them were covered in dust and had clearly been here a while.

I flipped the lid on the nearest metal box and used the penlight to illuminate the interior.

It was full of money.

Notes, wrapped in plastic bundles.

I removed one, turning it in my hand. It was difficult to tell for sure but each bundle looked like it had about £5,000 in it, and there were twenty-five of them stacked side by side.

I put the money back, closed the lid and moved on to the next box. It was the same; so was the next one, and the next one. The only difference was that, in the last of the boxes, one of the bundles had been ripped open and about half the notes were missing. I looked back along the shelf, at all the metal containers, at the money inside them.

That meant there was close to a million in here.

Originally there could have been more, though: on the next shelf down, almost cast aside, were two other, matching metal containers, both lids open, both empty. It suggested that Pierce – or someone else – had already been through both of them. They'd already spent a quarter of a million pounds.

Where did all the money come from?

I thought of Chris Gibbs, of the profit he and Laura had made from the sale of the houses at Black Gale. That had been nearly a million, but according to their financials, everything they'd spent had been accounted for. I clamped the penlight between my teeth and pushed on, dragging the first of the large cardboard boxes on to the floor. Dust mushroomed up into the spaces around me. As I removed the lid and set it aside, it took me a second to work out what I was looking at.

Muddied clothes.

Running leggings. A training top.

An old pair of Asics.

Ensuring my gloves were still on properly and intact, I reached in and took out the trainers. Women's running shoes, size five. Even without knowing exactly what was going on, I felt every nerve ending fire, a charge scattering along my spine. The trainers looked like they'd clocked a lot of miles, the pattern on the soles worn along the edges. When I took the leggings out, I could see mud caked to one leg, spattered in a line from ankle to hip; on the training top, there was mud on the same side, from hem to armpit. It was all on the left, not on the right.

The woman had hit the ground on that side.

I checked the pockets of the training top, found nothing, and then returned to the box. There were more clothes underneath, male and female, these much smarter: a jacket, two pairs of tailored trousers, a dress, a skirt, tracksuit bottoms, a selection of shoes. There was an iPad and a series of leads. I pulled the iPad out but it didn't work; the back had been separated from the screen, smashed, levered apart in order to neutralize it. There was a phone too, reduced to pieces – the casing splintered, its battery and its SIM both gone – and a power bank, but again it had been destroyed.

Uncertain if these things belonged to two people or ten, I pushed it all aside and – conscious of time – switched my attention to the second cardboard box.

Inside were even more clothes.

New jeans. A collared shirt.

Size eleven boots.

I found more men's clothing under that: a shirt, a pair of tailored trousers, a second pair of jeans, and then a woman's dress, red with blue trim, a pair of heels, some brown cords and polished brogues, a man's checked shirt, another dress – this one floral – and a green V-neck sweater. And, as I looked at them all, at even more shoes stowed underneath, my heart dropped. I knew who these clothes belonged to. I'd seen them in the photographs that Chris Gibbs had taken the night of the dinner party.

And I recognized what was lying underneath them too.

Five wallets.

Four purses.

Nine phones.

Martina: Part 2

Los Angeles | Monday 5 August

Adrian Vale sat down opposite Jo.

He was in a suit that he was a fraction too big for, the sleeves not long enough, the waistcoat struggling to deal with the width of him. It looked like it had been worn a lot, perhaps by his father before he'd died. As he shrugged off the blue jacket, he seemed to become aware of what Jo was thinking. 'This was Dad's,' he said quietly, looking down at himself. 'It was probably a nice suit twenty years ago.'

Jo nodded, her eyes taking in the Vales' living room, the things that surrounded them: things that he could make use of if it went south, if she cornered him and he started to feel trapped. Ornaments. Paperweights. Potential weapons. Or maybe even actual ones: maybe a blade somewhere close by, maybe a concealed gun.

Maybe nothing.

Even if things went well, there was every possibility that it might get back to Hayesfield. Vale might call the station and one of the other detectives might pick up Jo's phone. Or, perhaps innocently, and for whatever reason, his mother might. Valeria was in the kitchen, she was listening to them, she'd been here when Jo had arrived; by extension, she'd already become a part of this. Or it could go really badly and Vale might start throwing around accusations of harassment, citing circumstantial evidence and the word of a single, anonymous caller. Jo had gone back into old school records, had phoned the Kmart in Temple City that the caller claimed she and Martina Lopez – Vale's ex-girlfriend – had passed through at the same time in 1982, in an effort to try and find out who the caller was and if Jo could trust a word she was saying. But it was another dead end: there was such a high turnover of staff, no one remembered people who'd worked at the store three months ago, let alone three years, and the managers kept no records of former employees. Jo could have called the Department of Labor or the IRS and tried to trace the woman via them, but that meant official paperwork, and that definitely risked Hayesfield finding out. So here she was, feeling vulnerable and undercooked.

I could already be home by now.
I could be with Ethan.

Valeria brought out two tall glasses of home-made lemonade, ice cubes clinking. Jo hadn't asked for anything else but she let Mrs Vale busy herself, watched her return to the kitchen to collect some cookies and then bring them back out on a plate. Jo said she was fine, and then Valeria placed two on the arm of the couch, next to her son, without asking.

'I'll wait for dinner, Ma.'

'You've had a long day,' Valeria replied. 'You need the energy.'

Vale glanced at Jo, a half-smile on his face. But it wasn't a smile of embarrassment, it was one of clear and undeniable love for his mom.

'Okay, Ma,' he said, squeezing her hand. 'Thank you.'

And then Jo felt the panic set in again. This wasn't what she thought her first impressions of Adrian Vale would be like. It wasn't as if she'd expected him to be some snarling animal either; if he was even half as devious as the anonymous caller had made out – if he'd abandoned his girlfriend in the darkness at the top of a mountain trail, if he'd watched from the shadows as she dragged her shattered ankle for a mile and a half back down the slope, if he'd killed a man and left him to liquefy in a tub full of acid, and he'd got away with all three – he was good at hiding who he was: a liar, a killer. So she'd been prepared for some sort of act.

It was more that he carried it off so well.

It was that his display of love appeared so real.

Jo shifted in the armchair and felt her holster move against the top of her right thigh, the weight of the gun against her body. But that was just the thing. It didn't feel like she'd need it. This situation felt the total opposite of that.

'You said on the phone that this was about Martina?' Vale asked, laying his tie next to his jacket, loosening the top button on his shirt and then taking off his waistcoat. It felt even hotter in the living room than when Jo had first arrived.

'Martina Lopez,' Jo said, looking down at her notebook. She'd placed it on the coffee table between them, her notes small and difficult to read from where Vale was sitting. Not that he was looking at what she'd written: he was looking at her, his expression completely neutral. His voice had been the same when she'd called him at work earlier. Jo had phoned the house first, because that was the only number she had for him, and then Valeria had given her the number of the law firm in Pico Rivera. Jo looked at Vale. 'You dated Martina in high school, correct?'

'Right,' he responded. 'For seven months.'

Valeria sat down at the living-room table behind her son.

'Is Martina okay?' Vale asked.

Jo studied him, searching for minor giveaways and, when she failed to find anything, looked down at her notes again. In the corner of one of the pages, under Martina's name, she'd written, *DOD 10/13/84.* Jo had gone looking for Vale's ex in the time since the anonymous call and had found her almost instantly: on 13 October 1984, Martina and a friend had been smoking crack in a house the two of them had shared in Boyle Heights, when Martina started to develop breathing problems. She then went into cardiac arrest. Her friend called 911, and Martina was rushed to the ER – but she died before she got to the operating table.

'Detective Kader?'

'No,' Jo replied. 'No, unfortunately, Martina died.'

She watched Vale, but the only response she saw was shock. He just stared at her for a moment, as if struggling to process what she was telling him, and then he glanced at his mother, whose fingers had strayed to a necklace she was wearing: a tiny gold crucifix.

'She's dead?' he said. 'How?'

'A drug overdose. Crack cocaine.'

There was a sharp intake of breath from Valeria.

'An overdose?' he muttered quietly. 'I can't believe this.'

'She was such a sweet girl,' Valeria said, and worked the crucifix between her fingers. 'Adrian used to bring her over for dinner, and she was always polite, always so respectful . . . I never would have thought . . . Oh, this is awful.'

'When was the last time you saw Martina?' Jo asked Vale.

It took a moment for him to find his voice again.

'When we split up, I guess.'

'Which was when?'

'Late spring of '82.' He paused again, staring off into a space between Jo and the mantel. For a moment, she wondered if he was trying to formulate a plan, a route out of this, a lie, but – just like before, when she'd seen him interacting with his mom – it was hard to detect any deceit, if it was even there. His eyes came back to her. He was handsome, olive-skinned, muscular, but for a second he seemed pale and small. 'I'm sorry,' he said, 'I'm having a real hard time with the idea that . . .' He faded out again.

'The idea that what?'

He shrugged. 'That she's dead.'

'Was it her anxiety?' Valeria said from the table.

Jo glanced at her. 'What do you mean?'

Valeria looked guilty, as if she'd been caught gossiping.

'It's okay, Ma,' Vale said, holding up a hand to his mother. 'Mom just means, was it the drugs that killed her or did she develop breathing problems because of her anxiety stuff?'

'What anxiety stuff?'

'The panic attacks.'

Jo eyed him.

He frowned, looking confused, uncertain of what Jo's silence meant. 'She never took drugs when we were together – not stuff

276

like crack, anyway – but Martina used to suffer these . . . I don't know, I guess you would call them "episodes".' He frowned again. 'She'd get real panicky all of a sudden, irrational, impossible to calm down, and it got so bad that the doctor had to prescribe her these pills to take. Stuff like Xanax.'

Anxiety, panic attacks: Jo could see exactly where this was going, she just wasn't certain if Vale was deliberately guiding her there or not. The caller claimed that, according to Martina, Vale had left his former girlfriend at the top of the mountain and stalked her from the dark on the way down. Now it seemed obvious what Vale's version of that night would be if Jo actually asked him: they'd hiked to the peak, they'd watched the sunset, then, for whatever reason, Martina had freaked out. She'd had one of her episodes. She'd become irrational, mixed up, had spun out of control. What she thought she remembered was all wrong.

Jo made a note to chase down a medical history for Martina Lopez, to check for a detailed history of benzodiazepine use, including during the period she dated Adrian Vale, because that would be the easiest way to prove or dismiss Vale's claims. But, even without that information, she could feel things starting to shift: in Martina's autopsy report, the coroner had noted that there were faint traces of Valium in her blood. Jo hadn't placed much importance on that detail when she'd read it the first time – half the city was using tranquillizers – but now it seemed like a major bridge back to this moment. And, again, it framed Adrian Vale in a different light.

'Why did the two of you split up?' Jo asked him.

'I just found it hard to deal with her.'

'Her illness, you mean?'

'Yeah, exactly.' He pushed his lips together, a look of regret and of guilt. 'I know that sounds terrible. But she would just lose her mind for no reason, and it got more and more difficult to calm her down.' He stopped again, taking a breath, wiping at an eye. He wasn't in tears, but he was emotional – or appeared to be. 'Her parents weren't around, and she just wouldn't listen to me. I kept telling her she needed to go seek help: not pills – not more medication – but real help. A psychologist, or someone who could actually get inside her head. But I was seventeen, man. I didn't know anything about the world, so I was telling her to do this stuff, but didn't really have a clue what I was talking about. All I knew was that I wanted her to get better.'

'Did you split up after what happened at Big Bear Lake?'

Jo watched for a reaction.

'I'm sorry?'

'Did you split up after Big Bear?' she repeated.

He seemed disorientated by the change of direction – but then, slowly, he understood and his expression began to fill with remorse again, contrition. The starkness of his face, the almost complete lack of opacity, sent the panic charging through Jo's bloodstream again. He was going to tell her exactly what she'd predicted: Martina had freaked out at the top of the trail; he didn't abandon her, he helped her down. Maybe there was no ankle injury at all. Maybe he was there the entire time and the account the caller had given Jo was an account that Martina, confused and scared, had imagined, or embellished, or mis-remembered. Jo was here based on the word of a woman she didn't know, had never met and, ultimately, couldn't trust.

What the hell am I doing?

'Yeah, I guess that night was the beginning of the end,' Vale said, his big frame shuffling to the edge of the couch. 'She just went totally nuts up there – accused me of leaving her alone when I was standing right beside her the whole time. I was lit-erally looking at her, had my hands on her shoulders trying to calm her down, and she was screaming at me, calling my name like I wasn't even there. It was weird, but mostly it was just really upsetting. In the days after that, when she'd calmed down, we tried to talk about it, but she started bringing up stuff that never even happened. She said I was watching her from inside the tree-line, which was ridiculous, because why would I go hide inside the forest when she had the only torch and that place is full of bears?' He paused, picking up his lemonade. 'I don't know,' he said softly. 'It was just sad, that's all. I loved Martina. She was my first proper girlfriend. She was funny, sweet.' He drank from the glass. 'I managed to talk her around in the days after that, assure her that what she *thought* had happened *hadn't* happened at all, but I guess it was beyond rescue by then.' He looked up at Jo, a pained smile on his face. 'At least, it was for me. I just . . . I didn't know how to handle her.'

'So, once you split up, you never saw her again?'

'I saw her a bunch of times at the Kmart in Temple City. She got a job there after she dropped out of school, and I was working part-time in a supplies yard in Industry, which was three miles away. Sometimes I'd drop in. But she'd changed a lot by then.'

'Changed how?'

'Thinner, I guess. Gaunt. I figured that she wasn't sleeping properly – that she was on different, stronger pills – but I never knew for sure.' He drew a finger down the condensation on his glass, and then looked at Jo again. 'I started to worry that maybe she'd got in with the wrong crowd. There were a bunch of kids working there who'd dropped out at the same time as Martina did, and not all of them were . . .' He stopped, grimaced, looked at his mom. 'I'm starting to sound real preachy.'

'You're saying they were a bad influence on her?'

'All I know is some of those kids, they were pretty wild at high school, and not always in a fun way. So I remember being surprised.'

'Surprised she would hang out with them?'

'Sure, yeah. They would never have hung out together at high school.'

'You got names?'

'I think one of them was called Jessie.' Vale frowned. 'There was another guy who worked there who was in our year. Clark maybe – or that could have been his surname. I'm sorry. I never talked to those guys. I didn't talk to anyone, really.'

'How come?'

He opened out his hands, palms facing up.

'You'd have to ask all the kids who would call me names and never want a single thing to do with me.' It was said without rancour, but it was obvious it still hurt. 'But, you know, I understood. I was a nerd. I wanted to do well at school, I wanted to be a lawyer. I was interested in things like politics and history. Without sounding conceited, I could have got on to the football team if I'd really wanted it; I was a pretty good centre, I could have been a jock – I mean, look at the size of me – but none of that interested me. I think the fact that I actively *shunned* sports set other kids against me. I was the loner. I never had anyone to hang around with.' He glanced at his mother, who looked more pained at this admission than he did. 'I've always wanted to go and study abroad somewhere,' he said, 'even for a short time. I'd love to see London, Paris, the Italian cities, but you say those things out loud at high school and you get called a fag; and not just once – over and over again, on repeat. You paint a target on your back. So I kept myself to myself.'

Jo took a moment, spinning back to what Vale had said about the people Martina had worked with. If Jo could cross-reference the names Jessie or Jessica with girls who'd been in the same school year as Vale, it might be enough to zero in on who the caller was. Yet it was hard not to feel conflicted already: either Vale was one of the most frightening and confident liars she'd ever sat in front of, or the love he'd shown for his mom, the love he talked of having for his ex, the explanation he'd given for that night at Big Bear Lake, was all exactly as it looked and sounded.

Jo changed direction.

'You ever heard the name Gabriel Wilzon, Adrian?'

Vale frowned. 'Who?'

'Gabriel Wilzon – that's Wilzon with a *zee*.'

'No,' he said. 'Never. Why?'

She studied him for a moment. The eyes were normally where it began to break down first, where the rifts and fractures of a lie were initially exposed. But Vale's eyes hardly strayed from hers at all and were still sheened with moisture from where he'd got emotional talking about Martina. Jo pressed him again: 'Have you ever heard of the Star Inn?'

'Is that a hotel?'

'A motel. It's out in West Hollywood.'

He shook his head. 'No, never.'

'You ever spend any time out that way?'

'In West Hollywood?' He glanced at his mother, who appeared as puzzled as he was. 'No,' he said, 'Never. I can't remember the last time I went that far across town.'

'You weren't there on the weekend of 20th and 21st of July?'

He frowned again. 'No.'

'Do you remember where you were?'

'Two weeks ago?' He paused, thinking. 'I was probably just hanging out here. I haven't done much since I've been home. The last semester at Stanford was pretty intense, so I've been taking it easy. Do you remember what we did that day, Ma?'

'Days,' Jo corrected. 'Saturday and Sunday.'

Valeria's expression mirrored her son's.

Jo moved on.

'You used to work at Caraca BuildIt, right?'

'That's right,' Vale replied.

'Any chance you might have somehow got access to a maroon VW Quantum that belongs to the company in the time since you got back for the summer break?'

He looked at her like she was joking with him.

'I don't work there any more,' he said. 'I haven't worked there since I went to Stanford.' He was frowning again, genuinely confused. 'I haven't seen Mr Caraca for a couple of years, so I don't know how he does it now – but back when I was there, he was the only one who ever had the keys to the garage where all the vehicles were left.'

'What about Donald Klein? Does that name mean anything to you?'

'No,' he replied again. 'Nothing. Who is he?'

'You ever been to Runyon Canyon Park?'

This time, he looked frustrated at the constant swerving, at the lack of any sort of explanation. 'Never been there in my life,' he said, his voice tight. 'Not even once.'

At the table, Valeria was starting to look pale, clearly worried that her son had got himself into some sort of trouble; but there was anger as well, as palpable as the heat in the living room, her eyes narrowed and brow creased. She was ready to defend her son if it came to it, to fight for him. It was an instinct Jo identified with instantly.

I need to calm this down.

Jo raised the flat of her hand. 'It's nothing to worry about,' she lied, trying to head things off. She had to be careful. If she pushed too hard, this was exactly the sort of thing that could end up on Hayesfield's desk. 'Basically, it appears as if Martina purchased a particularly strong batch of crack cocaine and suffered a heart attack as a result of it, and we're still trying to locate the person who sold her those drugs last year.' She watched to see if the lie would divert them away from the questions she'd asked. Both of them, Vale and his mother, seemed to slump, their faces smoothing out, the fire in their cheeks fading, and then the full horror of Martina's death – her heart attack; the fact she'd become another statistic in the city's crack epidemic – hit home, and they both seemed to deflate. Valeria leaned across the table. Vale collapsed into the couch.

'I'm sorry for your loss,' she said, addressing the both of them, but keeping her gaze on Vale. He glanced at her, blinked again, and then sat up, wiping his eyes.

'I guess finding out that she died in that way . . .' he said quietly, embarrassed. And then his words dissolved – and a tear escaped, tracing a path along his cheek.

41

I looked at the clothes and the shoes in the second box.

The wallets. The purses.

The nine phones.

A heaviness settled on me, a sinking feeling that I couldn't cast off as I realized what it meant: it was highly unlikely I was looking for nine missing people any more.

I was looking for nine dead bodies.

Deep down, I'd always feared that would be the case but it didn't make it any easier to swallow. I rubbed my eyes, the adrenalin washing out of me, the sorrow of a doomed search, and then – at the very periphery of my vision – I saw the other box of clothes that I'd already opened. Was it worse than I thought?

Were there even more missing people?

Grabbing my phone – a cheap replacement for the one that Mills and his accomplice had stolen from me at the cottage – I quickly took as many photos as I could. I started with the clothes, then the boxes, then the money that Jacob Pierce had locked away in here. After I was done I packed everything up again, trying to return it in the vague order in which I'd pulled it out. The checked shirt belonging to Chris Gibbs. A T-shirt with the poster for *The Shining* printed on it, belonging to Mark. The brown cords that Randolph Solomon had arrived in. John Davey's blazer. Patrick's green V-neck sweater. Emiline Wilson's red-and-blue dress and the floral one that Freda Davey had been wearing. There was a small tube of painkillers too that Freda must have brought with her, her name printed in tiny letters on the side of it. In all that had happened, in the frantic search for answers, it was easy to forget that, a few months before she vanished, she'd found out that her cancer had come back.

The Black Gale residents' phones were as useless as the iPad

I'd found in the first box, destroyed in the same way. As I placed them back into the container, I tried to imagine why Pierce, or Mills, or whoever else was involved, kept everything hidden here and hadn't just dumped it all somewhere remote. But then I started to see a kind of sense in it: if it was all in here, it would likely never get found.

If everything was left out there somewhere, it might.

Clothes took years to degrade. Nylon and leather lasted forty years, the Lycra in the exercise gear upwards of a hundred. They wouldn't just disappear, not like human beings. We decayed. We atomized, sometimes – with the right conditions – in a matter of weeks. If a body was a skeleton, reduced to a series of disconnected parts over time, it became much harder to identify. If it was still clothed, and if those clothes matched the last description of what a missing person had been wearing, it opened up a pathway back to the disappearance, possibly to the suspect involved in taking them, and combined with DNA that might have been left in threads, on collars, on sleeves, investigators were suddenly armed. Keep the clothes, however, and another source of trace evidence was secured. Same with the phones: the batteries were gone, the SIM cards too, but a mobile still carried a model number, an IMEI barcode printed on the inside, and that made it possible to trace ownership. The wallets had driving licences, and bank cards, personal effects, and it all remained a risk if left out in the open.

I thought of Mills, of his reasons for giving me the key, and my mind spooled all the way back to the cottage, to when he'd had a shotgun pointed at me. He'd told me the story about the family of four who'd been murdered. I'd thought it was because he wanted to let me know that he knew who Healy was, and maybe that *was* part of the reason. But now I was starting to wonder if that wasn't just secondary to something else: perhaps he was telling me he had a conscience; perhaps he was telling me that no amount of money was quite enough to suppress his instincts as an investigator, as someone who intuitively cared for victims. He'd cared for that family, he'd cared for the shop owner he'd saved from being shot, he cared for the girlfriend I'd seen him with and her two kids, and now he cared about the lost lives hidden in these boxes. That made me think he'd only come across this room recently. It made me think that Pierce had been keeping him out of the loop, telling him only what he needed to know, and that the money Mills had been earning had been enough for him to ignore some of the things that didn't add up or sit right with him. But, eventually, Mills had got curious, and somehow he'd ended up here. And once he saw this place, it flipped a switch.

I stopped.

I'd been thinking so much about Mills, I'd almost missed something else entirely. It was rolled up in the green sweater belonging to Patrick Perry and had remained hidden there, even when I'd got the sweater out and set it down. But as I returned it the box, I felt it shift and slide towards me.

I unwrapped the jumper.

Inside was a Dictaphone.

42

The Dictaphone was digital, but it was an old model, large and cumbersome, and I immediately thought of Patrick Perry, of his years as a journalist, and then his weeks and months spent looking into the vanishing of Beatrix Steards. Had this been his when he'd still been at the *Manchester Evening News*? It was scuffed at the edges, suggesting it had seen a lot of mileage, and when I cycled through the folders on the display, I saw that almost all of them had been used, and each contained a recording. I eyed the device and considered the fact that it was wrapped in a piece of his clothing. The police had clearly never realized the Dictaphone existed, otherwise it would have been mentioned somewhere in the investigation. So either Patrick took it with him on the night of the disappearance – or someone went back to the village for it afterwards. But why?

I turned it over.

Something was written, in black pen, on the back.

G76984Z.

There was something about the sequence – in particular, the numbers – that got my attention, but I couldn't think what, and didn't have the time to waste here trying to figure it out. Instead, I went to the top of the steps, looking out into Pierce's office, making sure I was still alone, and then used the volume wheel on the side to push the sound down.

I pressed Play.

'*Okay. Are you ready to start?*'

It was a male voice with a Mancunian accent.

'*Yes, I'm ready.*'

A female, also Mancunian.

'*Did they explain to you about the online story?*'

'*Yes. They said it would be posted later.*'

'That's right. I'm just an old hack set in my ways but, as I understand it, they will post an edited version of this interview on to the website at the same time as the printed version goes out. That means I just need to do a very brief introduction . . .'

'Okay.'

There was a second's pause.

'I'm Patrick Perry, senior reporter for the Manchester Evening News and I'm here with Coralie McEwan, former girlfriend of city council leader Tony Eckhart.'

Straight away, I recognized the name of the woman: she was the mistress of the city councilman who'd been caught siphoning off public funds back in the 1990s. Patrick had hung a framed copy of the front-page story he'd written about this on his study wall.

'Thank you for talking to me, Coralie.'

I listened for a minute or so and then switched to the next file, and the next, moving through them as fast as I could, constantly pausing to make sure the office was still silent, aware that the longer I stayed here, the more I put myself at risk. But, at the same time, it was hard *not* to listen. I realized I hadn't heard Patrick speak before, so as he interviewed local politicians, victims of crime, protagonists in stories he'd written in his time as a reporter, it was a chance finally to match a voice to the person I'd read about and had described to me. I'd studied his life so closely and knew so much about him now that I found myself surprised at how he sounded, different from how I imagined, his voice deeper than Ross's, and scratchier, as if he had once been a smoker. But compelling as it was to hear him talk, as I kept going – one file after the next – I quickly began to realize I was no closer to understanding what possible interest any of this could hold for Jacob Pierce, or why the Dictaphone was in here.

But then I hit the second-from-last file.

The date of the recording flashed up every time I switched folders, and all of the other interviews had predated the point at which Patrick was made redundant in 2010. All of them, except this one and the next.

This one had been recorded on 15 October 2015.

Sixteen days before he and the others disappeared.

'Okay. We're recording now. You asked me not to write anything down, so getting everything on tape is the next best way for me to remember all that I need to. Not being able to take notes . . . it just makes it harder to remember important details, that's all, and details are the way you make progress with stuff like this. So just talk to me like you did all the other times we've met and don't worry about the Dictaphone. Everything else on here was recorded years ago, when I was still at the newspaper, so what we talk about will be safe. This thing's just been gathering dust until now . . .'

For a moment, there wasn't any response. I could hear movement – the squeak of a sofa, the rustle of clothes, the distant whine of the wind at a window somewhere – and, briefly, became worried it wasn't just coming from the tape but from the office too. I stopped the recording and inched into the corridor, looking into reception, towards the entrance. Nothing had changed. No one was here.

But I was still on edge.

I stayed where I was, in sight of the entrance, and pressed Play again.

'Okay, so you want me to just tell you what I remember?'

A woman.

'Exactly,' Patrick replied.

'I guess I remember being surprised her name was Beatrix.'

I froze, eyes fixed on the Dictaphone now.

'You don't think it suited her?'

'It wasn't that.'

'So what was it?'

'I don't know. She just never seemed like a Beatrix to me.'

There was a long pause, peripheral sounds fading in again, the clink of a mug being put down.

'What else do you remember thinking?'

'It was all such a long time ago.' The woman paused for a moment

and I heard her take a long breath, the sound of it heavy, almost uneasy. *'I don't . . . I just . . .'*

'It's okay,' Patrick said. *'Take a minute if you need to.'*

In the quiet that followed, I tried to imagine who Patrick was interviewing. Her voice gave few clues. She was from the south somewhere, but there was a generic quality to her inflection that made it hard to be more specific. It was even hard to put an age on her – her voice was smooth, her speech patterns unblemished. The lack of a northern accent immediately discounted the idea of it being one of the women from the village: Freda Davey had been born in Leeds, Emiline Wilson was brought up in Kendal and Laura Gibbs in York, while Francesca Perry hadn't moved to the UK until she was fifteen – and, according to Ross, had never lost her Italian accent.

'Sorry,' the woman said, *'it's still so hard to talk about.'*

'It's okay,' Patrick replied. *'So you saw Beatrix's picture in the media?'*

'Yes. In the newspaper.'

'After she was reported missing in 1987?'

'Yes. She was on page four of the Mail. *I remember that.'*

'How did you know it was her?'

'If you look at photos of her, she has a birthmark on the right side of her face, on her cheek, just below her eye. It's small and quite pale – but it's very distinctive.'

'You mean the shape of it?'

'Yes. I always thought it looked like butterfly wings.'

I'd thought the same thing.

I remembered the birthmark. I remembered the light green, almost grey colour of Beatrix's eyes in the photograph of her, how her mouth had been turned up in the merest hint of a smile, her slim build, her short, dark bob.

'How did it feel when you saw her in the paper?'

'I felt,' the woman started, but then stopped again. *'I don't know. I guess I felt surprised to start with. And then when I was definitely sure that it was her, I felt shocked, and a terrible sense of guilt. I think it was that, more than anything. Guilt is such a dreadful burden to carry.'*

'*What did you feel guilty about?*'

'*It's pretty obvious, isn't it?*' the woman said, although there was no malice in her voice, no disdain. '*I did an awful thing to Beatrix – an awful, terrible thing.*'

Absolute silence.

On the tape.

In the office.

'*I hurt her,*' the woman said, her words breaking up, '*and then I betrayed her, and then – when it was finally over – I buried her in the deepest hole I could find.*'

43

I buried her in the deepest hole I could find.

I was listening to Beatrix Steards's killer.

'Is there any part of you now that thinks what you did back then might have been justified?' Patrick asked, the twang of his Mancunian accent pulling my thoughts back into focus. *'It's easier sometimes to look at decisions we've made —'*

'No.'

The woman cut him off, her answer unambiguous, but, once again, there was no aggression in her tone, no sense that she was shouting Patrick down, admonishing him, even correcting him.

'Not a single part of you thinks there was any justification for —'

'No,' she repeated, cutting him short again. *'Not a single part.'*

I rewound the recording, so I could listen again. Patrick's question had been so jarring, I almost didn't process it properly the first time: how could he ask if there was a justification for murder?

'I've tried to forget,' the woman continued, *'but there's not a day that goes by when I don't think of what I did. My choices are like a disease eating away at me —'*

Suddenly, the woman stopped talking.

I expected Patrick to follow up on it, to ask her what the matter was, why she'd stopped, but instead — quietly, but audibly — there was a noise in the background of the interview. It took me a split second to work out what it was: a door opening.

'Uh, sorry, have you booked this room?'

Another male voice.

'I didn't realize you had to,' Patrick replied.

'I'm afraid you do. At reception.'

'Oh, I apologize. Just give us a second.'

The door closed again.

'*Bloody hell*,' Patrick muttered. '*Sorry.*'

'*It's okay.*'

'*I'm trying to get a sense of what went on, of what you did and how it happened, but it's so complicated. You can't come to me, I can't go to you, if anyone at Black Gale sees me with you, they're going to start to ask me questions, and that's exactly what you don't want to happen.*' A long, frustrated pause. '*I thought coming to the club would be a good idea on a day like this. I mean, look at the weather: who's going to come here today to play golf? But even here, it's . . .*'

He stopped.

They were at a golf club somewhere, in a reception room. A place that would raise no questions for Patrick and no questions for the woman.

'*I should never have asked for your help,*' she said.

'*It's fine. I want to help you.*'

'*It's wrong to involve you.*'

'*It's not wrong, it's just complicated.*'

More silence. As the recording whirred on, backed by nothing but the sound of rain against the windows, I tried to imagine what was going on and where this fitted in.

'*I'm going to have a think about –*'

Patrick turned the recording off.

I stared at the Dictaphone, watching as the numbers halted and reset again. A split second later, the next recording – the forty-third and final one – came to life.

'*Are you okay?*'

Patrick again. It was dated 29 October – two days before the Halloween dinner – and the background noise was different this time: no rain, none of the compressed sound that came with recording inside a room. I could hear birds, the rustle of trees, and yet they were still somehow subdued.

And then I realized why.

They were in a car.

'*I'm fine,*' the woman said. '*You?*'

Patrick sighed. '*I was coming out of the house yesterday, with this useless bloody camera, ready to walk down here to meet you, and then Fran got back early from work and started asking me what I was doing.'* The wind picked up outside the car. *'I hate all the lies.'*

'I know. I'm sorry.'

'It's okay. I understand why. I just . . .'

He didn't finish his sentence.

'You don't have to do this,' the woman said.

'It's fine. I want to help you.'

'I didn't want it to be like this.'

'It's fine,' he repeated. *'Honestly. Let's talk about what I've found out.'*

'All right. If you're sure.'

More background noise: birds, the very faint drone of a plane.

'Let's go back to the start.'

'Okay,' the woman responded nervously. *'Okay.'*

'Let's talk about Adrian Vale.'

Dead Ends

Los Angeles | Monday 5 August

With the traffic, Jo didn't get home till just after eight.

Ethan was already asleep, the sheets twisted around him. She leaned into the crib, brushed her son's hair away from his face and kissed him gently, before padding back through to the kitchen where Ira was serving up dinner.

As they ate, she asked him what they'd got up to and Ira said he'd taken Ethan to the beach. Jo felt a pang of jealousy as she listened, at missing out again, at the things Ethan had said that had made Ira roar with laughter, at the fact that – while the two most important people in her life were building sandcastles – she was eating shit from Hayesfield about a minor admin error she'd made on a log sheet; that, while Ira and Ethan were having ice cream, she was talking to a grieving family about the corpse on State Route 39; and that, while there was a water fight going on in her backyard, Jo was sitting in Adrian Vale's house, watching him cry, realizing she'd made a big mistake.

It was a mistake that had only got worse afterwards.

Once she'd left the Vales', she'd driven her department-issue Caprice back to the station as the keys for her Oldsmobile were in the top drawer of her desk. Inside, the changeover had already happened, day shift to night shift, briefings still taking place at the tables and in meeting rooms. The dominant conversation had been at the far end, where the Night Stalker task force were discussing a .25-calibre revolver used in the last attack in Sun Valley.

She'd slid in at her desk and found a xeroxed page sitting on her keyboard: it was the naked July model from a Pirelli calendar that hung in the kitchen – a calendar she'd told a couple of the detectives that she hated, that she objected to, and that she wanted taken down. Above the model, someone had drawn a speech bubble.

It had said, *I'm 34D Detective Kader.*

Jo had glanced around at the rest of the floor, but no one had been looking at her. The other detectives were leaving or working, or in the middle of a conversation – or just pretending not to know what was going on. She'd screwed up the xerox and tossed it into the trash, boiling with anger but trying not to let it show, and then – as she'd grabbed her car keys from her top drawer – her attention had switched: one of the operators had left a couple of message slips inside.

The first had been from Caraca BuildIt.

She'd been waiting on a callback from the assistant manager about whether any containers of acid were missing from their stock. The number listed was for the guy's home line, so she'd punched in the numbers and – once he'd picked up – had reintroduced herself.

'Ah, right,' he'd said, 'sure. I called you earlier.'

'Did you find anything?'

'No.' It sounded like he was in the middle of eating. 'I did what you asked and did an audit on the stock. It took a while – but everything's there.'

'There are no missing containers?'

'Not a single one.'

She'd put the phone down, drained, frustrated, and then turned to the second message. It was from one of the guys down in Records. Before she'd left East LA, she'd called him and asked him to see if he could find a Jessie or Jessica who'd dropped out of William Hay High School in Belvedere in 1982, and if that Jessie or Jessica had a record. Jo wanted to ID the caller because she needed to know if she could trust her.

The message she'd been left showed that she couldn't.

The caller was Jessica Cespedes, aged twenty. She was living at an address east of the river, in Downey. The guy in Records listed, in familiar department shorthand, some of the crimes on Cespedes' sheet: forgery, fraud, possession of narcotics. She'd done eight months for intent to distribute in Chino, at the California Institution for Women.

Jo's caller was a criminal.

'I've got to go and work,' Ira said, shaking Jo out of her thoughts and returning her to the kitchen, to the stifling air of the house, the locked doors and windows, the perpetual hum of the fans. She squeezed his hand, telling him that was fine, and watched him disappear through to his den. Ira had got the job he'd pitched for on his trip to New York a couple of weeks back, and he'd been right: it was worth a lot of money, and it would definitely pay for a nice vacation for the three of them next year. But the deadline was at the end of September. It was going to be tight, and although he played it down, she could tell already that he was stressing. He was waking up with headaches every day. He was panicky and restless. She didn't say anything, but Jo was worried as well about how they'd make it work when she was having to do such long days, when – just to keep her head above water – she was having to leave before Ethan was awake and was getting home after he was asleep. And it wasn't because of her caseload: she *was* overloaded, being dragged in a thousand different directions, but that wasn't the reason she was pulling fourteen-hour days. Or, at least, not the main one. Instead, it was because she was still having to prove herself, even after seven years in homicide. She was still having to bite her tongue and ignore the jibes. She was still having to try to predict how the department – and the men in it – might come at her. They were able to talk about things like instinct on cases, about knowing something intuitively, whereas she had to deliver the facts, or evidence, or both, if she didn't want to be dismissed out of hand. She was still having to contend with two different rule sets – one for them, one for her – and it was grinding her down. She didn't want it grinding Ira down too.

She didn't want him to forget what it was like to have a wife.

She didn't want her son to grow up without seeing her around.

44

By the time I got back to the car, I was soaked through.

I switched the ignition on, turned the heaters to full blast and then checked that I hadn't been followed. I'd left the Audi in the corner of a near-empty multistorey so it should have been easy enough to spot a tail – but there wasn't one. There was only one other car on the floor, at the far end, close to the down ramp, and it had clearly long overstayed its welcome because its windscreen had a yellow parking ticket on it and the left front wheel was clamped.

As mine began to warm up, I shrugged off my coat and went through the pockets.

In one of them was Patrick's Dictaphone.

I held it in my hand for a second, my pulse thumping in my ears, wondering if I'd just made a terrible mistake. There had been dust all over the boxes in the hidden room because they'd gone so long without being looked at. I'd found no itemized list of objects anywhere, no indication that anything in the room had been individually numbered, but that did little to settle my nerves. After what had happened at the cottage, it was obvious that whoever was behind this was on high alert, and that meant, sooner rather than later, they were going to start searching for potential vulnerabilities, ensuring they hadn't been compromised. They were going to check the room.

And when they did, they were going to find the Dictaphone missing.

That meant I had to work fast.

I looked again at the sequence written on the reverse of it in black felt pen: *G76984Z*. It had taken me the entire walk back to the car to realize why I recognized the sequence, and in particular the numbers in the middle.

It was in Isaac Mills's handwriting.

The alarm code for Seiger and Sten had been *459822* and the sequence on the dictaphone was *G76984Z*, so they shared some of the same digits – *4, 9, 8.* Mills's *4* was distinct: the horizontal tail went up slightly, the vertical line kicked out to the left, and his *8* had a small loop at the top rather than at the bottom. It was definitely him. So had he written on the Dictaphone in anticipation of me finding my way into the room? Even if he did, what did the sequence mean? Was he giving me another access code?

I didn't know yet, but as much as taking the Dictaphone was a risk, I tried to tell myself that it was less of a risk than leaving it behind. If I had, someone might see what Mills had done, and although I still wasn't sure what to make of him, still wasn't sure if I even trusted him, what he'd done for me felt less and less like a trap and, in getting me the key for the room, more like a massive personal gamble.

I grabbed a USB-to-stereo jack from the glove compartment and plugged one end into the car's Aux slot and the other into the Dictaphone. After that, I swung the car out and headed for the down ramp, pushing Play as I did. The muted sound of birdsong started to fill the car's speakers.

And then Patrick.

He began discussing Adrian Vale, his background, the fact that he'd been bright, on a fully paid scholarship and on the same Politics course as Beatrix. After a while, he veered away from Vale to discuss the details of Beatrix's disappearance, the search for her, and what he'd had passed on to him from a source in the Greater Manchester Police. That was Kevin Quinn. He didn't name Quinn, but I knew that was where all of this had come from, and not only because Quinn had already confirmed as much, but because everything Patrick talked about was pretty much lifted directly from what I'd already seen in Beatrix's case file. And then he said, '*I got through to Robert Zaid last week.*'

Zaid was the guy that Beatrix Steards had been through university with, first as they'd studied History, then during the

Politics postgrad. The Met had talked to him about Beatrix, about Adrian Vale, and as I recalled that, I recalled something else – what Zaid had said to DS Smoulter during an informal interview: *Beatrix, me and a couple of others were walking back from the pub and one of the guys said, 'Isn't that Adrian?' And we all looked around, and it was definitely him, but when he saw us, he darted off into this side street and didn't appear again.*

Smoulter had always liked Vale for Beatrix's disappearance but had never had enough evidence to pin it on him, and then two years later, on 12 October 1989, Vale's body was discovered on a beach in Sussex after he committed suicide. So was it possible that Beatrix's killer was Vale after all, not the woman talking to Patrick on this tape? Could he have jumped to his death because he felt so guilty about what he'd done? I listened to the buzz on the Dictaphone, to the faint hum of background noise filling the space between conversation. It was possible. But it was just as possible that this woman's confession was real, and that Adrian Vale had ended up on that beach because he was depressed and grieving. His mother, who he was close to, died the January before he did, something he'd mentioned in a half-finished suicide note left on the beach. He was lonely and reclusive, which was backed up by the fact that not one person – not even the men he shared a house with – realized he was missing.

'*So what did Zaid say?*' the woman asked.

As I listened to her voice, I thought, *Who are you?*

Were you really the one that killed Beatrix Steards?

If you did, why didn't Patrick go to the cops?

'*Pretty much the same story we already know,*' Patrick replied. '*Zaid said Vale could be weird around Beatrix. Not aggressive as such, more . . .*' It sounded like he was grimacing, sucking in breath through his teeth. '*I don't know, he just used the word "weird". Like, Vale would try to talk to Beatrix when she was in the middle of talking to someone else; or he'd follow her around. But, then, I also managed to track down a couple of the other people who did that Politics postgrad and they told me Vale was a bit of a loner but was relatively harmless.*'

'*Do you think Vale was in love with Beatrix?*'

'*He could have been, yeah.*'

'*But the police saw it more as an obsession?*'

'*Well, Smoulter definitely did.*'

'*Okay,*' the woman said. '*What else did you find out?*'

'*Well, as I mentioned, I got in touch with this Robert Zaid guy last week, and, after finally getting his PA to actually do her job properly, the two of us ended up talking over Skype a couple of days later. He's still down in London; lives in Highgate. He works in the Foreign Office as some kind of diplomat, which he's been doing for years, although I've no idea why: his dad was Iranian and made tons of money from oil back in the seventies, so Zaid was already "don't have to work" rich. After his parents died, he used his inheritance to invest in a load of Internet start-ups, and now he's not just rich, he's* Sunday Times *Rich List rich – which is why I guess it was hard to pin him down.*'

I thought of the money I'd found in the room at Seiger and Sten, and tried to force a connection between Jacob Pierce and Robert Zaid – an easy explanation for how hundreds of thousands of pounds had come into Pierce's possession. But Zaid had been an irrelevance up until now, a minor side story, and it was Adrian Vale, not Zaid, who had an established connection with Jacob Pierce, using him as his solicitor when he'd been pulled in for questioning after Beatrix vanished. Being wealthy and then knowing Beatrix Steards weren't the same things as buying Jacob Pierce's silence and then abducting and killing someone, and on a postgrad, at a good university like King's College, and in one of the world's most expensive cities, Zaid wasn't likely to be the only student who came from money. In fact, it was just as probable now that the postgrad was a redundant line of enquiry – not least because the woman on the tape had already admitted to killing Beatrix.

I passed a small airfield, the runway lit up by orange lights, and then the dark swallowed everything again and all I could see were cat's eyes, winking in the middle of the road, and a sign saying that it was three miles to the village the cottage was in.

The woman's voice brought me back.

'*And this Zaid guy still thinks that it was Adrian Vale who killed Beatrix?*'

'*He says he's always believed that's the most likely explanation.*'

'*Does he ever talk to anyone else from back then?*'

'*No. He says he kept in touch with a few of the other Politics students for a while after they graduated, but then they all started to drift apart, and now he doesn't talk to any of them. Because of Zaid's money, his net worth, the amount of cash he's got plugged into these big companies – and, I suppose, the potential for him to be blackmailed and got at – he admitted he tries to keep a low profile. He never does interviews or profile pieces.*'

Again, there was nothing suspicious about a very rich man choosing to limit his exposure to publicity, but the mention of *blackmail* made me wonder if this might actually be a lead worth chasing up. Pierce had got that money from somewhere, and there was no reason why it couldn't have been from a man like Robert Zaid – a businessman, a diplomat, a government official, whose reputation and professional interests could be damaged severely over a mistake he might have made in the past: drugs, an affair, the wrong money to the wrong sort of people.

'*So, anyway,*' Patrick continued, '*Zaid reckons that trying to keep himself out of the spotlight never helped very much when it came to staying in touch with the people he went to university with – but he also said that he felt Beatrix's disappearance had begun to damage the friendships they all had, even before that.*'

'*In what way?*'

'*Basically, I think they were all affected by her going missing in the manner she did. Zaid said she was always the life and soul, the glue that kept them together, and after she vanished – and especially after rumours started spreading that Vale might have had something to do with it – it created tension, resentment and paranoia.*' Patrick paused and I listened to the rain on the roof, my windscreen wipers sloshing back and forth. '*Zaid reckoned that a few of the guys he did the course with began turning on Vale. They'd refuse to speak to him. Vale would try to engage with them and they'd*' call him a "rapist" or a "killer". Zaid says he tried to avoid getting involved, but it was hard because he felt so upset by what had happened to Beatrix, and admitted being seduced by the pack mentality a couple of times. He said part of the reason it got so bad was because, a lot of the time, Vale would just sit there and take it; he'd just let them throw all these accusations at him, point fingers at him, sometimes push him around. Vale was a big guy – six two, seventeen stone – but Zaid said his temperament was the opposite. He looked like someone who'd been bullied for years and was conditioned to it. He was your classic loner.'

Either Patrick or the woman shifted position slightly.

'So,' Patrick continued, 'as I said, after Beatrix went missing, it sounds like it got messy: arguments, anger, a lot of fighting and accusations, and almost all of it was directed at Adrian Vale. The irony is, when Vale turned up dead on that beach in Sussex, Zaid said he read about it in the papers, then spent months feeling like he and the others were responsible. In his suicide note, there's a line where Vale mentioned being unhappy during his time at uni, so it's possible Zaid is right. He might not have pushed Vale that day, but all of them on that course – by virtue of how they behaved towards him – probably got Vale to the edge.'

'Or maybe they didn't,' the woman said.

'Right. Maybe Vale really, genuinely, was responsible for Beatrix going missing, he knew what happened to her afterwards, and he made that jump because he couldn't live with himself.'

I glanced at the Dictaphone.

Something had changed.

The trajectory of the conversation had altered.

I looked up at the road and then back to the passenger seat, the digital display a faint orange, the numbers slowly ticking over. Now the two of them were talking as if Adrian Vale *was* actually the man responsible for Beatrix's disappearance, not simply the man who'd taken the fall for it. I wheeled back in my thoughts to what the woman had said on tape when I'd first switched the Dictaphone on at Seiger and Sten: *I hurt her, and then I betrayed her, and then, when it was finally over, I buried her in the deepest hole I could find.* It had sounded so much like a confession, so obvious a proclamation of guilt. I'd been so on edge at Seiger and Sten – so conscious of being found there – that at the time I hadn't even stopped to consider an alternative, even though the fact that Patrick had seemed to go along with it – had even seemed accepting of the crime the woman was saying she'd committed – had always bothered me. But now everything was starting to jar.

'*Are you okay?*'

It was Patrick, his voice soft.

And then, slowly, as the silence rolled on, something else faded in, barely there at first, and then louder and louder until it was all I could hear.

Sobbing.

'*I know this is hard,*' Patrick continued, and I heard him move, and then the rustle of clothing as the two of them embraced.

'*I let her go,*' the woman said quietly.

'*You did what you thought was best.*'

'*I let her go,*' she repeated, the sentence dulled slightly by her mouth being so close to Patrick. '*I let her go. I never should have let her go . . .*'

'*Dave and Mira, they were good people. They really loved her.*'

'*I know,*' the woman said.

'*She had a happy childhood.*'

'*I know she did. I know they were good to her.*' The woman sniffed, coughed a little. '*But that doesn't make it better. I still gave her away.*'

'*You were fifteen.*'

'*She was my baby, Patrick.*'

Everything else faded except the voice on the tape.

'*Beatrix was my baby,*' the woman repeated, her words gluey and pained. '*She was my daughter – and I gave her away.*'

PART SIX
The Mother

I can hear a noise.

It's not what I've always assumed is a generator. It's not in my head either. The first few times, I started to worry that it was — that this was some consequence of my isolation, the start of an illness, except not one that would consume my body, but one that would demolish my mind. That's something that has troubled me since the very first moment I woke up here. When all you can see is darkness, when most of your time is spent in complete silence, when scenes from your life, faces you've pictured or conversations you've replayed aren't real, but imagined — constructed in the space behind your eyes — sudden noises aren't a reason to rejoice. They're a reason to be fearful and to panic.

Because you want them to be real.

You're just terrified they're not.

This one, though, is different. It feels different. When I clear my head, when I let the portraits of my family go, of my parents, of friends and people I worked with, of every single face I'm using to try and keep me sane, I can still hear the noise. It's not some remnant of a memory. It's real. It's here, as much a part of this place as this floor and these walls are, as I am. When I move, my muscles stiff, my body doughy from the lack of exercise, I can still hear it. When I eat — and the sound of my eating fills my ears — it doesn't go away.

I need to find out what it is.

I get on to my feet, arms out in front of me, and shuffle forward into the dark, in the direction of where I think it might be coming from. I don't know how this place looks in the light, if there was ever light here, but I know there must be doors, even though I can't find them, and I know it's fifty-two paces north to south and forty-seven paces west to east. I have no idea what's actually north, south, east or west, but I know which wall is which, so I give them compass points to help me navigate.

As I keep moving, following the direction of the noise, I can feel the uneven concrete floor beneath my feet. I've stopped wearing the shoes I was left: they're too uncomfortable, my toes too sore from where they didn't fit and kept rubbing. When the concrete gets too cold at night, and it can become as chilled as an ice rink, I use one of the blankets to wrap my feet up. I have two blankets now: a second was left for me a few days ago. Maybe a week. I didn't understand why to start with, but then I could feel it: the air, still and stale as it is, is mutating. The temperature's dropping.

One of my hands – out in front of me – hits the north wall and I realize I've allowed my thoughts to wander and lost count of my footsteps. Refocusing, I pause where I am and listen: this is the part of the room closest to where I think the sound is coming from. For a second it seems to stop, but then I press both hands to the wall, and I stand motionless and silent, and I hear it again. It's less frequent now, more distant, but it's here. Readjusting, I begin sidestepping to my right, keeping both hands on the wall. The walls are made from wood – oak, I think – huge, heavy slabs of it that stretch up higher than I can reach. I'm pretty tall, but even on tiptoes I can't feel the right angle where the walls must eventually meet the ceiling. One day, I tried launching one of the shoes into the space above my head, to see how far the room went up: in the centre, the only sound it made was when it landed on the floor again; at the edges, though, it was different – it hit the top with a brief, dull thump.

That was when I realized the room has a sloped ceiling.

As I think about the design of this place, I think about the man who put me here, who drugged me, picturing him in the final moments before my blackout. It's hard to remember much after that. I remember being blindfolded, gagged, my ears covered, but whatever he gave me, it messed with my head. My perspective, my reality. I had the vague sense of being carried somewhere, perhaps into the boot of a car or the back of a van – it felt like I was there for hours – except it seemed almost coffin-like, smaller than a boot should have been; certainly smaller than the back of a van. There was maybe the high-pitched hum of a vehicle engine at some point later on, but I'm not certain of that. Over the time I've been a prisoner in this room, I've started to worry that what I think was the sound of an engine is, in fact, an embellished moment, something that never took place, a recollection added because

I've been alone for so long, replaying the same memories so often that they've distorted and twisted out of shape. But then, at other times, I force myself to stick to what I remember. I tell myself I'm not mistaken. I did hear the drone of an engine. I was in a small, narrow space. And wherever I am, it's not a town or a city. There's nowhere in a city where the noise just stops like this. Wherever I was driven to, wherever this place is, it must be way out in the countryside. Somewhere remote.

So I don't know where I am, I just know who took me.

I know who he is.

But here, alone in this darkness, there's no one for me to tell.

45

The sun came up just before seven, bleeding out across the horizon, the sky blooming orange, and then pink, and then mauve. I sat at the window, watching it, bone-tired but unable to sleep, and waited for Healy to finish up in the kitchen. Apart from the sound of the kettle boiling, and the occasional moan from the cow sheds, it was quiet.

He limped through, the injuries Isaac Mills had inflicted on him still evident. He'd been awake when I got back, sitting alone in the pre-dawn blackness of the living room, waiting for me to return, and I told him about what I'd heard, and then played him the things that Patrick Perry and the woman had discussed during their meeting in the woman's car. That was where Patrick must have been going during his walks and why he always went alone. The two of us sat and listened to the tape in silence, to the sobs of Beatrix Steards's birth mother, her tears, the words she couldn't express. She'd never been a killer.

She'd just been a parent.

She was the woman who'd brought Beatrix into the world in March 1965, the woman who'd carried her for the nine months before that, and what she'd said to Patrick made perfect sense, because the hole she'd talked about burying Beatrix in had never been a physical one. Instead, the hole was the deepest, remotest part of her. It was a place in which she could try to inter the trauma of giving her baby away.

'So why would she want to know about Beatrix now?' Healy asked, half covered by shadows, his knuckles red from trying to fight off Mills. 'How did she even know Patrick to ask for his help?'

I tapped the top of the Dictaphone. 'She says why in a second,' I told him, because I'd heard the next ten minutes in the car before I'd got back to the farm. I'd heard her explain to Patrick the reasons why she needed to know the truth.

The answer to that was coming.

And so was something even bigger.

I continued to hear the same words being spoken for a second time – '*She was my baby, my daughter, and I gave her away*' – and then the woman said, '*Sorry. What a state I must look . . .*' I heard her sniff, clear her throat; imagined her getting herself together, trying to collect her thoughts. Eventually, she started speaking again, and though her words were soft, they were warm: '*I would never have thought of Beatrix for a name. It's actually lovely. I'm glad they called her that.*'

'*What did you want to call her?*'

'*Sophie.*'

'*That's pretty too.*'

'*It had been my grandmother's name. After the birth, after I held her in my arms, I looked at her and thought, "Sophie". It suited her so well.*'

'*What did your boyfriend think?*'

'*Not much, really. Simon Lenderith, his name was. We were both teenagers. The moment he found out I was pregnant, he basically abandoned us, so I did the whole thing on my own. Well, me and my mum. My dad didn't speak to me for five months after I told him I was going to have a baby.*' She made a sound: a short laugh, bereft of any humour. '*A teenage girl getting pregnant: that gets frowned upon even now, so imagine what it was like back then. But, you know, Dad was just a product of his time . . . I didn't blame him.*'

'What about this Lenderith guy?' Healy asked me. 'Is he relevant?'

'I don't think so,' I said. 'I tried looking him up just now, and the only Simon Lenderith I could find, who's about the right age, died back in October 2011.'

'*I always dreamed she would come and find me.*'

The woman had started talking again.

'*Beatrix?*'

'*Yes. When she was eighteen, I prayed that she would want answers, that we could sit down together and I could explain everything. I just wanted the chance to meet her, even if only once. It was so crazy: it started, quite literally, the moment I gave her away, the idea that I needed to explain why, that I needed to tell her that – despite what I'd done – I loved her. And that obsession with telling her, it would colour everything.'* Her voice had collapsed almost to a whisper, making it harder to hear now, even with the volume up. *'I was born up here, but because my father was in the air force, we moved down south when I was two years old. So by the time he retired and decided to move us all back up to Yorkshire again, I was seventeen, and do you know what I kept thinking? I kept thinking, "How will Sophie be able to find me in Yorkshire?" I mean, it was a naive, childlike thought, but it would keep me awake at night. I had no idea where she was living, if she was even still in the London area, but that was what I was thinking: "How will she find me if I move counties? How will she find me up here?" In my teens, my twenties, it troubled me so much . . .'*

Healy glanced at me.

I could almost see the gears cranking behind his eyes.

'I've been so lucky in my life otherwise,' the woman said, still wounded, still distressed, her words cut through with the weight of her history. *'Well, for the most part. I mean, we all have our battles, don't we? Life sometimes treats us in a way that isn't fair. But I live in a beautiful part of the world and have neighbours I adore. I have a wonderful husband who I love. I have two amazing kids. But what I did to Beatrix, it kills me. I try not to show it in front of John, with Ian on Skype, when we visit Rina, but it cuts me so deep. I think sometimes it's worse than the cancer.'*

Healy glanced at me for a second time.

We'd both been wrong.

Because of the southern accent, because these meetings had taken place away from the village, because all the women in Black Gale, except Francesca, were born – and, we'd assumed, raised – up north, we'd thought that this woman was entirely new to us.

But she wasn't.

She'd been right there all along.

It was Freda Davey.

46

'Freda,' Healy said softly, almost to himself.

I remembered the Skype call I'd had with Rina Blake where she'd talked about her mum: how Freda had never placed much importance on a career because she'd just always wanted to be a mother. I remembered what Ross had said right back at the start, about how she could be a mother-hen type. Now it seemed obvious why.

Her southern accent had thrown me when I'd heard it on the tape, had me looking in another direction, away from Black Gale. But, instead, the answer about who the woman was had been at our starting point all along. Patrick's investigation hadn't been triggered by a request from a stranger, and it wasn't an affair with someone mysterious and unknown. It was a friendship built much closer to home.

Literally next door.

'So now we know who she is,' Healy said.

I paused the recording and the cottage became quiet.

'And we know who Beatrix Steards was to her.'

His eyes fell on the Dictaphone again.

'That just leaves the question of why Freda went looking for Beatrix after all this time.'

I shook my head. 'We know why.'

'Do we?'

'She got cancer again.'

Healy frowned. He looked tired, like me, but he was beaten too, bruised and in pain, and it was stopping him from thinking as clearly as he would normally.

'From what I've been able to find out,' I said, 'she went to see her GP in the middle of August and was then back at the hospital in September. She told Rina that doctors reckoned it was early days and the cancer was treatable, which was why she decided to delay treatment for a few months. You remember she told that nurse she wanted to go on holiday?'

'To Australia.' Healy nodded. 'Her dream trip.'

'Right. It was in the Black Gale file. Thing is, though, I don't think she ever had any intention of making that trip. That wasn't why she delayed treatment.' I tapped out a rhythm on the table, trying to put it all together in my head. 'Rina said her mum was scared about the idea of more chemo because the first round had been absolutely brutal, so a more likely reason is that she wanted to give herself some extra time to prepare physically and mentally for what was coming.'

'But it was the holiday thing that became the narrative,' Healy said quietly.

He was starting to get it now, just the same as me.

I looked at the wall, where photos of Freda Davey had hung the day before. 'None of the Black Gale investigators so much as even *spoke* to Freda's oncologist. It was a line of enquiry that got missed entirely in the middle of a frantic search for nine people, and also because they already had an explanation for her delaying – she'd planned to take a holiday. And, ultimately, as bad as the news was for Freda, getting cancer again wouldn't have seemed like a starting point for a whole village disappearing. So, her delaying her treatment made sense, whether for a holiday – as she'd told a few people – or because she was scared, as Rina suspected, and after that the search became about everything *except* her illness –'

'When, in fact, her illness was where it all began.'

I nodded, glancing at the Dictaphone again.

I'd heard the next part once already, so I knew exactly what was still to come, including the final truth.

It was just that a part of me didn't want to have to listen to it again.

I pushed Play.

'*Like I told you before,*' Freda said, '*in my teens, into my mid twenties, the idea that Beatrix might not be able to find me, it played on my mind so much. But then I had Ian, and Rina three years later, and that feeling . . . I guess it sort of went away for a while.'* She stopped, sounding unconvinced at her choice of words. *'Well, not away. It never went away. Not really. I suppose what I mean is I could pretend to forget it all, because I had a son and a daughter who I didn't ever have to let go of, who I loved without apology, without having to justify or rationalize it. But then, in the middle of August, when I started to suspect the cancer had come back, I realized something: I'd never buried her memory at all. I didn't bury her memory when she was born, I didn't do it after I saw her face in the papers. Ever since she vanished, it's been a crushing weight I can't shift.'*

Silence: sombre, bleak.

'I just want to know what happened to her,' Freda said.

'I know,' Patrick responded softly. *'I promise I'm doing my best. I've seen a copy of the original police report. I've spoken to Robert Zaid, to some of the others she was on that Politics course with. I've got another call lined up for tomorrow afternoon. I'm going to use a payphone – I've bought one of those calling cards – so there's no record of it at home. I told Fran I'm meeting a client.'*

'I'm so sorry I'm asking you to sneak around like this.'

'It's fine. Like I said, though, I hate lying to her. I'm starting to think that she suspects something's going on – that she knows this whole photography thing is just a smokescreen for something else – and it's so hard not being able to tell her the truth.'

'I know. I know it's hard.'

It sounded like Patrick was drumming his fingers against the dashboard.

'The thing is, Freda, Fran would understand if I told her what's going on. She's a mother too. She'd instantly get it – the need to find out what happened to Beatrix, the search for closure. I mean, you've seen what she's been like since you told everyone the news about the cancer. She's a nurse. She helps people.'

Everything went quiet for a moment.

This was what had been missed.

This was what no one but Patrick, Freda and her oncologist knew.

'*I know Fran would want to help.*' Freda's voice had started to become muted. I reached over and turned up the volume. '*But no one can do anything for me now.*'

'*There must be something.*'

'*It's okay. I've made my peace with it.*'

'*But I can't . . . I just . . .*'

'*It's okay, Patrick. Really.*'

'*But it's not, is it? It's not okay.*'

'*No, it's not. But sometimes that's how life is.*'

Healy glanced at me, fully understanding now.

There was another lull, this time for longer, and it was unmistakably a kind of mourning. Because, in reality, Freda hadn't delayed her chemo due to the overwhelming nature of the treatment, or because she was frightened, and she definitely hadn't delayed it for a holiday. She'd done it because she didn't want to tell her husband, or her children, or her friends, the devastating truth – a truth that only her, her oncologist and Patrick Perry ever knew about.

The doctors hadn't caught it early.

The treatment would never cure her.

Freda Davey's cancer had been terminal.

47

This had all begun with a woman's illness.

The recording continued, the numbers ticking over, Patrick and Freda silent. The lull in conversation spoke eloquently of a friendship – one soon to be over.

'It's okay,' she said eventually. *'It doesn't matter about that. I've been over it and over it, and it's not going to change. So now I just need to know about Beatrix.'*

Again, Healy and I looked at each other across the table, but this time neither of us said anything. We didn't need to. We recognized the pain in Freda's voice, the fear of what was coming, of going to her grave without doing all that she needed to do. I'd seen the same look in my wife's face before her death; Healy had seen the echoes in his own reflection in the months after his daughter had been murdered. The fights they'd had that he wished he could take back. The things he'd said that he'd have given his life to erase.

Death was about love, and about grief.

But more often it was about regret.

'Patrick?'

Our attention returned to the Dictaphone.

'Yes, of course,' he replied, his words delivered in a rush of breath, a sigh which seemed to, once again, impart how he felt towards Freda. *'Like I say, I hopefully might get somewhere with this call I'm going to make tomorrow afternoon.'*

'Okay. I appreciate it.'

'I just want to do the best job I can for you . . .'

'I know. And you are.'

A pause. *'Why don't you just tell him?'*

There was no response from Freda.

'You should tell him,' Patrick said again, more forcefully, but

without any sharpness to his tone. '*You're sick, and before . . . you know, before you . . .*' His words fell away. He couldn't bring himself to say *die*. '*Before it happens, you want to find out what happened to Beatrix. Everyone will understand that, Freda. Everyone. You told us about the illness, and you saw how we all rallied around, and John loves you more than anyone. Beatrix was your daughter, you were her mum. He'll get it.*'

'*I can't,*' Freda replied.

'*John's your husband. He'll understand. He will.*'

'*No.*' It was said with strength this time. '*He can barely even cope with the fact that the cancer's back, let alone it being terminal. I mean, I can't look him in the face most of the time these days because it just sets us both off. So, me running around, destroying any hope of prolonging my life as I spend my time trying to find out what happened to the daughter I gave away . . .*' I heard movement again: the creak of a seat. '*No. I'm not telling John.*'

'*Does he even know about Beatrix?*'

'*No. When I saw her photograph in the newspapers, that birthmark on her face, when they said she disappeared the day before her birthday, I knew it was her. I knew it. And that was when I should have sat John down and told him. He would have accepted it, I know he would. He's such a good man. But I just . . .*' A sniff. '*I should have told him from the start, I know that, but I was just so ashamed.*'

'*You have nothing to feel ashamed about.*'

'*I gave my daughter away,*' she replied, her words subdued, '*and I never told my husband about it. I never told my kids. I have plenty to feel ashamed for.*'

It was obvious why she'd turned to Patrick to try and bring some closure. The police hunt had hit a wall back in 1987 and had lain dormant for twenty-eight years, and Patrick was a talented journalist, a friend she could trust, he had huge experience in hunting down leads, and he would want to help. Plus, she knew that if she asked him not to tell her husband – or mention it to Francesca, in case it got back to John that way – Patrick would do that as well. He was a man of his word.

If he knew anything, it was how to keep secrets.

Finally, the tape came to an end.

Quietly, Healy said, 'Something makes sense now.'

'What?'

'When we found those audio bugs in the houses, there were five in each, but the Perrys and the Daveys had different *types* of devices from the Gibbses – different designs – and to Randolph and Emiline as well. You remember that?'

I did.

'The Perrys' and Daveys' were smaller,' he said, 'harder to find; and in the other two houses, they were bigger, without the equalizer bars on them.'

'Now we know why.'

'The Perry and the Davey bugs went in at a different stage to the other two.' And then he followed the idea to its natural conclusion: 'They probably went in earlier because it was Patrick and Freda that were the focal point.'

I nodded. 'Because they were looking into Beatrix Steards's disappearance.'

Healy squeezed his eyes shut, as if he didn't want to have to think about where this was going. But he knew, the same as me: it was bad now and was only getting worse.

'So the bugs were in their homes before they even disappeared,' Healy said.

Tori Gibbs had said something, back at the start, that I'd filed away and almost forgotten about. I couldn't refer to the actual quote in my notebook, because the page had been torn out by Mills and whoever he came with, but I recalled enough. She'd been talking about Chris, about her brother actually building the houses, and had said something that didn't seem important at the time.

The village had only just got decent broadband.

I called Tori. It was early, but she was already up, so I reminded her of what she'd said and asked what she knew about the Internet at Black Gale.

'Not much,' she said. 'Chris just mentioned they were all being upgraded.'

'At the same time?'

'No. I think he said they could only do it in blocks because everything was so far from the telephone exchange. I mean, you know how remote that village is.'

'Do you know what he meant by "blocks"?'

'Like, a house at a time, I guess.'

Or two.

I had the phone on speaker.

Healy and I glanced at each other.

'Do you remember when that upgrade started, Tori? It might be important.'

'I don't know.' She sighed. I could hear the journalist in her, the texture in her reply as she realized she was being led. 'Probably not long before they all vanished, I guess. A week maybe? Ten days?'

I flicked a look at Healy again.

'Why?' she asked.

'I'm trying to work out who upgraded their broadband.'

'You don't think it was the phone company?'

'No, it's not that,' I lied, 'it's just a gap in my paperwork, and I'm trying to make sure we've got as complete a picture of the run-up to Halloween as possible.'

It was fiction, and maybe she knew it, but I needed time to process what Healy and I had just found out before I was ready to share it with anyone else.

Healy rubbed at his forehead as I hung up.

'They posed as engineers from the phone company,' he muttered, so quietly it was almost like he was telling himself. He looked up. 'Do you think it was Mills?'

I shrugged. 'There's probably no way of knowing now.'

Healy was looking at the empty wall, studying it so closely it was like all the information we'd gathered was still up there. Eventually, he said, 'So I get why Patrick and Freda were targeted.

They started looking into Beatrix Steards.' He was still staring at the barren wall. 'What I don't get is, why bug all four houses and why take all nine people from Black Gale? It's miles more complicated, it's much riskier, and it didn't need to be done, anyway. You reckon it was wrong place, wrong time?'

'You mean, they were all at the farmhouse, so it was just easier to take all nine of them when they came for Freda and Patrick?' I shook my head. 'I don't think so.'

Abducting nine people was hard, it had the potential to go badly wrong very quickly, and none of the others posed a threat – so why bother involving them? Plus, whoever it was who'd come to Black Gale that night – whether it was Mills, Pierce, someone else or all of them – they wouldn't have come unprepared. They'd been listening and watching Patrick and Freda for at least a week, possibly more, so they would have known about the dinner party; and even if, as unlikely as it was, they hadn't known about the gathering until they actually arrived at the village, they'd have seen it and surely decided that any abduction was too risky.

'Maybe the other villagers knew,' Healy said.

'You mean, they knew about Freda and Patrick's search for Beatrix?'

He shrugged. 'That would explain the need to take all nine of them.'

It would, and although Freda had been adamant she didn't want anyone knowing at the time Patrick had recorded her, that she didn't want her family thinking that her focus was on anything other than spending time with them and getting better, it didn't mean she hadn't changed her mind in the two days after. She'd already told the other villagers she was sick again. She could easily have gone on to tell them the cancer was terminal.

And maybe, at the dinner, she'd spoken about Beatrix as well.

'But why wouldn't she have told her kids first?'

Healy shook his head. 'Maybe it was harder for her to do that. Sometimes it's like that: when you love someone, you don't want them to hurt.'

I looked at him, surprised at the tenderness of the comment: it was a response that went way beyond this moment, back to decisions and situations Healy had long since left behind, but what he was saying was true.

Sometimes the hardest conversations were with the ones we loved the most.

Even if that turned out to be the case, though, there was still so much about that night that didn't make sense. Why were there no tyre tracks belonging to any other cars? Why were there no footprints except the villagers'?

I took a breath, trying to clear my head.

'What about the other box full of clothes?' Healy asked.

It was a good question. There had been two large cardboard boxes in the hidden room at Seiger and Sten, one full of items belonging to the Black Gale villagers, the other packed with random clothes, a smashed iPad, phones and a power bank.

'You reckon it might be more victims?'

We looked at each other.

It was the first time we'd used that word.

Victims.

'I hope not,' I said, but it was a response without much conviction, because I didn't know what the box meant, how many people its contents belonged to, over what period of time they had been collected – or where we'd find the owners.

Maybe in the same place we find the villagers.

'What's on your mind, Raker?'

'I just don't know where other missing people would fit in,' I said. 'I don't see where they sit alongside what went on at Black Gale and what happened to Beatrix Steards.'

And I stopped short of saying the rest.

That a part of me didn't *want* to know.

'What about this Robert Zaid guy?' Healy pressed.

'What about him?'

'You still think he's worth speaking to?'

'I just know he's a link to Beatrix Steards,' I said, 'and that Beatrix is a link to Black Gale.'

'So you're going to try and arrange a meeting with him?'

'Yes,' I said, nodding.

My eyes went to what was left of my notebook.

'But there's something else I'm going to try and do first.'

The Photograph Album

Los Angeles | *Wednesday 19 May*

'Detective Kader? Are you okay?'

Jo didn't hear the voice to start with.

She was miles away, watching cars pass on Temple Street, three floors below, the sun winking off their roofs as they moved between the dual shadows of City Hall and the Federal Courthouse. After fifteen years as a detective, she'd been back and forth to Downtown so many times, to the DA's office here, to the Halls of Justice, out to the county jail and Twin Towers Correctional Facility, she could probably make the drive blindfolded.

'Detective Kader?'

Opposite her, a woman in her late thirties leaned forward in her chair, and Jo remembered where she was and what they'd been doing before she'd drifted off. On the desk, next to a PC, was a nameplate: DR LEILA BARNES, EMPLOYEE SUPPORT SERVICES UNIT.

'Are you okay, Detective Kader?'

'Sorry,' Jo said, and held up an apologetic hand.

'I was asking about your son.'

'Right.'

'How's he doing?'

'He's doing fine. He's in fourth grade now.'

'So he's – what? – nine years old?'

'Correct.'

'It won't be long before he's off to middle school.'

'And then he'll be a teenager and I'll officially have to sacrifice my sanity.' Jo smiled. 'No, Ethan's a good kid.' She felt something flutter in her throat, like a filament about to burn out. 'Have you got children, Dr Barnes?'

'One. A daughter. She's three.'

'Well, enjoy it. The time goes by so fast.'

Barnes nodded. 'Do *you* enjoy it?'

'Of course. I love being a mom.'

'I sense a "but"?'

'No buts.' Jo shrugged. 'Or maybe one. With the job that I do, sometimes it can be hard to find an equilibrium.' She glanced out of the window again. 'What if, huh?'

Barnes frowned. 'What if?'

'What if I'd made different choices?'

'From looking at your file, your choices seem pretty good.'

'They were choices,' Jo replied. 'I don't know if they were good.'

She looked at Barnes and knew what the psychologist was seeing: the hint of something in Jo's face – monochrome where it should have been colour.

Barnes said, 'You told me in our last session that perhaps one day you might like to teach.' She flipped through the pages of her pad. 'Does that still interest you?'

'Maybe. Lecturing, that sort of thing.'

Barnes nodded. 'Do you think you would miss being a cop?'

Jo let out a long breath. 'I don't know. It would be different, obviously. I mean, I wouldn't be getting calls at one in the morning because some asshole has blown a hole in his wife's chest, but I imagine that buzz you get on cases – you would miss it sometimes.' She watched as Barnes made notes. 'Although, I don't know if "buzz" is the right word exactly. I've been a cop for over eighteen years, and at some point that buzz became more like a . . .' She sighed, searching for the word.

'A debt?'

Jo glanced at Dr Barnes.

'Exactly,' she said. 'Exactly.'

Her eyes stayed on the psychologist, trying to read her, finding something in Barnes's choice of phrase that she identified with instantly. *A debt.* That was exactly what it was.

'But for now,' Barnes said, moving on, 'you're still a cop?'

'I'm still a cop, yeah.'

'Did you always want to work homicides?'

'Always,' she said. 'I never wanted to do anything else. I guess, to start with, I wanted to be a cop because I was an obstinate jerk and needed to prove that I was just as capable as any man. It was hard, though. When I graduated from the academy in '74, it was still compulsory for female deputies to wear heels, skirts and lipstick.' She flashed Barnes a humourless smile and, for a second, the psychologist broke from her professional sobriety and rolled her eyes. 'That rule got tossed in the trash soon after – but there was plenty more garbage to go around. You remember the Night Stalker?'

'Sure. It's pretty hard to forget a man like Richard Ramirez.'

'You probably know all this already then, or you've heard, but while he was busy putting the city on its knees in '85, the push to track him down turned into one of the biggest manhunts in the entire history of US law enforcement. Plus, we were in the middle of a crack epidemic too. What I'm saying is, I'd been a detective for seven years by that time, and I alone was catching at least one new homicide every week. So, after seven years, I had a ton of experience. But do you know when I got asked to join the Night Stalker task force?'

Dr Barnes shook her head.

'Never,' Jo said. 'I did zero hours on that. They didn't trust me.'

'Because you were a woman?'

'Sure, that was most of it. But also because I had the temerity to rely on instinct sometimes. I mean, I know police work. I *know* it. I know when something doesn't feel right, even if I don't have the proof; even if the evidence *says* it's right. But, after a while, I stopped saying stuff like that at the station. I learned that lesson – probably too late, actually.' Jo came to a halt, not liking the anger rising in her voice. 'But you know something? Since Rodney

King, since the riots, the old guard – the old way of thinking and doing things – it's starting to get dismantled, and things are slowly starting to change. I don't want to be some token appointment, have never wanted a job just because some arbitrary quota system says I should have it. But it's 1993, I've eaten a whole hill of shit in the LASD for more than eighteen years because I'm a woman, and probably set my career back another five just by having the sheer impudence to get pregnant, so you know what?'

Barnes shook her head.

· 'When I got a call from the LAPD last week and they started telling me they're pushing for better race relations, as well as more senior female officers, and that they'd admired my work in the Sheriff's Department, you bet I sat there and let them make their pitch. I listened to them offer me a job in Robbery-Homicide – a *lieutenant* in RHD, no less – and I didn't spend one single second interrupting them, even though I knew the whole thing was purely driven by politics. You know why I kept so quiet?'

'Why?'

'Because I would deserve every dollar I got.'

'You sound like you might take it.'

Jo shrugged. 'I might, or I might not.'

Dr Barnes worked in the Employee Support Services Unit – or what LASD staff more commonly referred to as 'Psych Services' – not out on the front lines, so this news was going nowhere: it was all protected by doctor–patient privilege.

It was exactly why Jo kept coming.

Originally, she'd agreed to the counselling because it gave her a chance to vent to someone who knew how the LASD worked, and it got her out of the office a couple of times a month. But now it was more than that: it was an ongoing conversation about life, about her choices, about acceptance and loss.

'How long have the LAPD given you to decide?' Dr Barnes asked.

'A couple of days. I told them I needed time to think about it.'

Jo reached forward and picked up her glass of water.

'And *have* you been thinking about it?'

'Pretty much constantly.'

Barnes was studying Jo, a slant to her face as if she knew something else was coming. 'Detective Kader?'

'I think I've been coming long enough for you to call me Jo.'

Barnes smiled. 'Jo, then. Was there something else?'

'It can be hard, that's all.'

'What do you mean?'

'I mean, it's the job I deserve, but I don't know if it's the one I should take.'

'Why not?'

Jo thought of Ethan, pictured him that morning at the table, eating his cereal while telling her about a book they'd been reading at school about a lonely wolf pup.

'My son, Ethan,' she said, one hand on her water, 'I reckon he'd probably say I was a pretty good mom. A definite pass, but maybe not top marks. Parenting is one of those jobs you never really master. It's got a learning curve like this' – she held up her spare hand at ninety degrees – 'so anyone who tells you they've got it figured out is a liar. All you can really hope for is that you make more right choices than wrong ones.'

Jo looked out of the window again and could make out a vague reflection of herself, her face pale, ghostly, her eyes painted with blobs of light.

'I'm not sure I ever told you this,' she said, quieter now, the words harder to say, 'but a long time ago, my husband gave me this picture album for my birthday. Ira was really good at taking pictures – and so, up until Ethan was six, he took all these photographs of us on outings we'd have, on vacation, even while we were sitting around at home. And so he gave me this album as a present, and I thought it was a sweet thing to do, but as I opened it up and started flicking through the pages, I began to realize something: there would be months between pictures of me. It was all about Ethan, obviously, so there were a ton of pictures of him, and Ira was the one with the camera, which meant there were shots of them at the beach, in parks, on jungle gyms, in bounce houses, playing soccer, having frozen yoghurt, a whole bunch of things. But, whenever *I* was featured, we were at home, Ethan was always in his PJs, and he was usually full of snot or running a temperature or sick from some bug. Man, I remember feeling really annoyed about it to start with – how this album featured all these photos of them doing fun stuff, and then me with Ethan when he looked sad, and tired, and grumpy – to the point where I thought, "I'm definitely going to say something to Ira." And then a couple of weeks after that, late at night, as I was driving back from the station, something suddenly occurred to me. Ethan was always sick in the pictures of me and him because, when he had a cold, or he couldn't breathe, or whatever it was, he didn't sleep. The illness would knock him out of his routine, and so he'd be getting up earlier and going to bed later. But once he was *back* in his routine, I'd be leaving before he was up and getting home after he was asleep.'

Her eyes dropped to her glass of water.

'There were no pictures of me doing the fun stuff – going to the beach, or eating ice cream – because I . . .' Jo's voice faded. 'Well, because basically I was never around.'

There were no tears in her eyes.

Not yet.

But she could feel them coming.

'There are cases I've had that I've found impossible to let go.' She stopped, dug around in her jacket pocket and came back with a small notebook. Its edges were tattered. She laid it down on the table between her and Dr Barnes, slid a finger inside and flipped it open to a well-worn section in the middle. Her handwriting was small, detailed, deliberately hard to read, but the title at the top was bigger and much clearer.

It was a case number.

#4729-81.

Underneath that was an address.

Star Inn, 1005 La Cienega.

'That,' she said, putting a finger to it, 'that's the one that got away.'

Barnes came forward in her seat, laying her legal pad down on the table next to her, trying her best to make out Jo's handwriting.

Under the address were three lines.

Gabriel Wilzon. Donald Klein.

Acid. Bathtub.

~~*Vale?*~~

'The thing is, though,' Jo said, her throat taut, her emotions much harder to suppress now, 'you have to make a decision. I still think about this case now. I think about what I might have missed, what I could have done better, how I might have wasted time chasing the wrong person for the wrong crime. But that debt you talked about earlier – that commitment you feel to the dead – at some point, if you don't want it to rip your family apart, you have to make your peace with it and let it go. As hard as it is, and it's *hard*, you need to accept that you're not going to be as effective as a cop, you're going to be twenty, thirty per cent less engaged than you should be, but you're going to have a kid that actually talks about you as if you exist, and looks at you like you aren't a total fucking stranger.' She paused. 'I just realized it all way too late.'

'Because you were working this case?'

'It definitely contributed to my blindness,' Jo replied. 'The whole time I was trying to figure out the truth, even years later, I overlooked things I shouldn't have.'

'Like what?'

'Like, periodically, all the way through those first six years of Ethan's life, Ira would complain about these headaches he was getting. I just thought it was his job, or working from home, or looking after Ethan during the day, so I told him to take painkillers and then left him to go to the next crime scene, and the next one, and the next one. Two months after he gave me that photo

330

album, I got home one night, and Ethan wasn't asleep in bed, he was lying on the floor of the living room, just sobbing.'

'Because of Ira,' Barnes said delicately, shuffling back in her seat.

'Right.' Jo nodded. 'He'd suffered a brain aneurysm.'

Jo pushed a smile to the surface, an attempt to show some stoicism, but it was a phoney reaction, one that didn't belong, and it vanished almost as soon as it formed.

'I went into the living room, and I found my son lying next to his dad, his face literally scarlet from all the tears he'd shed for Ira, and I tried to comfort him, tried to take him in my arms, but he wouldn't even let me touch him. He wriggled free from me every time I tried to hug him. He kept going back to Ira's body, over and over, and just kissing his dad on the face.' This time, her eyes blurred. 'He didn't want me because he didn't really know me any more. It was like my son barely recognized me.' She looked down at the notebook, still open between them, at her words, the ink, the blemishes on the pages. 'Once things had settled down, Ethan and I grew closer. I've made it up to him, I've sacrificed that twenty or thirty per cent at work and have become a worse cop in order to be a better mom – and it's been worth it. It's been totally worth it. I mean, I could have already been an LT, not only getting there now – but I made a choice and sacrificed that chance because I love my son.'

Slowly, she drew the notebook back towards her.

'But you know what the worst thing is? Despite all the lessons I had to learn, all the heartache and guilt I had to endure when Ira died, how much I *love* Ethan with every atom in my body, there still isn't a month that's gone by – not a single one in eight years – when I haven't opened this up, and . . .' She stopped, shaking her head, pressing a finger to the names most prominent on the page. *Gabriel Wilzon. Donald Klein.* 'I can't forget it,' she said, wiping her tears away. 'That's all. I need to solve it. And I know I won't find any peace until I do.'

48

Her full name was Amelia Griffin.

She and her two children lived in Undercliffe, a small suburb to the north-east of Bradford city centre. I'd got her address from the registration plate of her car and now I was sitting in the front of mine, watching her house from a bend in the street about two hundred feet further down. I'd already been to Isaac Mills's, because the initial plan had been to confront him, but his Lexus was gone and his house alarm had been set.

I'd come for answers, not codes.

Not keys.

We were past that now.

I'd spent two hours outside his house, had gone to Keighley town centre, to the mill again, walked the streets and parks surrounding his property, before returning to his house for another three-hour sit-in, and he hadn't come up for air once. I'd phoned Seiger and Sten and, when one of Jacob Pierce's staff had picked up, I'd pretended that I'd recently done some work with Mills but had lost his contact details, and they told me they'd never heard of him. It had sounded genuine too, the woman's confusion hard to fabricate, so — as a final move — I'd tried phoning Mills's mobile. It went straight to voicemail.

After I rang off, I started to realize something: because whatever Mills was doing for Jacob Pierce was completely off the books, so was anything that happened to him as a consequence. I'd looked at his empty house, its shutters closed, and had started to wonder if someone had discovered what he'd done for me. I was so conflicted about Mills, I didn't even know how to process the feeling. I still wasn't sure if I could trust him. And yet he'd given me the alarm code and the key to Pierce's hidden room.

He'd led me to the clothes.

The conversation between Patrick and Freda.

I looked down into my lap, at his handwriting, the sequence he'd written on the reverse of the Dictaphone: *G76984Z*. I still hadn't worked out what it meant, but he'd put it there for me to see. It was there, too, because he didn't want to be found out. That was why the clues were so subtle: he was trying to fly low.

But maybe they hadn't been subtle enough.

Someone opened the front door of Melia Griffin's house: it was her fifteen-year-old daughter, her face fixed on the screen of her phone. I watched her go, head down, still staring at her mobile, and then – ten seconds later – her mother came to the door, opening it a sliver and looking out to where the girl was going. She didn't want her daughter to see her, to know that she was checking on her, conscious of embarrassing her. The girl was long past waving goodbye as she walked away – didn't even look up from her phone – but her mum watched her all the way to the end of the street and, when she was gone, Melia lingered there for a second. It was such a delicate and natural moment, a mother still finding it hard to let go, even now, that – for a second – I lost sight of my reason for being here, thinking of my own daughter instead, almost twice the age of Melia's. I pictured Annabel, and then Olivia. I wondered what they were doing.

And then the door closed again.

Back in the present, I decided to drive all the way to Keighley again, to see if Mills had returned, but the house was exactly as I'd left it, and when I got back to Melia Griffin's place again, I slipped into the same holding pattern as before, filling my time by replaying sections of the conversation between Patrick and Freda. I listened to their voices and then looked at my notebook, at the frayed margins where some of the pages had been torn out, at others that I'd filled up in the hours since. I got my mobile and went through the pictures I'd taken in the room at Seiger and Sten: the clothes, the smashed iPad and phones, the driving licences behind windows in wallets. And then I looked up and the sun had begun to set, the brightness of the sky giving way to a mauve sweep. The daughter was arriving home again, her eyes still fixed on her phone.

As she let herself in, reality started to hit me: no matter how long I sat waiting – or how patient I was – Mills wasn't coming here.

He wasn't going home either.

But that didn't mean Melia couldn't tell me where he was.

49

Melia and her kids lived in an end terrace, a short alleyway running along the left edge of the property, their back garden ending at a row of high laurel bushes, as thick and as opaque as a wall.

I moved along the alleyway first, giving myself some time to think: just knocking on the door was never going to cut it. It would put her on edge. I had to know exactly what I was going to say. At the petrol station, when we'd first met, she'd struggled to remember me, and I had no idea what Mills might have said in the meantime if she'd asked who I was. He could have lied and said that I *was* the person I'd pretended to be, a guy she and Isaac had bumped into in town a few weeks before that. Or he could have told her that he had no idea who I was.

I doubted that he'd told her the actual truth, though.

I stopped, level with the end of the back garden, using the gathering shadows as a way to take in the property. Because it had been warm this afternoon – or, at least, a lot warmer than previous days – the kitchen window was open, and so was the window of one of the bedrooms on the second floor, and in both I could see movement: Melia was standing at the sink, and her son was in his room, playing video games.

I waited some more, watching.

She was leaning against one of the kitchen units now, her body side-on to me, her head bowed, her face painted a soft, pale grey.

It looked like she was texting.

Upstairs, a second light came on and I saw the daughter enter the next room along from her brother's, still doing something on her mobile. Below her, Melia had exited the kitchen and was heading into the living room. I couldn't see much of it, but I could see enough: the television was on in there and she'd collapsed into the sofa, curling her legs up and under her.

A side gate opened on to the back garden. It wasn't locked, just latched, so I pushed at it, left it ajar, and then stopped short of the ground-floor window. When I peered in, looking through the kitchen into the living room, Melia was still where I'd last seen her.

But she'd left her phone on the kitchen counter.

Maybe I didn't need to find a way to speak to her after all.

I glanced around me, along the row of terraces, making sure there were no eyes on me, but I was at too tight an angle for anyone to see. The only danger came from people walking along the alleyway that connected Melia's street to the next.

I looked at her phone again.

Using the open window, I reached in and grabbed it.

As soon as I had it, I hurried back to the car – but then, almost instantly, it started chirping as a series of texts came through, their sound catching me totally unaware, resonant in the stillness of the evening. I tried to suppress the noise by closing my fist around the handset, but then it beeped again, and again, Whats-App alerts blinking on the display, and as I got to the Audi, I looked back at the windows of the property, at the homes adjacent to it, expecting to see Melia looking out at me, or one of the neighbours, or both. But there was no one.

The street was still quiet.

I unlocked the car and slid in at the wheel, knowing what a risk it was taking the phone. I had no sight of Melia or her movements. She might already be looking for the mobile. That meant I needed to go through it as fast as possible.

There was a numbered passcode but, by tilting the phone to the light, I could see tiny clusters of fingerprints where – over a long period of time – she'd repeatedly put her password in. I tried entering the code, following the pattern of prints.

It didn't work the first two times.

But on the third I got it.

As soon as I was in, I went to her texts, looking for Isaac Mills. His was the fourth name down. When I tapped on the thread,

336

I saw that the last conversation between the two of them had taken place the evening before. I swiped up, trying to get to the beginning of it. For the most part, it had been pretty low-key, the two of them talking about the lunch they'd had at the mill the day before, Melia joking that seeing Mills had saved her from the ritual boredom of another Inset day, which was why the kids hadn't been at school.

And then I got to the end – and the reason Mills wasn't there.

I've got to go away for a couple of days with work. Sorry. I should be back by the w/end.

The old "work trip", eh? ☺

Ha ha. Yep, that old excuse. If it's any consolation, it'll be exceptionally boring.

Doesn't sound boring to me! Where are you going?

I've got to go and see someone in London. Highgate. It's a bit posh there, just like me ☺

I stared at the screen.
He'd made light of it, but it wasn't a joke.
Highgate was where Robert Zaid lived.

50

By the time I arrived home the next day, London was fading into dusk, my house consumed by the dark. I pulled on to the drive and paused for a moment, looking at the SOLD sign in the front garden, blown to an angle by the wind. After the case I'd had at Christmas, something had changed here: a psychological rot had begun to infect the rooms I'd once shared with my wife, and now it was hard for me to look at it, let alone live in it. This building was no longer a home, it was just a place I'd come back to, a space I slept in and left as soon as I could. I knew that, deep down, the connection I felt to missing people was most of why I'd agreed to go to Yorkshire. I wanted answers to what had happened out at Black Gale. I wanted to help the families. I wanted the truth. But there had been another reason as well.

A more selfish one.

I didn't want to be inside these walls any more.

I unlocked the house and jumped straight in the shower. I felt the water run off me, turned the temperature up and let the heat scorch my skin, and – afterwards, as I sat on the edge of the bed, surrounded by the gathering darkness – I looked at the inky bruises Isaac Mills had left me with.

I texted Annabel to tell her I was back in London and that I'd give her a call in the morning as I had a meeting over in Highgate and probably wouldn't be back until late, and then – just as I was getting dressed – my phone started to buzz on the bed.

It was the number of a hotel just outside Luton.

'Shame you're not earning loyalty points for all these rooms you're paying for,' Healy said when I answered. That made me smile, despite myself. 'I'm checking in.'

'Is everything okay?'

'Yeah, everything seems fine.'

'Okay,' I said. 'Stay where you are until I call.'

'And when'll that be?'

'I don't know. Just sit tight.'

He didn't respond to that.

'You all set for Zaid?' he asked eventually.

'Yeah,' I said. 'His PA called an hour ago to confirm everything.'

'So what time are you seeing him?'

I glanced at the clock. It was just after 6 p.m.

'I have to be at his house in an hour.'

As I was locking up, someone entered the driveway.

'Mr Raker?'

I spun around, immediately on the defensive.

It was a man in his thirties, thinning on top and dressed in a suit that didn't fit. I vaguely recognized him, but my head was so full of noise about the meeting with Robert Zaid, I couldn't place where from. He'd stopped on the other side of my car, his eyes shifting to the damage at its front. 'You're a hard man to pin down,' he said, 'you know that?' He dug around in his pocket for something and brought out a business card. 'It's great to finally meet you in the flesh.'

I felt a rush of blood to the head: suddenly, I remembered who he was – and, as I did, my throat closed.

He held out the card to me.

Connor McCaskell. Reporter, Daily Tribune.

'I expect you remember me now.'

'What the hell do you want?'

I almost spat the words at him.

'I thought we could discuss my story.'

'Yeah? What story's that?'

He smiled. 'The story I'm going to write about you.'

I brushed past him and unlocked my car.

'I'd really like us to work together.'

I smirked. 'I bet you would.'

He didn't seem surprised by the response; in fact, from his

expression, it looked like he'd been expecting it. 'You just keep fighting me, David.'

I almost laughed. 'Are you serious?'

'You don't answer my calls –'

'Are you *actually* serious? I don't owe you anything. We're not in a relationship, I don't have to answer your calls, I don't have to spend one second of my life acknowledging you exist. I told you last time I made the mistake of picking up the phone to you that I had no interest in appearing in your story *or* your worthless fucking newspaper, and nothing's changed.' I stopped, realizing that my voice had become loud. Out on the street, a man and his wife turned and looked at me. I leaned towards McCaskell. 'I don't know what the hell you're doing, what story you think the world needs to hear, or what you think I have that's worth following me around like this, but the one thing I can tell you with absolute certainty is that I'll never – *never* – choose to work with you.'

He nodded. 'That's unfortunate.'

'For you maybe.'

'No,' he said. 'For both of us.'

I eyed him.

He'd come with a plan.

'That case you had before Christmas . . .' His teeth pressed into his bottom lip and he winced, as if he felt something genuine for me; as if, by osmosis, he too could feel the way that case had turned me inside out, the way all my cases had carved out deep troughs in my life. 'That was when I realized that this had the potential to be big. People would *want* to read about this hero, this man who had suffered so much in his personal life but who still had the drive and the desire to help others. Roll in these other, huge investigations – some of which Joe Public doesn't even realize you were involved in, let alone single-handedly solved – the fact that the Met *hate* you, basically see you as an enemy of the state, and, well . . .' He whistled gently. 'That's a spicy story.'

I felt my guts twist but tried not to show it, getting into my car and pulling the door shut. As I started up the engine, he gestured to the crushed bonnet and shouted through the glass: 'I know you've got secrets, David, and not the kind that are going to paint you in a flattering light. I mean, let's take your mystery pal Bryan Kennedy as an example. He has no bank account, he's not on the records of the utility companies, he has no National Insurance number, so he's never been treated at a hospital anywhere, *ever* – and he doesn't have a driving licence or an official passport. He's a ghost. *Your* ghost.'

I shook my head, as if all of this were ludicrous.

He came forward, putting a hand on the wrinkled bonnet, on the roof, trying to get in the way of me – trying to stop me – even as I began to reverse off the driveway.

'One way or another,' he said, pointing at my window now, pressing a finger to it, 'your secrets are going to come out, and they're going to be a part of this story, but *how* they're a part of it is up to you.' I had to slow down, unsure if the gates were even wide enough for me to get the car past him. McCaskell pounced on the opportunity, coming at me again: 'So you can give them all up to me voluntarily, you can talk about them, justify them and defend yourself, and I'll quote you directly on everything. *Or* you can keep hiding from me, you can keep running and I can keep chasing, and when I find out what those secrets are – and I will, David; I always do – I'll put in absolutely everything I have. And it'll hurt you, I promise you that. What I write, it'll rip your life apart.'

I accelerated away.

Empty

Los Angeles | Thursday 15 August

They left the house before the sun was up. The car was quiet. Neither of them had slept well the previous night, but for different reasons: Ethan, because he was so excited about starting the next chapter of his life; Jo, because her son was leaving for college and, secretly, without ever having shown him for a single second, it was tearing her heart in two.

'Are you going to be all right, Mom?' he asked when they stopped to pick up coffee in Santa Clarita, both of them lit by the red-and-yellow glow from a Carl's Jr. sign.

She smiled at him and squeezed his arm. 'I'll be fine, baby. I'll get to do all the things I always dreamed of, like gardening and yoga.' She winked at him, and he returned her smile, and when they got back to the car he'd already moved on, talking breathlessly about how the computer science portion of his degree could lead to all sorts of things, including designing video games.

Back on the interstate, she just let him talk, loving the sound of his voice. He'd always been like this, as far back as she could remember: at eight and nine, he'd sit at the breakfast table before school and tell her everything he'd learned the day before; at fifteen and sixteen, he seemed to bypass the sullen teenage years entirely, never hiding away in his room, never cutting her down with a comment, or fighting her over homework, or girls, or going out. They'd definitely had their moments, times when they'd irritated one another, when Ethan snapped, when Jo did, but they were rare, certainly in comparison to other parents she'd talked to. She didn't know if she'd just struck lucky with Ethan or whether his good nature, his relative calm, was somehow tethered to what had happened to his father. He claimed not to remember much of that night, of clawing at Ira's body in the hours before Jo got home late from another shift, but she often worried – irrationally, like parents so often did – that the memory had lodged somewhere deep and was just waiting for the right moment to come out.

They stopped again after about three hours and had breakfast in a dust-blown diner at the side of the freeway. Ethan ordered a three-egg omelette with bell peppers and Swiss cheese, Jo the corned-beef hash, and as they waited, they talked some more about the year ahead, about Ethan living on campus, about his plans for the holidays.

'I don't think I'm going to make it back home for Thanksgiving, Mom,' he said, a mouth full of food. 'That sort of round trip, it's just too much hassle for a weekend.'

'Absolutely.'

He gave her an apologetic look and then searched her face for signs he'd upset her. She gave him nothing, not wanting him to feel in any way bad. If being a cop for twenty-seven years had taught her anything, it was how to sustain a good poker face.

'Save the turkey for Christmas, okay?'

'Sure,' she said, and winked at him again, her standard response when she was hurting. She didn't blame him for not wanting to come home on Thanksgiving, it was simply that, for the first time since Ira had died, she'd be spending it alone. Ethan ducked his head slightly, as if trying to read her again, a movement that reminded Jo of Ira, of moments when Ethan was still a kid and Ira would give Jo pep talks before work. *You're a pioneer, honey. You're out there in your wagon, crossing those plains by yourself, having to deal with all the dangers of unexplored territory.* She always remembered that one. He'd called her Davy Crockett, just with better hair.

'What's up?' Ethan asked.

Jo realized she was smiling.

'Oh, nothing,' she replied. 'I was just thinking about your dad.'

'Do you think he would have been proud of me?'

'Are you kidding? Of the two of us, *he'd* have been the one sitting here in tears.' She took one of her son's hands and squeezed it gently. 'He loved you so much, Eth.'

Ethan nodded. 'I know he did.'

'I wish he was here to see the person you've become.'

'Thanks, Mom.'

They went back to their food for a while and, when they were done, asked for some fresh coffee and just sat there in the booth talking about the news, about books and movies, about stuff that had nothing to do with Ethan leaving home or Jo's work. But then, just as Jo asked for the cheque, her son glanced at her across the table, that same echo of Ira in his face, and said, 'So what are you going to do about your job?'

Jo looked out the window: between the diner and the edge of the blacktop, a dusty haze had kicked up, whorled and churned by the passing traffic.

'I'm not sure,' she said finally.

'You've fallen out of love with it.'

'Have I?'

'That's what you said.'

'I don't remember that.'

'Admittedly, you'd had a couple of glasses of wine at the time.'

Jo laughed and he smiled back at her, but she was only pretending. That *was* what she'd said, and it *had* been fuelled by a bottle of wine: Ethan had been out somewhere with a bunch of friends and, when he'd got home, she was watching reruns of some old show she'd long forgotten and on the table in front of her had been her notebook.

Old cases from her time at the Sheriff's Department.

And, in the middle of it, *the* case.

'Mom?'

She looked at Ethan. 'I don't know if I've fallen out of love with it exactly – it's more that, over the years, it's just . . .' She stopped again, trying to articulate what she felt, conscious of dousing the excitement of Ethan's day. 'I guess what I'm saying is, I struck lucky when I took that job at the LAPD because it came at a time when I had more leeway in dictating terms – they wanted more women, they were trying to change, and I wanted to spend more time with you; all of it worked out for the best.'

Ethan frowned. 'So you've fallen out of love with it because . . . ?'

The waitress brought the cheque to the table.

'Mom?'

'It doesn't matter.' She waved him away. 'It's boring, Eth.'

'It's not. I want to hear.'

'Today isn't about me being a cop.'

'Tell me, Mom.'

She looked at him for a moment, his eyes on hers, his big frame in the booth, acne scattered at the tops of his cheeks: there were only hints left behind now of the one-year-old she'd watched sleep in his crib, of the boy she'd found banging his fists against the dead body of his father five years later, who'd told her stories about lost wolf pups at nine. He'd always be her son, she'd always love him, but this was a man.

He deserved to hear what she carried.

'Okay,' she said, and pushed aside the tray with the cheque on it. 'Okay, so fast-forward nine years and I'm now a captain, and what that means is that I get to spend most of my day behind a desk looking at stats, dealing with petty politics and breaking up arguments between grown men about which of them has the biggest dick.' She smiled. Ethan gave her a *Men, huh?* look. 'My point is, I'm not even really out there on the front lines. The cases, they're my concern, I have ultimate responsibility for everything, but it's not me walking the scene these days – or very rarely – it's not me in the room with the witnesses, it's not me having to do the hard graft in order to take it all to the DA, packaged up, and get it over the line. And yet I still feel *exactly* the same as the very first day I started as a detective. I can't let it go. I'm pulling my detectives in and asking them where we're at with cases, not because I give a single damn about how it's going to look in a spreadsheet, but because I've still got this crushing sense of debt.'

'Debt?'

Jo shrugged. 'I used to see a shrink in the nineties, after your dad died. She kind of became this sounding board for me. She coined that phrase, and she was right. The main reason I moved to the LAPD was because of you. I needed to make sure I had enough time with you, that I got to see you growing up, that I wasn't some spirit passing through your life. But there was another reason as well. I thought, by getting a promotion, by chaining myself to a desk, I'd be able to shake off this feeling I had.'

'The sense of debt.'

She smiled. 'Right.'

'But you haven't?'

'No,' she said, and thought of the notebook she'd dug out at home, of the two names written in the middle. *Gabriel Wilzon. Donald Klein.* They weren't the only unsolved murders in her career as a cop, they weren't the only case of hers that had hit the skids, but they were the first, and they'd always stuck the hardest, and she'd always known that there would only ever be one way to shift the weight of them.

It was the same way you shifted the weight from any case.

You found the killer.

'Mom?'

She tuned back in.

'Do you think we should get going?'

'Yeah,' she said, 'Of course.' She laid out some bills on the tray and then flashed her son a big smile, telling him everything was fine. 'Let's get my little boy to college.'

Jo didn't get back home until after 9 p.m.

At the screen door, she froze, her key in the lock, as if there were something bad waiting for her on the other side, and then she opened up and moved through to the hallway. The silence of the house crashed past her. She went further in, to the door of Ethan's room: back when she'd been at the LASD, standing here had been the thing she'd done – the goodbye she'd given – as her baby had slept. Now the crib was long gone, and so was the LASD; so was Ira, so was Ethan. She took in the emptiness of the space, hated how unnaturally clean it was, from the perfectly stacked bookshelves to the flawless bed linen. And then her eyes were drawn to the other side of the room, to his desk, where – in a frame – there was a picture of him and Ira. It was taken on Ethan's fifth birthday.

It didn't matter how much you loved a person.
Eventually, you had to let them go.
Jo burst into tears.

PART SEVEN
The Diplomat

51

Robert Zaid lived at the end of a winding cul-de-sac, the entire road cut off from the outside world by a pair of five-foot-high security gates. At 7 p.m. I pulled up in front of it and pushed the buzzer on an intercom. From this side of the gates, the cul-de-sac looked quiet, and the road I'd come in on had little in the way of through traffic, but I could still hear vehicle noise from Highgate High Street, the wail of sirens, the low drone of planes in the sky. London was never silent. It made me think of how different it was from Black Gale.

'Yes?'

The intercom crackled into life.

'Mr Zaid? It's David Raker.'

'Oh yes, of course.'

With a clunk, the gates began to open.

'Come in,' he said. 'I'm down at the end.'

Either side of me, hedges became thicker and higher as I made my way down, but intermittently driveways would appear and, when I looked along them, every building was huge, a series of vast, pristine properties with broad, sweeping gardens, the grounds supplemented with tennis courts and outdoor pools. The further down I got, the bigger the houses became, until eventually Robert Zaid's drifted into view, the gates already open. The house itself was a faux-Victorian mansion with pillars either side of the front door, and gabled windows on the top floor.

Zaid was standing in the doorway, waiting for me.

I nosed the Audi through the gates and up the driveway, and thought again of what I knew about him. *Born in London to an Iranian father and Hungarian mother. Educated at a private school in Gloucestershire, and at King's College where he'd got a BA in History and an MA in Politics. A diplomat at the Foreign Office and a hugely successful investor and entrepreneur in his own right. Seventy-second on last year's* Sunday Times *Rich List.* I pulled in next to a year-old Aston Martin. A Porsche and a Land Rover were parked next to it.

He knew Beatrix Steards.

Knew Adrian Vale too.

I switched off the engine.

Still works for the government, despite his vast wealth. Hard to find online, except for the blandest of profile pieces. Protects his privacy vehemently. Yet I'd called his PA early this afternoon and he'd immediately agreed to meet me.

He started coming down the driveway in my direction, and behind him I saw two other men fanning out on either side, heading in the direction of parked cars – much less lavish than Zaid's – as if getting ready to leave. They were big and brawny, wearing the same black suits; one of them was yanking an earpiece out, the wire snaking under the collar of his jacket; the other glanced at me but didn't seem particularly interested, apparently already briefed on who I was. They must have been Zaid's home security team. He was letting them go for the evening.

I watched them for a moment and then got out of the car, still going over what I knew about Zaid: *No obvious links to Jacob Pierce. No links to Isaac Mills either. But he spoke to Patrick Perry in a Skype call in October 2015, when Patrick had come asking about Beatrix Steards, and, in a reverse of my experience, it had taken Patrick a couple of days to arrange a conversation with him.*

So why had Zaid made himself available so quickly for me?

Not knowing the answer put me on edge. The fact that, a week or so after that Skype call, Patrick was gone, and eight others along with him, put me on edge too.

I was anxious and tired, right down to my bones.

But I was clear-headed enough to see what I needed to.

Something didn't feel right.

52

Robert Zaid's home was every bit as beautiful on the inside as it was out. Polished wooden floors led from a foyer into a sunken living room – modern and airy, the furniture a mix of homely and contemporary – that, in turn, swept through to a huge, all-glass garden room. Beyond that was a tiered lawn, dotted with lights, and an outbuilding with a slate roof that appeared to house a swimming pool. I could see the reflection of the water on the walls, shimmering softly.

Outside, I heard the crunch of gravel as Zaid's security team headed away, the sound of their vehicles quickly swallowed by the night. Once they were gone, Zaid used a sensor to close the gates and pushed the front door shut, cranking one of its locks. The moment he did, I heard a long beep from somewhere deeper in the house, and realized every entrance, every lock and every latch, was wired into an alarm system. There were clearly significant advantages to being as wealthy as Zaid was – but having to live like a prisoner wasn't one of them.

I followed him further in.

'Can I get you something to drink?' he asked, and stopped at the edge of the living room, where three steps descended towards a low coffee table surrounded by a white rug.

He was in his early fifties, olive-skinned and dark-haired, with a neat beard. I'd managed to find a limited collection of photographs of him online, taken over a decade before, but there were more recent ones on the wall to my left, shots of him that hadn't ever been publicized, and the one pattern I'd noticed was how much Zaid's weight had fluctuated over time. In some of them, he was well-built and lean, muscular, strong, and in others, he'd totally gone to seed, the heft gathering around his face and in a band along his midriff, his belly straining against his shirt or lifted away from his beltline entirely by the sphere of his stomach. Right now, though, he was strong and angular, dressed in a pair of tracksuit trousers and a training top, and, as I looked at him, I had the weirdest sensation that we'd met before.

'I like to box,' he said, and gestured to the wall. 'It's why my weight goes up and down. I could see you were wondering, but you're too much of a gentleman to say. It looks like you've been in the ring yourself.'

He was talking about the bruise on my cheek. 'Just a little accident,' I said, returning the smile. 'So are you prepping for a fight now?'

'Next week. When I work with my trainer, I always scrub up pretty well, but my body – if I don't work hard in the gym and don't eat properly all the time – packs it on quickly. Sometimes it's hard to find the motivation to live the perfect lifestyle twenty-four seven.'

I nodded. 'I can imagine.'

'Now, that drink?'

'Just water would be great,' I said.

I followed him through to the kitchen and stole a look to my right, along one of the two corridors that led from the living room: in this one were more glass walls, segregating the hallway from a gym – a running machine visible – and what looked like a shower and sauna. There was steam on the glass next to the shower, and I could see a pair of dumbbells on a mat in the gym. He'd obviously just finished exercising.

He handed me a glass of water.

'I appreciate you seeing me so quickly, Mr Zaid.'

He waved me away, as if it had been no trouble at all. 'Robert's perfectly fine.' His accent was elegant, his words refined. 'Today is one of the rare days when I've been relatively unencumbered by meetings, so when Jackie told me yesterday that you'd called and asked to see me, I confess I did spend a moment Google-stalking your name to see if it was a meeting I should take. But as soon as I saw what you did for a living, I was intrigued as to how

354

I might be able to help. I don't know that I've ever met a missing persons investigator before.'

'Well, this is what we look like.'

He smiled again. 'So I see.'

He directed me to the sofas in the living room and, as I sunk into one of them, I could see along the opposite hallway. There was a bedroom at the far end.

'You've got a beautiful place here,' I said.

'Thank you.' He looked around the room, out to the garden and the swimming pool. 'I've been very lucky, I know that. My father was wealthy, I was fortunate to get an extremely good education, I've had a very interesting and varied career at the Foreign Office – those things shouldn't be underestimated. But I like to think I've not relied on the fact that I was given certain assistances. I hope that what I've done with my advantage is to help people from less auspicious backgrounds than myself.'

In the profile piece I'd read about him, it said he'd done an enormous amount of work with charities and had ploughed millions of pounds into a state-of-the-art cancer research facility in south London, neither of which it was even remotely possible to criticize him for. Otherwise, his comments didn't entirely ring true. Most of his wealth – not including the property portfolio he inherited from his parents, who died a year after he finished his Politics MA – was accumulated via his father's stakes in two vast multinational oil companies, and in a media group that went on to create the world's largest video-sharing platform. He'd made money of his own by funding Internet start-ups, some extremely successful, but all of it was built on the mountains of cash he was still making from his father's old investments.

'Ever think about giving up the day job?' I asked him.

'You mean, at the Foreign Office?' He pursed his lips. 'I've thought about it.'

'But Whitehall is just too much of a pull?'

This time he laughed. 'I wouldn't say that exactly. It's not really a day job in the proper sense of the word. I have a desk and an office there, I do a couple of days a week most weeks, and, yes, in the 1990s and early 2000s I chose to spend a lot of time abroad, working in various roles for high commissions and embassies – so, in that respect, I *have* been a bona fide diplomat. But I have lots of other business interests, more now than ever, and they suck up a lot of time, so over the past ten to fifteen years I've had a much looser brief with the FCO. I turn up at events, I wine and dine, and I leverage my contacts in order to advance the UK's standing.' He stopped, frowning, as if realizing how that came across. 'That sounds terribly boastful. What I mean is, I do what I can to help them.'

It was hard to know if that was any less immodest.

'I actually think a day job, a proper day job, can give you purpose,' he went on. 'My parents always said it was important to have a routine – something to get up for and something to come home from – otherwise you risk becoming lazy. And, as we all know, you should always listen to your parents, especially ones as remarkable as mine.' He smiled again, glancing at a picture of his mother and father on the wall behind him. 'But, seriously, working at the FCO, it's not to everyone's tastes, I understand that, and not everyone understands why I still do it, but my work as a diplomat has been so interesting. I've been to places I wouldn't have even *thought* to go to otherwise. In the nineties, I was posted to Hong Kong for a while, after that I spent three years in Jakarta, and then another two in Muscat – I mean, *Muscat*; why would I *ever* have gone to Oman if not for this job? – then Moscow, Nairobi, Pretoria . . .' He opened out his hands. 'I loved all of those places. The FCO, it's full of boring politicians – but sometimes, and I know it's a cliché, there really *are* things money can't buy.'

I looked around the room and out to the garden.

But it can still buy a lot.

'So what is it I can help you with, Mr Raker?'

'David,' I said, taking out my pen and pad and setting them down. 'I was hoping to talk to you about a woman who was on the same Politics MA as you back in 1987.'

I watched for any sign that he knew what was coming.

I didn't have to look hard.

'You want to talk about Beatrix Steards,' he said.

'You remember her?'

Zaid frowned, as if the idea of forgetting her was offensive to him.

'Of course,' he responded. 'I remember her very well. I remember the day she went missing, the aftermath of her disappearance. But, mostly, whenever I think of Beatrix, I remember the man who murdered her.'

Retirement: Part 1

Los Angeles | Friday 30 October

Her retirement party was at a Mexican place in Irvine. The university staff had hired a room at the back and decorated it with balloons and banners, and while a part of her had worried no one would turn up – an irrational fear given how many friends she'd made during her twelve years of teaching at UCI – it was packed. So she drank too much and ate too little, she danced to songs that she'd thought she'd forgotten a long time ago, and then she left just after midnight in an Uber one of the staff had organized for her.

The drive back to her apartment had taken thirty minutes, the driver apparently not big on conversation, but Jo welcomed the silence. She'd enjoyed watching the city pass at night, the lights blurred, the windows lit; she knew she would probably be back in Irvine again at some point for lunch, perhaps back at UCI for a one-off lecture, but she wouldn't be doing this journey every morning and evening. For the first time in almost half a century, she wouldn't have any commute at all.

She thought about the first job she'd had, straight out of college, doing basic administrative work for the clerk at the federal courthouse; about her first day at the Sheriff's Department as a deputy; about when she moved to the LAPD as a lieutenant in 1993; and finally, she recalled the day she'd left law enforcement for good, after twenty-eight years.

That day had felt similar to this one.

Similar, but not the same.

She'd known it was the right thing to do then, just as she knew now, but twelve years ago she hadn't been tired of it all. Now she was exhausted. For the last six months she'd been waking up every day feeling like she was done. After forty years, she didn't want to have to talk about crime or criminals any more, whether it was purely theoretical and in front of a lectern, or out on a sidewalk as she stood over a body. She was still fit and healthy, still felt as good now as she'd ever done, but emotionally she had nothing left to give.

She wanted a vacation.

She wanted to go and visit Ethan and Claire in San Francisco.

She wanted to sit and hold her granddaughter.

After the driver had dropped her off, she let herself in and dumped her bag on the couch, then went to the kitchen and got herself a glass of water. She noticed the answer machine was blinking red, its display showing one message waiting.

It could wait until morning.

She woke with a crashing headache at 8 a.m.

As she stumbled through to the bathroom with one eye squeezed shut, she tried to remember the last time she'd felt as terrible as this. It could have been twenty years ago. It could have been more than that. She'd pretty much given up drinking after Ira had died, except at the occasional social event: she'd stopped out of grief to start with, and then stayed that way because of Ethan. She'd been a single mom with a young kid, and she'd had a career that had taken every ounce of whatever she wasn't giving to her son.

And whatever she wasn't giving to Ethan never felt like enough.

So drink had never ranked high on her list of priorities, even if – some nights – it would have been an easy way to go after her son had gone to bed. In those first few years, the house had seemed massive, its rooms empty, the bed as big as a football field. Drinking herself into blackness may not have been the worst thing in the world, even if it didn't seem like it now.

She washed her face, popped a couple of paracetamol, then

wandered into the kitchen. The blinds weren't twisted all the way shut and, from where she was, she could see across the rooftops to the beach. Out the front of one of the stores down there she could see a huge inflatable skeleton and remembered that today was Halloween. She watched the sea for a moment, moving metronomically, blue and calm, and then the brightness of the sky started to make her eyes sting, the sun pouring in through the slats of the blinds.

Suddenly, the phone started ringing.

She filled a glass full of water, took a long, deep mouthful, and then shuffled across, assuming it would be Ethan. He'd called the day before, to tell her he was thinking about her on her last day at work, and said he'd call her this morning to talk about how it had gone. He'd find it hilarious that she had a hangover.

As she picked up the phone, she saw the machine was still blinking, reminding her that she had a message she hadn't listened to yet.

'Jo Kader,' she muttered.

'Ah, Detective Kader. Brilliant.'

It was a man, English accent.

'I'm not a detective any more,' she said sharply. 'Who's this?'

'Excuse me. Of course. I've had my head in this investigation far too long. Let me start again. Ms Kader, my name's Patrick Perry and I'm hoping you can help me.'

She'd never heard of him.

'We haven't met before,' he went on, 'although I left a message on your machine yesterday. I'm not sure if you've had the chance to listen to it, but it doesn't matter if not.' He paused. Jo couldn't hear anything beside his voice: wherever he was, it was either quiet or deliberately secluded. 'I live in the UK, but I'm looking into a case that might possibly have a connection to something that you worked on a long time ago.'

'How did you get my number?'

'Uh, well, I found a profile of you on the University of California website.'

It was simple, and obvious, and she felt like a fool for asking. She sank another mouthful of water and willed the paracetamol to kick in. The hangover seemed to be getting worse.

'But before that,' Patrick Perry said, obviously trying not to make her feel like she was being stalked, 'I called the LA Sheriff's Department, and then the LAPD, and that was how I eventually found you. To cut a long story short, I've been trying to see if I can find out anything more about a man called Adrian Vale.'

Jo blinked, shocked to hear his name after so long.

She hadn't thought about Adrian Vale for months. She hadn't looked at the notebook, packed away in one of the drawers in the spare room, for even longer.

But she'd never forgotten.

'What about Vale?' she said.

Perry continued: 'Well, I was shunted around from pillar to post for a while – but then, eventually, I managed to get someone in Cold Cases at the LAPD to do a search for Vale and his name came up in relation to the murder of a man called . . . uh . . . Donald Klein. Apparently, you were the last person to add anything to Klein's file. It was in 2003 – on your last day at the LAPD, I think.'

Jo went to the window and twisted the blinds shut. Her head was banging so hard, white spots were flashing in front of her eyes.

'Ms Kader?'

'I remember,' she said.

And she did: on her last day in Robbery-Homicide she'd told one of her detectives to pull the Klein file for her. Unlike the murder of Gabriel Wilzon, it had never been closed, chiefly because Ray Callson's parting gift to the casework was a note saying that he didn't believe Klein was the killer and it wasn't a murder-suicide. So, while Hayesfield shut the LASD's half of the investigation down, the LAPD had kept theirs open. No one was working it, no one was likely to work it any more – and any potential evidence was lost in the passage of time – but, even after so long, Jo had still felt that sense of debt to the two dead men: so she'd gone in and entered Adrian Vale's name as the probable murderer of both. She'd had her doubts about him – and there was never enough evidence to convict – but he'd remained her best, and only, lead. Now, though, none of that seemed to matter. Squeezing her eyes shut, she said, 'I thought Vale was dead.'

She'd gone looking for him in the months after Ethan left to go to Berkeley, the house she'd shared with Ira and her son in the Valley too overwhelming by then, big and empty and forlorn. Whenever she'd get home from work, she'd hate the silence of it, so she'd kept herself busy by looking into Vale again, and after weeks of Internet research and long-distance phone calls she'd managed to speak to someone at East Sussex County Council in England, who pulled a death certificate for her.

'He *is* dead,' Perry responded. 'He died in 1989.'

'Then I don't understand.'

She felt like she needed to puke now.

'I think he might have been involved in the disappearance of a woman called Beatrix Steards. The two of them were at university together in London.'

Grabbing a pad off the counter, Jo said, 'Steards?'

'Yeah. S-T-E-A-R-D-S.'

'So this girl disappeared and never turned up?'

'No. Never. She vanished in March 1987.'

Jo retched; and then again.

'Are you okay?' Perry asked her.

'Look . . . Patrick, is it?'

'Yes, that's right.'

She started hurrying through to the bathroom.

'Patrick, you're going to have to give me a few hours, okay? I definitely want to hear what you have to say – *definitely* – but I'm . . .' She got to the bathroom, covered the mouthpiece of the phone and heaved into the toilet. Nothing came up. 'I've woken up with a bug or something, so could you call me back in a couple of hours?'

'I've got to get back for a dinner tonight.'

She remembered then that it was 4 p.m. in the UK.

'Okay. How about tomorrow morning?'

'That sounds great,' he said. 'I'll speak to you then. I can't promise you anything new – and Adrian Vale is still the best fit for a suspect – but I don't know. I just think . . .'

Jo felt dizzy now, unsteady even with a hand on the basin.

'You think what?' she muttered, bile burning at the back of her throat.

'I think there's something even worse going on here.'

53

'You said you remember the man who murdered Beatrix?'

'*Probably* murdered,' Zaid responded. 'Adrian Vale, his name was. He just always seemed the most likely suspect.' He uncrossed his legs and shuffled forward on the sofa. 'Actually, this isn't the first time someone's come asking me about Beatrix in the last few years – and it's not the first time I've tried to put it all together in my head.'

'Who else wanted to talk to you about her?'

He rubbed a hand against his mouth, thinking.

'It was a man from up north. Manchester, I think.'

'Do you remember his name?'

He nodded. 'Someone Perry.'

'Patrick Perry?'

'That's the chap,' he said. 'That's him. We talked over Skype. He was some kind of journalist – or used to be. I'm afraid I don't recall the specifics of what we discussed. I mean, I'm trying to think when we actually chatted.'

I waited, wanting to see how this story unfolded.

'I guess it must have been two, two and a half years ago,' he said.

'So around October 2015?'

'Yes, I think so.' He whistled. 'It's hard to remember things I did two and a half *weeks* ago. He asked me about Beatrix, I know that, about when she went missing – probably what I talked about to the police too. I'm sure I would have spoken to him about Adrian.'

From somewhere else in the house, I heard a noise.

'Cats,' Zaid commented, waving a finger in the vague direction of the second hallway. 'They belong to a friend. Stupidly, I said I'd look after them while she was in Italy with work – but

I never realized I'd be allergic to their hair. The day after they arrived, I just couldn't stop sneezing, so I've had to quarantine them in the spare room.' He pointed to my pad. 'So, are you also looking into what happened to Beatrix?'

'In part,' I said. 'She might inform another disappearance I'm working on.'

'Oh,' he responded, 'I see.'

'I know it was a long time ago, but do you remember anything specific you might have said to Patrick?'

He took a breath, as if going back to 1987 hurt him, a physical pain he couldn't shift, and he began going over the account of what he remembered from the time. It matched almost exactly with the timeline DS Smoulter had put together three decades ago, and then the account he'd given to Patrick over Skype in October 2015. He asked me if I wanted something else to drink, and when I said I was fine, he stood and went to the kitchen. I watched him as he grabbed a bottle of whisky from one of the cupboards, pouring himself a measure, his movements slower somehow, maybe burdened by the memory of Beatrix. He looked at me and then sank the whole thing, before pouring himself another one.

'So you're still adamant that Adrian Vale was behind Beatrix's disappearance? You think he killed her?'

'Yes,' he said.

'What makes you so sure?'

'Sure?' A forced smile. 'I don't think we can be one hundred per cent sure about anything.'

He downed the second glass of whisky.

'But Adrian . . .' He almost mumbled the name, as if he didn't want to form it on his tongue. 'Adrian was always struggling to fit in. Always. It wasn't that we actively left him out – we never overtly avoided him; well, not until after Beatrix disappeared, I suppose – but he didn't belong. You know how some people are. They just don't fit in, however hard they try to – and you never take to them, despite your best efforts.'

'So he was always on the outside of your group?'

'Yes. I mean, he tried hard, but . . .'

'But what?'

'We didn't talk much, because I always felt there was something about him. All the abuse he got, all the name-calling, being physically shoved and pushed sometimes, most of the people doing it mistook his silence and lack of retaliation for weakness. But I never did. Right from the start, from the moment I met him, I could see something.'

'What sort of thing?'

His eyes were back on the bottle.

'The sort of thing that could bite you,' Zaid replied.

54

'You were scared of Adrian Vale?'

He shrugged. 'Wary.'

'Why?'

'Like I said, I think he disguised who he really was.'

I watched him for a moment, replaying what he'd just told me. I wasn't certain he was lying to me – I just wasn't sure he was telling me the truth either. The way he talked about Vale, the way Vale had scared him: it felt erroneous somehow, insufficient, as if he'd left something unsaid.

'Did you go to his funeral?' I asked.

Zaid seemed surprised by the question. 'Yes. Yes, of course. It was a very small occasion. His mother had already passed on and so had his father, and anyone else he might have been connected to back in LA had long since stopped talking to him, so he was cremated in a cemetery in Brockley.'

Zaid came back to the sofas.

'Have you ever heard the name Jacob Pierce, Robert?'

He thought for a second.

'No, I don't think so.'

'He's a solicitor, based up in York.'

'Oh, wait a minute: yes, I have heard of him.'

I studied him more closely now. His head was slightly ducked so I could see his eyes, but not as clearly as I'd have liked.

'How do you know him?' I asked.

'I don't really know him, I just know the company he used to work for. Before he moved up north, Jacob Pierce worked for Franklin Habash down here in London. They were the law firm that my dad used to use, run by an ex-pat Iranian, like him.'

'Jacob Pierce was Adrian's solicitor back in 1987.'

'Yes,' he said, 'that's right.'

'Did you recommend Franklin Habash to Adrian?'

He shrugged. 'He asked if I knew a solicitor. I said I did.'

'But you said the two of you didn't really talk?'

'We talked enough over time.'

'You mean, you grew closer?'

'No, not closer,' he replied, shaking his head, as if the idea offended him. 'Adrian and I were never close. But we would talk a little on occasions, so when he asked me if I knew any solicitors, I gave him the one I knew. At that stage, in the hours after Beatrix went missing, I wasn't really thinking about allegiances. I wasn't even thinking that Adrian might know where she was. I was naive, I suppose. I thought maybe Adrian knew something that could help the police.'

'So why would he need a solicitor?'

Zaid frowned. 'I was twenty-two, David. I'd never even been *close* to anything like that. I didn't think about it all that much. He asked, and I obliged.'

There was silence now from Zaid.

Silence in the house as well.

'Have you ever heard of Black Gale, Robert?'

He frowned again.

'It's in Yorkshire,' I explained. 'It was in the news a few years back.'

'Doesn't ring any bells with me.'

'The entire village went missing on the same night.'

A spark of recognition in his eyes this time.

'Wait,' he said. 'Wait, I think I do remember. "Just like the *Twilight Zone*."'

I nodded. 'That's the one.'

'Is that the case that you think Beatrix might be tied to?'

'Patrick Perry lived there,' I said, by way of a reply.

'Oh, I didn't know that.'

'He never talked about it with you?'

'The village? No.'

'Okay.' I pushed on. 'Okay, so what about –'

368

The sound of a phone shattered the silence. As it rang, its tone seemed to be coming from three or four different parts of the house.

He looked at me and rolled his eyes. 'I'm sorry, David. I switched off my mobile, but I forgot to put the house phone on mute.'

'Can it wait?' I asked. 'I'm almost done.'

'I won't be long, I promise,' Zaid replied, and then he hauled himself up off the sofa. 'There's beer and wine in the fridge. Help yourself.'

He smiled and headed down the second hallway, towards the main bedroom at the end. As he got there, he grabbed a phone off the wall just inside the room, and I heard him say, 'Robert Zaid,' before pushing the door shut with the edge of his foot.

The house quietened again.

I looked at my notes for a moment, annoyed at being made to wait, and went back over what Zaid and I had just talked about. That lingering sense that something had been left unsaid didn't go – but I couldn't see the deceit in what I'd written down.

I took out my phone, checking for messages.

There was no signal.

There was Wi-Fi – and an invitation soon popped up to join Zaid's home network – but it required a password I didn't have. Other than that, I had no bars at all. How could I be right in the heart of London and have no reception?

Getting up, I went through to the garden room, standing at the doorway that led out to the lawn. Nothing. I tried the door, hoping it might open – that I might be able to go outside – but as soon as I pressed down on it, I heard a gentle beep from elsewhere and remembered how Zaid had locked up the house after I'd first arrived. At the time, it had seemed like the understandable actions of a wealthy man concerned about his security; now, being sealed in, it only fed my sense of unease.

I moved around the sunken living room, into the hallway with the gym and the shower room, trying to find a signal in there, then headed back out again. Opposite me, I could see along the hallway where Zaid had gone, the door of his bedroom still shut. Behind me was the wall of photographs, full of shots of Zaid – bigger, smaller, fatter, thinner; shaking hands, standing in front of landmarks – that I'd noticed earlier on.

This time, though, I was much closer to them.

I was looking at the pictures in detail, seeing people Zaid had shared time with, the places he'd worked in and visited, the experiences he'd had. For the first time, from just inches away, I was properly able to take in the chronicle he'd mounted of his life.

And, as I did, I felt a sudden twinge of panic.

Something wasn't right.

55

There must have been over forty photographs on the wall, different sizes and in different frames, arranged in a series of vague, concentric circles. It should have a looked a mess, but it didn't: when I'd first come into the house, I'd thought how warm it made the place feel, a document of Robert Zaid's life that quietly suggested, despite his wealth, Zaid was a normal guy.

He'd had family he'd loved.

He'd done things he was proud of.

In the very centre was a shot of Zaid and his parents. Zaid couldn't have been more than eleven or twelve. They were on a veranda, sea in the distance behind them, the whitewashed walls of Spanish villas dotted about in the greenery in between. This must have been the home that Zaid's father had owned in Marbella, a place – according to the profile piece I'd read – that Robert had sold when his parents died in a helicopter crash in 1989. They'd come down in the Pyrenees after a weekend skiing.

Something about the picture didn't add up.

In it, Zaid was tall and thin, a good-looking kid but a scrawny one. His father was the same: even in adulthood, he'd remained slender, his height – six two, six three – appearing to narrow him even further. And he was incredibly dark, his hair and moustache jet black, his eyes like blobs of ink, his skin almost sepia, as if some artificial filter had been added. Except it hadn't: Zaid's mother was beside his father, holding her husband's hand, as physically different from the man she'd married as it was possible to be. She would have been in her forties at the time the picture was taken, but her age seemed immaterial: she was absolutely beautiful, timeless, her skin pale – almost pearlescent – her eyes a deep, ocean blue. In front of them, Robert was smiling, his father's hand on his shoulder, and it was easy to note both his

371

parents in him: his father's stature, his mother's eyes, skin colour that was a near-perfect mix of the two.

So what could I see?

What didn't feel right?

My eyes switched to three shots on its left.

None of the photos was ordered chronologically, so in these ones Zaid ranged from early fifties to early thirties, then back into his forties, and in two of them he was overweight, the shirt and jacket he was wearing straining at the stitching.

In the first, he was outside the front of a home he owned in the south of France: I couldn't see much of the house itself, but I could see its name written on one of the gateposts in Arabic – a nod to his father's Iranian roots – and knew that what I could see of the building tallied with the description of one of the four houses he owned.

In the second, he was on the tarmac at some kind of airfield, smiling for the camera, his arms opened wide, presumably in celebration of the fact that he'd just bought himself a plane. In his left hand was a large, inflatable ignition key with a key fob reading 'The Zaid Express'. I didn't know much about jets, but I knew enough: even second-hand, even conservatively, he'd have probably dropped £20 million on it.

In the third, he was on a ski slope somewhere, among a group of what must have been friends. He had his arms around two of them and he looked fit and tanned.

My gaze lingered on the pictures.

Again, something stirred in me.

I took in what I could see of his house in France, its Arabic name, and then switched to the airfield – it was definitely somewhere in the UK: in the distance I could see a long row of 1930s terraced houses – and then to the shot of him on the slopes. He was fitter on that trip, sculpted, but in the other two his face was bloated and red.

I looked at other photos, taken in his twenties when he was assigned to the British Consulate in Hong Kong and to the embassy in Jakarta. There was a shot of him, overweight again, in Dubai in the mid 2000s, presumably when he'd been working further along the Arabian peninsula in Oman. More photographs of him, this time in Russia, in Kenya, in South Africa, all of which tied into the locations of jobs he'd said he'd had while working for the Foreign Office. As I looked at a portrait of him on Cape Town waterfront, I thought again about his reasons for still working at the FCO, despite having enough money not to work for twenty other lifetimes: *You should always listen to your parents – especially ones as remarkable as mine.*

I stepped back from the wall.

Out of forty-five pictures, there was only one of his parents: it was the frame in the centre, the one of the three of them, with Zaid as a boy, at their place in Marbella. So if his mum and dad had been so remarkable, where were they? Zaid had just one portrait of them, and yet I could see lots of photos of the same, less important faces – friends, colleagues, business partners, someone who had probably been a nanny. Other than the one of him with his parents in Marbella, there were four shots of Zaid as a boy: at the age of one or two, at his fifth birthday party, at about ten, and in his early teens.

I stepped in closer again, trying to get a better look at one of the shots nearest to me, but the moment I did, I saw something else at the very margins of my eyeline.

It was right in the corner of the room, wrapped in shadow and fixed as high up the wall as it could conceivably go, ensuring that – without a ladder – it was impossible to get at. I moved away from the photos, glancing along the hallway at Zaid's closed door, and stopped beneath the object on the wall.

It was about the size of a credit card, and looked like a cross between a wireless router and an electric key fob. There were three small antennae on top of it.

My stomach dropped.

I looked at my phone, still in my hand – still with no bars

showing, no hint of a reception – and then back up to the object on the wall.

Zaid had installed a signal jammer.

56

I spun on my heel, panicked, looking at Zaid's closed bedroom door, my heart pounding in my chest.

Moving towards the hallway, I kept my eyes on the door, then stopped again, listening. Over the sound of my heart, all I could hear was the hum of the central heating and the wind pressing at the windows.

I started inching forward again, approaching the doorways on the left and right. In one was a bathroom with a Jacuzzi, a wet room and two marble basins. In the other was an office, modern and immaculately decorated like everywhere else. There was a computer, shelves of books, files. On the desk beside the computer was an in-tray. My eyes were drawn to what looked like a printout on top, something typed across it in bold.

G76984Z.

I quickly moved into the room and picked up the printout. It was an email that Zaid had received from someone called Carson Connolly. *G76984Z* was the subject line, and Connolly worked for a company called Parsonfield. I vaguely recognized the name of the company, but couldn't remember where from.

The email itself seemed short and trivial.

From: carson_connolly@parsonfield.co.uk
To: rz@robertzaidholdings.com
Subject: Ref – G76984Z

Hi Mr Zaid –– just to let you know that I've managed to move your slot forward, as requested, to 10 a.m. tomorrow. I'm not in, but it should all be absolutely fine. Just in case, though, why don't you bring a copy of this email with you?

It was sent four hours ago.

I grabbed my phone, took a picture of the printout, then put it back where I'd found it. As I did, I noticed something on the next shelf down.

A photocopy of a driving licence.

I reached in and took it out, then realized it wasn't a photocopy but a fax. There was a machine behind me, on a desk in the corner, but it wasn't connected to the Internet, running instead off an old-fashioned phone line. Using technology this old only had one real benefit: it couldn't be intercepted digitally. It couldn't be hacked. If Zaid put the faxed document through the shredder tomorrow, there would be no record of it left.

I looked at the black-and-white licence.

The face of a woman in her sixties looked back at me: shoulder-length hair cut into a bob, an elegant mix of black streaks and natural greys; green eyes, glasses. In the bottom right, it listed her height as five nine and her weight as 140 pounds. In the top right was a bear icon.

The driving licence was Californian.

Her name had been circled in black pen, and an arrow went from that to a note at the side of the sheet. It was in Isaac Mills's handwriting:

Source at North Yorkshire police says she's been in touch. She's ex-LAPD. Been asking questions about Patrick Perry.

I froze.

Patrick Perry had talked to Freda about having one more call lined up. He'd said he was going to use a payphone and a pre-loaded calling card, ensuring there was no record of the conversation at home. So was this who he'd called? An ex-cop in Los Angeles? Most pre-loaded cards were for making international calls, so it wasn't a stretch, and the woman was from the same city as Adrian Vale. So had she known Vale? Had their paths crossed? And did she know that Patrick was now missing?

I took another look at the woman's face, her name, took a

photograph of the licence, then put the photocopy back and moved out into the hallway. I stepped to my right, trying to get a better angle on the staircase in front of me, but wasn't able to see much more than a couple of paintings, so I kept my eyes fixed on Zaid's door as I approached the next rooms along.

They were both spare bedrooms, stylish and clean but with the unlived-in feel of empty wardrobes and permanently made beds. I'd stopped short of the stairs but could see all the way up them now: at the top was a closed door, and visible through the balustrade was another. There had to be more rooms up there, but my attention had switched again.

Why was it so quiet in here?

I moved to his bedroom door, could see it had been left marginally ajar, and pushed at it. It swung back, revealing some of the furniture I'd glimpsed earlier: a huge bed, a pair of wardrobes, and a bay window looking out at nothing but darkness. There was a walk-in wardrobe on the other side, its door also ajar, and an en suite where I could see a shower and half a basin.

'Robert?'

In the bathroom, I heard someone move.

I realized I was holding my breath, my head swimming, nerves firing in every part of me, and as I came around the bed I found a cordless phone discarded on the carpet, abandoned between the end of the frame and the start of the bathroom's wooden floors. It was the one Zaid had been using earlier.

All I could hear now was the drone of a dial tone.

I took another step forward, and then another, and – in the bathroom – a man came into view: he was standing on the opposite side, leaning against one of the walls, waiting for me.

He had a gun aimed at my chest.

'Mills?'

An expression filled Isaac Mills's face. I wasn't sure what it was to start with. Anger? Sorrow? Pain? And then I realized – too late – that it wasn't any of them.

It was guilt.

It was a warning.

Someone's behind me.

The second I started to turn, it felt like the side of my head imploded. The butt of a knife handle cracked me in the temple – I could see the flash of a blade, facing up, out of a palm; an arm; a shoulder – and then I lurched sideways, landing awkwardly. When I tried to look up, to get on to my back, I felt the same arm jam against my throat, the crook of an elbow clamping against my windpipe.

I was in a chokehold.

I tried to move, to thrash around – tried to punch and kick my way free – but there was nothing to grab on to – and, even if there had been, the chokehold was too tight, the arm like an iron bar I couldn't shift.

My vision began to smear.

I glanced desperately left and right as everything turned grey, was conscious long enough to hear Mills say something to whoever had hold of me, and then finally everything shut down.

I slumped sideways and hit the floor.

Black.

Retirement: Part 2

2015

Los Angeles | Sunday 1 November

Her cellphone woke her, buzzing furiously across the nightstand. Turning over – aching from sleeping in the same position for hours – Jo glanced at the clock.

7 a.m.

Who the hell would be calling her so early on a Sunday morning?

She scooped up her phone, wondering if it might be Ethan, and then grabbed her glasses, sliding them on.

'Hello?'

'Ms Kader?'

'Yes.'

She rubbed at an eye.

'It's Patrick. We talked the other day.'

She frowned.

Patrick. The British guy who'd called about Adrian Vale.

'Ms Kader?'

'Uh, yeah. I don't think we agreed seven in the morning, did we?'

'No, I'm so sorry for calling you so early. Something's come up here that I have to take care of, but I still wanted to make sure that I got back in touch in order to follow up on what we talked about. You know, Adrian Vale and Beatrix Steards, and all of that.'

Jo sat up in bed and then hauled herself to her feet.

'Ms Kader?'

'Yeah, I'm here, I'm here.'

She wandered through to the living room, wiping the sleep from her eyes, and looked around for the legal pad she'd used during their phone call the day before. It turned out she hadn't written much down, mostly because she'd had a crashing hangover and about two seconds after she'd ended the call with this guy, she was puking into the toilet bowl. But at the top she'd written his name: *Patrick*.

'Do you remember what we talked about?' he asked.

She glanced at her notes again. She'd written down the name *Beatrix Steards*, but aside from that there wasn't much to jog her memory.

'I think we're going to have to start from the beginning, Mr, uh . . . ?'

'Oh, okay.' He didn't offer his surname. 'How come?'

'I wasn't feeling so good yesterday.'

'I see.' A pause. 'That's why I said I'd call back.'

This time, it was Jo's turn to pause.

'Do you remember anything at all?' the guy asked her.

It was a weird question: he hadn't framed it as an insult, more like some kind of a test. She frowned, fully awake now, her brain kicking into gear.

Was he the same as this yesterday?

'Ms Kader?'

'You mentioned Adrian Vale possibly having a connection to a disappearance over there in the UK.' She glanced at her notes. 'Beatrix Steards.'

'Ah, of course,' came the reply.

There was something else now too: she wasn't any expert on British accents, but she knew enough, and the guy yesterday had been from the north. Even with a hangover, she remembered thinking how much he'd sounded like a character from *Game of Thrones*.

But this guy didn't have the same accent.

'What did you say your surname was, Patrick?'

No response this time.

'Patrick?'

The line went dead.

Jo looked at her phone. Had he been cut off? Or had he hung up on her deliberately? She looked at her legal pad, at the name *Patrick*, and then waited a couple of minutes to see if he was going to call again. When he didn't, she switched to her land-line, dialled the number logged in her cellphone and waited for it to connect.

But it didn't even ring.

The number he'd called from was completely dead.

57

When I came around again, it felt like no time had passed at all and yet I was tied to a chair in the corner of a room I hadn't been into. My knees were touching the walls and all I could see was wallpaper. No furniture. No doors. No way out.

I felt drowsy, my head a fog of pain and confusion, but I knew enough: I was upstairs. I could hear the same noises outside – the city, its hum, the occasional car engine and siren – it was just the carpet and wallpaper that had changed.

I tried moving.

My hands were tied to the arms of a large oak chair, impossible to shuffle or move on the carpet, and my ankles were bound at the legs. I turned my head, pushing as far as I could to my left, and – at the fullest rotation of my neck – I saw him: he was right at the periphery of my vision, sitting in a chair on the opposite side of the room.

Zaid.

'I'll let you in on a little secret, David,' he said.

My neck was starting to ache already, but I held it there, watching him. He'd changed: he didn't have his tracksuit on any more, or his training top, he was dressed in a suit – all black, except for a charcoal shirt. He'd been sitting with his legs crossed, but now he uncrossed them and came forward in the chair, his elbows on his knees.

'I still don't know if I trust Isaac.'

I was forced to face the corner of the room again, my neck stiff, the unnatural position I had to reach to even look at Zaid sending sparks of pain into my skull.

'I mean, I suppose he's off getting things ready for me now,' he said, his voice maintaining exactly the same speed, rhythm and pitch, as if he were reading off an autocue. 'He's doing what

I asked. But he's not my man. He's Jacob Pierce's. Jacob vouched for him, Jacob was the one who said they'd worked together once on a case up north, and Jacob was the one who said Isaac was susceptible, that he could be turned. But that's the thing, isn't it? In my experience, most people can have their head turned with money. That's why rich people generally do whatever the fuck they want. You wave enough pound notes in front of someone's face and it's amazing what they'll forget. Their memories, their morals, it all goes out of the window. But then, after a while, you start to earn so much, so often, that, in a weird way, the money helps you see more clearly. Instead of making you *lose* your morals, it brings them back into focus.'

I looked again in his direction, but he'd deliberately placed his chair directly behind me so that, whichever way I turned, I could only see the very edges of him.

'Discussing money, its power to corrupt, always reminds me of another story. It's about Adrian Vale. What I said downstairs about him, most of it was true. He was a loner, he was weird, people didn't really get him. But the idea that I gave him the name of a solicitor when Beatrix went missing, well, that isn't quite true. That was an embellishment. Because, actually, I was the one who called Jacob Pierce.'

I frowned. 'What?'

It was the first time I'd spoken.

I sounded groggy, hoarse.

'Did you have a good look through my things, David?'

I turned, trying to see him behind me.

'Is that what took you so long to get to the bathroom? Were you nosing around in my office, looking at my things?' He made a soft *tut, tut, tut* sound. 'Joline Kader,' he said, forcing a breath out with her name. I thought of the driving licence with her picture on it. 'Is that who you were looking at?'

She'd been asking questions about Patrick.

'That bitch was like a dog with a bone.'

Again, he paused.

But this time it was because he was moving.

By the point I'd actually realized he was on my other side, it was already too late: a hand clamped on to the back of my skull, holding it in place, forcing me to face forward. The power in his hands was immense.

'I'm not really a boxer, David,' he said flatly. 'A sport in which you're confined to twenty-four square feet of space – I mean, where's the fun in that? No, the reason I lose weight and gain it again isn't because I'm training for fights. It's because weight – or the lack of it – has proved to be an effective disguise on the rare occasions when I've allowed myself to be photographed in public. People can't get the measure of you when you never look quite the same. A beard, or not. A new hairstyle, or a shaved head. Those things help. But you know what the greatest disguise of all is, David? You know what convinces people more quickly than almost anything else?' He dug his nails so hard into my scalp I could feel them draw blood. 'It's the way a person talks.'

He released his grip and came around to the side of me, and as I looked at Robert Zaid, as I processed what he'd just said to me, it hit me like a sledgehammer.

I finally understood why the photos on the wall of the living room felt wrong.

I understood why there was only a single picture of his parents.

I knew the nanny who Zaid had been photographed with as a boy wasn't a nanny at all, and I knew why – the moment I'd entered the house – I'd felt so strongly that I'd met him before, even though I hadn't: because I'd seen his picture in a police file.

'It's the way a person talks,' he repeated, slower, smiling this time.

But now his accent wasn't English.

It was American.

Because this wasn't Robert Zaid.

It was Adrian Vale.

384

PART EIGHT

The Forest

I can hear a noise again.

But it's different.

It's not coming from down here.

It's coming from above me.

I tilt my head slightly, trying to give myself the best chance I can of hearing whatever it is, but the moment I do, the noise stops.

When it does, all that's left is a ringing in my ears, a faint background noise that I've slowly got used to after weeks in the silence of this place. But now it acts as interference, an intrusive element that makes me less confident about what I'm hearing from above. Is something finally happening? Is he coming for me?

Or is it a fault in my ears?

In my head?

Is everything I'm hearing – as I'd always feared – entirely built in my mind? The thought scares me, because my mind used to be everything to me. It was what defined me, what I used to survive and stay ahead.

It was how I found missing people.

When Derryn was dying, her body, and then her voice, and then her breath, fading into memory as she was swallowed by a disease I couldn't fight for her, my lucidity was how I survived. And nearly a decade on, before this darkness, it was still keeping me safe: my days and nights were still filled with the faces of the missing, with the echoes of their voices, with stories in whose tragedy I sometimes saw no light. Deep down, I knew that finding people allowed me to fix things: the ragged fractures created by a disappearance; the ambiguity when someone vanished; the continual, unanswered sense of loss. Sometimes, when I brought people home alive, I got to raze grief to the ground entirely. I wanted families to feel that. I wanted them to remember what it was like to breathe, because when you lose someone you love, it just completely hollows you out.

You barely exhale; you barely exist.

I never wanted anyone else to feel the way I did.

So, even in times when I've doubted myself, when I've glimpsed the absolute darkness in men, the terrible things they're capable of doing to one another and the tremors their choices leave behind, I've had my mind. I've had a clarity of purpose. I've kept working, searching, taking the next case, and the next, and the next. And when the police would hit a wall, when the questions were thriving like weeds, I was always there for the families with a way forward.

But where is the way forward from here?

How do I fix this?

How will I ever find my way home?

58

For what felt like weeks, all I knew was darkness and silence.

In a place bereft of light and sound, I had no choice but to replay the moments before he'd drugged me, pausing and rewinding the image of him standing next to me; of my wrists and ankles bound to a chair; of him speaking to me in an accent he'd kept hidden for nearly twenty-nine years. On some level, I started to wonder if maybe I'd known what was coming before it had even got to that; maybe I'd seen through the disguise the second I stood in front of the photos that had covered an entire wall of his home.

But, if I had, I'd been too slow to stop him.

Instead, imprisoned in a blackness I couldn't escape from, I started putting it all together in my head, a jigsaw puzzle of stitched pieces that I grew to know intimately. The disappearance of Beatrix Steards in London at the start of 1987. Nine people vanishing from a remote village in Yorkshire. And, somewhere among it all, the body of a man on a beach in Sussex in October 1989.

Back then, DNA analysis was still in its infancy.

And that was exactly how he'd got away with it.

Because it was only being used in high-priority cases at the time, the suicide of a depressed student, his corpse discovered – decomposed and forgotten – at the bottom of a five-hundred-foot cliff face, was never going to make the cut. It appeared open and shut. The victim had a wallet on him, containing ID, there was a half-finished suicide note confirming other personal details, and what hadn't yet decayed into the shingle bore a striking similarity to Adrian Vale.

Not only were Adrian Vale and Robert Zaid a close match in terms of build – in adulthood, Zaid had filled out, shaking off the boyishness of his youth – Zaid also happened to be, like

Vale, olive-skinned, dark-eyed and dark-haired. He was half Iranian, Vale was Latino, but while their roots were thousands of miles apart, their colouring and physiques were nearly identical. The fact that, when investigators found the body, the teeth had been smashed during the fall only helped muddy the waters even more: dental tests proved inconclusive, but inconclusive was exactly what the teeth were going to be when a body hit the floor, face first, at ninety miles per hour.

Having inherited a fortune after his parents' deaths, Zaid was living the sort of lifestyle that Vale envied and would never have. And so with Vale's own mother dead by that time, and no other attachments in his life – nothing to draw him back to LA, especially with Joline Kader still sniffing around him – Vale made his move.

He killed Robert Zaid.

And then became him.

It was why Vale drifted away from anyone he'd attended King's College with – not, as he claimed to Patrick Perry during their Skype call in 2015, because they were all so upset about Beatrix Steards going missing, but because Vale knew that the other people on the course would ID him the moment they saw him pretending to be Zaid. It was why Vale also withdrew almost entirely from the public eye, why he hated having his photograph taken or posted anywhere, and it was also likely to be why he'd taken up a role at the Foreign Office. It was a move I hadn't been able to figure out: Zaid had so much money – why would he work for the FCO?

The answer was simple.

It wasn't Zaid.

Vale's time in government, especially at the start, had given him all the breathing room he'd needed. He'd deliberately got himself posted abroad for the first decade after Zaid's murder, working in countries where no one knew him or had met him before. By the time he came back to the UK, the lie was so embedded and he'd so successfully severed any connections to Zaid's former life back home that he settled into his existence in Britain totally unhindered, and with no one suspecting a thing.

He took Zaid's money, his inheritance and his identity, and he lived a life that didn't belong to him. The one photograph on his wall at home of the actual Zaid, with his parents at the house in Marbella, was just for show, for the rare visitors he had. Zaid and Vale had looked enough alike as kids for any disparities to pass relatively unnoticed, especially at a superficial glance – or, as with me, for people to note that *something* wasn't right in the pictures on that wall, but not be certain of exactly what.

The photos of Vale's mother that were mounted among the others – the woman I thought had been a nanny in the real childhood pictures of Vale – were what really mattered to him. When he'd said to me that his parents were remarkable, he'd never meant his father. His dad was an alcoholic, a failure, lost to him and his mother way before he drank himself to death. His mother, though, was different. As much as it was possible for a person like Adrian Vale to love someone, he loved her.

It might have been the only authentic thing about him.

Suddenly, I was back.

In the darkness. In the silence.

I was in the same place I'd been kept for weeks, this prison with no doors and no escape. I could still hear the same noise – the fault in my ears, the hum that was either inside my head or somewhere above me. But now something had changed.

Something was different.

It's the darkness.

It wasn't much, but it was there: a grey square directly overhead, maybe twenty feet above me, shifting across.

A hatch.

I'm in some kind of hole.

It moved again, opening further, and the minimal, charcoal-coloured light was enough for me to see that I'd been right all along: the roof in here was triangular, too high to reach with just my arms, and there were no doors anywhere, no windows, no exits at ground level.

Only above.

A rope tumbled down from the hatch.

59

The end of the rope hit the floor.

I didn't move.

I just stood there and watched. I was frightened, frozen. I couldn't work out what was happening. All this darkness, all this silence – weeks, maybe months of it – and now this.

I stepped closer to the rope.

There were knots all the way up, large enough to get a foot on to and aid an ascent. This system was obviously how the food, the water and the blankets had come in; not this exact rope perhaps, but one like it, secured to some kind of platform or container so that the meagre supplies they left for me could be lowered all the way down.

And always when I was asleep.

If the rope had been dropped in while I was still awake, I'd have noticed the hatch and the marginal change in the light. The fact that I hadn't made something else obvious: if the supplies only came in once I'd gone to sleep, I was being watched.

There had been cameras in here the whole time.

I grabbed hold of the rope.

Did I go up?

Was it a trap?

I hesitated a moment longer, looking to see if Vale might be waiting out of sight at the top – but then the overwhelming need to escape took over. I had to go up. I had to try and get out of here.

I started climbing.

As I did, I thought of the boxes I'd found at Seiger and Sten, the others who must have spent time here before me. Did they make this climb too?

The closer I got to the hatch, the more I could see of the

room around me, the grey light leaking in from above to show a camera – as I'd suspected – off to my right. I only noticed it as I got to the very top, one of my hands gripping the edge of the hatch, the other clamped on the rope. There were no LEDs on the camera, no hint it was there at all, the outside cased in black. For a moment, I looked down into the room I'd been in all this time. I could see the shoes I'd kicked off because they didn't fit and were too uncomfortable. I could see my discarded blankets. I could see a river of old water bottles flowing against one edge of the room, and then hundreds of paper plates. They were scattered everywhere, a map of my captivity.

I reached towards the hatch with my other hand – and then, finally, lifted myself all the way out.

Breathing hard, I looked around.

I was alone in another room.

It was low-lit and narrow, maybe 120 feet long. The walls were chipboard, the wood scratched and dirty, and there was one other hatch like mine between me and what looked like the exit door. The second hatch was already fully opened, had maybe been that way for some time, rope snaking out of it and clipped to an iron loop bolted to the floor.

Beyond it, the exit door was ajar.

Even in the subdued light, my eyes struggled to adjust after so long in darkness. They watered and blurred, tears breaking out across my cheeks, and as I wiped them away I got to my feet, moving around the other hatch, peering into its empty darkness.

I headed for the door.

It was ajar enough for me to see a sliver of what lay on the other side: some kind of slatted wooden veranda, with a flight of steps down to a sloped patch of grass. Ringing the grass were trees.

Forest.

Where the hell was I?

I placed a hand on the door and pushed at it very gently, trying to give myself a wider view of what awaited. It was either dawn or dusk. The light was weak, the sky like ash, and although I could hear birds far off, the forest was absolutely black beyond the initial treeline. It was cold too. There was no wind yet, but I knew that when it came, it would cut through me like a knife – and as I thought about that, I looked down at myself: I was in a T-shirt and a pair of ill-fitting trousers that weren't mine. I didn't have anything on my feet. Not even socks.

I turned, thought about going back for my shoes, but didn't want to waste time, so pushed at the door instead, inching it open.

Heart beating faster, I moved even further out on to the veranda, the slats creaking under my weight, and glanced both ways: the room with the hatches was part of a bigger structure – some sort of windowless house – but, compared to the immensity of the forest surrounding me, it was just a mote of dust. Everywhere I looked, there were trees, millions of them: immense soldiers in an infinite line.

A thump from somewhere else in the house.

Movement – or maybe a door closing.

I looked behind me for something to use as a weapon, couldn't see anything, and then switched focus. On the opposite wall to the hatch I'd climbed out of, there was a panel, high up. It was some kind of heating vent. I hurried across to it, reached up and quietly levered the plate off. As I did, I paused; there was no sound from the other side. All I could hear was birdsong, deep into the trees, and then a stark silence.

Wherever I was, it was miles from anywhere.

Placing the panel on the floor, I grabbed the edge of the vent and pulled myself up high enough to see into it. At the other end, vague, gloomy, was another room.

Some kind of lounge.

It was dark but I could make out a stone fireplace, the mouth of the chimney licked black with soot. There was an armchair next to it – pale, threadbare – and a low coffee table stacked with books. A bottle of whisky and a glass were on it.

Movement.

My eyes were drawn to the opposite side, as far to the right as I could see from where I was, and in the murk beyond the fireplace, I realized there was a shape in the shadows, hunched over, leaning on what looked like a walking stick.

Vale.

He was a half-turn away from me, perched on the edge of a dark sofa, a thick winter coat on, a beanie, snow boots.

At his hip was a knife.

The blade glinted despite the lack of light, and that was when I looked at the walking stick again and realized it wasn't that at all.

It was a rifle.

He was loading it.

60

I headed back out, along the veranda, trying to prevent the wooden slats from moaning under my weight. I ignored the cold, the fact that every inch of exposed skin was freezing and I was starting to lose sensation in my feet, but it was hard: even as I focused on what was ahead, I could feel my teeth wanting to chatter, the gentle vibration of them in my jaw as the air carved through the thin, torn cotton of my clothing like it wasn't even there.

Ahead of me, the veranda bent around to the right and then continued for another fifteen or twenty feet. I could see a window now, dusty and opaque, and a door. The building looked a lot smaller than I'd imagined: one bedroom, maybe two at most, the living room that I'd seen Vale in, and then probably a kitchen and a bathroom. It was all built from the same dark wood, even the roof. Only the stone chimney that I'd glimpsed through the heating vent in any way deviated from the main design: it broke out like a grey finger, and – from the top – smoke drifted faintly upwards.

Beyond that, it was just forest, so dense and tall that there was no view other than the trees. On the opposite side of the building from where I was, banks of pine were so huge and close to the house that they brushed against the roof, almost seemed to be reaching across it, and whenever the wind picked up, their needles made a soft whisper, like someone was talking to me.

I moved quickly towards the front door, stopping short of the window to look inside. The kitchen was bare and stripped back: to the right, a door exited into a hallway, dark and difficult to make out; to the left, a portable gas stove was on top of one of the worktops, disconnected, a plate beside that – scraped free of food – and a plastic beaker.

Ducking under the sill, I headed to the door.

The wind came again, moving the trees, rousing the voice of the forest – but as soon as it was gone again, there was nothing. No sound at all. No traffic close by, no planes in the sky, no voices. It was eerie, as if we were above the atmosphere, drifting through space: when I moved even slightly, looking around for something I could use as a weapon, the faint wrinkle of my shirt, the soft pop of my stiff, underused joints, shattered the silence. I tensed, waiting for Vale to react, to burst out of the front door – but he didn't.

Only branches moved.

Only the trees made any sound.

Another weapons search soon proved fruitless: there was nothing close by, nothing serrated or edged, and certainly nothing to compete with a rifle.

I'd have to improvise.

Reaching over the side of the veranda, I scooped up a handful of hard, crumbly earth and stepped back, beside the door, so that I would be behind it when it opened. Delaying for a moment, trying and failing to still my pulse, I took a breath and wondered if it would have been better to have run, and taken my chances among the trees. But it was too late now.

I launched the dirt up, on to the roof.

As soon as it hit the wood, it scattered and spread, a noise like waves crackling across a shingle beach, and then there was movement – instant, quick – from inside.

The door creaked open.

I turned, my back against the wall, and watched it inch out in my direction. It had no glass in it, but two of the wooden slats had slightly warped and, between them, I glimpsed the vague hint of a man.

A hand came to the end of the door, fingers along the edge of it, holding it in place, and then the barrel of the rifle drifted into view, pointing down towards the veranda. *Come on. A bit more.* A creak sounded and he took another step forward, more of the gun barrel extending out past the door: the fore-end, the tip of the scope.

More.

At the bottom of the door, I could see his boot now.

Halfway up, the zip on his coat.

A bit more.

A smooth, unblemished hand on the fore-end.

Come on, more.

I needed to trap his arm in the door.

Force him to drop the rifle.

More.

Instead, he stopped, as if he'd seen something.

I looked out at the forest, trying to imagine what, but all that stared back at me was the twisted darkness behind every trunk.

And then I realized something.

I turned, looking through the warped slats of the door.

It wasn't something in the forest he was looking at.

It was me.

61

I didn't have time to think.

As soon as I saw the flash of an eye between the slats, I smashed into the door with my shoulder. It snapped back, whipping on its hinges, and Vale got jammed between the door and the frame.

Grabbing the door handle, I yanked it towards me and smashed into him again. It gave him a fraction of a second to try and move, to retreat even further inside, away from the door, which he did – but not all of him made it. I crunched the door into his arm, just below the elbow. He yelled out in agony, his grip instantly loosening on the rifle.

I kicked at it – his hand, his wrist, the gun. Anything.

The rifle spun off and hit the veranda floor.

As soon as it did, he pulled his arm in and my weight – still against the door – forced it back into the frame. The door clattered into place and clicked shut.

I reached down, picked up the rifle and pointed it towards the door, gripping hard – and then the wind came again, rigid as bone, and I realized how cold I was. I couldn't feel my feet at all now, could hardly feel the ends of my fingers. My skin was starting to turn blue and my head was swimming: I was hungry and tired, confused, still unbalanced by weeks and weeks of darkness. *Keep it together*, I told myself, *keep it together, keep it together*, but it didn't matter how many times I repeated it, I could barely clear the fog. Every limb felt heavy, every muscle arthritic. I was so frightened I could barely even breathe.

The wind picked up again, the chant of voices, the crackle and scratch of pine needles on top of the house, and as it did, I looked down at the rifle: I hadn't held a gun like this for decades – not since my dad had taught me how to shoot as a kid on our farm.

Keep it together, I thought again, *keep it together, keep it –*

I could hear his voice.

I stepped closer to the door, to the warped slats through which I could see nothing except darkness, but now it was quiet again.

Reaching down, I grabbed the handle.

My fingers were trembling.

I stepped back, arching my body slightly, desperately trying to calm myself but nothing worked. The cold and the fear were too deeply embedded. I didn't know what other weapons he had. I didn't even know where he was.

I'm going to die out here.

I forced the thought down, forced everything else down with it, and gripped the handle as tightly as I could. Bringing the rifle across my chest, I quietly sucked in a breath and looked down at my hands.

Do it.

I yanked the door open, instantly raised the rifle and jammed the butt into my shoulder. But Vale didn't rush me. As I looked along the scope, through it, either side of it, the house remained utterly still. Ahead of me, a hallway branched off into three rooms. A bathroom on the left. A kitchen on the right. A living room straight ahead. I'd been wrong: there was no bedroom. Instead, in the living room, I could see a sofa bed, pulled out and set up, the sheets untidy on top. There were some books on a stand next to it, some candles too. There didn't seem to be electricity here, but if there were surveillance cameras, the house wasn't without power: there was probably a generator somewhere.

My bare feet hardly made a sound on the floorboards, just a velveteen murmur. The more I edged in, the more I could see: the fire in the living room, little more now than a pile of smouldering ash; the kitchen; a bathroom with a free-standing bathtub and a bucket. No basin. No toilet. The taps on the bath weren't connected, they were just for show: if Vale wanted to bathe, he'd have to use a water butt I'd seen out front. Maybe a generator heated the water, maybe it didn't, but one thing was obvious: wherever we were, no one was going to find it.

We were off the grid.

A noise, in the living room: I gripped the rifle even harder and tilted my head to the side slightly, looking past the muzzle. Something popped in the fire – a spark glowing for a second before dying again – and that was when I heard the same noise. It was clearer this time and much easier to place.

A door, banging against its frame in the wind.

A back entrance.

I took another step forward, trying to see into the living room, then stopped again.

A floorboard creaked behind me.

62

Instantly, I swivelled, swinging the rifle around.

The length of the weapon saved my life: Vale couldn't get close enough with his knife, the long barrel of the rifle – caught in the space between his bicep and his ribcage – keeping him an arm's length away. He had his knife out in front of him, its blade flashing silver, and he awkwardly slashed it from left to right, off balance and trying to avoid the gun. I felt the knife rip through the cotton of my T-shirt, slicing a shallow cut in my skin, but as I stumbled back, I was alive – I knew it, and so did he.

I fired.

The shot was off target: behind him, wood splintered, a flute of dust erupting out of a door frame. I fired again, and again: I didn't know where the first shot went, but the second hit him in the chest and the impact sent him staggering away, out of the door, to the veranda. Propelled backwards, he hit the handrail and toppled over it.

I heard a low, dull thump.

Scrambling to my feet, I followed his path out of the house, his blood dotted up the walls around the door, on the floor, over the veranda. When I got to the handrail, he was already on his knees, trying to get to his feet, one hand clutching his chest.

There was an exit wound on his back.

The shot had gone right through him.

'Stop!' I shouted, the word carrying all the anger of however long I'd been kept here – the days, weeks, maybe months of living in darkness, alone and abandoned.

He turned.

His eyes were wild, terrifying – even though I was the one with the gun – his fingers wriggling at the grip of the knife he was still holding. He finally stood, but then rocked forward on the balls of his feet, unbalanced, wincing, trying not to show me that he was hurt. But the chest wound was bad: against his coat it seemed almost black, the shape of it spreading like a charred flower. He staggered to a stop six feet from me and looked up.

'That fucking *prick* Mills,' he said, dots of blood on his face, saliva foaming at the corner of his mouth like a rabid dog. '*Mills!*' he screamed into the forest, and I looked beyond him, realizing now that Vale wasn't the one who'd opened the hatch. Mills was. Vale had been preparing for it, which was why I'd seen him loading his rifle – he'd been getting ready to finally put me down – but Mills had got there first.

Mills was here.

I looked out into the forest again, then behind me, into the emptiness of the house, and as I turned back Vale moved, staring at his chest wound, at the blood spilling over his fingers, as if the injury were Isaac Mills's fault, not mine.

'He was so *persuasive* about keeping you alive,' he said, wiping his face. He must have been talking about the night at the cottage, about Mills warning me off rather than cutting me down. Vale was the one who'd torn our investigation from the walls. He was the one on the phone who'd listened in to Mills and me talking.

'Where are the people from Black Gale, Adrian?'

He didn't respond, dropping to his knees again.

Frozen grass crunched as he hit the ground, and then his eyes swept across the vastness of the forest, his expression almost serene.

'Are they buried out there?'

He swayed.

'Adrian?'

'No,' he said.

He was suddenly different now, as if he could feel the end coming.

'So where are they?'

'I never buried them.'

He said it quietly, matter-of-factly.

'You mean, you just left them where you killed them?'

He didn't even look like he'd heard the question. I stared at the colossal sweep of the forest. Where the hell did I even start to search?

'You just left them where you killed them?' I repeated.

He nodded. 'No one's going to find them here.'

My whole body sank: I'd known it was coming, I'd known that there was little chance any of them would still be alive – but hearing it was different from imagining it.

'It began somewhere like this,' he said, his voice muted, as if it were coming from miles away. 'That's why I always liked it here. It's the silence.' He shifted on his knees, flinching, and looked up at me; it was hard to know what to make of him now – the threat was gone, the rage, the animal in him. 'Big Bear Lake. That's what it reminds me of.'

'In California?'

He nodded. 'I took a girl up there once, right back at the beginning. Martina. I liked her, I suppose. We had so little in common but I found her fascinating.'

'Is she dead too?'

'Yes,' he said, but there was a sadness to him. 'She overdosed.'

I watched him.

'Tell me where the bodies are, Adrian.'

He shrugged. 'I don't remember.'

'You don't remember where you left nine bodies?'

'Do you know how long you've been here?' he said by way of a response.

I looked out at the trees, a part of me scared to know the answer.

'Do you know how *long*?' He grimaced.

'How long?'

'Forty-six days.'

The news hit me hard.

Forty-six days. It had been the middle of March when I'd last seen daylight; now it was almost the end of April. I looked around me, at the trees, the frosted grass; felt the chill of the air against my skin. This had to be somewhere up north: it would explain why the weather was still so cool, the remoteness of the place, and it made sense of the vague memory I had of being enclosed inside a boot for hours – heavily sedated and tied up – and driven somewhere.

'G76984Z.'

It took me a couple of seconds to find my feet again.

'G76984Z,' Vale repeated. 'You recognize that?'

The sequence Mills had written on the Dictaphone.

The sequence I'd seen in an email at the house in Highgate.

'Do you know what that means?' he asked.

His fingers fell away from the wound.

'You don't, do you?'

He laughed, caustic, broken.

'So what's it mean, Adrian?'

He turned to the forest again and it was like I could instantly see his concentration wane, a light malfunctioning at the end of its existence, its power almost gone.

'Adrian? Is it some kind of map reference?'

'Do you know why I left you here so long?' he said distantly, the question he'd asked me forgotten. 'I've been out of the country for almost five weeks. Endless shareholder meetings in places I fucking hate, and then some Foreign Office bullshit I couldn't get out of. If I didn't go to those things, I would have let people down, and then they'd have started asking questions, and questions are what I've spent my life trying to avoid.' He sniffed, blood specked up his cheek in an arc. 'So I got you here and left you. I would have preferred to have just got rid of you straight away – walked you out to the forest like everyone else – but there wasn't the time to do it, to make sure it got done properly, and I thought to myself, "If nothing else, a little stay will soften him up a bit." I thought it would be fun to see you emerge from the dark a month and a half after I put you down there. But I guess I underestimated you. Or Mills. Or both of you. I thought nothing could touch me.' His words fell away. 'It's another thing I found out about being rich. You start to think you're invincible.'

'So if you weren't here, who was feeding me?'

'Mills,' he said mutedly. 'He was babysitting you until I could get here. He probably spent the entire time trying to work out his little plan of attack today: using you to get to me was the only way he could be free. He's tried to walk away before, but I've always had too much on him – too many insurance policies ready to kick in if he fucked me.'

'Tell me where the bodies are, Adrian.'

He didn't move.

'What difference does it make to you now?'

No response.

'Is Beatrix Steards out here too?'

He took a breath, the sound rattling in his chest.

'What about Joline Kader?'

This time, I got a reaction.

'Kader,' he said, almost whispering the name.

I took a step closer.

He glanced at me. 'You and her, you'd have got on. That bitch had the same' – he waved his bloodied hand around in front of him, searching for the word he wanted – 'obsession as you. The same eyes. Always searching for a fucking lie.'

I tried again: 'Why take all nine of the Black Gale villagers?'

He was growing smaller, sinking in on himself.

'Why not just take Patrick Perry and Freda Davey?'

His eyes closed.

'*Adrian?*'

He opened them again, but his body was shutting down.

'Is Beatrix Steards here too?'

He shook his head.

'Where's Beatrix?'

'London,' he said.

'Where in London?'

He touched his fingers to his wound again, like he'd only just noticed it was there.

'Adrian, where in London is Beatrix buried?'

He collapsed forward, hitting the grass.

He was motionless now.

'Adrian?'

But there was no answer.

Just the quiet of the forest.

And, somewhere among its trees, nine people from Black Gale.

Circle

London | Two Weeks Ago

The flight landed at Heathrow almost twenty minutes late.

She followed a family out, into the corridors of the terminal, watching as the son and daughter – neither more than four or five – discussed the films they'd been watching when they should have been sleeping. The flight had been turbulent, the eastern seaboard like a rollercoaster, so Jo hadn't managed to sleep much either, and now her eyes felt dry and her throat scratchy. She grabbed a bottle of water from her backpack and hurried past the family, trying to get ahead of the crowds spilling out of flights all the way down the walkway.

The lines in immigration were still huge, a snaking queue that went across the hall and back again. She got out her phone and waited for it to connect, then texted Ethan to let him know she'd arrived safely. She told him to give Claire and Maisie a big hug from her. After that, she went to her Dropbox and accessed everything that she'd collated on the village of Black Gale.

She moved forward in the queue, inch by inch, footstep by footstep. It had taken her a long time to get here.

Almost two and a half years.

She remembered the call she'd got the day after she retired from UCI. If the British guy hadn't mentioned Adrian Vale, maybe she would have forgotten about it entirely, despite the things that bothered her. She was sixty-five at the time, exhausted, actively looking to leave the reminders of her working life behind. She'd been worried about whether she'd find a similar sense of purpose in retirement, the same drive to get up every day, but not worried enough not to do it. Soon after the call, she'd flown up to San Francisco to see Ethan and his family, spent four weeks with them, and, when she'd come back, allowed her retirement to take over in earnest and the ghosts of her working life to wither. She'd actively gone out to meet friends, she'd invited old LAPD colleagues around for dinner, she'd taken up Pilates and tried her hand at golf. At weekends, she'd gone on walks with other retirees she knew at Seal Beach, along the coast into Sunset and Huntingdon, into the rolling hills of Crystal Cove, sometimes on the ferry across to Santa Catalina Island. She'd been out on some dates too, although none of them ever felt quite right, even after so many years. They were perfectly nice men, polite and interesting, but they weren't Ira and, eventually, she stopped.

She spent more of the holidays with Ethan, Claire and Maisie, either up in San Francisco or at home in her apartment, and she eventually gave up golf because of mild arthritis in her shoulder. And then, slowly, the coffee mornings and social events and dinners started to become a little more sporadic and she found herself spending more and more time at home, in her own company. As her life became less hectic, she began retreating into her own thoughts, going back to her career, to things that she wished she'd done, or done better. Finally, she found herself digging out her old notebook, flicking through its yellowed pages, and – in the middle – stopping at the names of the ones that had got away: Gabriel Wilzon and Donald Klein. Once she saw them, everything came full circle.

She remembered the call she'd taken about Adrian Vale.

She remembered the man called Patrick.

In the first conversation he'd had with her, he'd given her his surname. She recalled that clearly, she just didn't recall what it was. She'd never written it down. Her hangover had been so bad that day, her stomach churning, her head thumping, that the notes she'd made had ended up being worthless. She'd been banking on the follow-up call to fill in the blanks.

But the follow-up had been totally different.

Because whoever had called her the second time hadn't been Patrick.

Even then, she sat on that knowledge – the certainty that a deception had taken place – for a long time doing nothing about it, anxious about letting her old life invade the sanctity of her retirement. But with every passing week, the more she denied herself, the more it ate away at her and, eventually, she found it impossible to resist any longer. At the point she finally started looking properly into who the call *had* been from, and who the real Patrick was, over sixteen months had passed. But, immediately, she started to hit barriers. The name was too common, the search parameters too wide. Was she looking for a Patrick who knew Adrian Vale? Was she looking for a Patrick who knew Beatrix Steards? Or was she looking for neither? All three routes ended up in dead ends so she then decided to switch tack.

She went back to landline phone records she'd already pulled from AT&T and zeroed in on the second call on 1 November 2015 from the man claiming to be Patrick.

The number was listed as UNKNOWN.

But the first call wasn't.

The number listed for that had a +44 international code and, when she reverse-traced it to its source, she discovered it was a payphone in a place called Sedbergh, a small town in the county of Cumbria. She had no idea where either of those were, but this time she didn't let anything else get in her way. She spent hours researching the area and looking for Patricks in it.

When she still couldn't find him, she started massaging the truth. She called the police forces in Cumbria and North Yorkshire, and told them she worked for the LAPD. *Worked.* It was technically correct, she just hadn't worked for them for almost fifteen years. To her surprise, it started opening some doors – slowly. Cops in both police forces said they would call her back, and the Met said the same thing when she got in touch with them about the unsolved disappearance of Beatrix Steards. After that, it became a waiting game. Weeks and months would pass, and then she would chase again, and then she would get the same vague reassurances about a response, wait some more, and would have to chase anew. Eventually, though, she got the answers she needed. The name Patrick was a dead end and so was the town of Sedbergh.

But Beatrix Steards was different.

Two years after the phone call from Patrick, after being passed between different detectives, someone at the Met agreed to talk to her in detail about Beatrix Steards. She sat at a window thousands of miles away, overlooking the Pacific Ocean, and made pages of notes, and at the end, when she asked for the name of the last person to access the case, the cop told her: Detective Inspector Kevin Quinn.

She chased him for months, emailing him, leaving messages for him, and in the end she figured she was going to have to try some other route. But then Quinn called her back one day, at the start of April, almost two and a half years after she first picked up the call from the man called Patrick.

'Are you a mate of Raker's?' he asked her.

'Who's Raker?'

There was a pause on the line.

'You haven't talked to him?'

'I haven't talked to anyone,' she said. 'Who's Raker?'

'David Raker. He called me about this same thing a few weeks back.'

She dragged her iPad towards her, swiped it on, and put in a quick Google search for *David Raker*. She found him easily: he was a missing persons investigator, based in London.

'Did this Raker enquire about a guy called Patrick?' she asked Quinn.

'Patrick? You mean Patrick Perry?'

A few days later, armed with the information that Quinn had given her, she started looking into Black Gale, the disappearance of Patrick Perry and eight other people in the same village, and then the names associated with the Beatrix Steards case, trying to find the links between those two and Adrian Vale; between everything she had and the deaths of Gabriel Wilzon and Donald Klein. And that was when she stumbled across Robert Zaid, captured within a few, solitary photographs.

Except the moment she saw his face, she knew.

It wasn't Robert Zaid at all.

Inside an hour, she'd booked a flight to London.

63

I went to the very edge of the veranda, the adrenalin washing out of me, woozy from the cold. Vale was completely still, only the grass moving faintly around him.

Turning, I looked back at the house.

'Isaac?'

Out in the forest, it was silent too.

'Isaac, are you here? It's Raker.'

I headed back to the house, moving along the hallway and into the living room. Even though the fire had died out, it was still warm, and – as I paused in the doorway – I took it all in for the first time. There was hardly any furniture, just the sofa bed, a rickety wardrobe, and a bookcase filled with old paperbacks.

And another mattress.

Off to my left, I could see the rear door that Vale had used in order to come back around on me. It was moving slightly, massaged by the wind.

Mills has made a run for it.

I quickly went to the wardrobe and yanked it open.

Men's clothes were on hangers – coats, woollen jumpers, trousers – and there were T-shirts in an untidy pile at the bottom, alongside summer and winter shoes. I grabbed a jumper, some trousers and some socks, and then levered my freezing feet into a pair of hiking boots. Nothing fitted, but all of it was warmer and more comfortable than anything I'd been dressed in since waking up in the black of Vale's prison.

I grabbed the rifle and headed for the rear door.

It opened on to a small porch with steps that led directly to a narrow mud path ringing the property. The path was totally hemmed in on one side by the forest. I was literally on the edge of the trees, staring into the shadows beyond.

There was no sign of movement anywhere.

I moved around the building in the direction of the veranda, keeping my eyes on the trees, then stopped on the parcel of grass where Vale's body still lay. His eyes were open and his blood had washed the frost-flecked grass a pale pink.

A noise.

I followed the sound, off to my right. The trees were moving now in the wind, their branches swaying, and with it came the sound of pine needles scratching the roof. I raised the rifle and looked through the scope, sweeping the gun from left to right in an effort to see beyond the treeline.

And that was when I spotted him.

A distant figure, in the forest.

He was heading away from me, his movements jerky and unstable, as if the ground were uneven, and as he took a furtive glance over his shoulder he almost lost his footing entirely.

I broke into a sprint.

It took me ten seconds to get to the treeline, and as soon as I passed the first row of pines the sound seemed to deaden completely. It was like going beneath the surface of a lake. In front of me, to the sides, everywhere I looked, massive trees went on for ever – spruce, yew, aspens, their trunks as high as cathedrals – and while the temperature wasn't as raw beneath the canopy, the ground was like concrete. Every step jarred my muscles and joints, the weeks of inactivity weighing on me now.

But I kept going, pushing on, looking up, way ahead of me, as Mills drifted in and out of sight. The trees were rammed together so tightly there was no defined path, every possible trail packed with leaves, debris from branches and exposed roots. The limbs dipped and bowed, swiping at me as I passed, and on the ground – pockmarked with pine needles and bird tracks – there was still a thin blanket of snow.

I heard the snap of twigs up ahead, the crunch of leaves, but couldn't see him at first. Then I passed through a narrow gap between two huge pines and spotted him up ahead, maybe only eighty feet away now, a dense fog gathering above him.

Was he really tiring already?

I picked up the pace, pushing down my own exhaustion, concentrating on my own footsteps, where they fell, trying to gain more ground and more distance on him.

And then I looked up to check where he was.

He was gone.

I stopped, watching the spaces ahead of me. When he didn't appear, I moved towards the tree closest to me, the bark gummy with sap, and peered past it. There was no sign of him. I rounded that tree and went to the next, quietly, but still couldn't see him.

Where the hell was he?

Instantly, the size of the forest seemed to pull into focus and I felt a flutter of panic. I'd come a quarter of a mile, maybe even more, but it was nearly impossible to be sure: I couldn't see the treeline any more, let alone the clearing or the house. I wasn't even certain if I was looking in the right direction.

I gathered the rifle in close to me and moved forward, in through a U-shaped hole between two sprawling spruces, their mottled trunks like diseased skin, and then again, weaving a trail between three others. Ahead, I saw scuffs in the ground: leaves, twigs and needles, all scattered where a boot had landed, dragged – or stopped dead.

I heard a click up ahead.

'Don't come any closer.'

I tried to figure out where the voice was coming from.

All I could see was trees.

'I will shoot you,' Mills said. 'Drop the rifle.'

I crouched, keeping my eyes ahead of me, and placed the rifle down on the ground. I had no idea if he was bluffing: the only thing I could see was a maze of wood, an endless repetition of timber that eventually became a grey, opaque wall.

'Isaac?' I said. 'I just want to talk.'

Silence.

I still had one hand on the rifle.

'Isaac?'

'Let go of the rifle, Raker.'

This time, the voice sounded like it was coming from slightly behind me, to the left.

I didn't move, just glanced in that direction.

'Let *go* of the rifle.'

I did as he asked, standing again, keeping my gaze fixed on the same part of the forest as before. Wherever he was, he was definitely to my left, hidden by the gloom.

'Isaac?'

'Shut up.'

I could see him now, shadowed.

'Let's talk,' I said, trying to sound assured.

I spotted the gun in his hands, the unmistakable silhouette of it at his side. He came into view beyond a massive pine, lingering there for a moment, a spectre, and then he moved. A step to his right, another, then one forward, then another and another. He started walking faster, the gun aimed directly at me, but he was limping, and it was obvious now why he'd run out of breath so soon.

Vale had ruined one more life before his had ended.

Mills had a knife in his stomach.

64

'Get on the ground,' he said.

He jerked the gun towards a patch of earth about six feet from where I was standing. I looked at him as I moved, hands up, trying to tell him I wasn't a threat: he suddenly looked older, his dark grey hair wiry and uncombed. But he held the weapon straight and true, and it was obvious that he knew exactly what he was doing with it.

He'd fired it before.

Maybe he'd killed with it.

He used his free hand to sweep his hair back from a face drained of colour, a face marked by worry, and secrets, and what seemed to be the lucid acceptance that this might be the last hour of his life playing out, here in the middle of a forest.

'On the ground,' he said again.

I dropped to my knees, the forest floor hard beneath me, snow caught in the folds of a spruce tree to my left, and he stopped just in front of the rifle. He was dressed in a thick winter coat with a fur-lined hood, a pair of combat trousers and an old, scuffed pair of black boots. The knife was in the right-hand side of his stomach, embedded to the side of the hip. As he kicked the rifle away with his heel, he winced.

'Is Adrian dead?' he asked.

His voice sounded desperate.

I looked at the gun he was holding, a white finger on the trigger, the blue of one of his eyes just above the sights as he angled the weapon down at me. I could hear my heart in my ears, feel my pulse in my throat. I didn't know what the right answer was.

'Yes,' I said simply.

He nodded, looking off to a spot over my shoulder, and, as he did, I saw that his eyes were wet. It was marginally warmer under the canopy, but still freezing, the cold bedded in, so it could easily have been the temperature. But the muted flicker in his face told me it wasn't.

It was relief.

He looked at me again, wiped one of his eyes with the tip of his thumb, and then – his face creased, pained – crouched down and got on the ground. Shuffling back, bringing the rifle with him, he leaned against the thin, marbled trunk of a cedar tree.

I watched him, saying nothing, as he started hunting around in his pocket, and when he found what he was looking for he brought it out, clasped inside the hollow of his palm. I was eight feet from him, maybe as much as ten, and initially it was hard to see what he was holding, but then he said, 'You used to be a journalist . . .'

He threw across what he'd been holding.

It landed in a mix of dirt and frosted grass beside me: a small notebook, a pen clipped to the spiral binding. I picked it up and opened it. It was new, totally empty.

'You know shorthand?' he asked.

I frowned.

'Do you or don't you?'

'Yes,' I said.

'Then write this down.'

I studied him, his eyes, his expression, understanding what he was asking me to do but not understanding why. But then he gestured to the notebook with his free hand, and I unclipped the pen and turned to the first page.

'What's going on, Isaac?'

'Just write down what I say, or I swear to God I'll kill you where you sit.' He stared at me, his eyes hard. 'You think I won't do it?'

I held up a hand. 'No, I believe you will.'

'Then do what I say.'

As I clicked on the pen, Mills looked down at himself, at the knife reaching out of his stomach like an arm. Keeping it in was helping to stem the blood flow.

'Okay,' he said, 'let's start at the beginning. Write this all down, just the way I say it.' He pointed at the notebook, the chill air fanning its pages. 'July 1985. Write that.'

I did as he asked.

'You know anything about Vale before he came to the UK?'

'Not much.'

'Well, he killed two people out in LA. He told me all about it once. By then, I'd got myself in too deep with him, accepted too much money, had blood on my hands, so all I could really do was sit there and listen. He wanted to talk to someone about it – confess, I suppose – and I'd gone beyond the point where I could say no.'

'What do you mean, blood on your hands?'

'What do you *think* I mean?'

Black Gale.

'Did you kill them all or did he?'

'Just write down what I'm saying,' he said, waving the gun at me. He couldn't even look at me now. 'Like I just told you, he killed two people out in LA.'

'Who were the victims?'

'One of them was called Pablo something or other. He was an illegal immigrant from Mexico who lived in the same neighbourhood as Vale, and who Vale used to smoke pot with sometimes. Anyway, this Pablo kid, he tells Vale about this guy he knows who sells extra-strong weed out of a motel room somewhere – I think Vale said it was in West Hollywood. So Vale, playing it safe and not wanting to take his mum's car to a drug deal, goes to see this guy he used to work for part-time: this old man, Caraca, thinks Vale's being nice, coming back to say hello and see how he's doing, but what Vale's really up to there is stealing a key to the place, so he can come back later and borrow a car without the manager ever knowing. Which is exactly what he does, and then he takes Pablo with him to this motel to score some of this magical pot that they can't get in their part of the city.'

Mills adjusted himself against the tree, grimaced.

'Donald Klein,' he said. 'That's the name of the dealer. The other victim. But he used the name Gabriel Wilzon to rent the room.'

I wrote the name down and watched as Mills glanced beyond me, deeper into the forest, in the same direction he'd looked before.

'Something goes badly wrong,' he said, his eyes slightly narrowed, as if he were struggling to remember everything that Vale had told him. 'Basically, this Pablo is a hothead, and when Klein tells him the price of the pot, he realizes he's gone all that way and doesn't have anywhere near enough money. So Pablo suddenly thinks he's Tony Montana and starts venting, shouting and screaming that the weed's overpriced, and *then* he starts stuffing his pockets without paying; when Klein pushes him away, Pablo pulls out a gun. Klein, he's just a stoner selling weed out of a motel room – not some criminal mastermind – so he shits his pants on the spot, and Vale, believe it or not, is initially trying to act as peacemaker.' A smile traces the corner of his lips. 'Vale as peacemaker. Like that makes any sense.'

'So Vale *wasn't* playing peacemaker?'

'Vale was smart. Like, Hadron Collider smart. He scanned that scene like the Terminator: if it got too loud, the people in the adjacent rooms would remember; if a gun went off, the cops would turn up; and if the cops turned up, they'd find all the drugs, then Vale would get charged and there'd be no Stanford for him. There'd be no travelling abroad, like he always dreamed of. At that time, in California, they had some of the harshest drug laws going, so the only place Vale was heading if he got found inside that motel room – or if anyone saw or heard him there – was prison. I mean, why do you think he "borrowed" that car from the old man in the first place? It was all one big insurance policy, a way to insulate himself and protect his identity. But he had another problem: while Vale enjoyed his company, Pablo had a quick temper and a big mouth, so even if they walked out of there with everything sorted, and no one saw or heard a thing, there was no guarantee that Pablo wouldn't be parading around in the days after, telling the story.'

'So Vale just killed him?'

'No. He said he tried to talk him back, told him to calm down, tried to get the gun off him, but Pablo was too pumped up by then. They wrestle for control of the weapon, Vale uses his power and weight to overwhelm Pablo, and then he gets carried away: he knocks Pablo out with the butt of the gun.'

Mills paused, looking down at himself.

The blood glistened around the blade.

'Now he *really* has a problem,' he said. 'Klein's panicky and scared, Pablo's out cold and is going to totally lose his head as soon as he wakes up. The scene that Vale was hoping to de-escalate, he's made a hundred times worse. So he finds some old rope and ties Klein to a radiator, gags him, and then drags the Mexican kid into the bathroom, ready to tie *him* up in there. He needs some thinking time. But then Pablo starts coming round on the bathroom floor. As soon as he does, he's spitting, so full of rage Vale knows there's no way he'll ever keep quiet about what happened. And not only that, but Pablo's got pals back in their neighbourhood who would look dimly on the idea of Vale having knocked him unconscious.'

I flipped to a new page and Mills waited for me to catch up.

'Vale knocks Pablo out again, grabs a pillow from the bed, puts it over the Mexican kid's face and pulls the trigger.'

As he stared at me, a breeze moved through the trees.

'Just like that?'

Mills shrugged. 'Vale hadn't killed anyone else before then, but that didn't mean being capable wasn't already in his blood. He was off. A part of him was just broken. He was the best liar I ever met in my life – he could lie to you about *anything* and make you believe it – and anyone who can lie like that, and be that good at it, isn't right in the head. He never made friends easily because he never found anyone who could hold his attention – there was never anyone that could compete with him intellectually – and all the shit he probably told you while he was pretending to be Zaid – that he told Patrick Perry in 2015 – all that shit about how everyone on that Politics course just turned on Vale after Beatrix Steards went missing, it was him playing games. His whole life, from the moment he became Robert Zaid, has been a lie, so those games – the lies he told – I think he enjoyed them. He never wanted to expose himself, but it was a thrill for him to carry this secret: how much he could get away with, how much he could gild the truth without anyone noticing.' Mills closed his eyes for a second, the pain obvious in his face, in the rigidity of his body. 'So, yeah,' he said, opening his eyes again, 'he shot Pablo through the face just like that.'

He looked out into the trees, recalling the rest.

'Trying to dissolve a body in acid: pre-DNA, that was his first smart move – and it wasn't like getting hold of the acid was hard for him, because he had a key to the builder's yard where they sold hundreds of gallons of the stuff. He said he went there and picked up what he needed, made an insanely good job of fudging the stocklists so it looked like nothing was missing, and then removed the labels so no one would know where the containers had been bought from once they were found later on. All of this from a first-timer.'

'And Klein?'

'Vale said the original plan was to put Klein in the acid bath too, one of them on top of the other. But then – after he left Klein tied up in the motel room, and after he'd picked up all that acid – he deviated from the plan. He used Klein's driving licence to locate his house instead. Vale decided he needed to discover whatever he could about Klein – which, again, is pretty smart for an amateur. It's pretty lucid and cold-blooded. That's what I mean about Vale. He wasn't right.'

'So he goes to Klein's – then what?'

'When he gets to the house, in the front room, there's Klein's mum. She's badly disabled, wires coming out of her everywhere. So he gets inside the home and just wanders around while she's sleeping, and he sees the sort of relationship that Klein has with his mother, how close they are – all these photos of the two of them – and that was when the plan changed direction. That was when he knew he could get Klein to take the fall for Pablo's murder. I mean, Klein was just a kid selling drugs to pay for his mum's medical bills. He wasn't some criminal mastermind.'

Mills coughed, the movement hurting him.

'He manipulated Klein by threatening the mother,' he went on, hoarser now, 'maybe because he recognized himself in Klein and knew how to push the right buttons. Vale loved his mother too. He was fucked in the brain but that much was human about him. And the mum, she was how he got Klein up to some park in LA on that same night; she was how he put Klein on his knees up there. Vale pulled the trigger for him but the mother was the reason Klein put the gun in his mouth. He said to Klein that he'd kill her. Vale said he'd make the old bitch suffer.'

A terrible, prolonged silence settled between us.

Eventually, Mills said, 'He was a killer before he ever killed, and he stayed that way after. You could see it if you looked for it. So, you know, the other students on that Politics course, I'm sure they did whisper behind his back when Beatrix Steards went missing, maybe even passed a comment in front of him, but they didn't stand up to him. No one bullied or pushed Adrian Vale around like he said. Most of them were probably as shit-scared as Donald Klein was that night at the motel.'

He let out a grinding breath.

'You need a doctor, Isaac.'

'Yeah? And what am I going to tell them?'

He looked down at the knife again, the blade, the grip.

'Just write down what I'm saying,' he said sharply.

He raised the gun off his lap, reminding me it was there.

'I always knew what kind of a person he was,' he said, his voice

424

trapped inside the trees, its bleakness and remorse somehow at home here, 'so it wasn't naivety. The very first time Jacob Pierce brought me on board, the first time I took money from Vale, I knew exactly what I was getting myself into. But the money was so good. I thought, "I'll just do this for a while, and then get out."' He shook his head.

'How much does Jacob Pierce know?'

'Enough to take his share and keep quiet.'

I thought of Seiger and Sten, of the boxes full of cash.

'You know what's funny?' Mills said, smiling, his eyes returning to me. 'There *isn't* a Seiger and Sten. There's no Mr Seiger and Mr Sten, and there never was. That's just the name that Jacob gave his practice because he said it would make it feel like it had been going for years. It's why he's got that place in the Shambles, so it looks all olde worlde and established.' He looked down at the gun, at the hands holding it, pale and bloodied. 'It's a measure of who he is, I suppose, a measure of who Vale was as well: they even lie about the simple things.'

'And you?' I asked.

He looked across at me.

'You haven't lied about the simple things?'

I expected a reaction of some kind, a flash of anger, but instead he just rolled his shoulders in acceptance, an admission of guilt.

'I lied,' he said quietly. 'But mostly I just tried to forget.'

I watched him, pen poised above the page.

'I tried to forget what Vale told me about those two kids in LA, I tried to forget what he told me about Beatrix Steards – and, for two and a half years, I've been trying to forget what we did to the people from Black Gale . . .'

65

At the mention of Black Gale, the forest seemed to still.

'I was there that night,' Mills said. 'And then I was here when we took them all out to the forest. I know everything.'

He swallowed, looked up at me.

'But Beatrix Steards, that's more of a mystery. He never really told me much about her. What I know, I've pieced together over the time I've worked for him, and from what Jacob Pierce has let slip over the years.'

'Vale told Pierce the truth about Beatrix?'

'Enough of it.'

'And the truth is what?'

'She spurned him,' he replied mechanically. 'Isn't that where most of this shit begins? Half the cases I worked in my time as a cop were because a woman said no.'

'So Vale asked her out?'

'He liked her, he wanted to date her, but she found him weird – definitely too weird to date – and then he got his signals all mixed up and made his move on the night she vanished, when the two of them were alone at that party. When he came on all hot and heavy, she was taken aback, wasn't polite or subtle about it – probably saw what I saw, a stone-cold psychopath – and she told him no. But not *no*; more like *no way, not ever.*' His silence filled in the gaps. 'Anyway, he's so besotted with her that instead of just taking it like a man, he gets angry.'

He sighed, the sound like fat crackling in a pan.

'He'd learned something from what happened back in LA: taking his former boss's car made it hard to put him at the scene, so he did the same the night he took Beatrix. This time, he borrowed a car belonging to one of his housemates – did it without the housemate ever knowing. And, of course, that was clever because why would the cops look at a car that didn't belong to him, and there was no evidence of ever having been taken, when they were searching for Beatrix?'

'How did he get her into the car?'

'He never told me, and Pierce doesn't know, but I know where she's buried. He drove her into the Chiltern Hills . . .' The timbre of his voice was low and robotic now: he was hurting, but he was trying to remember, trying to get it all out, perhaps atone in some way. 'It's an hour out of London, but it's like a different world. I drove up there once to see if I could find her, but I had no idea where to even start. There were these woods he'd found: the head of a pin compared to this place, but big enough.' Mills looked down at himself again, his hands, his fingers on the gun, the hard ground beneath his body. 'He told Pierce he hid her inside the hollow of this old tree – shoved her in there like she was some piece of old junk. She was still dressed. He hadn't . . .' He ground to a halt. 'She wasn't naked. He hadn't done anything like that. But he said she had two bullet wounds in her: one above the knee – that would have been to slow her down when she was running away; and one through the back of the head – that would have been when he'd had enough of her.'

When he'd had enough of her.

We both lingered on the dreadful nature of that statement.

'Jacob Pierce knows enough,' Mills said. 'Make sure that prick burns.'

The wind came again, harder this time, the trees creaking softly, their branches moving like the arms of a conductor. I asked if I could stand: I was cold, in pain, and my hands were freezing. Mills watched me for a moment, eyes narrowing, as if this were a trick I was trying to play on him. But then he nodded, and I hauled myself up, and so did he. It was slow and painful for him, but he kept the gun on me.

'Why are you making me write this, Isaac?'

'You'll see,' he said.

His response sent a prickle of fear along my spine.

'You know how Vale found out what Patrick and Freda were doing, right?'

I nodded. 'Patrick called Robert Zaid to ask him about Vale.'

Except Zaid and Vale were the same person.

And that was when everything changed.

It was the catalyst for what happened at Black Gale. It was why the listening devices were installed in the houses. It was why Vale started watching Patrick and Freda from the shadows – and, on Halloween night, it was why he'd taken them both.

Except he hadn't just taken those two.

'Why did you take all nine villagers?' I asked Mills.

'Because they all knew.'

'All knew what?' I said.

'They all knew about Beatrix Steards.'

I frowned. 'Patrick and Freda told them?'

He was staring down at the ground, digging at the crazed earth with the toe of his boot. 'Patrick and Freda had one conversation about Beatrix in their houses. It was the morning of the dinner party. It was the only time we ever actually heard them talk about her, even though we'd had the houses bugged for a week by that time, ever since Patrick went to see "Robert Zaid". It turned out they always met away from Black Gale, where none of the other neighbours would see them or suspect anything.'

'So what changed?'

He sighed. 'Patrick started to see the links.'

'What do you mean?'

'After his interview with Robert Zaid, something started to rub at him.'

'He figured out Robert Zaid was Adrian Vale.'

Mills shrugged. 'I don't know if he figured it out, but he told Freda something was up with Zaid. Francesca Perry was at work, John Davey was out at the shops somewhere, and so Patrick and Freda spoke on her doorstep. She was starting to go downhill by then, and while Patrick was working as hard as he could trying to find answers for her, he wasn't working fast enough, and he knew

428

it. And *then* there was this voice in his head niggling at him about Zaid. So he comes up with an idea.'

'He says to Freda they need to tell everyone at the dinner party,' I said.

'Exactly.'

'Because he thinks they can help?'

'Laura Gibbs seemed bright, she was tenacious, she spent a lot of time online; when he wasn't farming, her son spent even more, always on forums and all that shit, websites like Reddit where you could crowdsource an entire missing persons search using a bunch of Internet sleuths with too much time on their hands. Francesca had patient records at her fingertips and – who knows? – maybe Patrick could try and persuade her to call in a favour if they ever needed access to someone's history in another hospital. John Davey was a historian, and good research skills were what they were after; even Emiline, the part-time librarian, was smart – bookish, academic. Plus, Chris Gibbs's sister was some kind of writer for *FeedMe*, so she knew how to unearth a story as well. It was an intelligent move. Believe me, there were brains at that dinner table. But then, by looping everyone in, Freda had to tell them why she was doing it – and that meant telling them the truth.'

'That she was looking for a daughter they didn't know about.'

A breath of wind in the trees.

'And that her cancer was terminal.' Mills nodded. 'That was the only thing holding her back.'

'Because she hadn't even told her husband or her kids.'

'Right. They just thought she was delaying her treatment.'

Around us, the trees moved again and, for the first time, I could see the sun, winking through the canopy at a low angle off to my left. I'd wondered earlier if it was dawn or dusk, but now I could see the answer: the sky was lightening and the light improving.

'But, in the end, she went ahead with it?'

Mills nodded again. He was propped up against the tree now,

weakening every second we spent out here – not bleeding profusely, but bleeding enough for it to make a difference. He blinked, as if struggling to focus, and said, 'Vale was paying some kid to sit and listen to these people, all day, every day, and not to ask questions why, and when I called in to check on him about a week in, the kid mentioned a dinner party. So he reads back what he's heard. At this point, it was already 5 p.m. . . .'

He stopped, guilt embedded like shrapnel in his face.

'I called Vale.' He closed his eyes, winced. 'I picked up the phone and I called him to let him know, thinking he'd just want to sit on it and hear the recording from the dinner party first, get a sense of what they all discussed. We'd only been listening in for a week or so by then. It was no time at all, really. But he didn't. As soon as I told him Patrick was getting suspicious about who Zaid was, he went totally fucking nuts. The idea of even more people looking into Beatrix, and then looking into Adrian Vale, and then asking questions about Robert Zaid, it just blinded him. He told me we were going to go to the village straight away. I said, "This is a bad idea. We're not prepared for this. You'd be better off biding your time," and he said he didn't give a single shit what I thought, and that he already had a plan in place. It was too late to stop the dinner party from happening, too late to stop Patrick and Freda discussing it there, but it wasn't too late for Vale to stem the bleeding.'

At the mention of blood, he looked down at himself again, and then off at the trees behind me again, deeper into the forest. It took him a moment to rediscover the thread of the conversation, his eyes distant, his expression fixed and difficult to fathom.

'He had to come up from London, so they'd had a lot to drink by the time we got there. A *lot*. Randolph, he didn't drink as much as the rest of them because he had some sort of a liver thing, but Patrick, John, Francesca, Emiline, the Gibbses – they'd all piled it in. Freda had had plenty to drink too: not as much the others, but enough. She'd told John before they even left for the party, which was probably a lot of the reason. She'd said she owed him the truth before anyone else heard it. I sat there and listened to her telling him about Beatrix, about the fact that she was dying, before Vale and I left for the village, and, honestly, it was one of the hardest things I've ever had to do. It was fucking horrible. And just as they'd got themselves together and cleaned themselves up, put a brave face on everything, she went down the track and did it again for seven other people. I remember it so clearly. They were all totally shocked by what she told them – tears, denials, the sort of reaction you'd expect from friends – and then she started talking about Beatrix Steards and it galvanized them.'

'The mood changed?'

'Instantly changed. She didn't have to persuade any of them because they were all on board from minute one. Patrick sat there and talked to them about what he'd already done, what the new plan of attack was, who was going to do what, and once they were all clear on their roles, they cracked open the wine and the beer and got drunk.'

'So what time did you and Vale turn up?'

'I don't know,' he said, looking out beyond me again. His eyes kept going to the same spot. 'Nine, maybe. Nine thirty. They'd just made coffee.'

'And then what happened?'

We looked at each other – me wanting to know, him not wanting to relive it – as frost drifted through the air, blown from the branches by the stirring of the wind.

'I'd been to the village before that, posing as an engineer from BT, spouting some bullshit about needing to upgrade their phone line.' He paused and I could see it fitted into what I knew already of how the bugs were installed. 'We did the Perrys' and Daveys' first, and then a few days later, Vale decides he wants all of them bugged, so he comes with me and we do the Gibbses' and then Solomon and Wilson's place as well. I'm in there, sneaking around the houses, trying to install these bloody listening devices while everyone's still at home, and he's off doing I don't know what the hell else, keeping out of sight. I figured he was just looking around the homes when he could, getting a feel for who these people were. And, in part, that was true.'

I frowned. 'What do you mean?'

'Halloween night, we hire a van and drive it up there, and then park it outside the boundaries of the village, so there are no visible tyre tracks. He's brought these brand-new wellington boots with him, not even in his size, and a pair of new walking shoes, and it takes me a few seconds to catch on. Then he hands me the walking shoes and tells me to put them on, and that's when I get it.' Mills glanced at me, seeing if I understood where this was heading, and I did: when Mills was installing the bugs, Vale had already been thinking about the endgame. 'The walking shoes,' Mills went on, 'were an exact match – make, size, everything – for a pair John Davey had. The wellies were exactly the same: Chris Gibbs had a pair, same size, same make, same print on the bottom . . .'

Now it all made sense.

Footprints and tyre tracks were found that night, but all of them belonged to the villagers. The tracks matched up with tyres on the cars belonging to the Daveys, Perrys, Gibbses and to Randolph Solomon, and the same was true of the shoes. When the police cross-referenced the footwear found inside the houses with the footprints found around the properties, everything matched up.

'That was why he left the van on the main road,' I said quietly.

Mills nodded. 'It was tarmacked, so there would never be any evidence of us out there. Inside the village, though, it was different: the track was mud and loose stone.'

'So whose car did you use to get them to the van?'

'Solomon and Wilson's camper,' Mills said. 'It was why we never put it back on the driveway. It was why we took it that night and sent it to the crusher. By the end of the evening, it was full of nine people's DNA – full of ours too – and not only that: we figured, if the camper van was the only vehicle missing, it would point the finger of suspicion at Solomon and Wilson.'

It was so simple.

'And no one put up a fight?'

Mills looked down at his gun. 'We went there in masks, we were armed, we were shouting and screaming at them the whole time, putting weapons to their heads and telling them we'd blow their brains out if they did anything stupid . . .' He sniffed, glanced at me. 'They were just ordinary people. Four of them were pensioners and one of them was barely even an adult. They were terrified. Vale tied them up, gagged them and took them out two at a time to the camper van, then he drove them back up to the main road, dumped them in the van and returned. Four times he did that, and then the fifth time he took Patrick. And do you know what I did? I just stood there in the kitchen throughout all of it, pointing my gun at these people I knew weren't ever coming home again, and tried not to hear them begging.'

The emotion played out in his eyes.

'Why didn't you stop Vale?' I asked.

'And then what?' he fired back, anger flashing in his face now. 'I'd taken over three hundred grand from him already, sorting out all these little problems for him: when people asked too many questions, or started sniffing around, or he just decided that he didn't like someone, there I was to shut them down: this anonymous voice at the end of an untraceable line, waving some past indiscretion in front of them that would land them in deep shit. That's what I was. That's all I did for him. I dug into lives, found these ruinous things – and I used them to help Vale maintain his lie.'

'You were scared of him,' I said.

He looked at me like I was insane: 'Of *course* I was fucking scared of him. He was a monster, and I was in debt to him. If I walked away, he'd ruin me or kill me. He told me he kept a hidden record of everything I did, so even if I made a move, there was all this shit on me, just waiting to be found, even after he was six feet under the ground. I'd taken all that cash from him, I'd kept silent, I'd destroyed lives. There was no escape.' Except, perhaps, through someone else, which was why he'd left the key for me.

Finally, almost dreading the answer, I said, 'And after that?'

'I'd left my car in Skipton, so he dropped me there and then I didn't hear from him again for almost two weeks. He had properties all over the place, including empty units he'd bought with a view to developing them into businesses, so I expect he took them to one of those. He would have drugged them at some point, to keep them quiet and pliant: I don't know where he got his supplies from, or where he learned to use that crap, but he was good with it. He always knew the right amounts, how much kept you under for how long, the risks. Like I said, he was bright. That was what made him so dangerous. Anyway, a fortnight later, he calls me up and tells me to come to London.'

I frowned. 'For what reason?'

He swallowed, his throat like a broken piston. 'He says he's put them all somewhere no one will ever find them. So I meet him at his house, and I ask him where this place is, where he's planning on taking them, and he says to me, "They're already there. Why do you think it's taken me two weeks to call you?"' Mills looked off into the forest. 'He brought them here one by one to lessen the risk. That was why he was so quiet for so long. I don't think he trusted me not to screw it up, which is why he never involved me until they were actually here and it was too late. The smaller things, maintaining his lie, sorting out his problems, digging into people's lives, he'd seen enough of my work to know that I could handle that. But transporting nine people to their execution? That takes a different type of person, and he knew that person wasn't me.' He swallowed a second time, and a third, as if the taste of that moment was ash in his mouth. 'And so he brings me here. This place is just another part of Vale that no one knows about.'

I looked around the forest.

'There are others out here.'

434

'What?' I eyed Mills. 'What are you talking about?'

'Somewhere in the trees, he's put others in the ground. People who've got too close to knowing the real him, people who've endangered the lie he tells. I don't know how many, or over how long, but I've seen their clothes in that box at Seiger and Sten, I've seen emails, paperwork, notes, little things that just don't make sense. I've seen people disappear who I know he has dealings with, and I know it was him. I know he must have put them out here because, this place, it's all his – and it goes on for ever.'

'Where are we, Isaac?'

'You ever heard of Parsonfield?'

I had. It was on an email I'd seen in Robert Zaid's study.

'Is that what this place is called?'

But he didn't seem to have heard me.

'Isaac?'

He wrapped his hands around the knife handle.

'Isaac?'

'Shit,' he said softly, fresh blood spilling out of his wound.

He moved the blade in his stomach, crying out, and then shifted against the tree again, pushing himself away from the bark. As he did, he staggered slightly, almost losing his footing. Once he'd recovered, he used the gun again, gesturing at the notebook in my hands, and said, 'You finished there?'

I looked down at my notes and then back to him.

'I don't know,' I said. '*Have* I?'

'Throw me over the notebook.'

I looked at him, uncertain what was going on.

'Throw over the *notebook*,' he shouted.

I did as he asked and he caught it with his spare hand. Once he'd wriggled it back into his coat pocket, he raised the gun and said, 'We're going to start walking in that direction.'

He looked at the forest behind me, at the same spot as earlier.

'What's in there?' I asked.

I tried not to sound panicked, but it was hard.

'Isaac?'

'Shut up.'

'Isaac, where are we going?'

'Shut *up*,' he spat. 'It's over.'

He looked at me, sorrow carved into his face.

'This is the end for you now.'

66

The forest closed in around us.

'Isaac, you don't have to do this.'

'Don't speak, don't turn around.'

As we walked, Mills trailed behind me, the gun out in front of him, telling me where to head. It all looked the same in front, the ground frozen, the branches reaching out, the canopy preventing much in the way of sunlight from hitting the forest floor. Whenever I looked over my shoulder, Mills would wave me forward with the gun, but his legs were barely carrying him now and the crimson bloom around the knife wound was expanding, crawling away from his stomach towards his hip, down to his groin, up to his chest. He stumbled a couple of times and quickly reset himself, but he couldn't go on like this. Even if the knife hadn't hit his organs, he'd still been stabbed. He was losing blood, he was in shock, his skin was greying and his breathing was getting shallower.

I just had to wait for the right moment.

About twenty minutes later, we hit a small clearing, a wooden shack at one edge, next to a stream. The shack was padlocked from the outside, a pitchfork and shovel propped next to the door, and what looked like a plastic groundsheet beside those. The pitchfork and shovel had mud caked on them.

I looked from the shack to Mills, and watched as he stopped at the edge of the clearing, pale against the trunks of the pine trees that flanked him. He followed my eyes, to the plastic, to the tools, and then he pointed beyond the shack, to where the forest continued on the opposite side of the stream, and said, 'They're all in there.' He blinked, as if he were struggling to focus. 'All nine of them are in there.'

I looked beyond the stream, into the trees.

This is the end for you now.

He'd meant the case, not my life.

'Vale didn't give a shit about them once they were dead,' Mills said, his voice so low now it was barely even a whisper. 'He would have happily left them where they dropped. No one would have found them. No one comes out this far. But I couldn't.'

It took him a moment to find his words again and for the first time he dropped the gun to his side, as if he didn't have the strength or the energy to hold it any more.

'I couldn't leave them like that.'

'You buried them all yourself?'

He nodded: a single, painful jerk of the head.

'He kept them in the same hole you were in, and then, once I arrived here, we took them out and walked them down to this spot. He'd done all the prep himself – travelled here with them, one by one – but he wanted to kill them all at the same time, and he knew he wouldn't be able to handle nine people alone, even armed. There was too much risk. So that was what he brought me for. When I had doubts, he told me he would kill me. When I tried to beg him not to do it, he put a gun in my mouth and told me he would pull the trigger. I think a part of him liked the idea of me being here too: it gave him something else to use. I'd be complicit, even if I never fired a bullet. I'd be so deep into the swamp there would be no way out.'

'So you went along with it.'

He nodded. 'I stayed silent and listened to him explain to me how killing nine people at the same time was easier. He said he'd already been away from work longer than he should have been.' Mills smiled, an anguished, distressed twitch of the mouth. 'Longer than he should have been – like he'd been talking to the neighbours and hadn't realized the time.' Tears flashed in his eyes. 'So, yes, I stood about where you are now and watched him do it all. I stood and did absolutely nothing. I just watched them drop, one after the next, *bang, bang, bang, bang*. I was a fucking coward.' More tears, and then more. 'All I could think about was getting out of here; getting it done, going home, trying to forget any of it had ever happened. All the money I'd taken from him up until that point, all the shit he had me do, none of it was anywhere *near* as bad as this. I knew what I was doing for him wasn't legal – but I wasn't hurting or injuring people. I was just keeping him insulated. Because of his money, there was always someone out to get him, blackmail him, always someone trying to twist him in whatever direction they thought would get them what they needed – so that was all I was doing: twisting things back. It was mucky, it was grey, but it was never like this.'

He wobbled a little from side to side, the quiet filled by the sounds of the forest. 'And then I came out here with him, and I watched him do this, and my complicity became the catalyst for him to tell me the truth, for him to reveal he was actually Adrian Vale. And that was what he wanted: he wanted to *tell* someone, because lies become so heavy, even if you're as good at them as he was.'

I looked into the trees again.

I could see something now.

'He was the devil.'

I could see the nine graves, shallow mounds against the forest floor, speckled white with frost.

'I don't sleep any more,' Mills sobbed. 'I just lay awake at night and I see the nine of them lined up here. I hear them too. That's even worse, hearing them. I hear them crying and begging for their lives, and then the crying and the begging gets worse each time Vale kills one of them – they start moving around, running, going to one another – and then I remember Freda Davey was at the end of the line . . .' He stopped, his speech fractured. 'She just stood there, and turned and faced him before he shot her. She just looked him in the eyes.'

There was nothing except the sound of Mills crying.

No wind. No birds.

'I stayed behind and buried them all,' he whimpered.

I moved forward, towards the stream, knowing that there was no threat from Isaac Mills any more. Leaping from one bank to the other, I passed from the clearing back into the trees, the light closing off instantly above me. But I could see enough.

He'd made makeshift crosses for each of the graves.

My throat trembled with emotion.

I reached out to the nearest tree for support, my legs suddenly weak, tired in my muscles and sinew and bones in a way I couldn't ever remember being. I'd found them, I'd got to the end – but it didn't feel like a victory.

Only a loss.

And then I noticed something.

There were ten graves, not nine.

I turned and looked back through the trees towards Mills, across the stream to where he was still standing in the clearing, lopsided, suffering. In his face, though, it was obvious he knew exactly what I was thinking and what I needed to ask.

'Who else did you bury with them, Isaac?'

He didn't reply, just wiped his eyes.

'Isaac? Who is this?'

'Kader,' he said. 'That one was Joline Kader.'

An Ending

London | Two Weeks Ago

In the arrivals hall, she found Kevin Quinn waiting for her. He had a sign with her name on it, and was checking his cellphone with his spare hand.

'DI Quinn?'

He looked up. 'Detective Kader?'

'*Ex*-Detective Kader,' she replied, smiling.

Quinn returned the smile and they shook hands.

'Once a detective, always a detective,' he said.

'Well, it's very kind of you to agree to meet me, anyway.'

'No problem. I'm as keen as you to find out what's going on.'

He led her out of the terminal, across to an adjacent parking lot, and they talked politely about her flight, about her career at the LASD and LAPD, about his, in Manchester and then in London at the Met, and then Quinn said, 'I just want to find out what the hell has happened here. Black Gale, Beatrix Steards, this case you had, it needs some closure.'

She nodded. 'I agree.'

'Patrick Perry was an old, uh . . . colleague.' He hesitated and looked sideways at her, as if he wasn't sure whether to reveal the true nature of his relationship with Patrick.

But it didn't take much in the way of imagination to figure it out.

Quinn was a cop; Patrick Perry had been a journalist.

She held up a hand. 'It's okay. I had "colleagues" too.'

Quinn broke into another smile.

'Thank you for digging me out of that one,' he said.

'Sure.'

'So, after you leave London, you're heading north?'

She nodded, following him into a packed elevator. 'Hopefully you and I will be able to get somewhere with this Beatrix Steards stuff over the next couple of days – maybe look deeper into the connections between her and Black Gale – and then I'm going to get the train up to York, hire a car and take a drive out to the village myself.'

All of that was true – she'd just left out one thing.

Robert Zaid.

She hadn't told Quinn what she knew.

She hadn't told anyone that Zaid wasn't Zaid.

Someone called David Raker had come looking at exactly the same things she had and now she couldn't find him anywhere. The phone number she had for him went to voicemail. Her emails to him went unanswered. She'd managed to track down his daughter and she was in a state of absolute panic about where he was. She said her father had been silent for three and a half weeks, and he never went quiet on her for this long. The last time she heard from him, he told her he was back in London from Yorkshire, and was driving to Highgate for a meeting.

Highgate was where Robert Zaid lived.

They reached Quinn's car and he loaded her suitcase into the back for her, and then asked if she wanted to check into her hotel first or just go straight to the station.

'Straight to the station is fine,' she said.

'Straight to the station it is.'

'A coffee might be good, though.'

He smiled. 'The best jetlag cure going.'

They were soon heading east into London. As they drove, he told her there was a service station about ten minutes away where they could get some coffee, so as Quinn asked her about LA, and then started telling her about a trip he'd made to the city with his wife in 2016, Jo allowed herself a moment of peace: no Gabriel

Wilzon or Donald Klein, no acid bath, no Beatrix Steards, no Black Gale.

No Robert Zaid.

No Adrian Vale.

She looked out the window, at a spring day full of watery sunlight and pale skies, and thought of Ethan, pictured him, Claire and Maisie at the kitchen table in their blue clapboard house in Oakland. She thought of the last time she'd been there with them for Christmas, how there had been so much laughter, so many times she'd held Maisie, or talked to Claire, and thought how lucky she was; so many times she'd sat and watched the outline of Ira in Ethan's face and actions, and had to pause for breath to appreciate how blessed she was to have the family she did. In her quiet moments at night, alone in the bedroom they'd made up for her, Jo tried not to think about how different it might have been if Ira hadn't died, not only because his death still hurt, even all these years on, but because there was a side to his passing that was hard to ignore: without it, she might have lost her son completely. And so the worst thing that had ever happened to her in her life had also made her better. It made those moments with Ethan possible, even so long after Ira's passing, because Ethan remembered her being there for him, all the way along. But she'd only been there because Ira suddenly wasn't.

It was something that she'd never quite reconciled.

Something brought her out of the moment, a twinge in her thigh, and when she checked the side of her pants there was a speck of blood on them. Confused, she looked out at the motorway, saw the signs for the service station pass them, and then she turned to Kevin Quinn. As she did, her vision spotted white, smearing and dimming.

'I'm sorry,' Quinn said.

She touched her thigh again.

'What's going on?'

And then she saw that he only had his right hand on the wheel.

His other was at his side, his knuckles resting against the edge of his seat, a syringe inside his palm.

'What the hell have you done?' Jo said, her words slurred.

'I'm sorry,' Quinn said again. 'I'm so sorry.'

For some reason, before the blackness, images of Ethan when he was a boy, of her standing in the doorway of his room looking in at his crib, blinked in front of her.

Her heart swelled with love for him.

For who he was, and who he'd become.

And then she slumped sideways against the door.

67

Mills fell to his knees, the gun resting against one of his thighs. He looked across at me, the two of us on either side of the stream: he was like a man who'd run a marathon, his breath coming in harsh, ragged movements that seemed to send convulsions through his body. He wiped an eye, and then again, blood mixing with tears, then said, barely audibly, 'I picked her up from the airport.' He sucked in another breath. 'An old source of mine in North Yorkshire Police called me to say she'd started asking around about Beatrix and Black Gale, so I started digging into her phone calls. I could see she'd called Quinn.' Another breath, so frayed and so broken, it was nothing but pain. 'I pretended to be him. I got her to trust me.'

He knelt there and sobbed.

'Vale decided it would be too dangerous to meet her himself,' he said eventually, the blood in his mouth now, smeared across his teeth. 'He suspected that she already knew who he was. He was supposed to come back to London for a couple of days midway through that five-week trip he made to see shareholders, but he cancelled it and stayed out of the country instead.' He made a small sound, like a grunt; maybe a snort of disbelief. 'All the shit he'd pulled over the years and you know something?' He glanced at me. 'He was scared of that woman. I think she was the only person he'd ever met who was as obsessive as him.'

Gabriel Wilzon and Donald Klein.

Thirty-three years, and she'd never let it go.

'So he asked me to take care of it, to bring her here, and said he would finish the job when he was done with that work trip.' He sniffed, using his wrist to wipe his nose, mouth, cheeks. 'Any sounds you heard down in the hole, that was probably her.'

I remember the clunks, the hums.

I thought it had been a generator.

It meant Kader hadn't been dead for long.

Maybe only days.

'There's a pipe in the hatch we kept her in,' Mills said. 'She would try to climb it.' He looked past me, to Joline Kader's grave. 'She was a fighter, right until the end.'

To the end.

The wind rose and then settled again.

The trees moved.

I turned and took a few tentative steps back into the forest, closing the space between myself and the graves. Kader's was slightly removed from the others, dug at a fractionally different angle, the wood of the cross newer, less battered by wind, by the rain that must have washed through here since the nine villagers were buried; by the frost, the snow, the pine sap. Beneath my feet, the ground was hard, my ankles aching, my legs as well, and so I dropped to a haunch in front of the mounds of earth and watched the wind move in again, the crosses all fluttering.

A gunshot ripped through the air.

Startled, I turned and looked back in the direction I'd come, out to the clearing in which I'd left Isaac Mills, but now he wasn't standing, watching me, he was on the ground: one arm under him, the other still holding the gun, eyes gazing up at the sky.

I left the graves and headed back to him, looking down at his body, the top of his head a mess of brain and blood, and then closed my eyes, trying to regain some measure of composure. I felt like I wanted to hide. I wanted to cry. When I opened them again, I saw that he'd taken the notebook out of his pocket and tossed it on to the ground.

It was the history of all this.

He'd made me write his confession.

The forest seemed to close in, the trees oppressive, and I backed away from Mills, from the graves, as if I needed some distance just to find my breath again.

And then I saw something.

The padlock for the shack was lying on the floor.

Realizing that Mills must have unlocked it when I'd been on my haunches at the graves, I moved slowly towards the wooden building, the door fanning back and forth in the breeze, and stopped at the entrance.

Inside was a fire, empty and unlit, a few shelves with a mix of old tin cans and rusting metal equipment on them, and then a chair in the corner, chained to the wall.

On the chair was a woman, gagged and bound.

I recognized her instantly.

'It's okay,' I said, holding up a hand.

She blinked, watching me, still uncertain if I was her enemy, her face streaked with dirt and blood, a lilac bruise below her cheekbone.

I took another, even smaller step forward.

'Honestly, it's okay,' I repeated. 'I'm not going to hurt you, Joline.'

68

We covered Mills's body with the groundsheet, took his notebook and went back to the house, following the vague path through the frozen trees. Neither of us said much about how we'd got here, but Kader – Jo, as she told me to call her – knew as much about me as I did her. It was enough for us to see clearly: we'd both gone looking for answers – we'd just been at opposite ends of Adrian Vale's life.

At the house, we patched ourselves up using a first-aid kit in the living room, and then I found some food in the kitchen and we ate out of cans in front of the fire.

'Do you know where we are?' Jo asked.

I shook my head. 'No. Do you?'

'No.'

I'd searched the house properly and had found a small, open lockbox in one of the wardrobes, but all it had in it was a car key for a Ford, and an old Nokia mobile phone, pre-touchscreen, with a black-and-white display. It was working, the battery charged, but there was no reception. Neither Vale nor Mills had brought anything else with them. Any wallets, IDs or bank cards they might have had must have been back at the car, which suggested they'd walked out here to the house, not expecting to be long. The question was in what direction they'd come. In her search, Jo had found a wrinkled, yellowing piece of paper with a hand-drawn map on it. It looked like it was Isaac Mills's writing and it appeared to show a path through the forest in a northerly direction, skirting the clearing and the shack next to the grave site. Yet I could tell, even without knowing her at all, that Jo was just as concerned about how we found our way out of the forest as I was: the map was a start, perhaps better than nothing, but it was still lacking in detail.

She moved in her seat, wincing.

Her wrist was sprained and she'd broken a finger.

'When he got me out of that hatch, I fought like hell,' she said quietly, her fork clinking against the tin of the can. 'He kept telling me, "Don't fight me, don't fight me, I've got a plan," but what was I *supposed* to think? This was the same guy who'd picked me up at the airport; the same guy who'd talked to me over the phone, pretending to be Kevin Quinn, and who told me he'd show me the Beatrix Steards case.' A flicker of torment in her eyes. 'Twenty years ago, even fifteen, I'm not sure I would have fallen for that crap. But I'm sixty-seven. I'm retired. Before this, I spent two and a half years having lunches, going to Pilates classes, meeting for coffee and playing golf. I spent two years having holidays with my son and his family. And before any of that, I was teaching for twelve years. I'd lost my edge. That drive, that obsession, that sense of debt, it never leaves you, but when you're not doing it every day, you do lose something. I don't know if it's focus. It's more like a loss of altitude.'

'The bigger picture.'

She nodded.

'So you injured yourself fighting Mills?'

She looked at her bandaged wrist. 'Yeah. Like I said, I fought like it was my last breath. I fought him so hard. Eventually, he got me in the face.' She gestured to a bruise on her cheek. 'Hell, he hit me so hard, it almost knocked my teeth out, and then he walked me into the forest, staying behind me with a gun to the back of my head, and told me he had a plan and I needed to play along.'

Mills's plan was to use me.

He couldn't release himself from Vale's grip because the moment he did, Vale would ruin him. Whether Vale really *had* kept a record of everything that Mills had done for him – as he'd claimed to Mills – was debatable, as it would be a huge risk to keep that sort of information lying around, but what was undeniable was that Adrian Vale had the money and power to leak, expose and manipulate the narrative when it came to Isaac Mills.

And actually going as far as killing Vale himself represented no sort of escape either: his death would invite the police in, and the police would find Mills.

With me, though, maybe he'd thought he had a chance.

I was pretty much the same build as Vale, so physically I wouldn't instantly be overwhelmed, and if Mills released me from the hatch early, I'd have another advantage, because Vale wouldn't see me coming. And if it all went to plan and I got the drop on Vale, Mills could immediately get back to London and begin the process of insulating himself from whatever Vale had on him before anyone even got a sniff that Vale – or Robert Zaid – was dead. It wasn't foolproof. It was, in fact, treacherous and difficult, but it was better than the life he was having to lead.

A life of lying, and of hurting people.

A life of burying bodies in a forest.

It was, though, a plan with one unanswered question: what had Mills intended to do with Jo and me? He hadn't wanted to kill us, that much was clear, but if we were still alive, we could tell the world what he'd done and been a part of, regardless of how much of it he managed to erase from history in the time it took us to find our way home again.

Maybe, in the end, he didn't know.

The man I'd followed to the mill that day, the man he'd been around Melia and her children, the man who didn't want to hurt Jo, who apologized to her even as she blacked out in his car, wasn't a murderer. But he *was* a survivor. He wanted to break free. He wanted a different life. He wanted to love someone. He wanted to be normal. When he'd made a run for it into the forest, even after he'd been stabbed by Vale, he was still thinking about the plan. The blood, the pain, it skewered his perspective entirely, his sense of what was possible from that point on. But then, when I'd caught up to him, reality had finally kicked in. He had a knife in his gut. He was dying in the middle of nowhere. He wasn't going to make it home to Keighley, to Melia, to her kids. The plan had failed.

All he could do was make his side of the story clear.

That was what the notebook was for.

'He dug a grave next to the others,' Jo said quietly, bringing me back into the half-light of the house, 'and then he went out and shot a deer. I had no idea what he was doing, but he dragged the deer back, skinned it, and then dumped it into the grave, before filling it all in again.'

I thought of the deer I'd hit with my car right back at the start of the case. If I hadn't done that, I might never have met Mills at all.

'After that,' Jo went on, 'he bound and gagged me and left me in this hollow. It was about forty feet from the clearing, behind that shack there, and it was full of fallen branches and sticks; leaves, mud. He told me that if I wanted us both to live, I had to stay quiet, whatever I heard.' She stopped, putting the can down, the glow from the fire like pigment on her skin. 'I heard him bring Vale down. They stood somewhere close to the graves and Mills told him that I'd pretended to be sick, and that was why he'd got me out of the hatch; then, once I was out, I'd made a break for it into the forest, and – after a long chase – he'd ended up having to shoot me. And that was when I felt the change. I'm not even kidding. I was forty feet away and it was just like static; you could feel Vale's rage like moisture in the air.'

She was silent for a moment, the fire crackling.

'Mills kicked some of the earth away, to show Vale the corpse, and that was when I realized what the deer was for. It was still bloody, fresh, and mixed with mud, I guess its belly would have looked enough like a human's.' She glanced at me, as if she were still struggling to understand her feelings towards Isaac Mills. 'Vale went insane. It was scary just listening to it. But that's what I did. I lay there under all the shit that Mills had covered me with, and I listened to that beast ranting and screaming, telling Mills he'd screwed up, that I was his, not Mills's. "That bitch was mine": that's all he kept saying – "That bitch was mine" – like I was some part of his destiny. Maybe I was, I don't know. Maybe, if you believe in that stuff, he and I were always meant to meet each other, and – when we did – one of us wasn't leaving again, but all I kept thinking as I lay there was, "I could have stopped this. I could have stopped this fucking monster thirty-three years ago."'

She was quiet for a while.

I put some more wood on the fire, stoked it a little, and thought about what to do next. It was five thirty in the afternoon now, and there was no way we could head out into a forest this massive and this dense with night only a few hours away.

We'd have to go at first light.

'Mills came back for me later, got me up and locked me in that shack,' Jo went on, her eyes on the flames licking the chimney, 'and when I tried to ask him what was going on, tried to talk through the gag, he just told me to stay put and stay quiet, and then he left me. I had no clock, no way of knowing how long I was there, but it must have been a day. I saw a sunrise and a sunset. And then, finally, I heard some voices.'

Mills and me.

'Do you remember much about how you got here?' she asked.

'This place?' I shook my head. 'You?'

'I was heavily sedated, so a lot of it was just background. Maybe an engine. Maybe some traffic noise. They blindfolded me, taped my mouth, put things over my ears, so even when I felt lucid, it wasn't like I could make use of my senses.'

'Do you remember being in a tight space?'

'That I *do* remember.'

'Do you remember anything about it?'

'Just that it was like being in a coffin, not a trunk.'

I'd thought the same thing.

'What about the sequence G76984Z – does that mean anything?'

She frowned. 'No. What is it?'

'I don't know,' I said, rubbing at my eyes. 'I can't figure it out.'

We talked some more, about who she was, who I was, our

families, our cases, about the double murder that had marked the beginning of her hunt for Adrian Vale. I talked about my search for answers at Black Gale, about Patrick Perry and Freda Davey, and then about the closure Freda had sought in asking for Patrick's help. As I spoke about it, I started to feel emotional again, the words catching in my throat, and I realized I was probably in a delayed state of shock, one that wasn't even necessarily provoked by this case. I'd barely got over what had happened to me at Christmas and now I was here, twenty minutes from nine bodies in the ground, mourning their loss, the loss of Beatrix Steards, and the forty-six days I'd spent in darkness and silence.

I thought I'd been ready for this case.

I'd told Healy I wasn't broken.

But I was.

I was hurting.

And the next morning, I found out how much.

PART NINE
Home

69

The morning that Jo and I left Adrian Vale's house in the forest, the sky was clear, pale as milk, the trees silhouetted against it. We moved across the grass in front of the veranda, heading in the same direction that Mills had taken me the day before, to the graves of the Black Gale villagers. As we did, we passed the body of Vale, still in the same place he'd died, but now covered in a tarpaulin we'd weighted to the ground with rocks to stop the animals getting at him. Once we hit the trees, the light began to dwindle and everything seemed to pull in towards us, huge trunks in vast lines in all directions. It was freezing cold, the forest floor like iron.

I grabbed a torch from my pack and switched it on.

Light scattered ahead of me, shadows lurching and changing direction, and we picked up the vague hint of the trail we'd come back to the house on after I'd found Jo in the shack. She was close behind me, her shoes making a heavy thump every time they landed: her build was small, her frame slender, but the only boots we could find in the house for her were men's, a size eight, so she'd had to make do. Both of us worried about blisters, about the discomfort of walking miles in footwear that didn't fit, but we had little choice. The clothes she was wearing were too big for her as well – but they were warm, and they were preferable to what Vale had put her in.

'Any reception on the phone?' I asked her.

She checked the Nokia. 'No, nothing.'

We'd divided up what we'd needed: I was carrying food and water, some spare clothes and a couple of blankets, as well as Isaac Mills's notebook, and she had more spare clothes, another blanket, a first-aid kit, and then the car key and mobile phone.

'How are the shoes feeling?' I asked.

'Like I should be in a circus.'

I smiled, and we chatted some more, Jo discussing her husband, me talking about Derryn, and then we fell into a comfortable silence until we reached the clearing. Mills's body was still under the plastic, exactly where we'd left it, the sheet weighted down with rocks for exactly the same reason as Vale's. After we got out of the forest and alerted the authorities, they'd want to examine the bodies, and we needed to preserve the evidence as best we could.

Once we locked the shack, we paused for a second, looking from the place in which Isaac Mills had died to the graves on the other side of the stream, barely visible yet in the low light of the forest. And then we nodded at one another, Jo asked me if I was good to go, and we headed out, past the graves, to where the hand-drawn map had shown a trail. This time, it was harder to follow, the trees inching in closer every time we moved forward, Jo ducking under branches with ease, the six inches I had on her forcing me to be more careful. Once or twice, the light was so subdued I almost walked right into a rigid limb, but mostly I was able to protect my face with an upturned arm.

After an hour, the forest had barely changed, except for the dark: the sun was up fully and we could see more of what was around us, but I was unsure if it was better like this or not. The more we could see, the more colossal the forest seemed, an infinite ocean of trees moving in all directions, so distant and so vast they eventually faded into mist. Previously, all we could see was what was immediately around us, and that had allowed us to think we were getting closer to something; that the trail was leading us somewhere good, away from this labyrinth.

Two hours in, we stopped for water and something to eat, and Jo said she had to go to the toilet – so I sat down, gave her some privacy, and got the map out again.

I didn't know if we were on the right trail.

I didn't know if the map was even accurate.

I looked ahead of me and felt the first flutter of panic. It was already after 9 a.m. and it felt like we hadn't even got anywhere. The trees were all exactly the same, the terrain hadn't altered; if anything, the canopy had grown thicker, not thinner, and the sounds of the forest had deadened. There wasn't a breath of wind any more. Any birds sounded miles away. It was just a perpetual hush all around.

'What are you thinking?'

Jo was beside me now.

I looked up at her, then out at the forest.

'I'm thinking I don't know where the hell we are.'

'Is the map wrong?'

I looked at it again, at the line that represented the trail from the house to what I hoped was a road. But maybe it wasn't a road at all. Maybe it was just another trail. Maybe what Mills had drawn here was totally worthless.

'This isn't the direction they would have come,' I said.

'No,' Jo replied, eyes on the trees. 'I don't imagine it is.'

She knew what I knew: there was no way Vale and Mills had carried one person this far, let alone the nine from Black Gale – not through growth this dense. So had they headed south from the house, not north? Was that where their car was? The way out?

Were we headed in completely the wrong direction?

'Do you want to turn around?' Jo asked.

I looked at her. 'I don't know. What do you think?'

She looked into the trees again.

'It'll mean we've just walked two hours for nothing.'

'I should have asked Mills how to get out of here,' I said, annoyed with myself, 'not relied on this.'

'He had a gun to your head, then he had a gun to his, then he blew his brains out.' She turned in the direction we'd come. 'Don't be so hard on yourself.'

I took a mouthful of water.

'I don't suppose there's any reception on the phone?'

She got it out of her pocket and checked it.

'Nothing.' She looked at me. 'Let's just keep going for a while.'

We started walking again.

Jo went ahead of me this time, but if I was hoping for a change of luck, we didn't get one. The trees didn't get smaller, they didn't thin out or break up. There was marginally more of a path now, and the sun was arcing through the branches, arrows of soft light spearing the mud, the twigs, the needles, but otherwise we could have been back where we'd started, only minutes from the house.

Another hour passed.

And then another.

After the fifth hour, I noticed something: the ground was beginning to change, the flatness of the earth leaning away from us, in a slant. Jo noticed it too, but her reaction was more muted. She'd long since started to flag, the boots hurting her, her gait uneven; she was holding her sprained wrist across her chest like a broken wing, and her damaged finger had bruised the colour of ink. She glanced over her shoulder at me, to check that I was seeing what she was, and then told me to go ahead of her, to see how far the slope went, and to where. Very quickly, I realized I wouldn't have to.

Through the trees, I could see a lake.

A road.

We both stopped, looking at the tarmac drifting in and out of view through the wall of branches and trunks. I glanced at Jo and could see tears in her eyes, and when I looked again, at the grey ribbon cutting around the lake, I began to get emotional too.

I'd started to think we were lost.

I'd started to fear we might never escape the forest.

'You ready?' I asked.

She wiped her eyes.

'I was ready five hours ago,' she said. 'Let's do this.'

We started moving again, with more purpose now, any pain forgotten, bruises, cuts, grazes, scars, all fading to nothing. The terrain beneath us continued to drop, a steep slope forming, the trees as thick as ever but the sounds fading back in: we could suddenly hear birds again, a breeze, the far-off murmur of water lapping on a shore.

'What's the first thing you're going to do when you get home?' Jo asked with a smile on her face, looking at me, then down at her boots. 'I'll be getting a foot bath.'

I laughed, moving even faster, the road maybe a mile away, maybe even less. The sound of our footsteps, the scuff of our soles on the forest floor, became quicker; I listened for cars but couldn't hear any, couldn't see any either, but it didn't dampen my excitement. We were a mile from the road; a mile from this hell coming to an end.

And then it all changed.

As I turned, Jo was already falling: she'd lost her footing, a tired leg catching the knot of a root, and she tumbled forward, hitting the ground about seven feet away from me, too far for me to stop her. She kept falling, propelled by the natural incline of the hill, her head hitting the ground, then her ribs, then her head for a second time. I lurched in her direction, sliding against the camber of the ridge, desperately trying to get to her before she passed me – but it was too late. She had built up way too much speed and all I could do was watch as she went beyond me.

She hit a tree about twenty feet down.

The impact was so hard, it seemed to send a tremor through the earth. Worse, the moment she made contact with the trunk, she was still: no sound, no movement.

'Jo?' I said, my voice frenzied, terrified. '*Jo.*'

She didn't even react.

I almost slipped as I ran down the slope, shoulder-barging a tree and spinning out from it in a desperate attempt to get to her faster. She was wrapped around the trunk, stomach facing in, her coat torn badly, her hair matted to her face with blood.

'Jo?'

I placed two fingers under her jaw.

There was a pulse.

Sliding my arms under her, I hauled her up and staggered into a clearing a little distance away. She moaned, her eyelids fluttering, and then I shuffled the backpack off her, tossed it aside and took off my coat, using it as a pillow. Without my jacket on, I could instantly feel how cold it was, the air like ice, so I took off my own backpack, unzipped it and removed both blankets I'd been carrying.

She moaned again.

'David?'

I heaved a sigh. 'Yeah, I'm here, Jo. It's okay.'

'I think I blacked out,' she said groggily.

'It's okay,' I said again, but – just as I was getting ready to put the first of the blankets over her – something fell away inside of me. I hadn't noticed it as I'd carried her here, but I could see it now: a sharp, compact branch embedded in her gut.

Shit.

Shit.

I glanced down the slope to the road.

'Go,' she gasped.

I looked at her again.

'Go,' she repeated, more forcefully this time, her hand on my arm. 'Go and get us help.' As she spoke, the wound bled, bubbles forming around the branch, her top already soaked. Her breath crackled and wheezed, and I started to realize she had a cracked rib, maybe a broken pelvis too. I looked from her to the road, then back to her. I didn't know what to do. How could I leave her here like this? But how could I not?

'*David.*'

I met her gaze again.

'You need to go.'

A tremble rippled through my throat.

This time, I nodded, yanking my backpack towards me, emptying my food out on to the ground next to her. I left my water bottles there as well, three of them in a line.

'You need to drink and eat,' I said.

'Okay.'

'I mean it, Jo.'

'I know.' She forced a smile. 'Take the phone.'

I fumbled around in her coat pocket for the Nokia, thinking that a signal might save us, and when I got it out, I discovered that we finally had something: a single bar, flickering in and out. I held it up to the sky, hoping it would hold, but then it dropped out altogether. Placing it in her hand, I said, 'You keep the phone. I'll be back, okay?'

She nodded.

'Stay strong for me, okay?'

A hint of a smile. 'Okay.'

I pulled the blankets up over her, held her eyes for a moment – her fear written across them like words – and then I headed down the slope, trying to move as rapidly as I could. I kept going, and going, using my arms to sling me between trees, my head down, watching every step I took, every movement, my entire focus on getting help.

Four hundred feet from the road, I finally saw something.

There was a car coming.

Family

The Forest | Now

Jo lay with her head against the ground, looking at the trees directly above. She wondered where David was, whether he'd managed to find anyone. She wondered how close they were to civilization. She tried to listen for car engines and voices. But all that came back was the whisper of the trees, the soft crackle of pine needles hitting the ground, and her own, shattered sobs: they shuddered out of her throat, as broken as the bones under her skin. She couldn't feel her legs. The pain seared across her stomach. Just breathing hurt her more than any injury she'd ever had in her life. She cried some more, letting it all come out, letting the tears run unhindered down the sides of her face, and then, when she'd gathered herself, she brought the cellphone in closer, still gripped in her hand.

She'd expected to find no bars.

But there was one.

Very slowly, trying not to move her hand, trying not to let the reception get away from her, she pushed *9* three times and then pressed Dial. It failed to connect.

She tried again: *999*.

Nothing.

The reception dropped out for a moment, then came back again. When she tried to get through to the police, a paramedic, anyone, anything, the same thing happened for a third time – it just kept refusing to connect. As she looked at the display, at the bar blinking in and out in the top corner, she began to cry again, a huge wave of emotion hitting her.

Confusion. Pain.

And then, just for a second, some clarity.

As quickly as she could, she raised the cellphone again – her arm juddering, a spasm of agony flashing across her chest – and, as steadily as she could, she began to put Ethan's number in. She was struggling to see properly, struggling to focus, but once it was in, she tabbed down to the message space. She blinked the tears away, steadied the emotion that was rocking her hand from side to side, and typed her message.

> Ethan, it's Mom. I'm in trouble.
> I need help. I don't know where I
> am but I'm hurt

She stopped, watching the cursor blink.

The text might not even send – and even if it did, how would anyone ever find her? What if this was the last message she ever got to send to her son?

It didn't matter how much you loved a person.

Eventually, you had to let them go.

She started typing again.

> I love you so much. I need to let
> you know that in case I don't
> make it home. You are
> everything to me. Absolutely
> everything. You are all that ever
> mattered. Be safe. Mom x

Jo pushed Send.

As she waited to see if it would go, she closed her eyes, tired now – and the second she did, she felt herself drift.

Darkness.

And then, gradually, something else.

A kitchen.

Suddenly, she was inside their old home in the Valley, and the three of them were having dinner, all exactly as they were now.

Jo, sixty-seven. Ethan, thirty-five.

And Ira.

Thirty-six, handsome, dressed in an LA Raiders T-shirt.

Exactly the same as the day he'd died.

'I'm so proud of you, son,' Ira was saying, reaching across the dinner table to Ethan, putting a hand on his boy's arm. 'You've made your mom and me so incredibly proud.'

Ethan smiled at his dad.

He didn't seem to notice they were the same age.

'Thanks, Dad,' he said. 'We really miss you.'

'I know.' Ira looked between them both and took Jo's hand in his, his skin warm, alive. All three of them were joined now. 'I know you do. I miss you both so much – more than you could ever know. But I've been watching, don't you worry about that.' Ira studied his son, blinking, and then glanced at Jo. He was becoming emotional, his voice trembling. 'I've been watching Davy Crockett here.' He smiled at Jo, and Jo couldn't stop herself this time: she began to cry. 'I told you that you could do it,' he said to her, tears welling in his own eyes now. 'I told you, Kader, didn't I?'

Jo laughed, nodded, gripping her husband's hand. 'You told me,' she replied, never wanting to let go of him, never wanting him to slip away again.

'I always told your mom,' Ira said, looking across at his son, his fingers moving from Ethan's arm to his hand. 'I always told her, " You're the strongest person I ever met." '

Jo looked at Ira, at a face she'd only been able to see in memories and photographs for so long, and suddenly some part of her knew this wasn't real. She knew it was a dream, a fever, some sort of hallucination that would soon be over, because she could hear wind passing through the trees of a forest, and it was growing louder every second. But she didn't care. Whatever this moment was, and however long it lasted, it was real enough.

It was Ira, and Ethan, and her.
It was her family as it was always meant to be.
For now, Joline Kader was home.

70

The car was coming from my right, a red blur emerging into view on the right-hand side of the lake. I picked up my pace again, waving my hands at it, trying to get the driver to see me through the trees, and then I slipped, stumbled, my hands hitting the ground, then my knees, and I slid forward and smacked into a tree. Not as hard as Jo had hit hers, but hard enough to wind me. It took me a couple of seconds to recover, and then I was back up again, finally moving from the forest into a sea of long grass. It whipped at me, frost-bitten, hard as glass, snow crunching under foot.

I looked for the car.

I could hear it but couldn't see it.

Trying to run faster, I kept going, even as my feet slipped, even as my skin throbbed, red-raw from the cold. I could no longer see the road because I didn't have the elevation of the slope: it was just sky above, hills emerging along the crown of the grass, and the slant of the forest behind me, its trees like the scales of a great dragon.

Faster.

Come on, you need to move fast –

I heard the car pass.

'*No*,' I shouted after it. 'No!'

Ten seconds later, I broke through the grass, on to the road, but by then it was too late. The car was too far away already. I could see a shape inside at the wheel, and the registration plate on the back, and it took me a couple of seconds to process both. To start with, all I could do was watch as it disappeared around a bend in the road, like a vision that was never even there; but then, as everything went quiet again, as the hum of the engine vanished and I looked out across the stillness of the lake, as I realized the hills I'd seen ahead of me were actually mountains – huge, snow-capped – something started to dawn on me.

I looked left, to where the car had gone, and then right: half a mile away there was a road sign, small, impossible to read from here. I dumped my backpack, not wanting to be slowed down by it, and started running – as fast as I could – towards the sign.

And, as I ran, I remembered.

I thought of what Isaac Mills had said about the nine Black Gale villagers, and how Vale had spent two weeks bringing them here one by one. I remembered my own experience of getting here, of the one that Jo had described too: engine noise, a cramped, coffin-like space. We'd both been drugged, been confused, disordered, our eyes had been covered, our ears, our senses suppressed, but we remembered the coffin. And then I thought of Adrian Vale pretending to be Robert Zaid, getting away with the assimilation of someone else's identity, and, despite Zaid's huge wealth, choosing to work a day job at the Foreign Office. It had always sat uncomfortably with me, but I'd just come to accept that it was because those first ten years he spent abroad at embassies and high commissions gave Vale the breathing room he needed. It gave him the space to properly convince the world that he was Robert Zaid, before he returned home again. And maybe that was a part of it.

But it wasn't all of it.

As I closed in on the road sign, I thought of the email I'd seen in Zaid's house from a company called Parsonfield, and I remembered recognizing the name but not being sure from where. And then, finally, I thought of the sequence I could never figure out.

G76984Z.

I stopped in front of the sign, out of breath, nauseous, and looked at the name of the nearest town to here, and the number next to it, the distance I'd have to go to get there: *43*. I could see the road unfurling ahead of me, a stripe of asphalt that extended so far into the distance, it eventually ceased to exist. There were no other cars coming. There were no towns anywhere close.

I dropped to my knees as everything rushed me at once: in the photograph I'd seen on the wall of his home, where he'd been standing in front of a Gulfstream jet, he hadn't just bought the jet, he'd actually learned to fly it; the reason he worked at the Foreign Office was so he could gain a diplomatic passport, allowing him to bypass customs checks and luggage searches; Parsonfield wasn't a company, it was an airstrip south of London; G76984Z wasn't a map reference, it was the tail number on Vale's Gulfstream; and it wasn't a real coffin we'd been transported in, it was a compartment inside his jet.

And then there was the car that passed me earlier, that I'd missed as I'd run so desperately through the grass: it had been left-hand drive. Its registration plate had been foreign. It didn't belong in the UK because we weren't *in* the UK.

We were an ocean away.

I looked over at the forest where I'd left Jo, at the mountains, the lake, the absolute emptiness of the road, then at the sign, at the name of a town I'd never heard of and could hardly pronounce, forty-three kilometres away.

This was how Vale had made an entire village disappear. He must have realized it was how he could make *anyone* disappear.

This was his final, awful act of cruelty.

He hid his victims on a plane.

And then he killed them in another country entirely.

PART TEN
The Aftermath

71

A month later, I met Ross Perry, Rina Blake and Tori Gibbs at Black Gale.

In the intervening period, the story about the village, about its connection to the abduction and murder of Beatrix Steards, about its tethers back to a double murder in Los Angeles in 1985 – and about the nearly forgotten 'suicide' of a young student in Sussex four years later – had already begun to burn out, the front-page headlines gone, the sensationalized accounts of what had happened all written.

The story, instead, had altered course.

It had become about Jo and me.

It had become about what happened to us after Vale was dead and Mills had killed himself. It was about what had happened to us as we'd tried to find our way out of the forest.

I'd spoken on the phone to Ross, Rina and Tori a couple of days after I finally got back to London. At the time, I was broken, barely functioning – physically and mentally – but I tried to give them the fullest and most detailed account I could stomach. The problem was, the lurid stories in the media had been so relentless in the time I'd been away that it became difficult to convince them that the whole truth wasn't necessarily in the newspaper accounts they'd read, so I suggested we meet at Black Gale. It was the place where everything had begun, the village in which the four families had lived so happily. It seemed like a place where I could give them some facts, some colour, and help them find some closure.

Tori Gibbs arrived first.

It was a bright day in late May, the sun cresting the peaks of the Dales, and, as we waited for the other two, Tori and I talked about Adrian Vale, a man she'd spent the last four weeks researching and writing about. She'd been writing about her brother, about

Laura and Mark, about the other Black Gale residents too, for her employer, *FeedMe*, in an attempt to give an accurate portrayal of who they were and what their lives had been like. A lot of the newspaper reporting about the villagers had been inaccurate, so it was an attempt to put the truth on record, and it was cathartic for her as well. But the Vale part of the story was harder to address because she was writing about a man for whom law and structure were just another lie.

His life as Robert Zaid – his casual murder of a fellow student back in 1989; the staggering act of bravura in becoming him – had fuelled much of what had run in the newspapers, on TV and online. I read and watched it all when I got back, every line on every page, every word out of the mouth of every reporter, dismissing the lies and using the rest to fill in some gaps and build a more reliable timeline of what I hadn't known. Annabel told me that she'd contacted the police when she hadn't been able to get hold of me for eight days, but hadn't officially filed a missing persons report until three and a half weeks in: the catalyst for that had been an American woman, Jo, calling her up to ask her if she'd seen or heard from me. And, while the Met did begin a proper investigation, despite all my history with them, it took an anonymous call to my daughter four days later for the case to find any actual traction.

The anonymous caller had been Healy.

He'd told her to go back to the Met and tell them that they needed to look into Robert Zaid. He knew that was the last place I'd been seen, and although he didn't know that Zaid was actually Adrian Vale, he knew I went there and never came back.

It had been a powerful, selfless act.

Annabel didn't know who he was, so when she went to the police, she simply told them the truth: a man with an Irish accent had phoned her about me, and when the Met traced the call back from her landline, they zeroed in on a phone box in Luton. They sourced CCTV footage, and appealed locally for witnesses, trying to figure out what relationship the unknown caller might have had to Robert Zaid, and then finally they found something on film: the back of a man – possibly in his forties or fifties, skinny, shaved head, with stubble or perhaps a beard. They didn't locate him, even after his picture ran in the papers.

But he was out in the open now.

And that made both of us vulnerable.

Yet Healy had put everything on the line by making that call, and he'd done it again in the days preceding it. He'd broken cover, gone to Yorkshire and got inside Isaac Mills's home, looking for copies of the audio recordings from the village. Or, at least, one recording in particular: the one of him and me in the farmhouse, in the hour after hitting the deer, where I said he needed to hide or we were both going to prison. The one in which I said he was supposed to be dead.

He found the recording on Mills's laptop.

Knowing that deleting the file wouldn't necessarily put it out of reach for ever, especially if any forensic techs came looking, he took the whole laptop instead. Again, his sacrifice moved me, not because I believed it got us out of trouble, or even that I thought it was the best thing to have done, but simply for the fact that he'd done it at all. In all the miles we'd walked over the years, it had always felt like it was me bailing him out, me trying to prevent him from self-destructing, me keeping him from being swallowed by the shadows – but in doing what he did, it felt like a repayment in full. His actions didn't insulate us and, in an uncomfortable parallel, in his faked death, in our lies, in our perpetual fear of being caught, neither of us was so far from the deceit that Adrian Vale had built his life on.

But there was one big difference.

Healy's actions were altruistic and noble.

In a way, given the fact that his daughter was dead and he could never talk to his ex-wife or sons again, it had been a heroic act for the only family he had left.

The offices of Seiger and Sten were raided within two hours of the first interview I did with the police. Jacob Pierce had already fled, his money gone, but the cardboard boxes full of clothes had been left behind. It turned out that what Isaac Mills had told me before he shot himself was right: the clothes in the first cardboard box belonged to other victims. Some belonging to Jo Kader had been found too, added after she'd disappeared. What she'd been wearing the day that Mills picked her up at the airport was in there; so were her iPad and her mobile phone, both of them destroyed.

But the rest of her things, the clothes she'd brought in her suitcase, as well as the suitcase itself, were eventually, painstakingly, traced back to a charity shop nine miles from Heathrow, via CCTV footage. The video showed Mills dropping all of it off within hours of her arrival in the country, and the fact that police had done that, and gone to those lengths, explained exactly why Vale kept the clothes his victims were last seen wearing in storage at Seiger and Sten. It was an extra insurance policy. Missing persons investigations always started with a physical description and a note on what that person had been wearing when they vanished – but both were irrelevant if neither could be found. And maybe there was another reason too: Vale didn't kill because he liked it or felt compelled to, but because it suited him, and it helped him. Was it so far-fetched to suggest that he might have kept the clothes for some other reason? Not as trophies, perhaps, but as reminders about the risks that came with living a life entirely built on a fiction.

One thing became obvious, though: the mud-spattered exercise gear I'd found in the box, the dresses and blouses, trousers and shoes, were all that remained of a business rival he'd had in the 1990s who had begun to get suspicious of him; a journalist who asked the wrong questions in 2002; and a man at the Foreign Office who saw something in Robert Zaid that wasn't quite right – all of them buried in the forest, alongside nine innocent people from Yorkshire.

Jacob Pierce himself was eventually located trying to board a flight to Moscow. He'd chosen Russia because the country had no extradition treaty with the UK. In interviews, he admitted that he'd met Adrian Vale for the first time in 1987, when he still worked in London, and had then developed a relationship with him, especially after Pierce moved back to York and started Seiger and Sten. He said, before Isaac Mills, he'd recommended other men to Vale who had done the same job for Vale as Mills had been employed to do – solving problems, making them go away – but none could protect him entirely. Because of that, Vale would become frustrated, and then angry. Pierce described Vale as a black hole, an impossible force around which things simply disappeared.

On the same day that Jacob Pierce was arrested at Heathrow, Connor McCaskell left a message on my voicemail.

'Wow, David, you're back in the headlines again.' He laughed, but it sounded forced, fraudulent. 'Who would have thought that a psycho like Adrian Vale would be the least of your worries in that forest, right? I mean, once he was dead, once Isaac Mills had blown his brains out, I bet you thought your nightmare was finally over.'

I could hear telephones, voices, office noise.

'Anyway, give me a call. Let's talk.'

Another pause.

'We can discuss the anonymous Irishman who phoned your daughter.'

After Annabel told them about Healy's call, the Met had spoken to Robert Zaid.

He'd had a rock-solid alibi.

He told them he was out of the country the night I went missing, and claimed that, although I called his PA about arranging a meeting, I'd never confirmed. That last part wasn't right, and in the end, once all the facts were known, it wouldn't stand up to scrutiny. But it hung together well enough until I finally arrived back home.

Again, it showed just how confident Vale was, how audacious,

477

how skilled as a liar, that he was able to convince the police. He spoke to them from Hong Kong, where he was attending a board meeting, and he offered them full access to his home and his office in London. He did that because, by that time, four weeks had already passed, and so memories of me were beginning to get sketchy among his staff. There was no record that any meeting had been officially scheduled with me, because he'd erased it from his systems, so while his PA remembered my call, the fact that my name wasn't in Vale's diary seemed to back up what he'd told the police about me never confirming. The two security guards who'd been there the night I went to his house didn't know who I was because Vale had never told them, and his plans for me were part of the reason why he'd dismissed them so early that evening – so while they both vaguely recalled Zaid having a visitor, they couldn't recall specifically on which night. Vale's lie wasn't watertight, but as long as I never came back from the forest alive, it was a lie that would hold perfectly well, and that was all he needed. He and Mills had cleaned his house down after I was there, wiping surfaces, erasing prints, scrubbing and scouring until there was no trace of me left. Vale disposed of any paperwork that might hurt him, as well as email trails, footage from surveillance cameras at his home, anything with a link back to me and Black Gale, which was exactly why he was so confident about letting the police come to his home and his business.

Except they never did.

It was the word of an anonymous caller who they couldn't trace, and – despite appeals for him to come forward – wouldn't come up for air, versus Robert Zaid, international businessman, an official in the UK government, a man who'd donated millions to charity, who'd built an entire cancer research facility. Zaid was a person people liked and responded to. After it all came out in the press, colleagues of his, the men and women he worked with, were profoundly shocked by what they discovered.

They never would have picked him as a killer.

He was so charming.

He was so benevolent and big-hearted.

'And that was how he got away with it,' Tori said, the two of us leaning against the drystone walls that surrounded Black Gale. I just nodded, because she was talking to me about a man she'd read about and researched, not a man she'd encountered in the flesh. In her voice, I heard a weird mix of disgust and reverence, the confliction between a woman grieving the lost lives of her brother, sister-in-law and nephew, and the journalist trying to write about them. I didn't blame her necessarily, because when someone you loved died, there was no right way to deal with it, but what I knew for sure was this: Tori hadn't stood opposite him. She hadn't seen the man Adrian Vale was. She could never fully understand the scale of what he'd done to Jo, to me, to all the others that he abducted and flew to that forest.

To her, he wasn't real, he was just someone built from things the police told her as a relative, and ideas she'd read, heard and researched herself.

If he'd been real to her, she wouldn't be writing about him.

If he'd been real to her, she wouldn't have ever slept again.

72

Beatrix Steards's body was recovered from the Chiltern Hills. It was left in a small but dense wooded area, close to a river, and when I saw shots of the grave site, it was hard not to see the similarities between the place that Adrian Vale had put Beatrix thirty-one years ago, and the place in which he'd put everyone else in the time since.

There was no one left to mourn for her.

Not properly.

Dave and Mira Steards, the couple who'd brought her up, died three years after she vanished, killed in a car accident on the road between their home in Woking and the nature reserve where they used to take Beatrix when she was a little girl. Her gravestone was placed next to theirs, in a cemetery on the edge of the town, but it was an ending much less than she deserved, much less than any of them deserved, and it had come three decades too late. It had come too late for Freda Davey too, the person – along with Patrick Perry – who had begun splintering the foundations of Beatrix's disappearance, the structure that Adrian Vale had built and kept intact from the night he drove Beatrix out of London, deep into woodland, and found a grave for her in a tree.

The funerals for the villagers took place within two weeks of one another, the Perrys first, then the Gibbses, then Randolph Solomon and Emiline Wilson, and then finally Freda and John. A memorial – the money donated by Ross Perry's firm – was built next to the Black Gale sign, with the names of all nine of the residents on it, and then a line underneath describing the thing they loved most about living there. As lovely a gesture as it was, as important as all four funerals were to the families left behind, it was hard to know, in the end, if any of it was better than the simple, unmourned gravestone that marked the conclusion of

Beatrix Steards's story. I didn't get the sense that Ross, or Rina Blake, or Tori Gibbs, felt any better after the ceremonies were over. There was no sense of relief, release or closure. If anything, the huge and domineering level of media coverage directed at them proved overwhelming, turning everything into a performance full of cameras and questions.

Five thousand miles away there was a memorial for Donald Klein too, although as he had no family left, and it had been so long since his death, it was undertaken at a local church, close to where he'd lived with his mother, and was only attended by a small number of people. And the man everybody had, incorrectly, always thought of as Gabriel Wilzon had long since been buried in an unmarked grave, in a cemetery in East LA, and – despite all the revelations that came to light in the weeks and months after I got home – something didn't change: Jo had never known what his real name was in 1985, and over three decades on, no one knew now. Isaac Mills had said it was Pablo, but that was as much of a christening as he would ever get.

And then there was Joline Kader.

When I eventually got back to London, I managed to find a few papers she'd written and had talked to me about, and a video from a speaking tour that she'd mentioned. It had been at Cambridge University, on the subject of equality and discrimination, and at the end of it she answered a question from someone in the audience about what it was like to be a female detective at a time when it was a male-dominated environment. She'd smiled before responding: 'I always remember something my husband said to me one morning, when I was having a meltdown in the kitchen before work. He said, "You're a pioneer, honey. You're out there in your wagon, crossing those plains by yourself, having to deal with all the dangers of unexplored territory. You're Davy Crockett and Daniel Boone – just with better hair."'

A ripple of laughter had passed across the hall.

She'd told me about her husband when we were walking through the forest, trying to find a way out. She'd told me about him again when I finally found help for her, ten kilometres along the road from where I'd left her. In the back of the car I'd flagged down, as the driver desperately asked me questions in broken English, she'd clung on to her life by telling me about a photograph album Ira had made for her. I think that was part of the reason I'd connected so easily with her: the way she'd talked about Ira, the way she'd felt about him, had clear echoes in my own life.

She was strong, and independent, and successful.

She'd constructed a life in the aftermath of his death.

But when you missed someone, when you hung on to them, there was a small part of you that was always trying to find your way home.

Author's Note

For the purposes of the story, I've very carefully altered some of the working practices of police forces in both the UK and US. I've also made some minor changes to the history of the LA Sheriff's Department in relation to its female detectives as well as the organization's real-life pursuit of the Night Stalker. Anything I've swapped out or adapted, I hope I've done with enough subtlety and care for it not to be noticed.

For anyone interested in the Night Stalker case, I highly recommend Philip Carlo's book *The Night Stalker: The Life and Crimes of Richard Ramirez*, which was incredibly useful in helping me paint a picture of what LA was like in the mid eighties. As well as visiting the city during my research, I also used *Ghettoside* by Jill Leovy and *The Killing Season* by Miles Corwin – great pieces of journalism that showcase the work of real-life LA detectives – to help answer any questions I forgot to ask while I was out there.

Acknowledgements

As with all my books, *No One Home* has been made possible by the brilliance of my publishing team at Michael Joseph (and Penguin as a whole), chief among them Maxine Hitchcock, who worked so hard with me on editing the novel. Her calm guidance, endless ideas and laser-focused attention to detail have immeasurably improved the story and this book simply wouldn't have been possible without her. I would also like to say a huge thank you to Tilda McDonald, Laura Nicol, Jennifer Porter, Christina Ellicott, Bea McIntyre, Liz Smith, Clare Parker, Louise Blakemore, James Keyte, Beth O'Rafferty, Jon Kennedy and David Ettridge for all their hard work, creativity, dedication and patience. Finally, a massive thank you, as always, to my copy-editor, Caroline Pretty, who does a peerless job of ironing out my terrible errors and fixing my equally terrible timelines.

Another huge, *huge* thank you goes to my agent, Camilla Bolton, who has been an absolute rock since before I even got a book contract. Not only is she brilliant at her job, she's a black belt in calming my nerves and a great friend. Thank you to everyone at Darley Anderson too, who work so hard on my behalf, particularly Mary, Kristina and Georgia in Rights, Sheila in Film and TV, and Roya and Rosanna behind the scenes.

So much love is owed to my family, both here and in South Africa. In particular, Mum and Dad, who are wonderfully, endlessly supportive; Lucy, who I still owe for doing my French homework in Years 10 and 11; Sharlé, who – for ten years – has shown a remarkable tolerance for writerly meltdowns every night over dinner; and Erin, for whom my books come a very distant second to YouTube videos about guinea pigs.

And, finally, the biggest thank you of all goes to you, my

amazing readers, for buying, borrowing, talking about and recommending my books. Without your support, I wouldn't get to do what I love every day – and I promise that never, ever gets taken for granted.

He just wanted a decent book to read ...

Not too much to ask, is it? It was in 1935 when Allen Lane, Managing Director of Bodley Head Publishers, stood on a platform at Exeter railway station looking for something good to read on his journey back to London. His choice was limited to popular magazines and poor-quality paperbacks – the same choice faced every day by the vast majority of readers, few of whom could afford hardbacks. Lane's disappointment and subsequent anger at the range of books generally available led him to found a company – and change the world.

'We believed in the existence in this country of a vast reading public for intelligent books at a low price, and staked everything on it'
Sir Allen Lane, 1902–1970, founder of Penguin Books

The quality paperback had arrived – and not just in bookshops. Lane was adamant that his Penguins should appear in chain stores and tobacconists, and should cost no more than a packet of cigarettes.

Reading habits (and cigarette prices) have changed since 1935, but Penguin still believes in publishing the best books for everybody to enjoy. We still believe that good design costs no more than bad design, and we still believe that quality books published passionately and responsibly make the world a better place.

So wherever you see the little bird – whether it's on a piece of prize-winning literary fiction or a celebrity autobiography, political tour de force or historical masterpiece, a serial-killer thriller, reference book, world classic or a piece of pure escapism – you can bet that it represents the very best that the genre has to offer.

Whatever you like to read – trust Penguin.